SUSANNA

In the carriage en route to Essex Square, Brent had taken Susanna's hand in his and they had sat in silence, watching each other, unaware of anything but their physical closeness.

I love him so, Susanna thought, I've longed for him so, I don't care about anything else . . . it doesn't matter that he doesn't love me enough to marry me. All the guile and coquetry she had practised, all her newfound sophistication were forgotten as every inch of her body responded to his nearness.

She dined with the English aristocrats as though she were one of them, to the manner born, Brent was thinking. There wasn't another woman in the room as exciting or beautiful. She was like a flamingo in a flock of sparrows. Every man back there wanted her, and tonight they'll imagine she is the woman lying with them, but she is mine.

Susanna

Joan Dial

CORONET BOOKS
Hodder Fawcett, London.

Printed in Great Britain for Hodder
Fawcett Ltd., Mill Road, Dunton Green,
Sevenoaks, Kent (Editorial Office: 47
Bedford Square, London, WC1 3DP) by
C. Nicholls & Company Ltd,
The Philips Park Press, Manchester.

ISBN 0 340 23834 8

"Her lines were easy and graceful, and she had a sort of saucy air about her which seemed to say that she was not averse to the service of which she was about to be employed."

Captain Raphael Semmes, describing the Havana, which was converted to the South's first cruiser, renamed Sumter.

SUSANNA

1

SUSANNA O'Rourke had long been aware of the exact nature of her Aunt Rhea's business in the mansion on Blossom Street. Although Susanna had always been restricted to the separate suite of rooms at the rear of the house, she knew what services the ladies of the establishment provided. Fortunately, Susanna spent most of the year in the cloistered halls of the Misses Elmrod's Academy for Young Ladies in faraway Richmond, where the teachers discreetly discouraged the other girls from becoming too friendly with Susanna or inviting her to their homes.

Aunt Rhea had instructed her doorman that should the child ever walk down the alley to the front door, she was not, under any circumstances, to be admitted. But Rhea O'Rourke had characteristically overlooked one fact. Although no other door led to the business side of the house, there was a sturdy wisteria-covered trellis reaching up the back wall to the upper-landing window.

Aunt Rhea's house, which was near the railroad terminal and the dock, was in an ideal location to service a traveling clientele. From the tiny patch of garden in the rear of the house, Susanna could sit on her swing and watch the trains carrying tobacco and cotton, could see the bustle of activity in the warehouses and the waiting ships in the harbor. Many of the gentlemen callers came from the trains and ships and knew of the shortcut to Blossom Street by way of the alley. Most of the traveling gentlemen smiled and called greetings to the lonely little girl on the swing, for Susanna was startlingly pretty and there was a sweet sadness about her that appealed to them.

The gentlemen who lived in the town ignored Susanna. They came skulking to Blossom Street under cover of darkness, in haste to be admitted to the house and jumped upon by Aunt Rhea's ladies. Susanna had noticed on her secret excursions into the brocaded and mirrored up-stairs rooms that the gentlemen of the town usually were jumped upon by the ladies, or were licked and bitten by them; whereas the traveling gentlemen were usually the ones who liked to do the jumping, licking and biting.

Susanna liked the traveling gentlemen—and one in particular. His name was Brent Chaloner and he was as different from the rough-tongued sailors as Mizjane, the black woman who had raised her, was from a fieldhand. His voice and manners were those of a gentleman, his knowledge of the world seemingly endless and his reluctance to speak of his origins enticingly mysterious. Even at Susanna's tender age, she knew Brent was good-looking as only a rogue or vagabond should be and was out of place either among his shipmates or in a world of dandies.

She had first met Brent on a sultry summer morning shortly after her eleventh birthday. Foolishly, wanting to while away the lonely hours in cooler surroundings, she had slipped away from Mizjane and wandered down to the beach. There she was quickly surrounded by a crowd of boys.

"Look out, it's the whore's whelp!" the oldest of them shouted, catching Susanna's pigtail. "Hey, you fellows, better watch out or you'll catch something you didn't bargain for."

"She should be run out of town. Her and all the tarts on Blossom Street," another said, flipping up the hem of her skirt with his foot.

She was in the center of a circle, wishing she had not left the safety of her garden, fighting back tears. "How brave you all are . . . picking on one girl," she said as scornfully as she could, trying to keep the terror from her voice.

"Why, we won't hurt you, honey," one boy said mock-ingly, "so long as you don't try to seduce us."

They all laughed loudly at his wit, and one, bolder

than the rest, reached out and untied her pinafore strings. Instantly there was a shifting of mood among the group that Susanna recognized as boding more danger than any jostling and pinching she had suffered in the past when she had approached the town's children seeking friendship.

Biting her lip, she looked into the eyes of her tormentor and swung her hand across his face with all of her might. She caught him off-guard and he staggered back with a howl of fury. "Why you little . . . I'm gonna fix you!"

Susanna's eyes went wildly about the deserted beach, then she lowered her head and butted the nearest boy in the stomach. He grunted and fell back and Susanna darted through the breached circle. She ran swiftly, feet skimming the sand, breath rasping in her chest, her ears filled with the shouts of her pursuers.

Suddenly her ankle twisted over an unseen rock and she sprawled face down in the sand. She could not escape now, and she lay panting, trying to think of the words to say to appease them, wondering if she had the strength to fight all of them. How many were there? Five? Six? Strong hands closed over her wrists and she felt herself lifted to her feet. A man wearing a Navy uniform was brushing the sand from her face and the boys were fading into the dunes.

"You're safe now, missy, the posse has gone," he said with a grin.

Susanna looked up into a face as sensually attractive as Greek statuary and for the first time was overwhelmingly aware of the chemistry of the male of the species. She stared unabashed and open-mouthed.

"Brenton Wilford Chalenor, at your service, ma'am. Perhaps I'd better walk you home? Where do you live?"

"Rhea O'Rourke's house on Blossom Street . . . in the rear." Her eyes never left his face.

Momentary surprise was quickly replaced by amusement in his dark eyes. "Yes. I know the place. I didn't know it had a rear."

"An alley. I'll show you. If you're coming from the docks it's shorter that way."

"Most convenient after a few months at sea," he said.

When next he was in port and came strolling up the alley bearing a box of Turkish delight he had brought for her, Susanna did not think about the possibility that the rear of the house was not his final destination.

It was the first of many visits over the years, and, in the spring of 1861, it was Brent who confirmed what Susanna had suspected from the whispered conversations between Aunt Rhea and Mizjane: the fact that the country was virtually at war. The Southern states were seceding one by one, first South Carolina, then Florida, Alabama, Georgia, Louisiana . . . and now Susanna's own Virginia was certain to follow suit any day. There were, after all, limits to the Yankee insults gentlemen could take, her Aunt Rhea had said, parroting one of her clients.

"I heard Aunt Rhea telling Mizjane that the war would be good for her business," Susanna confided to Brent, "but then she said she wished all the brave boys wouldn't have to get killed. It's so hard to take any two things Aunt Rhea says and fit them together."

Brent laughed. "Your Aunt Rhea's statements are usually made for effect, so pay no heed. But has she said what she will do with you when all hell breaks loose?"

"Why, I'll stay here with her, of course. She's all I have in the world except for Mizjane and I'd rather die than be parted from either of them," Susanna responded vehemently.

Brent frowned. "How old are you now, missy? I know it's not polite to ask, but I've been noticing lately that you are growing up."

Susanna looked down demurely. She had been afraid he had not noticed that her dresses were cut too childishly for her developing bosom and hung loosely about a newly arrived waistline, for she was not embarrassed by this fact as were the other young ladies at the Academy. The other changes in her body were no surprise either, for she had seen naked ladies long ago that first time she had fled from Mizjane's rage, climbed the wisteria trellis and hidden herself in one of the upstairs rooms.

Waiting for Mizjane's wrath to subside, Susanna had dozed off under the high bed, only to be awakened by thunderous crashes and creakings of springs above her. Alarmed, she had scrambled from her hiding place to see a portly gentleman of the town writhing happily beneath the capable thighs of Bella, the plumpest of Aunt Rhea's ladies, who sat astride him.

So engrossed were the pair with each other that Susanne was able to slip unnoticed to the door. There she paused for a second, astonished at the spectacle of so much naked flesh quivering in ecstasy.

This experience had aroused her curiosity about her aunt's business, and she was able to secrete herself in the upstairs rooms on a few other occasions when Mizjane's back was turned. Once she had found herself merely listening to the conversation of two of her aunt's girls, who were temporarily off duty. From their remarks it was clearly evident that her aunt's ladies were actresses of some sort, since despite their great outbursts of praise and enthusiasm for the gentleman callers' prowess, the girls were apparently quite unmoved by the gymnastic games they played.

Then one day Susanna had been dismayed to find she was spying on her Aunt Rhea and knew instinctively that her aunt was not play-acting with her French sea captain. Indeed, if she had not observed Aunt Rhea later secreting gold coins in a high-topped boot in her wardrobe, Susanna would have thought Aunt Rhea played the games just for the fun of it. Some strange pang of regret and longing deep inside Susanna told her that there was a great deal more to the games the ladies played than she had realized —that the services they offered, in fact, were only an imitation or substitute for something much more mystical.

After that, Susanna discontinued her investigations of her aunt's business. Later, when she had heard the girls at the academy puzzling over what exactly "conjugal rights" actually were, Susanna realized what was being imitated in the house on Blossom Street.

"Yes," she said now to Brent Chaloner, "I am growing up. I shall be sixteen this month and I shan't be returning to the Academy."

She looked up at him longingly, wanting to add that she was old enough to marry him now.

"Has your aunt made any plans for your future?"

"Sometimes she threatens to send me off to a finishing school . . . but I don't think Mizjane would let her."

Brent Chaloner glanced toward the kitchen window overlooking the garden. The familiar darkly inscrutable face of Mizjane was there as usual. "The ports and the shipping are going to be important to both North and South, Susanna. There's bound to be—" They were both startled by the sudden appearance of Rhea O'Rourke coming down the alley toward them.

Rhea normally never arose before noon, and Susanna's instincts had told her to converse with Brent only when her aunt was absent. Although disapproving, Mizjane would permit the lonely child a few minutes' conversation before calling her back into the house. On that particular morning, however, Rhea had awakened early from a troubled sleep and felt she would not be able to rest again until she had delivered the letter which had arrived the previous day for Susanna.

"Susanna!" she gasped, her eyes sweeping from the girl on the swing to the sailor lounging under the dusty dogwood. "Are you talking to that man?"

Immediately Brent was on his feet. "Morning, Miss Rhea." He smiled his slow and easy smile, dark eyes unconcerned. "Little Miss Susanna and I were just discussing politics. Seems that no one had explained that a seaport would be a bad place for a young lady in time of war."

Rhea's hand went to her throat, a gesture that implied shock, horror or outrage as the occasion warranted. "How dare you speak to my niece on any subject, sir? Susanna, go immediately into the house and tell that old darky I shall flay her alive for allowing this."

Susanna jumped down from the swing, praying that Mizjane had not heard herself referred to as an old darky. To outsiders, Mizjane had been a combination mammy, teacher and adoring slave, but she was a free woman in the legal sense, having been freed by Susanna's grandparents. Mizjane was not African; she had been taken from her native Caribbean island before her tenth birthday and educated in Europe.

"Hold on there now, ma'am," Brent said quickly. "Don't go taking it out on the child or Mizjane. If there's any blame in this it's mine. I've known the little lady for a long time now. . . . I guess I should have realized it was no longer proper for me to visit with her."

"You . . . you . . . you . . ." Rhea sputtered helplessly, then, seeing that Susanna had hesitated, swung a lacy parasol in the direction of the girl's derrière. "Go into the house *immediately*, Susanna," she said with an accompanying swat.

Susanna did not lose another moment in complying. She blinked in the sudden dimness of the kitchen and looked across the scrubbed wood floor to Mizjane, who sighed and shrugged her broad shoulders. Mizjane was a full six feet tall, her Amazon's body tapering from the shoulders to a slim waist and hips.

Outside they heard Rhea's shrill dismissal: "Good day, sir, your patronage is no longer desired in my house." Then Rhea's heels clicked across the brick and she flounced into the kitchen. Mizjane and Susanna remained standing while Rhea sat down and began to fan herself with a long buff-colored envelope.

"Really, Mizjane, I do declare you sometimes forget everything I ever told you. How dare you allow the child to consort with . . . with . . ."

"Apart from whatever else he is," Mizjane said slowly, her voice like warm honey spilled on velvet, "Brent Chaloner is a well-educated, well-traveled young man. Susanna can learn from him." There was an echo of English vowels and a musical Caribbean lilt to her accent, but thirty years in the South had taught her to choose words and phrases less likely to cause raised eyebrows.

"What, pray tell?" Rhea demanded. She was breathing heavily, partly from rage and partly from the tightly laced corset she wore.

"About the war . . . about what's happening up North."

"I do wish you wouldn't talk about war. You know how it upsets me. And there's only one thing any female ever learned from any male. You are never, ever again to allow the child to associate with the gentlemen callers, do you understand?"

"No, I don't," Mizjane responded flatly. "I don't see how it can be prevented."

Rhea chose to ignore her and turned instead to Susanna, who stood wide-eyed with horror at the discourteous dismissal of Brent, wanting to run after him and bring him back.

"This letter came for you yesterday, Susanna. I didn't get a chance to bring it around to you because we had an early party of gentlemen callers when the *Merrimac* docked. I'm afraid I took the liberty of opening the letter—which of course is my right and duty, since you are my ward."

Susanna took the letter from her, wondering if its contents could help numb the misery she felt at her aunt's treatment of her beloved Brent. The letter was from Richmond and was brief:

Madame:
We have been instructed to inform you that you are to be the recipient of a somewhat unusual bequest.
Mr. Rowan Marshall will shortly be calling upon you with details of the above. He will carry a letter of introduction from this firm.

Yours faithfully,
Davies, Hamilton and Son, Attorneys at Law

"A bequest?" Susanna asked. "Yes," Rhea said. "I've been wondering all night long what it could be."

Mizjane took the letter from Susanna's hand and looked at it. "It's dated early last month. We should expect their Mr. Marshall at any time. This would be a good time to buy Susanna's new wardrobe. In fact, you and the girls should buy some new clothes before the hard times come."

"Oh pooh! No hard times are coming. There'll just be a few more shouting matches and then everything will quiet down, you'll see. Though I do declare it might be nice to have some soldier boys come calling. . . ." Rhea's eyes strayed to Susanna and her train of thought was interrupted. "I suppose Susanna does need some new clothes. You don't suppose gentlemen will think I am older if Susanna dresses more grown-up?"

"It's time, Miss Rhea," Mizjane said firmly. "And time to put up her hair, too. You've kept her a child long enough."

Susanna retrieved the letter and read it again. "Who died?" she asked.

"Died?" Rhea repeated.

"Someone must have died, or there wouldn't be a will."

Rhea and Mizjane exchanged glances.

"It must have been my father. He must have died and I never knew him," Susanna said wonderingly.

"Oh dear me," Rhea said. "Let's wait for Mr. Marshall to arrive before we jump to any conclusions. If it is your father . . . well, we simply won't accept a penny of his money."

"Seems to me that will be for Susanna to decide," Mizjane said.

"Oh, hush. Haven't I always supported you all? Let me tell you, if that man is from . . . you know who . . ."

But Susanna was no longer listening. She was looking into the knowing eyes of Mizjane, for hadn't Mizjane told her less than a week ago to expect something important to take place with the advent of the new moon? Mizjane's "white" education had not been able to stifle the second sight she had inherited from her Caribbean forebears.

Although Susanna's surreptitious visits to the business side of the house had been discontinued before Brent came into her life—when she was still, in fact, a small child—she had eventually learned that Brent visited the house as a client. Once he had cut short a visit to the rear garden, explaining he had an appointment with Pansy, before he remembered he was speaking to Susanna. Pansy was the youngest, sprightliest and most bad-tempered of Aunt Rhea's ladies. Susanna had almost been caught by Pansy.

Velvet draperies covered the bay windows of the up-stairs rooms, providing uncramped hiding places. That evening Susanna had been waiting some time for the room to be put to use, and she was growing restless. Eventually she heard voices on the other side of the curtains. Carefully opening them a crack, she saw a gentleman of the town sitting on the bed and Pansy, recognizable by her cascading red hair, helping him undress. This was not an easy task, since the gentleman had obviously had too much wine and kept rolling around the bed in paroxysms of drunken mirth. Pansy at last managed to tug violently at his breeches and get them off. Disgusted, she looked down at his member, hanging limply between his legs.

"Why, you're not even ready!" Pansy exclaimed in annoyance.

This was a new development, and Susanna, interested to learn what had happened to cause such a catastrophe, opened the curtains a little more. Pansy slipped out of the transparent robe she was wearing, sat down on the dresser stool and began to roll down her black stockings. Her breasts were very white in the candlelight, and she showed small even teeth when she smiled across the room at the gentleman sprawled on the bed. Susanna knew instinctively that the smile was actually a grimace of rage.

"You're a pretty li'l thing and no mistake . . ." The gentleman was mumbling now. He stood up for a second, then promptly sat down again.

Still smiling, Pansy moved her legs farther apart to expose red-gold hair between her thighs. Susanna looked at the man, but there was no response from his organ. Pansy moved to his side and began to caress him, whispering all the ancient words of seduction, the invitations to ecstasy. Hidden in the window alcove, Susanna knew that Pansy was more accomplished than any of the other ladies in the house, yet still the gentleman did not respond. Then Susanna caught a glimpse of Pansy's eyes glittering coldly and saw that the caresses were not gentle.

"I'm sorry, Pansy darlin'," he muttered. "Give me a minute . . ." His speech was slurred and unintelligible.

After the first occasion of hiding in the upstairs rooms, Susanna's curiosity had been replaced by something else, at first undefinable. Susanna had slowly realized that warm longings deep inside her were floating to the surface as she learned the many ways ladies and gentlemen could play together. This night, however, Pansy's desperation and anger, coupled with the gentleman's dismay and embarrassment, presented a new and unwanted picture.

Susanna wanted to run from the room. This scene was not fun as it was when Bella lustily poured wine over a gentleman's pulsating member, then giggling, lapped it up like a kitten.

In her disappointment, Susanna carelessly pulled too roughly in an attempt to close the curtains on the spectacle and one of the rings broke away from the rod with a sharp sound.

After that all was confusion. Pansy screamed and leaped from the bed toward the window, became caught in the falling curtain and went down in a heap on the floor. The gentleman caller stumbled after her and promptly fell on top of her, eliciting more screams. Susanna quickly ran for the door.

As her sixteenth birthday approached, Susanna found herself lingering in front of her mirror, comparing her body to Pansy's and wondering if Brent would find her as beautiful. Susanna's waist was smaller, her breasts fuller. If there were faults, they were that her hips were narrow like a boy's and her hair, although a pretty chestnut color, was fine and straight, defying any attempt on Mizjane's part to coax it into ringlets. Susanna's eyes were green flecked with gold. He will come back, Susanna told her reflection, he will find a way to win over Aunt Rhea. When he saw her in the new dresses she had been fitted for he would fall in love with her and ask her to marry him.

She was filled with excitement when the boxes of clothes were delivered. The empty spring days that followed were an anticlimax.

Knowing that the girl missed her friend, Mizjane tried to interest her in the political situation and conjecture about what the Abolitionists would do next. One morning Mizjane had grave news. "Our batteries fired on Fort Sumter. I heard the fort surrendered two days ago and Mr. Lincoln's calling for volunteers."

"Volunteers for what?" Susanna asked, not really interested. How could one worry about such things when one's true love had been sent away?

"To come and fight us, of course. Honey, you ought to show an interest in what's happening."

Susanna poked her slipper into the worn grass beneath the swing. She was uncomfortable in her new dress and wished she were back in her pinafores. She had not realized that she would have to wear stays, or that the yards of muslin would be supported by uncomfortable hoops.

"But we don't own any slaves. Why should Mr. Lincoln want to send soldiers to fight us? Besides, Virginia hasn't even seceded."

"That's a foregone conclusion now, honey. And it doesn't matter who owns slaves and who doesn't, or who is right and who is wrong, because in a war everyone will be hurt one way or another—even the slaves who want their freedom so much."

"But you've always said slavery was wrong. Does that mean you're on the Yankees' side?"

"Oh, I want slavery abolished. If I were a man I'd go and volunteer. Only I'm a woman and not young, and I'm too weary to take up causes. All I really want any more is to see you settled and happy."

"How settled?"

"Married. And respectable . . . not living here."

It was the first time Mizjane had ever implied disapproval of Aunt Rhea and the house on Blossom Street, and Susanna was surprised. "But Aunt Rhea has always been so good to us," she protested, feeling her loyalty being divided.

"Honey, we've never talked about it, but you know what goes on up there, don't you? You know it isn't a respectable house and your Aunt Rhea's parties aren't like the parties respectable folks have. Used to break my heart that you never had any children your own age to play with . . . But then I guess it wasn't right for a black woman to be raising you, either."

"Mizjane! What would I have done without you? Aunt Rhea forgets I'm here sometimes. Besides, you know very well that black mammies are raising girls in every plantation and in all the richest houses in town."

"Well, I'm not a mammy, and to my way of thinking a girl needs someone she can model herself after . . . a real flesh-and-blood mother. All you got was an aunt who makes her living off the bodies of other women and a black woman bitter about being forced into a white world."

"Are you bitter, Mizjane? You never told me."

Mizjane's eyes softened and she reached out to touch Susanna. "Not since I had you, honey. I guess all of a sudden I realize you're growing up and there's a lot we haven't talked about and I have this feeling we don't have much time before . . ."

"Before what?"

"Tomorrow. Before tomorrow. Have you forgotten? It's your birthday tomorrow." Mizjane's tone of voice told Susanna the subject was changed, but she had glimpsed the sudden sorrow in the tired old eyes and was apprehensive about what Mizjane saw in the future.

The following day, April 17, 1861, several events took place in addition to Susanna Brigid O'Rourke reaching her sixteenth birthday. Virginia seceded from the Union. Mr. Rowan Marshall arrived bearing his letter of introduction from the attorneys in Richmond. And Brent Chaloner, resplendent in his Sunday best, came to ask Rhea O'Rourke's permission to call upon her niece.

2

RHEA O'Rourke was rudely awakened before ten that April morning by Emerald, her personal maid. Like her mistress, Emerald was out of sorts at being aroused before noon. Her attitude never let Rhea forget that Emerald had only reluctantly allowed herself to be trained as a ladies' maid, instead of in the work she had had in mind when she came to Blossom Street.

"Dey's a gempumun to see in de parlor," Emerald announced crossly, sleep still creasing her ebony cheeks.

"Go away. I don't see gentlemen at this hour," Rhea responded from the depths of her pillow.

"A Mistuh Rowan Marshall," Emerald persisted, "and he done come all de way from Richmond and he am a lawyer. He say it regarding yo' niece."

Rhea struggled, groaning, to a sitting position. "About Susanna? Oh, my gracious . . ." Her heart was fluttering nervously. Not quite awake, she had not yet remembered the letter about Susanna's bequest, and the nature of Rhea's business was always a matter of concern in regard to her niece. The legality of raising a young girl in a bordello, separate quarters nothwithstanding, was questionable.

"Go and make him some coffee and then come and help me dress."

"He doan' want no coffee. I already done asked."

"All right. Pass me the dark-green dress and help me into my stays. I suppose Mr. Marshall is . . . aware . . . of our business here?"

Emerald smiled slyly. "Ah specks he ain' nebber seen no pictures lak dem hanging on yo' walls in no respectable house."

22

"Well, Susanna doesn't know what goes on over here."
A lawyer . . . the name Marshall did sound vaguely familiar. Her mind refused to function properly at ten o'clock in the morning after a night of lovemaking with Henri. Her Frenchman had come into port determined they master an exotic new position in bed, and the acrobatics involved had left Rhea not only helpless with laughter, but also somewhat stiff in the joints this morning. Rhea smiled to herself at the memory as she went downstairs to meet the lawyer from Richmond.

The man who rose to greet her in the parlor was dressed in militia uniform of a butternut color. He was tall, lanky, with golden hair and mustache. A pair of level gray eyes regarded her politely, and Rhea was quick to notice the interesting cleft in his chin. Handsome rascal, Rhea thought, quite the dashing army officer. Pity he is not here as a client. Nothing in his demeanor suggested he was aware of the nature of his surroundings or Rhea's profession.

"Mr. Rowan Marshall?" Rhea asked.

"Lieutenant, ma'am, at your service."

"I don't understand. "What has the militia to do with my niece?"

"Nothing at all, ma'am, don't fret. I was in a hurry to join my regiment or I wouldn't have worn the uniform. I was formerly a junior partner in the law firm of Davies, Hamilton. I have a letter of introduction. Now a lieutenant in the Confederate army." The last was emphasized by a gleam in his light-gray eyes. "I guess you haven't heard, ma'am, but we're at war. Virginia has seceded and I'm headed north to fight the Yankees."

Rhea sat down abruptly, wondering what the immediate effect of this news would be on her business. The sailors who patronized her house were equally divided between Navy men and merchant mariners, Northerners and Southerners.

"About your niece, ma'am, Miss Susanna O'Rourke. I understand from your maid that your niece lives in a separate part of the house?"

"Very separate," Rhea said emphatically. "She would have to walk down the alley and then up Blossom Street to get here, and in any event Jason, my doorman, has orders never to admit her to this part of the house." Rhea had almost refused to give in to Mizjane's urging that there be no connecting doors to the suite of rooms added to the back of the house. But she had given in; Rhea had always been secretly afraid of Mizjane, and she knew she could not bring up her niece properly without Mizjane's help.

"I have always shielded my niece from . . . from my business. Susanna has been brought up to be a lady, and she attends a very good school, although she is home at present." *And insisting she be allowed to keep company with that sailor, Brent what's-his-name, damn his hide.* A common sailor and client in Rhea's house, no less, who had almost worn out poor Pansy, the youngest of her girls.

"I can assure you, sir, I have always taken good care of my sister's child."

Rowan Marshall cleared his throat and said, "I know this is a delicate matter, ma'am . . . but the child, Susanna, was born out of wedlock, wasn't she? The child's father . . . you knew who he was. Does Susanna know?"

Rhea went cold. "No, we never told her anything. Have you come from her father . . . after all these years?"

"In a way, yes. Lord Bodelon is dead. He left a bequest for his illegitimate daughter and hired my firm to find her and carry out his wishes."

"We don't want his money," Rhea snapped. "After what he did to my sister . . . and to me . . . if I hadn't been left with a babe to care for, I might have found a husband."

Rhea had taken the line of least resistance upon finding herself alone in the world except for the baby and Mizjane. She had become the mistress of an elderly merchant whose wife was incarcerated in an asylum. When he died, Rhea was left with the house on Blossom Street and unlimited debts. The few gentlemen who called on her after that quickly departed once they had coaxed her into bed. One of them was Henri Duvalle, skipper of a decrepit merchantman, a swarthy Frenchman who rhapsodized in a mixture of broken English and gutter French about Rhea's talents. When he left her the next morning, promising to return, he placed several gold coins on her dresser. He also sent several friends who did the same. It was soon evident that Rhea could not possibly entertain all of them, although for a time she managed by the simple expedient of taking two gentlemen to her bed at once and allowing the rest to watch from a peephole she had drilled in the wall of her boudoir.

Unfortunately, Rhea had never been able to put the lovemaking on an impersonal and business footing by detaching herself emotionally from it. She threw herself wholeheartedly into the act and managed to reach many moaning climaxes during the course of an evening. The Frenchmen taught her several innovations, and she was soon satiated with sex. At this point one of the sailors brought her a young Creole girl, who in time recruited her friends.

From these beginnings sprang Rhea's flourishing business, and the separate suite of rooms was added to the rear of the house for Mizjane and the baby. Mizjane had never set foot in the heavily perfumed, smotheringly curtained "entertaining" rooms. For all her perception in other matters, however, Mizjane never realized that Susanna was well aware of what went on in the other part of the house.

"If you will allow me," Rowan Marshall was saying, "to at least deliver details of the bequest to your niece in person."

"Very well, I'll get my parasol. We shall have to walk around to the back of the house."

"I have a carriage waiting," Rowan Marshall said.

Rhea could sense the suppressed excitement in the young lieutenant as she rode beside him and supposed it was the prospect of fighting Yankees that was stirring his blood; then she looked down the alley and saw her niece.

Susanna was sitting on the swing wearing a white dress with deep-pink trimming on the flounces and a very low-cut basque accentuated by tiny puffed sleeves.

Mizjane had managed to pull the girl's hair into a chignon, and silver earbobs danced in the sunlight.

Rhea's hand went to her throat. An afternoon dress in the morning, and earbobs! She would have to have a word with Mizjane. She saw the lieutenant straighten up as he caught sight of her niece, his hand going up to tweak his mustache into place and brush back a lock of hair from his forehead.

The carriage came to a rather jarring stop on the unpaved alley, and Susanna was at the gate instantly, smiling shyly. Rhea looked at the clear young skin, the brightly glowing eyes and tenderly curved lips and realized with surprise that her niece was beautiful. She noticed too that the lieutenant was having difficulty keeping his eyes from straying to the hollow just above the V of Susanna's basque, where young breasts strained against the silk.

Mizjane led them into the small parlor, and after the proper introductions, Rowan Marshall, suddenly aware he was staring at Susanna, hastily cleared his throat and began to speak.

"You are not aware that you are . . . that your father was Edward, Lord Bodelon, formerly of London and Sussex?"

"No, sir," Susanna answered quietly, eyes downcast. "I didn't know who my father was. No one would ever tell me about him. He disgraced my mother."

The young lieutenant looked awkwardly at his feet, but went on, "He died several months ago and toward the end was apparently filled with remorse about the way he had neglected you. We were commissioned to find you and inform you of a bequest."

"Yes, yes," Rhea said impatiently.

"It's a house in London, ma'am. And an annual annuity which will pay for taxes, maintenance, a small staff of servants and normal living expenses."

"Oh," Rhea said disappointedly, "is that all? What on earth would my niece do with a house in London?"

"She doesn't have to do anything with it if she doesn't wish," Rowan said, never taking his eyes from Susanna. "She has the use of it and the money for as long as she cares to live in it, then it will revert back to Lord Bodelon's estate. There is one condition. If Miss Susanna chooses to spend any time there, she may on occasion have to share the house with an old friend of her father's, a Mr. Nicholas Kirby, who may want to use a suite of rooms on the third floor when he is in London. Other than that, Miss Susanna is free to use the house as she wishes."

"I don't see any reason to suppose Susanna will ever use the house," Rhea said.

"That's for Susanna to decide," Mizjane put in, but Susanna's attention had been caught by a familiar figure sauntering down the alley, and she arose and went to the window to be sure her eyes were not deceiving her.

Coming up the brick path was Brent Chaloner, but not a Brent Susanna had ever seen before. He had always worn his Navy uniform, but this morning he was dressed in fawn-colored breeches, a fine ruffled shirt, embroidered vest and well-cut coat. His black hair was partly hidden under a dashing Panama hat, and his smile, as he caught sight of Susanna at the window, was different from the grin he customarily gave her. Before anyone else was aware of his arrival, Susanna had run into the hall and flung open the front door.

"Brent! Oh! Come in," she gasped delightedly, well aware that Brent had never come to their door before. Until now he had only stopped at the garden gate if she was on the swing.

Brent swept off his hat and bowed, taking her hand as his eyes went over her appreciatively. "You look beautiful, Susanna."

She led the way back to the parlor, her heart beating rapidly, vaguely aware that Rhea was rising from her chair in fury.

"I believe I asked you to stay away from my niece?"

Rowan Marshall stood up quickly and said, "I'd best be taking my leave." He handed Susanna an envelope. "Should you decide to use the house, you will find the address and the name of the solicitors in London who are handling the estate." He and Brent stared at each other for a long moment.

"Mizjane," Rhea said coldly, "will you see the lieutenant to the door? Good day, Lieutenant Marshall."

As soon as they were in the hall, Rhea turned her wrath on Brent. "How dare you come here against my express instructions? Why, I'll—"

"Miss Rhea, hold on a minute," Brent said stiffly. "I tried to see you several times, but your doorman wouldn't let me in. I want your permission to call on Miss Susanna. I believe she is old enough to have a beau? Naturally, I would expect her to be chaperoned . . . perhaps Mizjane?"

Stunned into silence, Rhea stared at him, and Brent pressed his advantage. "I thought perhaps I might take her for a buggy ride this afternoon?"

Rhea sat down weakly, her hand at her throat. "Brent Chaloner," she said at length, "we know nothing about you except that you're a sailor. I'm afraid that isn't enough to make me even consider your taking my niece out buggy riding. I do declare your impertinence is . . . is . . ."

Brent smiled easily. "I foresaw your objections, Miss Rhea, and took the liberty of asking Judge Horton to write me a letter of reference verifying my credentials. You know the judge quite well, I believe . . . he is, ah . . ."

"Yes, yes," Rhea said hastily. "I know the judge. And, of course, if he can vouch for you . . ."

"He knows my family well, ma'am. The Chaloners are one of Georgia's leading families, and although they disapproved of my running off to join the Navy, I can assure you I haven't been cut off without the proverbial penny. My personal finances are quite adequate, and I am the first son."

Susanna, her heart still beating wildly, could see her Aunt Rhea was suitably impressed.

"Oh, please, Aunt Rhea," she begged, forgetting that a young lady should not appear eager. "Do let me go."

Waiting, watching Susanna's shining eyes, Brent maintained his slightly deferential pose, his expression properly grave yet open. Somewhere in the depths of the dark eyes, however, was a flicker of arrogant self-confidence and a spark of primitive hunger that was, fortunately, lost on both women.

Afterward, Susanna never quite remembered the details of that glorious afternoon, sitting at Brent's side, giggling and looking up at him adoringly while he managed to say all the proper things for Mizjane's ears and at the same time convey to Susanna that he found her excitingly beautiful. Half-teasing, half-serious, he also let her know of his plans to see her alone, while at the same time regaling her with humorous anecdotes about his travels which sent her into peals of laughter until Mizjane pointed out that young ladies did not scream with mirth in the middle of a public street.

Later in the day when they sat in the parlor sipping tiny glasses of blackberry wine, Brent became ominously serious. "Susanna," he said, taking her hand in his and ignoring Mizjane's frown. "I'm afraid I shan't be seeing you for a while. I have to go away."

"Away? Oh, no, Brent, not to sea?"

"I resigned my commission in the Navy some time ago, and I've been waiting to see what the Confederacy is going to do about assembling a navy of our own. For a while I even considered joining the Confederate Army, so I wouldn't miss out on the fighting."

Susanna went cold. "Fighting . . . Army . . . Brent, no, you might be killed."

"They can't kill me, honey . . . I've a lot to do before I die. Anyway, now I have a couple of choices. We've got our first warship—named the *Sumter*, after our first victory—and if I'm lucky I'll be assigned to her. If not, they've called for Confederate naval officers to serve aboard privateers to sink Yankee ships."

"Privateers? You mean pirates?"

"Not really. We'll offer letters of marque and reprisal to owners of private vessels as we did in '76 and 1812. Lincoln's already ordered a blockade of our ports, and we've got to get our cotton out and supplies in. Until we can build our own ships we have to use everything that floats."

He did not add that he did not know, nor did anyone else, just where the South would build its own ships, having practically no shipyards or iron foundries.

"Susanna, honey, don't bother your pretty little head

about all this. The war will be over by Christmas, and I'll be back on leave before then."

Susanna was aware that Brent's eyes were darting to the clock on the mantlepiece and then to their hands, tightly intertwined, and she realized he was trying to give her a silent message. The time . . . he flexed his fingers, once, twice, then just two fingers. Twelve o'clock. He looked toward the window and nodded slightly. The message was clear. She was to slip away at midnight and meet him outside after Mizjane was asleep.

Susanna silently mouthed the word "yes," then said aloud, "I don't understand what this war is all about, Brent. The Yankees want to put an end to slavery . . . well, we don't own any slaves. What has it all to do with us?"

"My family owns slaves, Susanna," Brent said quietly. "And although I thought years ago that I was not cut out to be a planter, I still liked the idea that the plantation and more than a hundred slaves would be mine one day, when I became tired of the nomadic life. As a boy I used to feel stifled by county life, even though my folks also owned a house in Macon where we spent the winters. I wanted to see the world outside of Georgia. Oddly enough, as I get older I begin to see what my life was all about in Georgia—to see the order and purpose to it—and it is a way of life not to be found anywhere else on earth. Now that that way of life is threatened, I suddenly realize I want it again. Only I'm going to have to fight for it."

Brent had never before spoken of his family. Not having any real family of her own, Susanna had never wondered about this. Now she asked, "your family, Brent . . . tell me about them."

"I used to feel my father was a stern and unbending old rascal. I guess I'm not sure about that any more. My mother is the greatest lady I know, and I'm proud to say my two sisters are following in her footsteps. I have a younger brother too . . . probably as wild as me by now. I haven't been home for over a year, but I shall go and see them before I join my ship." Brent's eyes were not focused on her now, Susanna noticed; he was looking off into space, to some distant place in his memory.

Bent over her needlework, Mizjane coughed softly, and the two of them were again aware of her presence. Susanne realized with a guilty start that they had been discussing slaves. Mizjane—once a slave herself, but a mother and more to Susanna all these years. How tactless I am, Susanna thought, and how Brent is able to make me forget everything. But she must not hurt Mizjane's feelings, that was unthinkable.

"Well, of course, Brent, your family owning slaves is their affair. We don't personally believe in slavery," Susanna said.

Mizjane yawned very widely and looked at the clock. Brent took the hint, but not so quickly as to make her suspicious.

After he was gone, Mizjane lighted Susanna's candle and looked at the girl over its flickering flame. "He isn't the one for you, my lamb," she said gently.

"Why do you say that? Please don't say that, Mizjane. I love him."

"You'll love a lot of young men before you find the right one. Don't be in a hurry to fall in love with the first man who ever treated you as though you were grown up. Go on now, up to bed with you. We'll talk in the morning. My old bones are tired from riding all over the countryside this afternoon."

When she was sure Mizjane's breathing indicated sound sleep, Susanna slipped her new velvet cloak about her shoulders and went out into the garden. Brent was waiting for her in the shadows, and she felt a thrill of excitement as he came quickly to her side and took her hands in his.

"I've a carriage waiting at the end of the alley. Come on," he whispered.

As if in a dream, Susanna went with him, surrounded by the fragrance of the spring night, lost in the overwhelming feeling of love she felt for the handsome young man.

They huddled close together over a supper of cheese

and wine at one of the larger hotels, and then, all at once, were in a private room and Brent was popping the cork from a bottle of champagne.

Afterward, Susanna never remembered all the sweet, loving words he whispered in her ears, or even the happy plans they made. Brent took her in his arms and kissed her hungrily, and she clung to him, her arms pulling him closer until her bosom was crushed against his chest and all feeling drained from her legs. His lips grew more demanding, his tongue gently opening her mouth and his hand slipping from her waist to cup her breast. Somehow her breast was free from her basque and his mouth went down and took the pink nipple between his lips.

"Brent, Brent . . ." she whispered feebly.

"I love you, Susanna, I need you . . . my darling, I'm going away, I want you so much," he was mumbling against her white skin.

When he helped her undress it seemed to be the most natural thing in the world. Champagne bubbles were still exploding in her head, and the warm dusk seemed to be filled with the scent of him as he lifted her to the bed. There was a sweet, growing ache deep inside her as he caressed her body, sliding his hands from her breasts around the tiny waist to the soft mound between her legs, his fingers slowly seeking that dark, wondrous place where all her longing for him waited. She could feel her nipples tighten as she strained toward him, and the next moment his warm body was lying on top of her and she was parting her legs as his hardened member touched her and began to enter. There was a sudden dagger-sharp pain and wetness between her thighs. In her surprise and fear she tried to push him away, crying out, her body rigid. When he ignored her struggles and tried again to thrust his organ into her, she screamed and beat on his chest with her fists until he withdrew.

"Susanna, baby . . ." he was saying huskily, "it always hurts a little the first time. . . ."

But Susanna was crying into the pillow, deep racking sobs because she had never been told to expect such agony and had never suspected from the lovemaking she had long ago watched that fierce, tearing pain could quench the flame of desire so swiftly, so completely.

At last Brent said in a flat voice, "There's a commode in the powder room," and she went, moving stiffly as a puppet, to wash the streaks of blood from her thighs.

Silent and grim-faced, Brent took her home. When she tried to speak to him, to tell him how much she loved him, how she would die for him if necessary, but oh, please . . . perhaps there was something wrong with the way she was made, it hurt so much . . . he said shortly, "It's all right, Susanna. We'll try again. It will be better next time." And he stared out of the carriage window, not looking at her.

He stayed away for a week, and Susanna waited on her swing, her eyes never leaving the alley and the docks beyond, a dull pain in her heart and the sting of tears never far from her eyes. Then one afternoon he returned, smiling and greeting her as though nothing had happened and inviting her to go riding with him again. And when Mizjane was asleep that night, Susanna again slipped out of the house and went with him, knowing that this night she would please him, no matter how much it hurt, because she could not live without him.

Brent was impatient, and it seemed their clothes were quickly tumbled together in a heap beside the bed. Susanna was tense with anxiety, but she closed her eyes and bit her lips as he began again to consummate their love. The pain was not as great, and in her relief she opened her eyes and looked at him, at the pleasure and need on his handsome features, and her heart burst with love for him. They were rising and falling on the crest of a rushing wave, dizzily reaching the peak and sinking back before soaring upward on another tide that rose from a hot sea of love and sensuality. The waves were capped with fiery foam, champagne bubbles, words of love . . . and all at once everything became a kaleidoscope and, breathless, they were flung on the soft shore of spent desire.

For a long time she lay in his arms, content, and then eagerly she raised her head to look at him so that they could talk, make plans for their future together. His dark eyes were half closed, and she felt suddenly cold as she looked into his face, for she could see none of the love she felt for him reflected there. In her own happiness had she not been sensitive enough to his needs, had she been too concerned with expected pain? Perhaps he was disappointed? *She hadn't pleased him!* He must know how much she loved and desired him . . . she must prove to him how much.

Those secret visits to the entertaining rooms . . . all she had learned from watching Aunt Rhea's girls . . . she knew what men liked, and now was the time to put this knowledge into practice. She must overcome her shyness and reticence in order to prove to Brent how much she loved him. She pressed her lips against his chest, timidly ran her hands over his body. All the kisses and caresses in the world were going to be Brent's tonight. Never again would he need to seek Pansy's false embrace. Lost in worshipping him, she could not know that Brent was watching her with a different expression in his eyes.

Before dawn they went down the dark streets to the alley behind Blossom Street. Brent kissed her lightly at the gate and then, his finger to his lips to signal silence, pointed for her to go into the house.

Standing at the door for a moment, watching his tall figure disappear into the darkness, Susanna's ankle touched something cold, something caught in her petticoats. Bending, she drew out a gold chain and then a watch —Brent's watch. She remembered the tumbled heap of clothing on the floor beside the bed and smiled. No matter, she would return it to him when he called the next day. But Brent did not return the next day, or the next.

Before the spring of 1861 slipped away, the Confederacy seized the naval base at Norfolk. The Federals had scuttled the *Merrimac* before leaving and would soon regret not destroying her more completely.

Susanna, desolate because she had not heard from Brent, began to wonder why she was overcome by nausea every morning.

The men who visited Aunt Rhea's girls swaggered and boasted, and everyone was in high spirits. The Confederates had raised the *Merrimac* and she was their first ironclad, renamed *Virginia*, steaming out to sink Yankee ships at will. Troops were massing throughout the state, the Yankees would be licked in no time.

Susanna still sat on her swing, despite her biliousness, and searched in vain for the familiar easy stride of the broad-shouldered Brent coming up from the docks. Mizjane watched the girl with a sinking heart, just as she had watched another young girl sixteen years ago, and finally told Susanna what she had begun to suspect for herself. She was with child.

"Please don't tell Aunt Rhea yet," Susanna begged. "Not until Brent comes back and we are married. If it weren't for the war, he would have been back by now, I know. He must be at sea. I'll hear from him any day."

She looked so pale and woebegone that Mizjane had difficulty restraining her anger. "Susanna, baby, don't count on him coming back," she said.

"Oh, don't say that! He won't be killed, he can't be," Susanna cried tearfully.

"Not killed, honey. . . . Baby, he took his pleasure and he's gone. Men don't look at it in the same way as women. . . . I should have known better. I should have run him off long ago. I blame myself for this."

"He loves me," Susanna said pathetically, "and I love him. He'll come back, you'll see. It won't be the way it was with my mother."

Mizjane's arms enveloped Susanna and she rocked her back and forth. "Hush, child, hush. I'll take care of you and we won't tell Miss Rhea, not until it's too late."

"Too late for what?" Susanna asked.

"Never mind, honey. We'll tell her in July, late in July."

Late in July the Confederacy was jubilant over the defeat of the Union forces at the battle of Manassas; it was too late for Rhea to send Susanna to the old woman who took care of similar problems for the girls, and, waiting on the swing one day, Susanna spoke with an old shipmate of Brent's who brought news of him.

Brent was serving on the *Sumter*. They were cruising somewhere between the Gulf of Mexico and the Caribbean. The *Sumter* had distinguished herself by capturing a dozen Yankee ships, he told her.

"He's well, then? He's safe?" Susanna asked.

"And enjoying every minute of every day," his ship-mate assured her, beaming. "Young Chaloner always was a lad who thrived on excitement, and he's getting plenty of it now. Always bored he was, in the old days when there was nothing but sea exercises. I reckon he's hoping the war will never end. . . ."

So Susanna went into the house and eased her thickening body out of the binding corset and pretty dress, tried to hide her broken heart from Mizjane, and waited for the arrival of her baby.

3

THE pain had started in her lower back before dawn. All day she had thrashed about the bed as the contractions grew stronger and more frequent. Silently Mizjane mopped Susanna's damp brow and took her hands in firm brown ones. As a pain reached its crescendo, Mizjane would cry out in some strange language that needed no translation. It was an appeal to the heavens to spare her child this suffering.

Christmas had come and gone with a burst of nervous gaiety in the house on Blossom Street. The sailors knew and the girls suspected that the coastal ports were falling one by one. All the men talked about now was blockade running and the fortunes to be made from bringing in desperately needed supplies. Why let Englishmen reap all the profits? Sailors deserted and joined blockade-running ships under different names, and even those who remained loyal would occasionally slip off on a fast run between Nassau and Charleston or Bermuda and Wilmington. The risks were great, but the profits enormous.

There had been no further word of Brent's activities as Susanna labored to bring his child into the world. At first she had bitten her lips and dug her nails into her palms to keep from crying out, but as the day faded into evening the pains became too great to be borne and she hung onto the brass bedposts gasping and finally screaming her agony. The contractions gripped, twisted and contorted her body and the sheets dripped sweat, but still the baby did not come.

Darkness came and the night journeyed on into a vast valley of fear and pain. The last intelligible words

Susanna whispered that night were, "God damn you, Brent Chaloner!"

At that precise moment a sleek blockade runner was racing through the black night, course west by northwest, approaching Cape Fear. The ship was painted gray, there were no lights, and tarpaulins were thrown over the engine-room hatch, almost smothering the sweating engineers and stokers below.

Brent Chaloner and the pilot braced for the danger they knew was ahead, salt spray stinging their faces, hearts pounding, the deck heaving beneath their feet. To the howling of the wind was added a new sound, the crash of breakers on an invisible shore.

"Half speed," Brent said quietly into the speaking tube.

Suddenly a gaunt shadow loomed ahead. A Union cruiser; they had almost touched her.

"Port, port, hard aport," Brent whispered hoarsely, but a second shadow lay dead ahead. They were in the midst of a blockading squadron.

Out of the darkness, over the roar of wind and surf, came the shouted command, "Heave to, or we'll sink you."

A calcium rocket soared overhead, and the next second they were caught in the white glare of the Drummond lights.

"Full steam ahead," Brent yelled.

"There are men-of-war all around us—we'll never reach the bar," someone gasped at his side.

"Starboard, starboard," the pilot shouted. "You'll run us aground."

"Or else ram a Yankee gunboat. . . . For God's sake, heave to."

A shot whistled over the wheelhouse, followed by exploding shells from every direction.

"Full steam ahead," Brent repeated, and in the wild light his eyes glowed like those of some pagan god.

Silence and caution were flung to the wind now as the Confederate ship snaked through the threatening shadows, guided by the pilot's commands, the men urging the ship forward over the darkly heaving sea with muttered curses and silent prayers.

Another shell tore away the tip of the stern, but at the same moment a warning roar from the Confederate shore batteries slowed their pursuers and the blockade runner steamed ahead, leaving the shadowy vessels behind.

"We've come through—we're across the bar!" Brent shouted. "We're under the protection of our own guns." And he yelled the Rebel yell into the blackness of the night, not knowing that to the north in Virginia his son had just given his first enraged cry upon his entry into a dying world.

Susanna slept for ten hours and then, with the resiliency of youth, awoke asking for her baby and for food.

Smiling, Mizjane placed the pink-faced baby in the crook of Susanna's arm and a tray of food upon her lap—bacon and yams and hotcakes oozing butter. Shortages had not yet affected the well-stocked larders on Blossom Street, replenished as they were by the seagoing gentlemen callers.

"What are you going to call him, honey?" Mizjane asked as Susanna wolfed down the food.

Susanna swallowed hard and frowned. "Brenton Wilford Chaloner the third, of course," she said.

"I don't know that you can do that, honey . . . with not being married to his pa. Your ma just gave you her own family name. Why don't you call him Brenton O'Rourke?"

"No," Susanna said firmly. "Chaloner. Look at him, he's a Chaloner through and through." But her expression softened as she looked down at her son, and she bent and placed a kiss on a tiny nose.

"He's all right, isn't he? You counted his toes and everything?"

"He's perfect."

"He didn't get Brent's eyes, though. Little Brent's eyes are blue."

"They could change, Susanna. Most white babies are

born with blue eyes. Honey, now the baby's here we've got to think about leaving. It's only a question of time before the Yankees get here—they need the harbor. We've got to go to England, Susanna. You've got the house there and money to live on that you can't touch if you stay here. Honey, you don't want your baby to be brought up in a whorehouse, do you?"

Susanna's eyes widened. Mizjane had never been so blunt about Blossom Street before. "I'm not going to England. The time for that was when I was a baby— my mother should have taken me then. I'm going to do what she should have done. I'm going to take little Brent to his father's home."

"His father? You don't know where his father is."

"Maybe not, but I know his folks are well known in Macon—their plantation can't be far from there. We'll find Brent's family and take their grandchild to them. Even if they won't accept me . . . well, this baby has committed no sin, and he will have his birthright."

Mizjane looked down at the girl sadly. Through the long night of pain, childhood had ebbed from her, and it was a woman who lay in the morning sun holding her child and, eyes blazing, made this vow. Like sudden images caught by a blinking eye, Mizjane's own life came back to her . . . playing on the warm white sand while her parents sailed out to bring back the harvest of the sea . . . the raiding party . . . tossing endlessly on the ship . . . servitude . . . the bloodbath that was Haiti . . . the Englishman who took her to care for his ailing wife and educated her because her ignorance offended him, then abandoned her on the day of his second marriage . . .

"You'd give up the baby—give him to the Chaloners?"

"Perhaps I won't have to. Perhaps when Brent knows he has a son he'll marry me. But even if . . . well, if my mother had done the same for me, why, I'd have been brought up an English lady . . . and I'd never have met Brent Chaloner. Oh, Mizjane, I have to try, for little Brent's sake."

She cuddled the baby to her breast, feeling the fierce

love and pride surge in her veins. "I'll ask Aunt Rhea for some money. She'll help us. We'll leave as soon as I'm strong enough to travel."

Rhea O'Rourke cried and pleaded when told they were leaving. When she saw Susanna was adamant, she begged her to at least wait until the house could be closed down so she could go with them. "Just wait a few days until we can pack our valuables," she asked tearfully.

So the girls were given the news and Rhea began packing. Emerald decided to stay with her, and the other girls made their plans. Most of them had been planning to "refugee" somewhere far from the fighting anyway, knowing the Southern coastal cities were falling under the Yankee assaults. Rhea's "few days" lengthened into weeks, but when Susanna pressed her, she was never quite ready to leave. As always, Rhea found it impossible to plan beyond the present.

They still entertained the gentlemen callers, but spread the word that the house would soon be closed. Most of their clients were in uniform these days, and those who were not were given a poor reception, for despite their profession the women of the house were staunchly patriotic.

There was one man who had been a frequent visitor who was not in uniform, however. He called himself simply Johnnie and spent much time lounging at the bar, drinking and conversing with Rhea. Often he would ask her to go to the upstairs rooms with him, but Rhea would politely decline. Since the onset of the war she had confined herself to only one lover, Henri, her French sea captain. She felt vaguely that this was a gesture of patriotism, despite the fact that Henri was neither a Southerner nor even an American.

To offset her refusal of favors to Johnnie, or any other patron, she would politely converse and serve drinks while trying to divert their attentions to the charms of one of the other girls.

Henri would be gone for a while and then return. It was no longer necessary for him to make the long voyages to France because of the huge profits he was making running the blockade from Bermuda or Nassau to the Carolinas. When he traveled to Virginia, they fell into an almost domestic routine, which Rhea found comforting in the face of life's uncertainties, not least of which was her advancing age.

Unknown to either Susanna or Mizjane, Henri was the influencing factor in Rhea's decision to go south with them. Henri's first landfall was now Wilmington, North Carolina, and that was where Rhea hoped to persuade Susanna to settle, but while Henri still journeyed north to see Rhea, she felt no urgency in leaving Blossom Street.

It was Emerald who came pounding on their door that April morning, screaming for them to come quickly because the Army was arresting Miss Rhea.

Struggling from a deep sleep, Susanna heard Emerald's screams and the wail of the baby awakening to hunger. She pulled on a wrapper and ran quickly downstairs as Mizjane appeared on the landing above.

"Lordamercy, come quick! De Confedrut Ahmy done taking Miss Rhea off to jail!" Emerald sobbed as Susanna flung open the door.

"Jail! What are you talking about, girl? Stop crying and tell me."

Emerald's sobbing became more hysterical and she rolled her eyes and kept repeating, "Dey's taking Miss Rhea off to jail."

"You stay with the baby. I'll go with her," Mizjane said at Susanna's side.

"No. I'd better go. Maybe they'll tell me more than you—" Susanna was about to add, " . . . because I'm white," but stopped herself.

"And what if old Jason won't let you in?" Mizjane asked. Rhea's doorman was still under orders never to admit Susanna through the front door. Susanna nodded in agreement. The baby was howling anyway. She would have to nurse him and lose valuable time.

It was past noon when Mizjane returned, and Susanna had worn a path in the parlor carpet. The dark features were grave as Susanna helped her out of her shawl and bonnet. A whimpering and forlorn Emerald accompanied her.

"She's in jail, all right," Mizjane said, sitting down heavily in the nearest chair. "They say she's accused of treason. Giving information to the enemy about our ships."

"Our ships? I don't understand. Aunt Rhea wouldn't know a cruiser from a paddleboat," Susanna said, bewildered. "How could Aunt Rhea, of all people, be a spy? Why, she isn't . . . well, smart enough to know how," she finished lamely.

"They say she found out from the gentlemen callers when their ships would be sailing, then the Yankee gunboats lay in wait and sank them. They say they have a witness who heard Miss Rhea tell a man about two ships that were later sunk. They caught the man, too—called himself Johnnie and he's a Yankee spy."

"Oh! no! I suppose she could have . . . without realizing what she was doing," Susanna said. "What shall we do?"

"Nothing we can do. I talked to the officer's valet and he said they're waiting for someone to come from Richmond. Honey, we have to go ahead with our plans and leave here. I didn't want to worry you until you were stronger, but there's talk in town that the Confederates are going to evacuate Norfolk. They say they won't be able to defend us."

"I can't leave Aunt Rhea. There must be something we can do."

Emerald stopped sniffing and looked at Susanna. "You stay hyah and de Yankees gwine rape you and stick yo' baby on a baynut," she offered gloomily.

A chill of fear went through Susanna as she thought of her son asleep upstairs in his crib.

"Hush your mouth," Mizjane said to Emerald, but there was doubt in her voice. She had seen young girls used by soldiers once before in her lifetime.

"You will have to take the baby, Mizjane, and Emerald can go with you, to help you. Take him to Macon and find the Chaloners. Brent said they owned property there. Tell them he's Brent's son. And look . . . give them this." She ran to the rosewood secretary and, opening the drawer, pulled out Brent's watch, the watch she had found caught by its gold chain in her petticoats that morning so long ago when she had left her childhood behind.

"I can't leave you, baby. You must come too," Mizjane said.

"No. Not right away. But you must leave as soon as we can get you on a train. If the Army arrested Aunt Rhea they must be getting pretty desperate about the situation here. I promise I'll follow in a day or two. Is there anyone left in the house?"

"Jason, Bella and Pansy—the others are gone," Mizjane replied, a new look of respect in her eyes as she realized she no longer had a child to take care of, but a young mistress to serve.

"Let's start packing the baby's things. I'm going over there to get Aunt Rhea's secret stash of money so you'll have it for your trip. Emerald, you stay here and watch the baby while Mizjane does the packing."

Mizjane did not ask how Susanna knew where Rhea hid her money. Ever since the day Mizjane had realized that her charge had somehow managed an assignation with a man without anyone's knowledge, Mizjane's faith in her own second sight had been badly shaken.

Jason was not on duty at the door when Susanna walked boldly into the flamboyantly furnished hall for the first time. Curving around one end of the room was a semicircular bar under shelves of gleaming glassware. Couches lined the walls, their legs disappearing into thick carpeting, and an elegant staircase rose from the other end of the hall. Susanna glanced about, a quick image of the girls seated on the couches as the gentlemen callers drank at the bar flashing into her mind.

She went quickly up the heavily carpeted stairs to the second floor, then toward Rhea's room, which was set off by itself at the top of another short flight of stairs. Susanna knew from past experience that Rhea's room was the largest and most ornately furnished of the entertaining rooms, with a huge bed set upon a dais and gilt-framed mirrors covering most of the walls and even the ceiling. There were two large mahogany wardrobes, three dressing tables and several chairs, as well as a fur-covered chaise longue. In one corner of the room, behind an almost transparent silk screen, stood a hip bath, its four short legs decorated by alabaster cherubs, blatantly masculine.

Pushing open the door, Susanna saw that the hip bath was occupied. The silhouette of a tall gentleman bending over someone in the tub was clearly visible through the screen. Susanna hesitated, not prepared to find the room in use, and then realized angrily that it was Pansy in the tub.

Susanna's footsteps fell silently on the thick carpeting and she paused for a moment, torn between upbraiding Pansy for rushing to use Rhea's room the moment she was gone, and the need to extricate the hidden hoard of gold coins without either Pansy's or the man's knowledge.

Pansy was giggling drunkenly and the man was dabbing her body with a sponge and thrusting his hands down into the water between her legs. Susanna saw the outline of Pansy's arm and hand reach up to caress the source of his passion.

This was not the moment to disturb them, Susanna decided, and she went cautiously to the second wardrobe and eased open the door. On the wardrobe floor were rows of shoes, and at the back a pair of high-topped boots. Susanna reached for a boot and heard the jingle of coins as she picked it up. The next moment she saw the mirror reflection of the man bending, picking up Pansy and lurching toward the bed with her. Quickly Susanna squeezed into the wardrobe between the perfumed dresses hanging there.

Indignantly, she saw the man drop the wet bundle that was Pansy onto her Aunt Rhea's white satin bedspread. Pansy was shrieking with laughter as the man's face, tawny mustache and beard went down between her thighs. She seized the blond head between her hands and spread her legs wider to accommodate his darting tongue, her white hips rising and falling rhythmically. Susanna quickly turned away.

Despite her indignation at Pansy's use of her aunt's bed,

Susanna was impressed by the cries of ecstasy she was forced to overhear. Had she not known that Pansy felt nothing, she would have believed, as no doubt the man did, that Pansy was reaching a climax.

Unbidden, the memory of the wildly beautiful night she had spent with Brent leaped into Susanna's mind, the night that had produced their son. A faint stirring of desire, long forgotten during the months of her pregnancy, caused her to blink back the tears. She must not think of it; he had deserted her . . . used her even as this man now used Pansy.

Their voices were low now, muffled by the silks and brocades that hung about Susanna's ears. She wished they would be done so she could leave her hiding place. But she knew from their whispered conversation that they were slower, more deliberate in their movements now, that the man, having satisfied that first impatient urge, required other more exotic refinements to bring him again to his zenith.

Susanna remembered those long-ago nights in her childhood when she had watched from a similar hiding place, believing the men and girls were merely playing games. She did not want to watch, or hear, the spectacle upon Aunt Rhea's bed now . . . nor think of Brent and Pansy engaged in the same activities. Susanna's head was turned from them, her knuckles between her teeth, willing them to leave.

At last they slept and Susanna crawled from her hiding place, clutching the boot carefully to prevent the coins from jingling. As she sped silently from the room, she snatched up a reticule lying on a chair, hoping it belonged to Aunt Rhea and not Pansy, and, out in the hallway, she quickly transferred the coins from the boot to the reticule, which she hung around her neck from its leather strap.

The wintry sun was fading and night shadows were reaching for the house as Susanna went down the stairs again. Several boxes and trunks stood at the foot of the stairs, no doubt packed by Rhea in readiness for the journey. No use bothering with them—there was no telling what useless items they contained. There was no sign of either Jason or Bella.

Out on the street the sailors were beginning to come ashore for the night's entertainment, their clothes drab beside the handsome gray and gold of the Army uniforms in the crowds. Most of the men's eyes went appreciatively over the slender girl as she hurried down the street, but they did not call after her as they would one of her Aunt Rhea's girls, for it was obvious from her clothes and demurely downcast eyes that Susanna was a lady. She was halfway to the corner when a carriage suddenly stopped beside her and a thickly accented voice hailed her from within. "Mamselle . . . Mamselle O'Rourke, pleez, one moment."

Susanne paused, recognizing Captain Henri Duvalle. She had never spoken to him and had not been aware he knew of her existence.

"Your aunt . . . pleez, I cannot find out what 'as 'appened to 'er." There was genuine concern on the swarthy features as he jumped down from the carriage. He was shorter than Susanna expected, having seen him only in her aunt's bed on that previous occasion.

"Forgeeve me . . . may I introduce myself? I am Henri Duvalle, a friend of your aunt. I recognize you from the miniature she 'as. You are her niece, no?"

"Yes, I am. Captain Duvalle, I'm afraid my aunt has been arrested. They say she gave information about our ships to the Yankees."

"Mon Dieu! 'ow can zat be? Tell me, where is she 'eld?"

"She's in the jailhouse." Susanna's voice broke in the face of his sympathy. "Oh, Captain, will you help me get her out?"

"Of course I weel 'elp. Come, into ze carriage. I tek you 'ome and go to see what can be done. We must 'urry, for I 'ear ze Army plans to leave—zey cannot defend ze port."

Not feeling quite so alone, Susanna allowed herself to be handed into the carriage.

Mizjane awaited them, her lips bitten raw from the long afternoon's wait, and as they came up the brick path her fears tumbled from her in a torrent. "You have to come with us. Who will nurse the baby? What if the Yankees find you here? At least the Confederates have Miss Rhea, and if they leave they will take her with them.

I've seen refugeeing before—the soldiers will take all the trains and the streets will be full of carriages and cannon and there'll be no carriage for you, and oh, honey lamb, you have to come too."

Susanna nodded absently as Henri took his leave, realizing with a shock that Mizjane looked old. There was a tired droop to the once-proud shoulders, and the crisply curled black hair was turning gray.

"There, there, don't worry." Susanna patted the dear brown hand. "Emerald will find a wet nurse—there's bound to be some good black girl who will go with you. And Captain Duvalle has promised to help me get Aunt Rhea out of jail. But Mizjane, there's a strange feeling in town. I can't describe it, it's like just before a thunderstorm when the air crackles. And there are soldiers everywhere. I don't think you should wait. Look." She opened the reticule and poured the gold coins into Mizjane's hands.

"Buy train tickets to Macon. Where's Emerald? We must send her to find a nurse. And bring the baby to me so I can feed him now. Go on, dear, do as I say." Susanna's voice was sharp with the realization of her need to give rather than take orders.

Late in the evening of the following day, Susanna sat alone in the front hall sipping a cup of bitter coffee. Mizjane, Emerald and a young mulatto girl with a baby of her own were on a train. There had been no callers all day, and no word from Henri Duvalle. In the frenzy of activity Susanna had not had time to think of her aunt, and now that darkness was falling she was unsure what to do other than wait until Henri brought news.

When there was a loud knock on the door, Susanna went eagerly to open it, questions for Henri on her lips. But the lanky figure who stood in the shadows wore gray and gold. His blond mustache was pale in the lamplight, and he pushed back a lock of blond hair as he swept off his cap. Puzzled, Susanna looked up into the face of Rowan Marshall, whom she had not seen since he had brought the news of her father's bequest, all those long months ago.

4

LOOKING into Rowan Marshall's coolly appraising stare, Susanna was instantly aware she was alone in the house. "Lieutenant Marshall . . . I'm afraid the house is closed and my aunt is away." Her hand held the door defensively. Perhaps it was the setting that made her think that the girls would be disappointed to miss this particular client. No doubt the uniform and rangy body sent the thought flashing into her mind.

"I know. It's you I came to see, Miss O'Rourke. And I'm a major now." The thin blond mustache along the upper lip was like a punctuating mark above a wickedly grinning mouth. If the clear gray eyes had not been so devastatingly innocent and guileless, Susanna would have hesitated to allow him into the house.

"Won't you come in?" She led the way, acutely aware of their surroundings, particularly the gilt-framed erotic pictures which entirely covered one wall.

Trying to sound businesslike, she asked briskly, "And what is the nature of your business, Major?"

She did not ask him to be seated, but he strolled over to the bar and leaned against it, his eyes going over her much too boldly, and for a moment losing their reassuring guilelessness. She knew her dress was wrinkled and her hair in disarray. Her breasts were beginning to throb with the accumulation of milk left by the abrupt weaning of the baby. "I was just about to leave," she added.

"You've decided to accept your father's bequest and go to England?" His gray-and-gold uniform was handsome, Susanna noticed grudgingly. He looked quite dashing, in fact, with a boyish, eager look, despite the wicked mustache.

"No. I'm not going to England."

"Yes. I believe you are," his tone was almost apologetic. "That is, unless you wish to see your aunt executed for treason."

Susanna caught her breath. "Executed—" The word stuck in her throat.

Marshall's expression softened slightly. "Look, I know it's blackmail, but we didn't know if you would be willing to work for us without a little extra incentive. I'll come to the point. We know you have a house in London. You can be of service to the Confederacy if you go there, at least for a few months."

"What kind of service?"

"We need England's help. We'd like to have England in the war as an ally, but we'll settle for her allowing us to build warships in her shipyards."

"But I don't understand how I can help you with any of this. What do I know about such things?"

"You have a half-sister in England. Your father's legitimate daughter. She is a lady-in-waiting to Queen Victoria. She and her mother are well known in the highest circles in London. Through them you would meet members of Parliament and powerful men in their Foreign Office, to say nothing of customs officials and others we shall need to win over to our cause. There are many ways you can help merely by moving in their social circles."

Susanna flushed slightly and said coldly, "I still don't see. I'm sure if I do have a half-sister she will have no wish to acknowledge my existence."

"They are not aware of your true identity. They believe the bequest was made to honor a debt to an old friend in Virginia and that you are the daughter of that—fortunately deceased—old friend."

"But what exactly would I have to do?"

There are many things you can do. There are men in England who are ready to commit her to an alliance. You can help convince them."

"But how would I do that?"

"Come now, Miss O'Rourke. I'm aware of your youth,

but you are no longer the naive little virgin." A careful study of Susanna O'Rourke had been conducted by his superiors. Few details of her life had been overlooked. Rowan Marshall added, almost as though speaking to himself, "You are beautiful. Perhaps the most desirable woman I've ever met. There is a quality about you of combined innocence and sensuality few men will be able to resist."

Susanna felt herself blushing and turned her head quickly, wishing the interview were taking place in other surroundings. On the wall to Rowan Marshall's left was a large Japanese print of a warrior holding aloft an exquisite china-doll girl, while a second warrior, organ erect, stood waiting to be coupled with her. The three of them stood, frozen in time, the girl's legs apart as she was borne toward that bold erection.

"Then, too, we are plagued with Union agents in the British Isles who report every ship that sails. We can't afford to lose either the ships or the supplies they carry. If you can't bring yourself to consort with Yankees, at least you might be able to unmask them for us by dallying with the Englishmen who know their identities. There are some things a male agent just can't do." He was grinning in a diabolical way, and his frankly appraising stare made Susanna uncomfortable. There was an impertinent cleft in his chin and a lithe masculine power to his lean frame that seemed all at once suggestive of barely tethered virility.

Susanna's eyes flashed with anger. Drawing herself to her full height, she said, "How dare you suggest such a thing? Please leave immediately or I'll . . . I . . ."

"Come now," Marshall said quickly. "I'm not suggesting you lie with them. Just a little mild flirtation and free-flowing wine to loosen their lips. Miss O'Rourke, I'm afraid my superiors have made up their minds about this. It's the only way they will consider releasing your aunt. The charges against her are very serious."

"Who are your superiors, Major Marshall?"

"I am a member of the Signal Corps . . . headquartered in Richmond. You can, of course, go over my head, but every moment you delay, your aunt remains in custody."

Susanna was silent, wishing she had not sent Mizjane and the baby away.

"We would, of course, arrange for your baby and the mammy to accompany you."

Startled at his apparently being able to read her mind, Susanna blurted out, "My baby and Mizjane are not here. I sent them south today."

"That's too bad. We could still make arrangements to have them join you there if you wish."

"How long would I have to stay in England? And what guarantee would I have that Aunt Rhea would be released?"

"Just a few months. We're sure England will commit herself by the end of this year. If she doesn't, we're lost. The blockade will strangle us. As for your aunt, she will be home tomorrow if you give me your word you will remain here and be ready to leave on a moment's notice."

"Mizjane has gone to Macon to try to find a family named Chaloner. If I leave they won't know where I am. Could you send someone to see that they are safe and tell them? I wouldn't want to risk their safety by having them try to sail to England through the blockade."

"I could arrange to have them sent north to a Yankee port. They could sail on a Union ship."

"No. If I'm only going to be gone a few months I believe it would be better for the baby to stay with his father's family."

Marshall did not question this, but there was a flicker of understanding in his gray eyes. For a moment they were the most steely gray eyes Susanna had ever seen, great energy in their depths.

"How would I get to England?"

"I would take you. Probably sail at night for Nassau and board an English ship. You would tell your aunt nothing of this. Absolute secrecy is essential."

"Send my aunt home in the morning," Susanna said quietly. "I'll go to England."

Nassau lay bathed in sunlight at the end of a reef-filled channel where vicious currents surged beneath the surface of sparkling water and coral teeth had torn the hull of many a ship. Mecca of the blockade runners, Nassau was a brawling, dirty port of unbelievable affluence. Crowding the streets were descendants of roving pirates of a bygone day, keen-eyed blockade runners, fat merchants and prostitutes of every shape, size and color.

They shared a common bond. Their lives all depended on the sea and the bounty that came by way of those treacherous channels.

A hundred years earlier, pirates had sailed out to prey on Spanish galleons sailing northward with the Gulf Stream, for the island was an ideal haven for predators or fugitives. There were hundreds of coves in which to hide, and the waters were too shallow to allow the approach of deep-hulled ships of war.

The islanders were sympathetic to the Southern cause. Nassau was a huge storehouse of Southern cotton and every imaginable item of trade awaiting transshipment. Warehouses bulged with crates, boxes, kegs and bales, and vessels jostled one another at anchor.

Susanna blinked and raised her parasol against the brilliant glare of the sun, her skirts trailing the dirty quay as she followed Rowan Marshall through the crowds to the waiting carriage.

"We have rooms at a hotel. We'll spend the night there and be on a ship for England at dawn," Marshall said quietly as he lifted her into the carriage.

The driver of the carriage nodded to Marshall and laid the whip about the horses.

Susanna's eyes widened at the sight of the brazen prostitutes, drinking, shrieking and openly accosting the grinning sailors. She saw one man and woman sprawled in the street, sound asleep in each other's arms.

Marshall watched Susanna out of the corner of his eye, gauging her reaction to the wild, sun-drenched scene. If he expected shock or horror, it did not register beyond the widening of her green eyes.

"Your aunt's girls look like ladies by comparison, don't they?" he drawled, as they went by a group of sailors squatting in the dust gambling with gold pieces while several wenches casually retrieved unwatched gold and deposited it in grimy bosoms.

"What did you know of my aunt's girls?" Susanna asked icily. "You were only at the house twice to my knowledge—the day you brought the letter and the night you came to tell me about Aunt Rhea." The tropical heat was making her dress stick uncomfortably to her back, and her face felt flushed.

"Oh, I was there more than that," Marshall said casually.

"And which of the girls did you honor with your . . . with . . . " Susanna broke off, furious with herself for becoming embarrassed.

Rowan Marshall chuckled softly and the driver turned and threw them a glance over his shoulder, his face breaking into a grin.

"Miss O'Rourke," Marshall said, his grin matching the driver's, "please, ma'am, you are embarrassing me."

"Oh hush," Susanna snapped, and turned to stare out into the street, catching the dark eyes of a passing sea captain who smiled delightedly and doffed his hat to her.

They were alighting from the carriage when Susanna's eyes looked into another pair of dark eyes and her heart stopped beating. Brent Chaloner was pushing his way through the girls crowded about the hotel door and coming toward them.

He was more deeply tanned than she remembered, slightly leaner so that his broad shoulders were even more pronounced in the white linen jacket he wore. His eyes registered surprise and pleasure at seeing her.

"Susanna!" he exclaimed as he reached her side. "I couldn't believe my eyes. It's really you, isn't it? By all that's holy, what are you doing here?" He took her hands in his and leaned forward to brush her cheek with his lips.

Susanna's breath caught in her throat, he was so handsome. She tried to focus her gaze as the world spun dizzily and she heard herself murmur a greeting.

Rowan Marshall had been paying the driver and he turned and coughed slightly, his hand coming up to grip her arm in a proprietary manner.

"Brent, you remember Major Marshall? He came to

see us the day you . . ." Her voice trailed off.

"No. I don't remember. How do you do, sir?" Brent said.

The two men shook hands, each raking the other with a speculative look, and then, as the crowd jostled Susanna, Rowan ushered her into the hotel lobby, his eyes narrowing as Brent followed them.

"You still haven't told me what you're doing here," Brent said. "You're more beautiful than ever, Susanna."

"I'm on my way to England, Brent." She wanted to scream at him that he had never written, never come back to see her, that he had a son . . . but none of this was for Marshall's ears.

"England!" Brent exclaimed. "Don't tell me I'm going to lose you again as soon as I've found you." .

I was never lost, Susanna wanted to say. I was waiting for you, carrying your child. Oh, why did you come back into my life now, just when I thought the pain was going away? Aloud, she said, "Don't you remember . . . my father's bequest? I have a house in London. But perhaps I didn't mention it to you."

"When can I see you alone?" Brent asked with a pointed look in Marshall's direction.

"Sorry, my friend, that won't be possible," Marshall said, the steel showing in his eyes again. "Miss O'Rourke and I are sailing on the morning tide."

"What is he to you?" Brent asked, ignoring Marshall.

"Nothing, nothing at all. He is simply sailing on the same ship. Perhaps we could take tea together after I've had time to bathe and change clothes. I see there are some tables on the terrace."

"I shall be waiting," Brent said and bent to kiss her outstretched hand.

After he had strode off through the crowd, Marshall took her arm and guided her to the desk. As he signed the register he said under his breath, "You are a fool, Susanna O'Rourke."

Susanna did not answer until they were following a bellboy to their rooms. "Please mind your own business. I agreed to work for the Confederacy, not to answer to you about everything I do."

"You are still a fool. Well, never mind, you're young. You have time to learn from your mistakes, and believe me, Brent Chaloner is a mistake."

"You don't know anything about him," Susanna said.

"You don't really think I believed you acquired your child by parthenogenesis, do you?"

"Partho—" Susanna repeated, hating him for using a word she did not understand.

"I'm being facetious. A habit of mine when I'm trying to control my anger. I know that Chaloner is the father of your child. You didn't really think I'd approve of your seeing him alone again, did you? After all, you apparently—"

"Oh!" Susanna breathed in dumb fury, too angry to speak. Just before the bellboy unlocked her door, Rowan Marshall bent and whispered in her ear. "I'm sorry. I'm not judging you. It's just that I have a low opinion of a man who impregnates a virgin and then deserts her."

Wanting to slap his face, she slammed the door instead. Her single portmanteau stood forlornly on the floor. The trunk of clothes she had packed for the journey was still lying in the hallway in Blossom Street. Marshall had told her there would be no room for it aboard the fast ship to Nassau that would slip through the cordon of Yankee gunboats at night. New clothes would be purchased for her as soon as possible.

She was wearing a dark-gray travel dress, which was damp and wrinkled from the heat and far too heavy for the climate. There was a second travel dress packed in the portmanteau. It was forest green, trimmed with black braid, and, fortunately, it did interesting things to her eyes. She opened a bottle of cologne water, tipped it against a silk scarf and rubbed it over her hair.

A pretty dark-skinned maid brought water, and Susanna also sprinkled a little cologne into the hip bath so that when she was dressed she was surrounded by fragrance. She noted in her mirror that the heat had brought a flush to her cheeks that was most becoming.

Brent evidently thought so too, for he stood up as she came across the terrace toward him, his eyes glowing with admiration.

He had ordered mint juleps, and while they were not quite the same as those served back home, Susanna was grateful for the cool refreshment. Sitting under an umbrella of palm fronds with the man she loved, all the misery of the past months faded from her mind.

"Susanna, you'll never know how many times I thought of you, longed to see you again," Brent said. "Everything happened so quickly, I didn't even have time to go home and visit my family. I was on the *Sumter* for a while, then was sent to act as liaison officer aboard a blockade runner. When I was assigned back to a cruiser I missed the excitement of the Nassau trips, so every chance I got I made a run on my own time. . . . I couldn't get in touch with you, Susanna, because officially I'm not supposed to be here. I've been leading two lives, one as Lieutenant Chaloner of the Confederate navy and one as a blockade runner. There was never any time to get back up to Norfolk to see you. . . . But fate brought you back to me anyway. Don't go to England. Stay here and I will be able to see you—"

"Brent wait," Susanna interrupted. "Before you say anything further, there is something I must tell you. We have a child."

His face froze, at first into an expression or disbelief as his eyes went over her slender figure. Then, slowly, he composed himself and smiled. "A child. . . . A son?"

"Yes. I named him Brenton."

"Where is he? Can I see him? Oh, Susanna, I'm sorry . . . I had no idea . . . I thought . . ." Conflicting emotions were racing across his darkly handsome features, and for a moment Susanna thought he would say the words she longed to hear, but her hopes were dashed when he finished, "I guess I thought with your background . . . you would know how to prevent it."

He knows about our son and he isn't going to ask me to marry him, Susanna thought, her heart like lead.

"I sent Mizjane to take him to your family in Georgia. They were getting ready to evacuate Norfolk, and Aunt Rhea was in trouble, and I . . . well, I wanted him to be safe and I thought your family would take care of him."

Brent's eyes hardened. "Susanna, you had no right to do that."

"No right? He's your son as well as mine. Don't tell me I had no right," she flared back.

"And how do I know he's my son?" Brent asked angrily.

"You . . . you cad," Susanna said, her voice breaking. "You know you were the first. Oh, Brent, I thought you loved me. I loved you, I still love you, and we have a beautiful little son. We can be married and—"

"No," Brent interrupted. "Susanna, I can't and won't marry you. Listen to me. I'm sorry for what I said, and I believe you that I am the father of your child. No doubt my parents will make some arrangements for him. Susanna, I won't deny I think you are the most excitingly beautiful woman I've ever known . . . but you can't be my wife. If you will stay here, I'll provide for you and take care of you. Even bring the child here if you wish. But I won't marry you." His voice was harsh.

"But why?" Susanna asked in a small voice, all her pride gone, and a terrible knot forming in her throat.

"I told you . . . about my family. Susanna, my mother is from a very old Savannah family. My father's family trace their ancestry back to the seventeenth century and are one of the most powerful families, politically, in Georgia. I may have been a gypsy and a black sheep, but I'm proud of my family line, and it would be out of the question for them—or me—to accept someone with your background."

"You've used that word twice now, Brent. What do you mean, my background? What have I done that's so wrong? Only loving you, that's the only mistake I've made."

"Your Aunt Rhea—can you imagine my introducing her to my mother? And your Mizjane—how could I explain her? My family are used to black slaves, not black women who give orders instead of taking them."

"But you would be marrying me, not Aunt Rhea or Mizjane. What do they have to do with it? I'm not ashamed of either of them. Aunt Rhea did what she had to do to survive, and Mizjane has been dearer than a mother to me."

"All right, Susanna. I didn't want to say it. But how do I present *you* to my family? Mother, father, this is Susanna O'Rourke, who comes from a very fine brothel in Norfolk."

"Brent!" Susanna gasped, hurt beyond pain. "You know that Mizjane and I lived in separate quarters. I was never allowed to go through the front door of the house . . . and I spent most of the year in the Academy in Richmond."

"Susanna, I'm not a fool. Oh, I'll admit I believed you to be totally innocent that night I came for you. I'll admit I cared enough about you to want to take you away from Blossom Street before you were recruited by your aunt and moved into the business side of the house."

"You cared for me? You wanted to take me away . . . but then why . . . ?"

"I knew you were still a virgin, but that it was only a question of time before one of your aunt's customers made an offer for you she wouldn't be able to resist. I wanted to be your first and only lover, Susanna. I would have taken you south with me that night, never let you go back to Blossom Street, and I'd have cared for you, even though I couldn't marry you. But . . ."

"But what? Why did you change your mind? What did I do? Didn't I make you happy?"

His mouth twisted sardonically. "Oh, you made me happy. More joy than I've ever known. But you were too proficient, my sweet. No virgin ever heard of the tricks you performed . . . and most ladies and wives live out their entire lives without suspecting the existence of carnal pleasures such as those you take for granted."

"But I was a virgin, Brent. You know I was."

"Technically, perhaps. But I could only assume that you had already been trained for a future career among your aunt's girls . . ." His eyes moved abruptly over her shoulder and something like relief appeared on his face.

Turning her head, Susanna saw Rowan Marshall strolling toward them, a glass in his hand.

"So nice to see you again, Captain Chaloner," Marshall said sarcastically, bowing with exaggerated grace. "Miss O'Rourke, you look like a duchess among the trollops."

Angrily, Brent rose to his feet. "Are you insulting Miss O'Rourke?" he demanded.

Marshall looked taken aback. "On the contrary. It was meant to be a compliment. Evidently a poor one. Forgive me. I merely meant that the restraint of that gown against the exotic plumes of the other women present is quite arresting. I'm afraid I've never learned the gallant phrases of gentlemen. You see, I was just a clerk before the war, struggling to get an education in law. No fine family tree or white-columned plantation house. Unfortunately, I tend to speak to ladies in the same manner I address men. Which is probably why I am so unpopular with them." Uninvited, he sat down at their table, his eyes still appreciating Susanna.

Brent remained standing, glowering at Marshall. "I shall be waiting to hear your decision about staying."

Susanna watched as Brent walked away, the eyes of every woman on the terrace following him. Then she turned to Rowan Marshall, deciding he looked drab by comparison, the bright sun turning his blond hair to the color of wet sand and his eyes coldly gray whereas Brent's had been dark with passion and anger. For all that his words had cut her like a knife, she had been able to look into those dark eyes and see that he still wanted her. She could not imagine Marshall wanting any woman very desperately; he was too flip, too uninvolved and much too mocking to care.

She could not see the whiteness of the knuckles of Marshall's fists, clenched under the table. Nor did she notice that the glances of the bold-eyed women on the terrace were now directed at the good-looking Confederate officer opposite her. The gray and gold of his uniform were matched by his eyes and hair, and there was a reckless, devil-may-care attitude about his grin and rangy frame that was causing more than one feminine heart to flutter.

"So he wants you to stay with him," Rowan Marshall said. "I trust I don't have to remind you of your bargain? We kept our end of it. Your Aunt Rhea will be heading south by now."

"Don't worry," Susanna said, too stunned by Brent's rejection to think of anything but running away to hide. "I'll keep my word. We shall be on the ship to England tomorrow."

5

DESPITE the perfume of tropical flowers and the music floating on the heady air, dinner was a cold and silent meal. Susanna sat opposite Rowan Marshall, still wearing her high-necked travel dress, a sharp contrast to the other colorfully dressed women, many of whom were in the company of uniformed Confederate officers. In spite of her severely drawn-back hair and somber attire, however, it was toward Susanna that all eyes turned. It was almost as though she were saying, Look at me, I dare to be different, to dress plainly, to scowl at my escort instead of simpering, to drink my wine with a gulp instead of sipping daintily and to eat all of my food instead of picking at my plate . . . and, in spite of all this, I am the most beautiful, exciting woman here tonight. For this fact was reflected in every admiring glance and in the envious eyes of the women.

There was, however, an unnatural brightness to her eyes and a disconsolate droop to her lips that only Marshall noticed, and he kept up a steady barrage of conversation. When she did not respond to his attempts at humor, he changed the subject to speak of England and what they would be likely to encounter there.

"England is, of course, sympathetic to our cause," Marshall was saying. "And England holds the key to how the rest of Europe—and Russia—will react in the months to come. There are even those in our ranks who believe we cannot make a nation without England's help. If we can get it . . . ah, Susanna, if we can! And we might. It's not just a question of their needing our cotton. There's the British feeling for being on the side of the underdog for one thing, and for another their aristocracy feels we are the 'cavaliers' of the conflict, opposed by Northern power-seekers of a lower class. Lord John Russell made a speech and said the issue was not slavery at all." Rowan drank some wine and laughed softly. "But then, Lord John Russell has never met the likes of your friend"—he did not mention Brent's name, but went on quickly—"and I'd add to that the issue isn't states' rights either."

Although Susanna had steadily eaten her way through the meal as though she were alone, her eyes never meeting Marshall's gaze, as she laid down her knife and fork she said, "Then what, exactly, Major Marshall, are *you* fighting for?"

"Ah, I'm not fighting. I'm accompanying a lovely woman on a long sea voyage. An arrangement I find more appealing than eating hard tack and marching through the mud."

"And last year, why did you rush off to volunteer then?" Susanna persisted.

"Again, a question of alternatives. It seemed more exciting at the time than clerking in a musty office. Though I must admit I wasn't sure which side to volunteer for. Some of my relatives in West Virginia are on the other side, I believe." The last he added *sotto voce*, with a sly glance toward the next table where a group of Confederate officers were dining.

"All things considered," Susanna said, "I can't imagine why you were chosen for this mission."

"Because I look the part, Miss O'Rourke. I look like a dashing Confederate officer . . . all golden good looks and a slightly undernourished aristocratic air."

Susanna considered Marshall's conceit at believing himself to look like a dashing officer. Of course, in the right light his hair and mustache were clearly golden-colored and his features even. He was a trifle thin for his height, but he carried himself well and she supposed some people might find the cleft in his chin and his slightly rueful, faintly mocking expression interesting. It was an expression that seemed to make light of problems, obstacles or pomposity.

"Odd, isn't it," Marshall was saying. "Your Captain

Chaloner should look like me and I should look piratical like him."

At the mention of Brent's name, Susanna's composure cracked. She had not understood Marshall's remark, but hearing Brent's name conjured up not only Brent's irresistible image, but also that of their son. She thought of the tiny black-haired perfection of the baby and how far away from her arms he was at this moment. The green eyes slowly filled with tears, and the immediate flash of contrition and sympathy on Marshall's face was more than she could bear.

Leaping to her feet, she clasped her napkin to her mouth and tried to stifle the sob that rose in her throat. As she tried to walk she realized to her horror that her skirt was caught under the leg of her chair. Tugging futilely at the material, she could no longer quell either the visual or the audible signs of her misery. Heads were quickly turned in her direction, and a dark-skinned waiter came hurrying toward them as Marshall extricated her hem and slipped his arm about her waist to lead her from the dining room.

Susanna cried into her napkin and allowed herself to be led through the bobbing heads of the staring diners. Marshall walked without haste, patting her hand gently as they went. In the lobby he stopped and said, "Perhaps it would take your mind off . . . your homesickness if I were to show you a little of the night life of Nassau?" His expression was boyish and eager again, the mocking grin gone, and she could see her face with all its misery reflected in his clear gray eyes, forming an almost tangible bond of sympathy between them. But sympathy was the last thing in the world Susanna wanted from any man.

She blew her nose and said, "No thank you, Major. I shall be all right if you will just escort me to my room."

She had thought she could leave without seeing Brent again, but she could not sail on the morning tide without trying to explain to him. Explain what? That he must marry her, that she would make a good wife, that she loved no one but him, nor ever could. She had been wrong to lie with him, she knew now. The girls at the Academy sometimes whispered at night about how men would try to "compromise" a young lady and how careful one must be with one's reputation. Susanna had believed what they meant was that a woman should be true and not give herself to another man when she was betrothed. Too late she realized that even though men wanted to lie with a virgin, they wanted her to refuse them until after marriage, which seemed a devious situation at best. She had given herself to Brent in complete love and trust; why did he condemn her for that?

Perhaps Mizjane had been right—perhaps Susanna needed a mother to tell her what to do. Despite her aunt's profession, Rhea had never spoken of such matters to her niece, and neither had Mizjane. The girls at the Academy spoke endlessly of balls and beaux and marrying handsome suitors, but they did not seem to look beyond the wedding. Susanna had assumed that when they found the beaux they wanted to marry, they would make love. Later, after they were married, if it became necessary for the husband to travel, or if the wife were ill or in childbirth, or grown too old and ugly, then the husband would visit a house like Aunt Rhea's, because men's need for lovemaking was insatiable and they could no more go without it than without food. She had certainly not wanted Brent to take Pansy to bed after he and Susanna had discovered their love for each other.

She stood outside Brent's door, trying to think of the words to explain all of this to him. It had all seemed so simple. . . .

He opened the door and smiled, his eyes beginning to smolder as he drew her into the room.

"Brent . . ." she began, but the instant the door was closed his arms went around her, pulling her to him in a fierce, crushing embrace, his mouth coming down on hers and his hands immediately fumbling with her basque.

His lips were forcing her mouth open and she felt a numbing, dreamlike lethargy overcome her as longing for him seeped through her body, leaving her legs limp while her hands clutched his back, pulling him closer. He had her breasts free now and caressed them, setting her nipples on fire and bringing a swift response deep inside her that became a physical pain. As though with a mind of its own, her hand slid from his back, down over the tensed buttocks, around the muscled thigh, closing over the hard erection that strained against his breeches.

He was whispering words of love and passion and saying her name over and over. Her hair was loose and falling in her eyes, and she felt herself going down the warm abyss of complete surrender as he picked her up and carried her to the bed. But if her basque unbuttoned easily, her hoops, petticoats and pantalettes were a fortress not so readily conquered, and as he struggled to remove her clothes, a voice of warning was striving to be heard somewhere in the outer reaches of her senses.

"No!" She screamed the single word and struck him with all her might.

Totally surprised, Brent jerked away from her, his hand going to his cheek. Susanna scrambled to her feet, pulling her basque together.

"I won't lie with you, Brent. If I'm not good enough for you to marry, then you can satisfy your needs with one of those women down on the streets. I came to tell you I shall be sailing to England tomorrow and my son will be joining me there as soon as Major Marshall can arrange it."

"Susanna . . . please, don't go," Brent said, his voice husky. He reached out his arms for her, but she stepped quickly toward the door.

"Susanna, I love you. I need you. Try to understand about my family. . . . When I marry it must be to someone who will fit into our world. But I'll always love you, I'll always need you, my darling."

She had pulled open the door when he sprang to her side, his arm going quickly around her waist. "I won't let you go, Susanna. I can't," he began, but the next instant the door was wrenched fully open and Rowan Marshall stood on the threshold, gray eyes no longer lazily unconcerned, but flashing blue flame.

"Let her go, Chaloner," he said in a voice of deadly quiet.

"What the hell are you doing here? Why, I'll kill you . . ." Brent lunged at Marshall, who sidestepped as gracefully as a ballet dancer.

"Go to your room, Susanna," Marshall said to her, and she pushed between them and ran up the hall as several doors opened and other guests emerged to see what all the shouting was about.

In the sanctity of her room, Susanna undressed and bathed her body in the cold water from the pitcher on the commode. She brushed her hair and put on her nightgown and then paced the room, her body still afire from Brent's kisses, her longing a dull ache between her thighs and in her throbbing breasts.

When there was a light tap on the door she knew before she opened it that Rowan Marshall would be there. He was disheveled and had a cut lip. Susanna looked at him with distaste.

"What do you want? If it's thanks for rescuing me, or an I-told-you-so . . ."

"Not at all. I merely came to see if there is anything you need before you retire." The mocking light was in his eyes as they slid down the ruffled nightgown, and he grinned.

"Nothing. Good night," she snapped, aware that his glance was taking in the voluminous nightgown.

"Isn't that a trifle hot for a tropical night?"

"That is none of your concern. What time shall we leave in the morning?"

"Early. I'll come for you—unless you feel it would be better if I stayed here with you. To be sure you don't oversleep?"

"Will you please go?" Susanna said through gritted teeth, trying to close the door but finding his boot in the way.

"Are you sure there isn't something I could give you? To help you relax?" he asked lightly.

"No—I don't know what you mean. Oh, go away!"

"Yes you do. Susanna, my dear, I believe you are a woman who needs love. But you've got to distinguish between the kinds of love. There's love that is entrapment . . . I don't have to go into the details of that category. Then there's love that's a duty. There's love that can be bought . . . and by now you realize I use the word 'love' in its purely physical sense . . . and then there's love just for the fun of it. Such as you and I could have. Right now—this minute—so you could forget your longing for that blackhearted swine back there. They tell me I'm not bad in the love-for-fun department, and there'd be no heartache—or baby—in the morning. So why not be honest with yourself and give us both a great deal of pleasure?"

Susanna stared at him with unconcealed loathing. "You will remove your foot from my door and take your leave, sir, or I shall scream for help. Just as I could have screamed in Brent's room had I chosen to do so," she said, and as he withdrew his foot in mock alarm, she quickly slammed the door shut.

When they pulled away from the quay at dawn, Brent was standing watching the ship and Susanna stood at the rail looking down on him, her pain a great swelling bubble in her breast that threatened to burst at any moment. Her fingers were stiff as she clutched the rail, and a strand of chestnut hair whipped across her face in a freshening breeze. The shouted commands of crew and stevedores and the sounds of the port stirring beyond did not penetrate the mantle of hopelessness and despair that engulfed her as she looked across the chasm that separated ship from quay.

He had arrived on the quay after they were on board and made no attempt to board the ship himself, but merely stood watching, dark eyes implacable. Finding her cabin cramped and airless, Susanna had flung down her portmanteau and gone to the upper deck of the ship. She saw him immediately, black hair tousled and a dark bruise along one side of his jaw. Surely she had not caused the bruise when she struck out at him? She wondered what had happened between him and Rowan after she had left.

Their eyes were locked in a tormented embrace, but neither smiled, neither waved as the lines were cast and the ship began to inch away from the dock. She watched until he was a tiny figure, dark among the crowd, and then her eyes misted with tears and she turned away and made a silent vow. *I'll become a lady for you, Brent. I'll become the kind of lady even you cannot resist.*

The ship flew British colors and carried four other passengers, all men, all Southerners. Susanna was never consciously aware of it, but the crew was American also, and the colors they flew changed from time to time, depending upon the shipping lanes they traveled and the proximity of other vessels. She saw little of Rowan Marshall the first few days, as he spent most of his time in the company of the other men. They all wore civilian clothes as did Marshall, yet all bore the stamp of the military.

Susanna missed her baby desperately, and this, combined with her unbearable sense of loss at leaving Brent so far away, made her oblivious to sparkling green seas and cloudless skies. She was glad now that she had Marshall send a message for Mizjane and the baby to be intercepted in their search for the Chaloner plantation and brought instead to England. At least she would be able to look forward to being reunited with them at journey's end.

On the seventh day at sea the weather suddenly changed. The sky grew leaden and the sea began to roll toward the ship in threatening swells which were soon topped with angry foam. As they pitched and rolled, Susanna, partly out of fear and partly because of queasiness, retreated to her cabin and did not leave even for meals. The lamp suspended from the bulkhead swung to and fro in ever deeper arcs, and Susanna clutched her bunk posts as the cabin swayed each time the ship plunged forward into the deepening troughs of the ocean.

As darkness came so did torrential rains and howling wind. The ship's engines struggled to keep her moving slowly through mountainous seas, and with each pitch the propellers left the water and the shuddering vibration beneath Susanna's cabin added to her terror. Once she tried to leave the cabin to go in search of Rowan Marshall, or some other human being to cling to, but she was flung across the deck as the ship lurched and even when she reached the cabin door was unable to get it open against the pull of the ship as she rolled side to side, floundering in a vortex of battering waves and cascading spray.

Susanna struggled back to her bunk, panting between sobs, sure she was going to be drowned any minute as the vessel was torn asunder. She did not hear the cabin door open, but looked up to see the door swing closed and Marshall in the cabin with her. She wept with relief, although the ship was rolling more violently than ever and the engines seemed to be losing their battle with the surge of the ocean swells.

He was at her side, bracing himself against the bunk, and cradling her in his arms, stroking her hair and murmuring reassurances as she clung to him.

"I'm sorry, Susanna," he was saying into her hair, "I couldn't come to you sooner. It's all right, honey, we aren't going to sink, and we'll be out of the storm soon."

Now that she had someone to listen, her sobs became more hysterical and she screamed at him that it was all his fault that she was going to a watery grave, and who would take care of her poor baby?

"Well, since you're going to drown anyway," he drawled, "we might as well enjoy what time we have left," and his hand cupped her chin and turned her face up to his, and before she realized what he was going to do, he was kissing her. Not hungrily as Brent had done, but gently, almost carelessly, his mustache softly brushing her upper lip. She tensed for a second, ready to push him away, but then the stern of the ship rose from the water again and mixed with the vibration came the sound of wrenching timbers, so she closed her eyes and let him kiss her.

She had forgotten she was wearing only her chemise until she felt his hands, warm against her bare flesh, and he whispered, "Nothing like danger to spice up love-making and I'll wager your sea captain took his pleasure without much thought for yours. . . ."

"No! Let me go . . . get out of here . . . I hate you." She struggled against those insistent seeking hands, but it seemed the probing fingers were everywhere, the lips slipping from her mouth, tracing the line of her throat, moving to her breasts. His hands moved over her and into her with a sure and deft touch that brought an unwilling response. Between the swaying of the ship and the heady feeling of his lips on her body, a delicious sense of anticipation was replacing her terror.

"I don't love you!" she cried, despising herself for responding to him.

"Well, at least we're making progress," he said, his lips encircling her ear, his tongue darting lightly as he whispered, "A moment ago you hated me."

She turned her head, brought up her hands to push him from her and gritted her teeth so he could not kiss her lips, and he laughed and held her wrists as his mustache trailed down the length of her body and came at last to rest on the soft mound above her legs. She felt his warm lips and then his tongue and, finally, her own quivering response that was not to be denied. She was lying back, meekly allowing those warm hands to remove her chemise, brush lightly inside her thighs, move up her stomach and trace the contour of her breasts, press lightly on the tiny erections of her nipples.

Putting everything else out of her mind, she reached for him and drew him down on top of her in the narrow bunk, feeling the thrill of his hard body squeezing the breath from her lungs and his legs parting her thighs. She raised her hips as he entered her, and the storm receded into a faraway accompaniment of muted sound that blended with the rushing noise in her ears and the pounding of her heart. Now she was oblivious to everything but that warm rod of flesh that moved up and down within her and the magic of their movements as they soared away together, not even hearing as Rowan Marshall whispered, "Don't worry, Susanna, there'll be no pregnancy because of tonight . . . that is, if we stay afloat, of course . . ."

Oh, I'm a wanton. . . . The thought tried to intrude into her consciousness. I hate him, I shall never see him again. Oh, if only he were Brent! Then, as the lamp above them swung faster and faster and the ship's timbers groaned and creaked, she was climbing, climbing to the top of the wave and sliding down, down, shuddering, convulsively panting . . . Brent! Oh, Brent, my darling!

She felt suddenly cold and realized she was lying alone and naked on the rocking bunk. Rowan was standing looking down at her. "Shame on you, Susanna," he said quietly. "You're not supposed to let me know you are pretending I'm someone else. It's considered polite to let me make believe it is I who am giving you pleasure."

Before she could protest, he lurched across the cabin, pulled open the door and was gone.

Shivering, Susanna pulled a blanket over her. Now it was not fear of the storm that made her cry into her pillow, but shame. How weak her flesh, how great her need for Brent, that she could have let Rowan Marshall take her . . . and worse, enjoy it! Her flesh crawled with revulsion at her own wantonness. She had betrayed her love for Brent. Behaved far worse than any of Aunt Rhea's girls. At least they were honest. Everyone knew they were play-acting for the gentlemen callers' pleasure and felt no release themselves. For her, Susanna, to have felt pleasure and consummation with a man she despised was the greatest sin a woman could commit.

As if in agreement, the wind howled mournfully and another great wave lashed the ship, sending her sprawling from the bunk to the deck. But the warm glow of Rowan still lingered in her innermost places and secret little muscles contracted excitingly at the memory of him. She was also beginning to feel a lessening of her self-contempt, because it had begun to occur to her that Brent had been able to find satisfaction with the bad-tempered Pansy. What harm was there, therefore, in Susanna's finding solace with Rowan?

They sailed up the River Mersey and docked at Liverpool on an overcast afternoon, and Susanna fussed because of her limited wardrobe. The voyage after the storm had been uneventful, or so Susanna thought, not knowing that twice they had almost been identified by Yankee cruisers.

Rowan had brought her breakfast on a tray the morning after their wild lovemaking, greeted her with a joyful smile and eyes as serene as the summer sky. In return she had flung the tray on the deck and ordered him never to speak to her again as long as he lived. After that they were icily polite to each other and Susanna never went to sleep without locking her cabin door.

"How can I go ashore in this dress?" she greeted him when he came to her on deck to watch the miles of Liverpool docks slip past. "I have stains on the skirt and the trim is torn."

"You can remain on board while I go ashore and buy you a new one," he replied. "Come to the starboard side and I'll show you Laird's shipyard at Birkenhead across the river. That's where we are hoping to have our ships built."

"Go yourself," Susanna answered sullenly. "How can you possibly know what clothes I need?"

"Hoops are worn wider in England, I believe," he volunteered gravely, "and as milady walks they swing cunningly to show the pantalettes . . . which are usually trimmed with Irish lace. And speaking of lace, you know, Susanna, you hardly need to lace yourself into stays, your natural waist is so tiny. How you ever managed to have a child and keep your waistline is a mystery. . . . Are you sure the beetle-browed Brent Chaloner and his child are not just figments of our imagination?"

"If you don't leave me this second," Susanna threatened, "I shall fling myself overboard."

Rowan retreated quickly, smiling as he did so.

He was as good as his word and brought her two dresses before she disembarked. Also several petticoats, pantalettes and a cloak for, as he explained, she would find the English spring a little chilly. One dress was a deep burgundy color with a froth of fawn lace at the throat, and the cloak was black, lined with satin that matched the dress. The other dress was pearl gray, trimmed with burgundy ribbons which also matched the cloak. To complete the outfits was an outrageous concoction of a bonnet, all black and red feathers and streaming velvet ribbons to tie under her chin. She could not lace herself into her corset, but even without it the wider hoops made her waist look smaller than ever.

Her good humor restored, she went down the gangway with head held high, and every man within range stopped what he was doing to look at her. At her side, Rowan Marshall grinned and spoiled it all by doffing his hat to the onlookers as though they were royalty acknowledging the homage of the peasants.

She was disappointed to learn they would be spending several days in Liverpool before proceeding to London. Rowan gave her this news when they were installed in a small but fashionable hotel away from the waterfront area. When she protested that she wished to proceed immediately to London to her house, he pointed out curtly that they were not on a voyage of discovery, but were working agents for the Confederacy, and the Confederacy had work for them to do in Liverpool.

The next morning a box arrived containing a ball gown. Susanna caught her breath as she lifted the tissue and saw yards of oyster taffeta that mysteriously glinted with pink lights as she rustled the material. The bodice was covered with tiny seed pearls and pink rosebuds, and there was a long pink sash. Rowan, who arrived hard on the heels of the delivery boy, looked over her shoulder and said, "How do you like your working clothes?"

She lifted a pair of pink velvet slippers from the bottom of the box and, staring at all the finery, asked absently, "What do you mean . . . working clothes?"

"There's going to be a ball tonight, and we are invited. There are going to be many men flinging themselves at your feet, and we must discuss how you will deport yourself. At least you will be dealing with gentlemen. For myself, I must move among some of the tougher waterfront pubs and become acquainted with the ruffians who buy and sell information."

"I don't care what you are going to do. And as for my deportment . . . well, I believe you may rest assured I shall not disgrace you again by bursting into tears in public . . . or committing any other breach of etiquette."

Rowan sighed. "Since you bring it up, I do feel compelled to point out that while the Academy and your Aunt Rhea and your Mizjane have done a reasonable job in teaching you which fork to use and how to alight from a carriage and so on, you have never been out in the world and are, therefore, somewhat out of touch with modern customs. However, that was not what I meant about deportment. There is no need for you to hide the fact that you are a loyal Southerner. In fact, it would help if you talked about our nation's needs to some of the men who will no doubt be flocking about you. Of course, they are not to know of your connection with the military. You will let them think you are here solely because of your inheritance. Now sit down and stop fidgeting with that dress."

"No. You can leave while I try it on. I don't wish to talk to you."

"You're not going to. You're going to listen." Taking her hand, Rowan led her to a small pedestal table and pair of high-backed chairs nudging for space in the cluttered room. "It's time to stop thinking about yourself and start thinking about your country."

Susanna grimaced. "I'm not sure I have a country. My father, after all, was an Englishman. It seems what I have is an obligation. You may tell me briefly about that."

"All right. Let me tell you what's been happening. First of all, the Northern newspapers are already boasting that their sea power has crushed us. Norfolk and Hampton Roads have been evacuated and . . . I didn't tell you this before we sailed, but our flotilla defending New Orleans was destroyed." He paused, and when Susanna did not register shock, went on, "Our wealthiest city, Susanna, has surrendered. The coastal cities, the ports . . . the war at sea . . . the blockade . . . these are our weaknesses. If we lose the war it will be because we didn't have enough ships and open ports with supplies moving freely to support our armies. We can lick them on land—our boys know what they are fighting for, while the Yankees are mostly illiterate immigrants serving someone else's time. However, the news isn't all bad. Johnston and thirty thousand rebels licked Grant, who had seventy thousand troops, at Shiloh . . . and Lee is driving him away from Richmond. There's a vicious fight going on there now. But they've got to have supplies. That means ships. Ships, Susanna."

"You know, I never do recall giving you permission to call me by first name."

"Damn your name. Don't you care about anything but yourself? Thirty-five hundred men died at Shiloh. God knows how many will be killed defending Richmond." He stopped speaking and sighed again. "And about your name . . . I forgot to mention that we don't want you to use 'O'Rourke' while you're in England."

Susanna had been squirming in her chair, her eyes constantly straying back to the dress box with its glorious contents. Now she looked at him with narrowed eyes.

"Oh? And why not?"

"Because, my little ignoramus, it's an Irish name, and Ireland has been a thorn in England's side for quite some time."

"O'Rourke was my mother's name. My grandparents came from Ireland. I don't care how they feel about it in England. My English father never bestowed *his* name on me. Besides, what about the solicitors in London? Aren't they supposed to turn the house over to someone named O'Rourke?"

"It is at their request that your name be changed and your identity—that is, your relationship to the late Lord Bodelon, be kept secret. We thought we'd present you as my niece, Susanna Marshall. It has a pleasant ring to it, doesn't it?"

"No," Susanna said, "it hasn't. But tell me about the ball tonight. I'd rather talk about that."

"You did learn to dance at the Academy, didn't you?"

"Yes, But I've never been to a ball," Susanna answered somewhat wistfully.

Rowan's expression softened. "I forget sometimes how very young you are. I suppose it's that old-as-the-ages look in your eyes. Eve and Cleopatra and all the sirens of the seven seas look out from your eyes . . . yet you're little more than a child, aren't you?" A beautiful, vulnerable child, he thought, who wants what she cannot have and would scorn what was humbly offered. He reached across the table for her hand, but Susanna withdrew it.

"We shall be going to a country estate just outside Liverpool, the home of Sir Ronald Wain, who will be entertaining several of his millowner friends and a few shipyard men. The millowners need our cotton—the Lancashire workers are starving—and the shipbuilders are always interested in new contracts. We shall let it be known who they may contact to accomplish all of our ends . . . ships, supplies to the South and king cotton back to Lancashire."

"It can't be that easy," Susanna said.

"Yes, it can. I am the person who can handle matters. I am answerable directly to Mr. Bulloch."

"And who is Mr. Bulloch?"

Rowan grinned. "You really haven't taken much of an interest in the war, have you? James Dunwoody Bulloch is our Chief of Overseas Purchasing . . . and he's right here in Liverpool. However, some of his . . . negotiations . . . are handled by such as myself, with the help of my pretty little niece, whose eyes alone will eloquently plead our case. And, of course, she will suggest to all the English gentlemen present tonight that they bring pressure to bear in any way they can to get a commitment from England to build our ships . . . and maybe give more aid than that. Susanna, my sweet, you're a long way from Blossom Street and your aunt's whores. Every man you meet will believe you are the daughter of a fine old Virginia family, your parents deceased, of course, but from now on, you are a lady. They will look into those eyes and be ready to duel over you, leave their wives for you, or storm castles for you. Getting them to build ships for you will be a small matter."

Susanna looked at him, wondering if he was serious. She never knew for sure with Rowan. There was something about his eyes that was suddenly different; the gray had turned an icy blue, like the surface of a very deep lake, and lurking beneath the surface . . .

She dropped her own eyes, thinking that despite what Rowan had said about joining the Army to escape the boredom of an attorney's office, he was like all Southern men. What she saw beneath the surface, she was convinced, was the unleashed tide of patriotism. He would do anything to ensure victory for the Confederacy. Including using Susanna O'Rourke.

What Rowan was actually thinking was quite different. He was thinking that instead of taking Susanna to be admired by a crowd of men, he would have preferred to keep her all to himself. She would, however, definitely be the belle of the ball, and she needed to know this. It might help her overcome the feeling of worthlessness that the womanizer Chaloner had instilled in her. Rowan was painfully aware that there was little he could say or do that would count for much with Susanna beside a single kind word from Brent Chaloner.

6

ROWAN had not exaggerated the effect Susanna would have on the Englishmen. They fought to dance with her, brought her enough refreshments to feed an army and begged her to allow them to show her the rose garden. There were many beautiful women present, worldly women and young *ingénues*, but no one quite like Susanna. Half a dozen of the younger men asked to be allowed to call, even after she told them she would shortly be leaving for London, and to Susanna's complete astonishment, one young gallant impulsively proposed to her.

Watching the scene with an amused grin and slightly raised eyebrow, Rowan occasionally introduced people who Susanna assumed were the men she was to try to win over to the Confederate cause. As soon as she broached the subject, however, they assured her that they were sympathetic to the South and that ships would, of course, be built in England to sail to the aid of the embattled and beseiged Confederacy. Moreover, they told her not to worry her pretty little head because any moment now England would be recognizing Jefferson Davis and his new nation.

Later Susanna observed some of these men in deep conversation with Rowan, so she supposed some arrangements were being made. It was all too easy. She was the belle of the ball, and she discovered dancing was much more fun in the arms of a man than in an awkward pose with another girl from the academy while they argued over who would lead. Above all, the worshipful admiration of the men was soothing to her pride, wounded by Brent's rejection. How she wished he could see her in her magnificent gown, fresh flowers looped into her hair, surrounded by a dozen eager young men. It was an evening of music, laughter and a curious quickening of the senses at the ease and success of her masquerade.

Every young man she danced with became a substitute for Brent, and she practiced the beguiling glances and mischievous smiles she would bestow when next they met and he would realize she was a great lady after all. She would be so magically transformed when Brent saw her again that he would fall hopelessly, madly in love with her and they would be married.

Rowan did not ask her to dance, although she was aware that he watched her constantly. Surprisingly, Rowan was quite as much of an attraction to the ladies as Susanna was to the gentlemen. More than once Susanna noticed a milk-cheeked miss fluttering her eyes invitingly at the tall American with the reckless, teasing eyes. Moreover, Rowan had a quick wit and ready grasp of any situation, which put him at ease with the men, despite the differences of nationality. Even without the advantage of his uniform Rowan stood out in any gathering. His height, bearing and devilish grin were a magnet that drew the women without offending the men.

Susanna was never close enough to hear that although Rowan's conversation with the other women was pleasant and courteous, it was far from flirtatious. There had been plenty of women in Rowan's life, and each one had gone on her way wondering why a man who had so obviously been physically attracted to her had so desperately sought some other quality she evidently had not possessed.

Just before midnight, a late guest arrived—a tall, angular man with sunken cheeks and deep-set, almost colorless eyes. He had a shock of pure-white hair, although he was by no means old, and his clothes were not as well tailored as those of the other men. He appeared suddenly at her side and, in a low voice, asked her to dance. The invitation sounded most reluctant. He was American and, Susanna realized from his nasal twang, was probably from one of the Midwestern states —a Yankee.

"I'm sorry sir, all my dances are taken," she said coldly and allowed the young man on her other side to lead her out for a waltz.

As she danced she saw the latecomer in conversation with their host and several other men, while Rowan hovered near. At the end of the dance Rowan came swiftly to her side and told her they were leaving.

Susanna looked about the ballroom at the couples strolling from the floor and the eager line of young men waiting for her to be free to dance with them. She had never had such an evening of gaiety before and could not give it up so abruptly.

"Please . . . not yet, Uncle Rowan," she said sweetly, her eyes flashing a warning as he reached to take her arm.

"But I cannot allow you to overtire yourself, sweet little niece of mine. We have a long journey ahead of us." Rowan took her firmly by the hand and spoke in a most fatherly tone, but his eyes were filled with good-natured warning.

"No. I won't leave yet." Her voice sounded like escaping steam.

"Now, now, Susanna, let's not have a scene," Rowan said cheerfully as he began to propel her very forcefully toward the door as though she were a disobedient child.

"Oh!" Susanna gasped and, before she could stop herself, had stamped her foot in rage.

The dancing couple nearest them turned and stared in amazement, and Susanna could have wept with rage and disappointment but was too busy trying to keep her balance as Rowan rushed her from the room, his long strides eating up the floor as her slippers tripped along beside him.

After Rowan had thanked their host and they were in a carriage rolling down the narrow lanes of western Lancashire, Susanna unleashed her fury at being so unceremoniously dragged from the ball and humiliated like a naughty child in front of everyone.

"I'm sorry we had to leave early. But that white-haired fellow who arrived late began to ask me some very leading questions. I have a feeling he may be a Union agent. I didn't like the way he came sniffing around you like a hound dog, either."

"I can take care of myself," Susanna muttered.

"In the bedroom, possibly. However, Jacob Drost looked as if he would rather drown you in the Mersey."

"Oh, you're impossible!" Susanna fumed. "All you ever think of is . . . is . . ."

"Bedroom activities?" Rowan suggested for her.

Susanna ignored the remark and turned her head to look out of the carriage window. The deep-blue twilight had faded into the short English summer night, and the countryside was a shadowy green. The air was scented delicately by the wild violets growing under the hedgerows, and a nightingale sang sweetly in the rustling copse of trees that lay in the hollow of a meadow. Such a perfect evening, and it was wasted because there was no handsome prince to carry her off in a fitting climax. Oh, if only it were Brent at her side instead of Rowan. She checked her tears by surreptitiously dabbing her gloves to her eyes. Rowan must not have the satisfaction of seeing her woe.

When the carriage bounced over a cobblestoned courtyard and came to a halt in front of a Tudor-style inn, Susanne turned to Rowan again.

"Why are we stopping here?"

"We shall spend the night here. No train until morning. We could have stayed with Sir Ronald, but I didn't want to spend the night under the same roof as a Yankee," Rowan answered, watching her out of the corner of his eye.

An apologetic innkeeper, sleepily rubbing his eyes, said he hoped "your lady won't find the room too cramped . . . we've only one guest room left tonight, your lordship."

"My lady is so tired I'm sure she won't notice, landlord," Rowan said. "Will you, my dear? We are so grateful for a bed for the night on short notice, are we not?" And, under his breath to Susanna, "If you open your mouth I shall change my mind about sleeping on the floor."

They followed the innkeeper up the stairs and along a drafty landing to a small dormer bedroom. After the man had departed, Susanna turned to Rowan.

"You may take your leave too. You are not spending the night in this room."

"Ah, 'tis a hard woman you are, Susanna O'Rourke," Rowan said in an exaggerated Irish brogue. He glanced around the tiny room at the canopied bed, washstand, wardrobe and single chair. Prodding the seat of the chair, he grimaced at its unyielding surface, sat down and began to unbutton his jacket.

"The innkeeper said this was the last room, Susanna. If I tell him we're not man and wife, I reckon he'll throw us both out into the night. Of course, we could sleep in each other's arms in the woods . . ."

"No," Susanna said hastily. "You can have the chair. But you must leave while I undress. And I shall need hot water."

Rowan sighed and buttoned up his jacket again.

After he was gone, Susanna sat down on the bed, and resignation began to replace her sadness. It had been a wonderful evening, and she had not wanted it to end. The reality of the way things were was in this room she must share with Rowan, who was, after all, her jailer. If only she could have really been the woman all those men at the ball thought she was . . . a fine lady, with an unsmirched reputation. Why couldn't she have met Brent here, so he would not have known about Blossom Street? If only Brent could come calling for the first time again, to take her out riding . . .

She put the despondent thoughts out of her head. When she and Brent met again it would be for the first time, because she would be a brand-new Susanna, a woman who had learned how to fascinate and captivate him.

She pulled the pins from her hair and the still-fresh flowers dropped gently to her shoulders. She smiled as she remembered the impulsive marriage proposal the young Englishman had blurted out. Brent had come to her to take her as his mistress. If she had not lain with him that night . . . what then, she wondered. But to lie with the man one loved was as natural as breathing

the air. Besides, if she had not, he would have gone
to Pansy, and Susanna could not have borne that.
There had to be some way to win Brent, to wipe out
the mistakes she had made, to convince him that one's
origins were not important. Suppose, after all, that the
South lost the war? Then he would have nothing . . .
for wouldn't the Yankees free the slaves, and wouldn't
that be the end of the plantations? But he would still
have his fine old family name, she thought gloomily;
nothing would remove that. Besides, there was little
Brent. What kind of world would he grow up in if
the South lost the war? No, that was unthinkable.

She had been so lost in her reverie that she had not
realized she was absent-mindedly undressing until
Rowan came through the door carrying a pitcher of
steaming water. His eyes went over her chemise and he
smiled broadly.

"You may put that down on the washstand and leave."

"Perhaps milady would like some assistance with her
toilette?" Rowan suggested with that odd light in his
eyes that Susanna was beginning to recognize. It meant
that he was thinking about something serious, despite
whatever innocuous remark he happened to be making at
the time.

"Just leave while I bathe," she said somewhat wearily.

Rowan stood watching her for a moment, as though
about to say something, then apparently changed his
mind and left. When he returned she was in bed, breathing
deeply, her eyes closed although she was wide awake.
Rowan removed his boots, then slid his chair in front
of the door before sitting down.

When Susanna at last fell asleep, she dreamed she
was dancing with Brent and his dark eyes were adoring
her. As they whirled around she could see Mizjane
holding the baby, smiling and happy, waiting for Mr. and
Mrs. Chaloner to finish dancing so they could all be
together again. But suddenly everything was wrong . . .
Susanna felt fear clutch her heart and she looked up
into the sunken features of Jacob Drost, who held her
so tightly she could not breathe. Where was Brent? Brent!

She cried out in her sleep and tossed, moaning, on a

tear-soaked pillow. But strong arms were wrapped about her, whispering words of comfort. Shh . . . just a dream, go to sleep. No one is going to hurt you again, Susanna, and soon you'll have your baby in your arms and Mizjane to comfort you. There, there, sweetheart, go to sleep. . . .

Brent? Brent, is that you . . . ?

But it was not Brent who watched over her all night long, gray eyes wistful, body tensed to spring at any intruder.

In a time when most of the world's seaborne commerce moved with the wind, the steam-powered raider moved arrogantly along sea lanes to the crossroads of shoreline, current, wind and markets where merchantmen plied the water, their hatches bulging with rich cargoes.

"She's a Federal. Put a shot across her bow, Mr. Chaloner," the captain said, "and run up the colors."

"Aye, sir." Brent's eyes gleamed in anticipation. He had sailed the seas both as the hunted and the hunter . . . and hunter was better.

Disappointingly, after the first shot their victim came to an immediate halt and lay dead in the water, a fat prize cowering on the shimmering sea.

Brent was an old hand at boarding. Swagger past the shaking crew, their eyes downcast in fear . . . demand to see the ship's manifest . . . perhaps take the captain and papers back to the skipper for on-the-spot adjudication. . . establish enemy ownership of the cargo . . . remove crew and passengers and any usable equipment . . . then sink her.

Watching the orange flames leap from the doomed ship, Brent thought of his last trip into Cape Fear with his own ship afire as she limped perilously close to the shoals to escape the pursuing gunboat.

Strange, then as now, in moments of high danger or complete victory, when he felt most alive, he would experience that same quickening of the pulse he felt when he was with Susanna, and, in fact, he often thought of her in these moments of peril, wanting her most when his blood raced with the excitement of war.

There had been two females aboard the ship they were sinking. The thought crossed his mind that if it were a hundred years earlier, or if Captain Semmes had not been so unbending about his rule of Southern chivalry, then Brent could have taken one or both of the women to appease this sudden lust. Still, it would not have been the same as having Susanna. How many times he had tried to substitute other women . . . but none could lift a man to the heights as Susanna could, and just as he felt he was her complete master, the gossamer softness of her would grip him mercilessly and he was her prisoner. She was as dangerous as the sea or war, and equally fascinating.

Mr. Tweedye, of the London firm of solicitors handling the estate of the late Lord Bodelon, ushered Susanna into a small office filled with dusty books and sagging aspidistra plants. Rummaging through the yellowing papers which covered his desk, he produced a leather case and proceeded to unlock it with a key he carried on his watch chain.

"I requested you to come here before going to your house on Essex Square because there are certain matters Lord Bodelon wished me to convey to you personally, Miss O'Rourke. . . . I understand you will be calling yourself Miss Marshall? Very good. Lord Bodelon wished you to use a pseudonym whilst in London. Now, as you are aware, Lady Bodelon and her daughter, Emma, also have a house in London, not close to yours, but it will be inevitable that you meet, since they are aware of your bequest. What they do not know is your relationship to Lord Bodelon. They believe you are the daughter of an old friend of his lordship who was a Virginian. As you may know, Lord Bodelon traveled frequently to the colonies—I mean, to America—in connection with his business, which was, of course, shipping. The Bodelon Line was one of the first in England to begin to convert to steam, by the way, and their ships carry passengers all over the world, and cargoes too. . . ."

The old gentleman paused and studied the documents from the leather case for a long time. The office was airless and musty, and Susanna felt drowsy after the long journey from Liverpool.

At last Mr. Tweedye looked up at her. "For as long as you care to stay in London and are unmarried, the expenses of the house—servants, everything you need—will be paid for you. You will also receive a generous allowance for clothing and personal items. If you decide to return to America, you may keep any clothing you have purchased or jewelry you have received as gifts. Everything else is to remain in London. This will also be the case should you marry, although in that event there will be a handsome settlement."

"I see," Susanna said. "I am unmarried, of course. However, I have an infant son I expect to be joining me shortly."

Mr. Tweedye peered through his spectacles, blinking. "Oh . . . dear . . . well, perhaps you could say the child is a relative other than your son? Lord Bodelon also specified, you see, that no hint of scandal is to touch his name and that you must live properly and . . . ah . . . chastely. It is to this end that he wishes an old friend of his to have access to the house and . . . keep an eye on you."

"Nicholas Kirby—the man mentioned in the bequest," Susanna said. "Who is he exactly?"

"As I stated, an old friend of Lord Bodelon's. Apart from myself and the solicitors in Richmond, he is the only other person who knows you are Lord Bodelon's daughter. I feel it only fair to add that your bequest will go to Mr. Kirby should you decide to return to America and remain there in excess of a year. That is, he will receive the house and the annuity."

"Then I suppose he could report a scandal of some nature and have me removed?"

Mr. Tweedye rubbed his mustache thoughtfully. "You mean if he finds out the baby is yours . . . ?"

Susanna had not meant that; she did not believe Brent's son was a scandal. She had in mind Nicholas Kirby's reaction to Rowan's schemes on behalf of the Confederacy.

Taking her downcast eyes to indicate embarrassment,

Mr. Tweedye went on hurriedly, "Please do not distress yourself on that account, miss. There is no way he will find out. Might I suggest that since we are presenting Mr. Rowan Marshall as your uncle, you let it be known that the child is his . . . that he lost his wife in childbirth, possibly? I mean, as an explanation of why you are caring for the child? A single *man* with a child being less suspect?"

"Mr. Tweedye, I take it you are aware of Major Marshall's reason accompanying me here?"

The pale old eyes regarded her solemnly. "I do not wish to know. You may entertain whomever you wish. Were I a young lady embarking upon such a venture as yours . . . going to reside in a strange land . . . I should most certainly have looked for a protector. Since Major Marshall is from our counterparts in Richmond and evidently has some business of his own to conduct in England, I should say he is a logical and practical choice. Also, having met the young man, I would say he would be a splendid fellow to have on one's side in the event of trouble arising . . ." He coughed slightly, then pulled a large handkerchief from his pocket and blew his nose.

The interview appeared to be at an end, and Susanna rose hesitantly, feeling she should ask more questions about her father, yet still loath to speak about the man who had deserted her mother.

Rowan was waiting for her in the outer office, and before they reached the house on Essex Square Susanna told him of Mr. Tweedye's suggestion about little Brent. Rowan digested this with a strangely sardonic expression on his face, then shrugged his shoulders and agreed to the deception. They had not heard when Mizjane and the baby would be arriving.

An ornate carriage with a pair of fine horses was standing in front of No. 28 Essex Square. Almost as soon as he opened the front door, the butler announced that Lady Bodelon was in the drawing room. As an afterthought, he added that his name was Dobbs, that he was the butler, and that they were welcomed to London.

Rowan winked at her as he helped her with her cloak. "Want to freshen up before you see her?"

Susanna shook her head, anxious to get the meeting over with. To the butler she said, "Would you show me the way? Lady Bodelon is Lord Bodelon's widow . . . or his daughter?"

"His widow, mum. His daughter, Lady Emma, is lady-in-waiting to Her Majesty, you know." He looked a little pityingly at the ignorant foreigners who believed their arrival was important enough to bring a lady-in-waiting from court to greet them, and who did not know that Lord Bodelon's daughter was properly called Lady Emma, not Lady Bodelon.

From the glimpses of the house Susanna had as she followed Dobbs along an oak-paneled hall, she felt it was oppressively dark and cluttered with too much furniture, all of a massive scale and in somber colors. The carpets on the floors had evidently once been handsome Persian rugs but were now almost black with age and dirt. The windows were covered with dark draperies of an indeterminable color, and everywhere were oil paintings badly in need of cleaning and restoration. The drawing room to which they were shown was filled with more ugly furniture. Endless bric-a-brac covered every inch of table and shelf space, and china animals sat about the floor.

Lady Bodelon did not rise to greet them. Susanna's eyes widened as she saw the woman was strikingly handsome. Alicia Bodelon did not smile, although her greeting was courteous.

"Welcome to London, my dear. . . . You are Susanna? I'm afraid I know only your first name. Mr. Tweedye and his associates were exceedingly reticent about discussing you. I am Alicia Bodelon."

Moving to accept the outstretched hand, Susanna saw that although Lady Bodelon's clothes were black, they were hardly mere widow's weeds. The gown was well cut, flattering a small waist and full bosom, and a cameo brooch at the throat drew attention to a flawless white skin and large violet eyes. Her fair hair was dressed in an elaborate arrangement of curls. Susanna had never seen a woman whom black suited more.

"Marshall . . . Susanna Marshall. May I present my uncle, Rowan Marshall?"

Rowan bowed charmingly over the outstretched hand, and long eyelashes fluttered with much interest over violet eyes. "I came to invite you to dinner tonight. Except for Nicholas' rooms on the third floor, the house hasn't been used since my husband passed on and certainly will require some work to make it habitable. I've ordered Dobbs to see it is thoroughly cleaned. Only one bedroom is ready for use—we didn't know your uncle would be accompanying you. But we can find room for him at my house, I'm sure, until another room is readied here."

The invitation was extended with an ill-concealed glint in Lady Bodelon's violet eyes which Susanna was sure indicated more than politeness. Yes, Rowan was handsome, in a careless sort of way. Unreasonably, Susanna did not want Alicia Bodelon to have him. She is too old, Susanna thought. Youth and age should not mate. She had closed her eyes to the spectacle of the fat old men abed with Aunt Rhea's girls in Blossom Street, grunting and sweating like horses. That Alicia Bodelon was slim, beautiful and barely forty Susanna did not consider. Susanna herself had been battling the stirrings of desire ever since the night of the storm. She knew that Brent was far away. Now she wondered if she had been considering Rowan as a proxy all along . . . but he was so hateful, let Lady Bodelon have him!

Rowan and Lady Bodelon conversed briefly about their voyage, and, finding herself shut out of the conversation, Susanna interrupted to say, "I understand you have a daughter, Lady Bodelon?"

The violet eyes were dragged reluctantly from Rowan. "Yes. You will meet my Emma tonight. She comes to visit me once a week. Her duties are few now, with Her Majesty in mourning. Our dear Queen never leaves the palace. She loved Prince Albert so." She paused for a moment, then went on, "You will also meet Nicholas Kirby and some others of our set. Nicholas and your father were my late husband's dearest friends, although they apparently never met. Strangely, neither Nicholas nor I knew of your father's existence until the will was read." A faraway, dreamy look came into her eyes, as though to discount the importance of this statement.

Suddenly apprehensive, Susanna said quietly, "I shall look forward to meeting all of your friends."

Nicholas Kirby was a big, bluff man in his fifties with sandy hair and a somewhat slack mouth that did not go with his pale eyes, which seemed to dart in several directions at once. The darting eyes came back to her several times during dinner. She was seated next to Emma Bodelon, who had proved to be as unlike her beautiful mother as could have been possible. Lady Emma was pathetically plain, a small mouselike creature with flat chest and drooping shoulders. Where her mother's hair was gloriously golden, Emma's was wispy and dun-colored, and instead of possessing marble-white skin and magnificent violet eyes, Emma was inclined to sallowness and her eyes were hazel, and always, it seemed, looked downward.

Susanna made several attempts to draw Emma into the conversation, but the girl was obviously painfully shy. It seemed incredible that this frightened little girl was a lady-in-waiting to the most powerful queen on earth. For once, Susanna was glad of Rowan's easy charm and quick wit, for he was soon charming all of the ladies present, including little Emma. Lady Bodelon, seated at the head of the table, never took her eyes from him. Like a cat contemplating the cream, Susanna decided with a stab of jealousy. He wasn't Brent, but he certainly could be attractive when he wanted to be. Rowan's outrageous teasing and his rascally grin, no less than his remarkably clear eyes and vagrant golden hair, seemed to attract females from nine to ninety.

There were plenty of other men present, but they were not quite so appealing. Although that Tom Douglas with his flaming red hair . . . and the Bartlett brothers with their shy smiles and country-pink cheeks . . . Their father, Sir Edmund Bartlett, kept beaming at Susanna and extending invitations to his country estate in Surrey.

After the dinner of several courses, punctuated by fine wines, Susanna began to feel a languorous, well-fed euphoria steal over her, and when they retired to the music room to be entertained, she chose a sofa in an alcove on which to rest. She was instantly alert, however, when Nicholas Kirby came and sat beside her.

"So," he said in his staccato accent. "You are here at last, Miss Marshall. It took you some time to decide to come. Should I suppose that you now have a reason to be here?"

Taken unaware by the suddenness of the question, Susanna looked about the room for Rowan, but he was at Alicia Bodelon's side and she was fluttering a black lace fan below those enormous violet eyes.

"Your . . . uncle . . . seems quite entranced with our hostess. But it seems you would prefer he answer my question?" Nicholas Kirby said.

"Not at all," Susanna answered. "It was my decision to come to England, not his. He accompanied me because he has some business in England. I understand you have business in London also, Mr. Kirby. May I ask what your business is?"

His expression changed only imperceptibly, but Susanna knew she had just been reassessed as one not to be dismissed too lightly. "Imports and exports. My associates and I ship goods all over the world. We are called shipping agents. And what is your uncle's business?"

"Oh, my goodness, Mr. Kirby, Southern gentlemen never discuss their business with ladies," Susanna said, looking down at her hands, demurely folded in her lap, to hide the fact that her eyes were mocking him.

"And what do you suppose your Southern gentlemen will do when they have lost the war?"

Susanna looked up angrily. "The Confederacy happens to be winning the war, sir. Why . . . one of our boys can lick five Yankees . . ." She tried to remember what Rowan had told her about the battle of Manassas in order to back up her point, but she had not been interested enough at the time to remember. Now in the face of this foreigner's rude dismissal of her country's capabilities she felt for the first time a stirring of the blood that was almost patriotism.

"Of course. But there is the question of supplies. You have no factories or foundries or shipyards in your Southern states. Don't count on Pam, my dear."

"Pam?"

"Lord Palmiston." His face twisted into a damp smile. "You are not yet familiar with our nickname for Lord Palmiston? He is our Prime Minister."

Susanna was thinking that Nicholas Kirby reminded her of a large cold-blooded toad who had just finished eating a very greasy meal. She shuddered slightly and, turning her head, was grateful to see Rowan making his way toward them. At the same moment her blood seemed to freeze in her veins, for, looking beyond Rowan, Susanna could see Lady Bodelon at the music-room door greeting a newly arrived guest. The gaslight cast a yellowish glow on the white hair of the, tall, stooped figure in the wrinkled frock coat who was bowing to her. As he raised his face, Susanna looked again at Jacob Drost, the Union agent they had met in Lancashire.

7

Susanna looked across her bedroom at Rowan and wanted him to make love to her. Instead she said, "Who is he, and what does he want of us?"

Jacob Drost had been presented as a "fellow American" and no mention had been made of the fact that he was a Northerner. They had been spared further conversation by the arrival of the musicians, and Rowan had remained at her side the rest of the evening. He had declined Lady Bodelon's invitation to spend the night, and for once Susanna had been glad to have him near. Jacob Drost's presence had cast a pall of gloom on the evening, and at one point when Susanna realized that both the cadaverous Drost and the moist-lipped Kirby were watching her she had wanted to run in panic and hide.

Upon departing, Susanna had been surprised to find Emma Bodelon at her side whispering, "I do hope we can get to know one another. I'm very interested in learning more about your country. May I call on you?"

Susanna had agreed, absently, eager to leave behind the sinister Drost but more eager to be alone with Rowan.

"Did you know he was a friend of the Bodelons?" she asked him now.

"No, I didn't," Rowan said, "and it was as much a surprise to me as to you when he arrived tonight. But don't be afraid of him. I don't see how he can cause any trouble for us as long as we're careful not to let him know what we're up to."

"What are we up to, Rowan? I still don't know what I'm supposed to do, besides smile at a lot of idiotic Englishmen. Perhaps I should marry one of them and be done with the Confederacy."

"And desert your Aunt Rhea? Break your word? Have your son raised to be an idiotic Englishman? Shame on you, Susanna O'Rourke," Rowan said. "There are better times coming, always remember that. You're only licked when you want to be. Come on, my pet. Dobbs said the maids won't be starting work for a couple of days, so let me help you out of your stays and hoops."

"Why didn't you stay and help Alicia Bodelon out of hers?" Susanna snapped, then wished she had not been quite so vulgar when Rowan laughed triumphantly.

"So! You were a little jealous! I was hoping you'd notice how taken she was with me. Dare I hope you are beginning to care for me, my sweet?"

"No, you may not." Susanna scowled, but she did not resist as he led her to a chair and, when she was seated, removed her slippers and began to massage her feet. The wine had gone to her head, and there was a fire burning brightly in the fireplace to ward off the chill of the night.

Rowan left her for a moment and reappeared with two glasses. "A glass of port to help you sleep," he said.

Sipping the rich wine, she was so utterly relaxed her eyelids felt heavy, yet a flame was flickering ever more insistently inside her, and she wanted him to make love to her. Instead he was talking amiably, telling her she would have a great deal of freedom to do as she pleased while in London. That he would try not to be a bother, or endanger her in any way.

Susanna listened impatiently. Why did he not begin the suggestive teasing to which she had become accustomed? Then she could perhaps lead him into making love. He was, after all, the only man available, and the tightening of those secret muscles was becoming a sharp pain. Besides, he was so appealing tonight, for some reason . . . those long hard thighs and the way his mustache drooped so decadently . . .

"Perhaps I will remove my clothes—it's very warm in here," Susanna said in a low voice. "Would you help me . . . ?"

"Of course," Rowan said solemnly. He was as accom-

her head and kiss her, but he did not.

"There. You seem to be thoroughly brushed," he said. "Are you ready to retire?"

"Yes," Susanna answered dully and rose to face him. His expression was inscrutable. An iceberg, she decided, drifting in an arctic sea.

Susanna walked over to the bed, slipped between the sheets and tossed her dressing gown over the brass bedposts.

"Won't you be a little chilly, sleeping like that?" Rowan asked with great concern in his voice, gray eyes widely innocent.

Susanna could contain herself no longer. She sat up and flung a pillow at him, then leaped off the bed to beat on his chest with her fists, forgetting her nakedness.

"Oh, you are hateful! I hate you, Rowan Marshall! I hate you . . ." Her words died in her throat and she looked up at him maliciously. In their close contact she realized that Rowan had been aroused by her. There was a hard bulge in his breeches that belied the careful indifference of his conversation.

"You could have just asked me, you know," he said, grinning like the devil himself, eyes ablaze with mischief.

It was Susanna's turn to be casual. "Ask you what?" she said, walking back to the bed.

Following her, he stood beside the bed looking down at her with a faint smile. "Susanna, my dear, I've always believed that the enjoyment of lovemaking was as much a woman's right as a man's. Men ask for what they want, why not women? What a rare treasure such a woman would be in a world of blushing fools and brazen hussies looking for payment. As it is we are faced with the choice between a cowering wife who does her duty in the dark and avoids our eyes afterward, or a loose woman who is play-acting for us."

"You are forgetting one other kind of woman," Susanna said.

Rowan was slowly undressing, with elaborate care, folding his clothes and placing his boots neatly together. "And what kind is that?"

"A mistress . . . or a courtesan."

He straightened up abruptly. "Yes, I suppose to one of my station in life a mistress is an unheard-of luxury. I I doubt I shall ever be able to afford more than a wife. But you are right. I suppose that is what you were to the black-browed Captain Chaloner?"

"He was the first . . . oh, damn you, Rowan Marshall, it's none of your business." She bit her lip; the wine was making her dizzy and she did not want to talk. Especially not about Brent. The thought crossed her mind that if women could live like men, she would have Brent as a husband and Rowan as a mistress . . . but surely that wasn't the right word? She began to giggle and soon was laughing helplessly.

Unconcerned, Rowan sat down on the bed beside her and stroked her breasts gently, following the soft contours and tracing the nipple with his finger as lightly as a wind-drifted blossom.

"Someday, when we know each other better," he said, "you must tell me what it is you find so damn funny at this moment. Right now, I'm not sure I want to know. There are men, you know, who would lose all of their ardor . . . in view of such mirth."

"You don't seem to have lost yours," Susanna sputtered, choking with laughter as she reached out her hand to touch him.

His fingers glided slowly downward in widening circles, slid between her warm thighs, felt the moistness and gentle contraction as he penetrated the delicate passage. Susanna trembled as she leaned closer to him, her lips parted.

"My God, Susanna," he groaned somewhere deep inside his senses, "you make me feel like a god when it is you who are the goddess . . ."

Susanna's limited encounters in lovemaking had been hasty, almost without thought as to her own pleasure. This time, she was promising herself, it was going to be a leisurely, lovely experience. She wanted to feel, to explore, to know every nuance of this most supreme of all human experiences.

Rowan murmured again softly as she explored him with her tongue, lightly with her teeth, teasingly with her fingers. Then she pulled him to her, guided him as he entered her, and lost herself in a magically choreographed act of love.

The two of them were like dancers whose bodies touched, became one, pirouetted, plunged, soared . . . and laughing, whispering, slowing, quickening . . . joyously, in a burst of sun and stars and tides, lay limp in each other's arms.

At breakfast the next morning she thought about making the house livable and preparing for the arrival of Mizjane and the baby. In her own sense of well-being, she did not notice that Rowan was unusually silent, or that he watched her with a mixture of hope and fearful expectation in his gaze. Looking up once and seeing the waiting look, she said, "If you are going to daydream all day, I shall put you to work. Now be off with you, I have things to do."

She was busy the first weeks, replacing carpets and curtains, having bric-a-brac taken to the attic and some of the uglier pieces of furniture stored away. It did not occur to her that her life was more that of a well-to-do young matron than a Confederate agent. Rowan was gone much of the time and it was sometimes several days or even longer between his visits, but he never asked her to accompany him. A room had been prepared for him on the same floor as hers, and she told him casually to use it whenever he was in town.

Alicia Bodelon invited them to her parties and to the theater, and they were quickly accepted by all of the Bodelons' friends. Nicholas Kirby and Jacob Drost were often present at these gatherings, and although everyone else avoided mentioning the war in America, it seemed to Susanna that Kirby threw many veiled innuendoes her way and Drost watched hawklike for her or Rowan to give away some clue as to why they had removed themselves so far from the conflict. Kirby baited them continually about the hopelessness of a nonindustrial nation going to war against a superior foe, and Susanna was secretly proud of the way Rowan parried the attacks.

One day when Kirby was visibly losing an argument, his caustic thrusts tossed back lightly and with profound wit so that the barbs became the pointed edge upon which his viewpoint floundered, he suddenly ran his tongue over already moist lips and said, "But, of course, my dear chap, we are all very brave and daring when far removed from the actual scene of battle."

There was an instant hush in the room and everyone present shifted uncomfortably. Susanna jumped to her feet, expecting Rowan to drag Kirby outside forcibly, to tell him that the Confederacy had work for them here. Rowan's eyes became almost transparent for a second, but he merely smiled and said, "Quite right, sir," and turned to address a remark to someone else.

Susanna was outraged. How could Rowan have let Kirby humiliate him so? Later, when they were alone and she confronted Rowan with his "cowardice," he agreed with her completely and refused to quarrel.

"Of course, I am a devout coward. I should have called him out had I been half a man . . . informed him on the spot that I am a secret agent for my country and that if I am successful in my venture, I could be more valuable to our side than some poor devil being blown to pieces on some battlefield."

"Oh, you're impossible. I know you couldn't tell him that. But you could have done something instead of letting everyone think you are a coward and a fool."

"Did it ever occur to you, my wild Irish flower, that sometimes it is more difficult to remain silent? No, I suppose not. But I cannot change other people and what they think. I can only deal with myself. As I've pointed out to you before, we're only licked when we think we've been licked."

Susanna had left the room in her anger. She had not wanted to tell Rowan that the real reason she was disappointed in his handling of the incident was her growing fear of Nicholas Kirby. Kirby watched Susanna in the same way Alicia Bodelon watched Rowan, but Kirby's eyes were not the unspoken invitations that Alicia's were; his roved over Susanna's body like tiny weapons, and often he would wipe his forehead, handkerchief in thick fingers, as he watched her. Susanna would push back imaginary strands of hair from her face, pull down her skirts in case her pantalettes were showing, and squirm constantly under that relentless scrutiny. Yet even more than Kirby, it was Jacob Drost who filled her with real dread and a sense of doom every time she happened to meet his inscrutable stare. She was reminded of a cobra preparing to strike, and, even as she glanced away it seemed the flesh melted from his sunken cheeks and she could see the skull beneath.

Drost and Kirby were the only men in London who were not openly captivated by Susanna. Alicia Bodelon was patronizing to Susanna, charming to Rowan. Susanna wondered resentfully if Rowan were taking the violet-eyed beauty to bed, for he did not come to Susanna's room, although on one occasion she left her door ajar and a candle burning. Rowan had rudely stuck his head around the door and told her to close and lock it or she'd be giving ideas to Nicholas Kirby should he happen to use his rooms on the third floor. Susanna had slammed the door and locked it.

She was beginning to dread the lonely nights in her room when thoughts of Brent would come stealing into her mind and her body ached with longing for him. She would then, inexplicably, find herself thinking of making love with Rowan instead.

The wicked idea crossed her mind that if Rowan was no longer interested in making love, she would simply have to find another partner. This would merely be a matter of choosing the most handsome man of the throngs who came calling and squired her to parties and plays. That Tom Douglas . . . or one of the Bartlett brothers, perhaps.

As the weeks drifted by, Susanna began to feel uneasy over the fact that Mizjane and the baby had not arrived. When she questioned Rowan he said, "My superior in Richmond promised he would send someone to watch the trains arriving in Macon to find a Negro woman with a white baby. His orders were to intercept them if possible, but if not to keep watch on both the Chaloners and your aunt. I do have some news about your aunt.

She is living in North Carolina with Henri Duvalle. I understand he rented a house in Wilmington. Don't worry, honey, Mizjane and the baby are probably on their way here by now."

"Mizjane is very strong and resourceful. I know she will take good care of my baby," Susanna said. "I'd feel happier if they didn't have to sail from New York . . . but I suppose with the blockade they can't safely sail from a Southern port, and there won't be the problem of proving she isn't a slave in the North."

It was the quiet Emma, Lady Bodelon's daughter, who proved to be the biggest surprise to Susanna. Although Emma visited her mother only once a week, she slipped away frequently to visit Susanna and, shyly at first, offered her friendship. Susanna soon found herself confiding her worries about Mizjane and the baby to Emma, although continuing with the pretense that he was actually Rowan's son. Susanna had felt some satisfaction in announcing to Lady Bodelon that "Rowan's son" was shortly arriving from America.

"If Mr. Marshall feels they are safely on their way, you shouldn't worry, Susanna," Emma Bodelon said one afternoon as they were chatting over a cup of tea. "It is very sweet of you to feel such love for your little cousin. Your Mizjane—was she your slave?"

"No," Susanna answered sharply, and when Emma crimsoned with embarrassment she added, "I'm sorry . . . It's just that people here have very distorted ideas of Southerners. Mizjane was a slave, long ago, but she was freed before I was born. She was born on a Caribbean island and is very, very proud and dignified. When you meet her, you'll understand how I feel about her. 'Jane' is the name an Englishman gave her, but when I was a baby I always wanted to call her 'Mama' and somehow she became Mizjane all run together like one word."

"I see," Emma said and added, wistfully, "Your face shines with love when you speak of her. She is fortunate to have someone care for her as you do. Susanna . . ."

"Yes, Emma, what is it?"

"You don't mind my dropping in on you so much, do you?"

"Of course not. I'm truly happy to see you. It's nice having someone close to my own age to talk to. Especially someone in so exalted a position."

"I'm so glad . . . but if you mean my being at court, well, Mother tells everyone I am a lady-in-waiting, but that is a slight exaggeration. I'm only what one might call an apprentice lady-in-waiting. I would have become one in the real sense had not Prince Albert died . . . but now there's so little for us to do. I seldom see Her Majesty, and I'm glad, really—her grief is so terrible to behold."

"What about your grief, Emma . . . do you miss your father?"

"When he died, it was as if a shining light had gone out in my life."

Susanna looked at her in surprise. "You loved him?"

"Oh yes, very much. I think he loved me too, even though I'm so plain. I used to lose my tongue completely when he was home, trip over my feet . . . I wish I could have been more like Mother."

"Perhaps he loved you just as you are," Susanna said gently. "Were he and your mother very happy?"

A shadow flitted briefly across Emma's face, and she bent to stir her tea briskly with an Apostle spoon. Susanna had learned that Emma could not bring herself to tell a lie, and seeing the girl struggle between loyalty to her mother and avoiding the question, Susanna went swiftly to her rescue. "Of course they were. How foolish of me to ask." He probably loved my mother, she was thinking. Yet he did not divorce Alicia to marry her . . . or perhaps he knew my mother before he married Alicia? Aunt Rhea and Mizjane would never speak of him. Perhaps it was because my mother wasn't good enough to bear his name, as Brent feels I am not good enough to bear his.

Susanna could see a tear forming in the corner of Emma's eye and decided she had better change the subject. "Tell me, Emma, how do people in England really feel about the war in America? Are they taking sides? I have seen some dreadful political cartoons in *Punch* depicting the North and South as naughty schoolboys brawling with one another. And they always draw Jeff Davis looking so . . . hangdog."

"Don't pay any heed, Susanna. It is an outrageous periodical sometimes, even Her Majesty says so. I think people are secretly on your side. I know I am—especially after meeting that dreadful Mr. Drost. If he is a typical Northerner . . ."

"I heard," Susanna said, "that the Queen and Prince Albert had lost favor in England because they opposed the Crimean War in the fifties . . . and that perhaps the Queen is making the same mistake by not using her influence on Parliament to form an alliance with the South now."

"My goodness, Susanna! I had no idea you knew so much about English politics," Emma exclaimed, and there was admiration on her pointed little face. "I wish you could see the Queen . . . she is so lost in her grief over her Prince that I honestly don't think she is aware of what is happening outside the palace."

Susanna herself had not realized how much information Rowan had imparted to her about England. What a clever rascal he was, always teasing, yet all the while putting ideas in her head. At first Susanna had considered Rowan's attitude toward her vaguely insulting. She had observed that conversations between men and women were always punctuated by either extravagantly gallant phrases or slightly flirtatious undercurrents. Rowan spoke to her bluntly and without artifice, but there was no doubt he inspired her to think in terms of ideas rather than idle gossip. Then, too, since she had shown her ignorance to Nicholas Kirby about Lord Palmiston, who she had learned was a force more powerful in England than the Queen, Susanna had taken care to keep her eyes and ears open, although she told herself she was concerned with her goal to become a knowledgeable woman of the world more in order to dazzle Brent than in order to understand the maneuverings in the political arena.

"Oh, gracious me, Emma, we are getting serious. I

really wanted to show you the new gowns I've bought. Come on, I'll race you upstairs."

Giggling, the two girls ran hand in hand up the stairs, and Dobbs, the butler, coming from the servants' quarters, thought he had never seen the plain little Emma look so animated or happy. There was no doubt about it, that pretty young American girl seemed to bring out the best . . . and the worst . . . in everyone. Like most British servants, he knew more about the goings-on upstairs than those who lived upstairs did.

Dobbs knew, for instance, that Lady Bodelon was not as kindly disposed toward the American girl as was her daughter and that the fair Alicia would have been even less kindly disposed if she could see the way Susanna's uncle looked at the girl sometimes. Then there was that fat fly in the ointment, Nicholas Kirby.

Both Kirby and Lady Bodelon had approached Dobbs with thinly veiled offers of monetary reward for any information he or the other servants could pass on regarding the activities of the Americans. Dobbs liked his new mistress and her uncle and worried about the questions of Lady Bodelon and Kirby. There was more to those questions than any wish to have Lord Bodelon's will set aside, Dobbs was certain. It had something to do with the American war between the states.

As the days slipped away, Susanna realized there was something lacking in her life besides her baby and Mizjane. The birth of the child, Brent, and perhaps most of all, Rowan, had combined to turn Susanna into a woman, and her woman's needs were not being met.

She began to eye the young men who called more boldly. She even managed to maneuver Tom into giving her a brotherly kiss, but apart from this not one of them by word or deed even remotely hinted that they would like more from her, despite the fact they made it clear she was the most beautiful and desirable woman in London.

Had Susanna grown up in less uninhibited surroundings, or been less isolated from the world of social intercourse, she would have known that in the mores of the

day, young men did not make improper advances to
respectable young women. Young men were schooled
to take their pleasures with tarts and trollops, and if
they found this distasteful, society closed its eyes to liaisons between young men and married women. Such
liaisons were common in all the finest and outwardly
most proper families.

Although Susanna was always invited to Alicia's gatherings, she was well aware it was actually Emma who
requested her presence. Alicia Bodelon's violet eyes
narrowed noticeably whenever Susanna appeared, and
the older woman moved swiftly to break up the circles
of young men that clustered about Susanna. Alicia Bodelon seemed to go to great lengths to try to embarrass
Susanna; she quickly learned which English customs
were unknown to Susanna, as well as noting her American
lack of class consciousness,. Susanna had no knowledge
of the proper way of addressing titled visitors, or of the
hierarchy of English servants; she simply treated everyone in a courteous and friendly way and was aghast
when Alicia regaled a group of guests with the amusing
story of how the American girl had addressed the Duchess
of Wanford as "Your Highness" and in almost the same
breath called her own maid *Miss* Morgan! It did not help
that most of those present did not join Alicia in her
tittering.

When Susanna began to watch and listen closely to
avoid further *faux pas*, Alicia assumed the role of the
sophisticated woman of the world guiding the inexperienced young girl, but in such a way as to point up how
very gauche were Susanna's manners. Anyone less
resilient or adaptive than Susanna would quickly have
been reduced to tears of humiliation. In her self-styled
role of mentor, Alicia Bodelon took it upon herself to
drop in unexpectedly to see Susanna, a ruse Susanna
felt was used mainly to try to catch Rowan alone, and
one afternoon Alicia caught them both unawares.

Rowan had returned from one of his trips north and
was less grim-faced than usual when he paused at Susanna's open bedroom door. She had been trying on a
new ball gown and was standing clad only in her chemise

and petticoats, the flame-colored dress held before her as she studied her reflection in the dressing-table mirror.

"It's all wrong for you, my sweet," Rowan offered from the hallway. "The color is too bold, too flamboyant . . . it will make you look like a hussy."

"Oh . . . so you've decided to come back," Susanna said. "How you do pride yourself on your knowledge of women's clothes. I should think you would be afraid of being accused of being unmanly." She dropped the dress on the bed.

Rowan came into the room uninvited and sat down on her dresser stool. "Oh, I don't worry too much about what's unmanly. Or what's unwomanly, for that matter," he said.

"What do you mean by that?" Susanna asked suspiciously. Seeing him in her bedroom made her think longingly of the lean hardness of his body and how in his embrace she did not have to wonder if she was pleasing him. She put the thought aside, since it appeared inevitable they were headed for an argument. His eyes twinkled with devilment and his grin was preposterously audacious.

"Only that there isn't, in my opinion, as much difference between the sexes as there appears to be on the surface. We are equipped with the same five senses, after all. And that dress offends at least two of my senses. Send it back, Susanna. It isn't right with your hair and eyes."

"I shall do as I please with the dress," Susanna said.

"Of course you will. Just as I find myself unable to hold my tongue in my dealings with you, so will my pretty little Susanna blunder through life making the wrong choices."

"I suggest you try holding your tongue now. I also suggest you'd better leave before Morgan brings the water up for my bath."

"Do you believe, if I really tried, I could learn to say the right things to you, Susanna?" He got up suddenly and bowed dramatically, then dropped to his knees before her, his hand over his heart. "Ah, Susanna, fairest flower of the Confederacy . . . how my poor bruised heart has longed for you all the hours we were parted

. . . how many times I was reminded of the fire in your eyes when I saw sunlight in a deep-green forest, or the glory of your hair when the red-gold sun sank into the sea . . ." He pretended to twirl his golden mustache in a comically villainous manner.

Susanna picked up the flame-colored dress and flung it at him, the silk folds almost engulfing him except for his lower legs. Susanna was laughing, in spite of herself, and from beneath the flame cloud came plaintive gasps mingled with chuckles.

At that moment Susanna raised her eyes and saw the figure that had just moved silently into view in the hall outside her bedroom. Alicia Bodelon. She paused for a moment and then turned and went quickly back down the stairs.

"Rowan!" Susanna pulled the dress from him. "Alicia Bodelon is here and she saw us . . . at least I think she did, but she couldn't know it was you under the dress."

Rowan was on his feet, instantly serious. "Get dressed quickly and go down and talk to her. You've got to convince her there was no man in your room before she has you thrown out of the house."

"Me?" Susanna said indignantly. "What about you? It's all your fault. Besides, she's been making eyes at you ever since we arrived. I should think all you'd have to do is take her to bed and you could make her forget everything."

"There's only one woman in the world I would like to take to bed and make forget everything," Rowan said. "Go and make her believe you were simply giggling in here with your maid, who has rather large feet. I'll keep out of sight. Now hurry."

Alicia Bodelon was waiting for her in the drawing room, a triumphant smile hovering about her lips. Susanna's courage wavered slightly until she remembered that she hadn't actually done anything.

"Good afternoon, Lady Bodelon," Susanna said brightly. "It's Dobbs' day off and I suppose you had to let yourself in and come upstairs looking for me."

Alicia's smile faded. "Why . . . oh . . . yes. The place did seem to be deserted and I thought I would—"

"Search the house?" Susanna finished for her, speaking without thinking rather than from a real desire to anger her visitor.

"Not at all. . . . I was simply . . ." An angry flush was spreading across the camelia skin.

"Morgan—my maid—was helping me with my dress. I'm afraid you interrupted a little foolishness. I do keep forgetting what you have told me about not placing myself on the same level as the servants. We were being playful, as you could see. I really will try to remember not to fraternize—"

Alicia Bodelon recovered her composure. "My dear Miss Marshall, I'm not a fool. There was a man in your room. Your regrettable behavior cannot be tolerated in this house, which, of course, does belong to the Bodelon estate. I had been assured by the solicitors that you were a young woman of breeding and high moral character. In view of this episode—"

"How can you make such accusations?" Susanna exclaimed with more conviction than she was feeling.

"I don't know who the man is," Alicia continued, "but well-bred young gentlemen do not make improper advances to respectable young women. Whoever he is, he was in your boudoir at your express invitation. Miss Marshall, in case you do not fully understand my meaning, I believe you are a woman of low morals, certainly unfit to live in my late husband's house and associate with his daughter."

"Lady Bodelon," Susanna said, feeling anger rush hotly through her veins, "I must warn you that you had better be able to prove what you are saying, because if you say one more word I shall bring a suit for slander against you."

A polite cough from behind them made both women turn quickly to see Morgan, the maid, standing in the doorway with the flame-colored dress over her arm.

"Excuse me, miss," she said, "but you did mean you want me to take this dress back to the seamstress, didn't you? From your reaction upstairs when we were trying it on, I gather you don't want it?"

After Alicia Bodelon had murmured something about a misunderstanding and departed hastily, Susanna reflected that Rowan had very cleverly used Morgan to get his own way about returning the dress he disliked. She sat down and laughed at what a cunning rogue he was.

From that day on, Alicia Bodelon was openly hostile when they met, and she tried, in a well-bred way, to freeze Susanna out of her circle of friends, a situation Susanna found more tolerable than the previous pretense of motherly guidance.

As much as Lady Bodelon tried to shut Susanna out, however, Emma drew her in, making certain doors were never closed to her friend. Emma worried secretly about a conversation she had overheard between her mother and Nicholas Kirby.

"You should endeavor to overcome your jealousy," Kirby had told Lady Bodelon. "If we do not remain friendly, how shall we be able to report to our friends the information they seek?"

"Isn't there some other way we can get our ships into New York?" Lady Bodelon had asked.

"Getting them in is not the problem. Getting them out with their contraband cargo requires certain officials to close their eyes and not ask questions," Kirby replied.

Emma had decided that since they were discussing Bodelon ships, their conversation must not, after all, be about Susanna and Rowan, since they had nothing to do with ships and certainly no connection with New York, being Southerners. Still, her mother and Kirby bore some grudge against Susanna, as well as showing an extraordinary interest in her comings and goings. Perhaps it was the house, her father's bequest.

Susanna found the summer of 1862 particularly lonely despite the lively circles in which she moved and her anxiety about Mizjane and the baby had reached its limit when, at last, a letter arrived. The letter had been en route for a long time and was much the worse for wear, but Mizjane's copperplate handwriting brought tears of relief to Susanna's eyes.

> My dearest child.
>
> Little Brent is well and has grown so you'd hardly know him. His hair and eyes are dark and he can sit up now and hold a spoon. He's weaned to cow's milk—we parted from the mulatto girl who was nursing him—but more about that later.
>
> We miss you so much, honey. I curse myself for parting from you when they were evacuating Norfolk. Are you well, are you happy? When you didn't come to Macon, we met all the trains for days. We finally found out from Miss Rhea that you had gone to England, so I am sending this letter to those lawyers in Richmond to forward to you. I pray it reaches you.

Susanna looked up from the letter in astonishment. There was no mention of Mizjane and the baby sailing from New York. Had Rowan lied to her? She read on:

> You were right about the Chaloners, Susanna. They own a fine house in Macon and a large plantation somewhere—I didn't find out where. Some of the Chaloners are in trade and some in the state government. Now honey, don't be angry, but I didn't give them your baby.
>
> First of all, there were soldiers looking for us when we arrived in Macon. We heard the word before the train reached the station—that they were looking for a black woman with a white baby. Poor little Brent, I had to put him in the portmanteau and that mulatto girl pinched her baby to make him cry so nobody would notice little Brent screaming and somehow we got out of Macon Station. This was when the girl decided to go her own way. Seems that Miss Rhea had told Emerald, before we left, that at the first opportunity she would go to Wilmington, to the hotel where that Captain Duvalle stayed. Well, thinking Miss Rhea was still in jail, off Emerald went to find the Frenchman—as I gather our friend Henri Duvalle was quite fond of Emerald, if you know what I mean.
>
> Then little Brent caught a cold, from the journey and the sudden weaning, I guess. So I found a room for us

and took care of him because I didn't want to take him
to the Chaloners looking sickly. And all the while the
soldiers were looking for us. I didn't know what to do,
Susanna. I didn't know if you had been arrested too
and were in jail with Miss Rhea. White folks are all so
afraid there will be slave uprisings. With the war, I
was afraid to ask anyone to help us.

When the baby was well I set off to the Chaloners,
but when I arrived there was a soldier waiting outside.
I slipped around to the kitchen and talked to one of the
house servants, and she told me the master was expecting us because the Army had told him we were coming
and that he was going to turn us over to the soldiers,
because he didn't believe his son had sired a whore's
bastard. Forgive me, Susanna, but those were the words
he used. I couldn't give them little Brent, could I?

We left Macon at night and headed for North Carolina
to find Emerald in Wilmington, and that's when I learned
Miss Rhea was there. She and the Frenchman have a
fine house, but it was being watched by soldiers too. I
did manage to get a message to her, though, and let
her know the address of the house of some black folks
who let me have a room. I told her not to let the
soldiers know we are here, and I will try to get past
them and into her house at night.

Honey, I'm running out of paper. We are safe for the
moment although not in the best of neighborhoods. If
you are in England, you must send for us. Susanna,
honey, I pray to God you are in England.

Susanna wiped the tears from her eyes. Dear, brave
Mizjane. Why hadn't the stupid soldiers told her they
only wanted to send her to England? But, of course,
Mizjane had never given them a chance. Nothing in her
life had ever led her to believe she could trust soldiers,
or indeed any members of the white race. Susanna
hurried to her desk and began to write a reply. She was
engrossed in the letter when Rowan arrived back unexpectedly from one of his trips to Liverpool.

He listened silently as Susanna read him Mizjane's
letter and then berated him for not having arranged
things better. Gradually Susanna's anger subsided and
she became aware he had not spoken a single word.

There were dark circles under his eyes and his mouth was set in tight, weary lines. At last he slumped to a chair and said in a flat, emotionless voice, "I'll see to it that your letter reaches Mizjane and that she and the baby are brought over to you, I swear, Susanna. But I have some other news for you, and I must give it to you now because I have to leave again tonight."

"Tonight? But you only just arrived . . . what do you do on all of these trips?" Susanna asked petulantly.

"Nothing glamorous, I regret to say. I guess there's just no way I can compete with your dashing blockade runner, is there?" Rowan asked wistfully. "Not only am I not one of our Southern aristocrats, but my efforts for the Confederacy hardly bear comparison either. An agent in a foreign country sounds romantic enough, doesn't it? But in actual fact the work I do is sheer drudgery. Endless meetings with men who may or may not help us . . . or unsavory informers who may or may not be able to get inside the embassy and see what Dudley is up to . . . then hours spent poring over British maritime laws to look for precedents and loopholes."

"You know," Susanna said, "I've just realized that whenever you mention the law those cold eyes of yours come to life." What she really meant to say was that his amused glance became suddenly serious, but it would not do for him to believe she was becoming too friendly.

"Cold eyes? Not when I look at you, I'm sure. But the law does fascinate me. I've never told you of my humble beginnings, have I? My father was a dirt-poor farmer with a houseful of children. He was killed by the son of a local politician—accidentally, they claimed. Anyway, he was never brought to trial for it. Shortly afterward our miserable few acres of land were confiscated through some legal maneuvering. My mother died homeless and penniless, and we were all scattered among various relatives. I was just a small boy at the time, but I was determined when I grew up to find out why there was one set of laws for the rich and another for the poor . . . a question which I now know men have been trying to resolve since the beginning of time. Still, there will always be fools like me who keep trying." He managed to stop himself from adding that he wished he could tell a different story—be the kind of Southern gentleman Susanna so admired, instead of a lonely fool who spent his youth tilting at impossible windmills. Still, there was always a chance that even the most impossible windmill would eventually yield.

"So you went to those lawyers in Richmond?" Susanna was interested in spite of her fears for Mizjane. Rowan was so completely without self-pity in view of his tragic childhood that it occurred to Susanna that one could, after all, rise above one's beginnings.

Rowan had indeed gone to the lawyers in Richmond. When he had crammed as much of the law into his head as he could, they began to send him to the jail to interview the more rambunctious or dangerous of their clients. After all, he was young and strong, with a reckless disregard for danger or the threat of physical violence against his person. Lawyers often took their lives into their hands, especially when they lost a case.

To the surprise of Davies, Hamilton and Son, Attorneys at Law, young Rowan Marshall would often insist that a client was innocent, despite overwhelming circumstantial evidence to the contrary. He would then fight tenaciously for acquittal, sometimes against his own employers. On the other hand, he refused to use legal maneuvering to defend men he was sure were guilty. He also had the temerity to insist that men in high places were not necessarily above the law. These latter traits worried his employers more than the former. Still, young Marshall could be counted on to walk calmly into a murderer's cell and more than once had talked a violent man out of committing mayhem, so for this reason he was kept on in the capacity of clerk and later as a junior partner.

For Rowan's part, he simply answered Susanna's question by saying, "Davies, Hamilton . . . swept their floors and ran their errands and worked nights and Sundays doing odd jobs . . . and wore out my eyes reading law books. Maybe that's why you think my eyes look cold?

I wish you wouldn't tell me these things, Susanna . . . just when I start believing in fairy stories again and hoping I'm going to turn into a handsome prince in your eyes."

Susanna smiled. "Oh, you're not quite a frog even now, Rowan. I'm just worried about Mizjane and the baby, that's why I'm being so mean."

He reached out and laid his hands gently on her shoulders, looking down at her, and his eyes were not cold, but tender. "Will you always be the princess . . . and out of my reach, Susanna?"

Susanna squirmed out of his touch, not recognizing the tenderness and longing in his eyes. "Rowan Marshall! Just when I think you are beginning to behave like a gentleman you start teasing me again."

He looked bewildered. "I'm not teasing. . . ."

"Then you are being very unkind. I am well aware of my position in life, and it's the exact opposite of princess."

She was turning to leave when Rowan sighed deeply and said, "Susanna . . . wait, I haven't given you the news. You will probably be having a visitor within the next few days, and I don't know if I will be here to protect you from him . . . or even if you would want me to." Rowan's heart was heavy, and for once he was unable to disguise the anguish deep in his gray eyes.

Susanna did not see it, however, as she asked, "A visitor?" ripples of excitement starting deep inside her, although she kept repeating in her mind, it couldn't be . . . it couldn't be . . .

"Brent Chaloner," Rowan said, feeling as though he were pronouncing his own death sentence. "He's in England. I expect he will be calling on you."

He did not add that he had almost assaulted a superior officer for divulging Susanna's whereabouts to Lieutenant Chaloner of the Confederate Navy.

Looking into Susanna's shining eyes as she received this news, Rowan thought wretchedly that he had been a fool to hope she was beginning to get over her infatuation for Chaloner. Besides, what had Rowan Marshall to offer a girl who could take her pick among every young

aristocrat in London? Take the crumbs, Marshall, he
told himself sternly, and give her all the freedom she
wants.

8

ROWAN towered over most of the men present, but a childhood of never having quite enough to eat had left his frame spare, disguising the coiled-steel strength that was a stamina as much of spirit as of sinew. He believed in new beginnings and righted wrongs and the certainty that the sun would rise again despite the blackness of present clouds. His inborn optimism, however, was being sorely tried as he moved restlessly on the fringes of the men who had argued and schemed far into the night and who had reached a stalemate of ideas. Rowan knew only too well that defeat could begin in the minds of men as surely as in the actions of their enemies. Sometimes he battled in his own mind an occasional melancholy fear of not being granted enough time to accomplish all that must be done, telling himself sternly that this was merely the legacy of the violent death of his father and perhaps his own grandiose plans for life. He would need two lifetimes to do all he wanted to do. For the moment, the problem—if not the solution—was simple: how to get a ship out of a shipyard.

The man with the cigar that was fouling the air was thumping the table in accompaniment to his oft-repeated words. "Sure . . . sure we got the *Florida* out . . . and we were damn lucky. It's impossible to get another ship out. Especially not the 290. Hell, you've only got to look at her to know what she was built for."

"That's the trouble. The *Florida*. They *know* now."

"The British are too jumpy at the moment. It's hopeless. We'd have to get her out of Laird's yard and sail her down the Mersey before we ever got to the open sea. A ship of that size . . . crew . . . provisions . . .

we can't do it without the cooperation of the port authorities, and how the hell are we going to get them to cooperate after we brazenly sailed the *Florida* out and she's raising hell with Yankee shipping at this very moment? Sure, one time you can get away with it, but now the Yankees know and the British know."

They were all speaking at once, saying the same things, focusing entirely on one side of the argument.

"Besides . . . there's the question of fitting her with guns. Where do we get that, even if we get her out? What use is an unarmed cruiser?"

Rowan moved back to the table around which the men were seated and above which the cloud of cigar smoke rose in languorous swirls. The table was covered with curling drawings of the ship, scribbled notes and crumpled plans.

"Gentlemen," Rowan said, "you are overlooking one thing. British law."

"Law!" The cigar smoker spat out the word. "Here we go again, the lawyer in our midst with his obsession for the law. It's action we need, Marshall, not lectures on the blasted law."

"Nevertheless, the British are the most law-abiding nation on the face of the earth. They will not seize our ship without due process of law . . . and therein lies our opportunity," Rowan answered, pushing aside the ash-speckled documents and leaning forward over the table. "Because the wheels of legal machinery roll slowly, by the time a detention order has gone through all the necessary channels we could have the 290 in the Atlantic. That is, of course, provided we ever get out of this room."

James Bulloch's aide, who had been a silent observer for most of the long night, suddenly spoke. "We have an English sea captain and a crew we believe we can trust to take the 290 out into the open sea . . . if we can find a way to slip her out of the river."

"A second ship sailing from a different port—London, maybe—could carry all the supplies the 290 would need," one of the others put in. "A rendezvous somewhere where we could exchange the English captain for a Confederate captain—"

Rowan pushed his hair out of his eyes. "We know the British are considering the Federals' demand that they detain the ship, but maritime law is so cumbersome I believe there's enough time to get the 290 out before all the legal ramifications of a detention order can be carried out. I say, sail her out boldly—in full view of everybody—not only with an English crew, but with English passengers too, if necessary. If we start thinking about what we can do instead of what we can't . . . "

"If we knew exactly how much time we have before the detention order can be carried out by the collector of customs here . . ." Bulloch's aide said slowly. "What about it, lawyer? Can you give me a date? How far along are they with their legal ramifications?"

"I'm sorry, sir. I don't know."

"We must know. The exact date. We have taken the precaution of slipping some of our own naval officers into the country in the hope of putting them aboard the 290. We'll use them instead to sail a supply tender out. Marshall, you have to find out exactly when that detention order will be carried out. Mr. Bulloch has a vague plan in the back of his mind, and I believe from what you've said we can fill in the gaps for him. But time will be of the essence."

"The only people who know that are in London— the Foreign Office," Rowan said.

"Ah . . . the Foreign Office," the aide said. "At last I begin to see a use for an agent who has not been of much service to us since we brought her here . . . your little whore from the Norfolk brothel, Marshall . . . living in London and moving in the Bodelon and Bartlett crowd."

Rowan came slowly up from his chair, one hand on the table. "She is not a whore, sir," he said quietly. "And I won't ask her to act like one."

"Come now, Marshall, she is the only agent who can get close enough to someone in the Foreign Office to find out about the detention order for the 290. The only agent in all of England who can get the information we need. Besides, from what I hear we are going to ship her bastard and her slave over here to her. Seems she is heavily in our debt and has not yet made any payments in return. Not to the Cause, that is. . . . But perhaps you personally have been the recipient of her favors?"

Rowan was around the table and dragging the aide to his feet by his embroidered vest before the others present could recover from their surprise and pull Rowan back. Those nearest managed to galvanize themselves into action as Rowan's hands went around the man's throat. Four of them held Rowan by his arms and about his neck as the aide, panting and purple-faced, straightened his clothing.

"I could have you court-martialed and sent home in disgrace. Twice you have come close to serious assault within the last week. . . . And we'd use the girl anyway, so what would you have accomplished? For one who professes to believe in the law, you do show a regrettable tendency to flout it. What a paradox you are, Marshall—one moment the champion of law and order and the next a raving idiot trying to make a point with his fists."

"Are you going to bring charges, sir?" one of Rowan's captors asked.

The aide looked into Rowan's glacial stare for a long moment. "You will go to London and order the girl to get the information we need in any way necessary. Then you will order her to bring it here and be on hand in Liverpool to use her charms to keep the collector of customs occupied while we put Mr. Bulloch's plan into action. None of what has taken place in this room will be reported to Mr. Bulloch if we succeed in getting the 290 out to sea. It's all so asinine to get so angry . . . and all because of some prostitute."

"If you ever call her that again," Rowan said slowly, "I'll kill you."

Jacob Drost walked across the hall, his crooked shadow falling across the drawing-room carpet. Susanna shivered as he took her hand as though death itself had her in its grip.

"Afternoon, Miss Marshall. Nice day, ain't it?"

Susanna winced as he squeezed her hand tightly before dropping it. In the afternoon sunlight he looked like a corpse, with his skin stretched over gaunt bones, yet he seemed to exude an almost supernatural strength.

"What can I do for you, Mr. Drost? As you can see, I have company," Susanna said as he nodded toward Emma, who had stopped by to see if Susanna would attend a dinner party at the Bodelon townhouse that evening.

"Came to see your uncle. Butler says he ain't here. Figured you'd tell me where he is. Need to see him right away." Drost had a habit of speaking in fragments of sentences, so sparing of his words that Susanna had heard several of the ladies remark on his rudeness.

"I didn't know you had any business dealings with my uncle, Mr. Drost," Susanna said carefully. She was thinking rapidly of Rowan's long absences, the dark circles under his eyes that told of many sleepless nights, and when she had questioned him, he had told her only that "something important" would be finished soon. He had come to see her the previous evening only to let her know about Brent—he had made the long journey from Liverpool for that reason alone. She wondered if Rowan's superiors in Richmond knew he was working alone, for he had never asked her to help in any way.

"Where is he?" Drost demanded, his cold eyes raking her body, not with lust but with contempt for her weakness.

"I don't know. And if I did, I wouldn't tell you."

"Look, if you know what's good for you . . . and him . . ." Drost took a step toward her as though to wrench the information from her physically. He pointed a finger at her, inches away from her eyes.

Susanna stood her ground, chin tilted defiantly. "Are you forgetting yourself, sir? Or where you are? This is a neutral country, not a battleground. Oh yes, we know you are a Yankee, but you and my uncle and I are all guests in a foreign country, and nothing we do can have any significance to you."

"That a fact?" Drost said, his thin lips twisting in his

own expression of amusement. "Well, I know all about you and your uncle, Rowan Marshall. If he ain't here, I reckon I know how to find him. Now maybe you and me will have a little talk—privately—instead." He cast a malevolent glance at Emma, who was cowering behind Susanna.

Susanna picked up the bell from the table and rang it until Dobbs appeared. "Mr. Drost is leaving, Dobbs," she said firmly as the butler appeared, her eyes never leaving Drost, although her fingers were clammy as they clenched the bell tightly.

Drost glared at her and then turned on his heel.

"Oh, that dreadful man!" Emma exclaimed behind her. "I don't know why Mother tolerates him."

"How long has she known him?" Susanna asked, still trembling as she sank into a chair.

"Not long. Nicholas brought him to one of her musicales, just before you and your uncle arrived. Nicholas said it would be nice for the Americans to have a fellow countryman around. Though I do recall Nicholas laughed in a rather unpleasant manner at the time."

"I'm sure he did," Susanna said grimly. "Emma, from what you've told me about your father, it seems strange that Nicholas Kirby was his best friend."

"Well, he wasn't, really, but he was—and is—the biggest of the shipping agents who use Bodelon ships. Mother never liked him, but since Father died she puts up with him because now that our ships aren't carrying cotton from your country we would be in very dire straits if Nicholas were to give his business to another line. You see, Bodelon ships sailed almost exclusively to and from your Southern ports and the Caribbean."

Not for the first time, Susanna wondered privately how much Nicholas Kirby—and Jacob Drost—knew about her background. That Kirby was informed of the details of her birth she knew from the solicitor. What more he knew was uncertain. But Brent was on his way from Liverpool, and Susanna was too happy to care about anything else. He would arrive today, she was sure.

She dressed carefully for dinner, leaving instructions with Dobbs that any visitors were to be sent directly to

Lady Bodelon's house. She had considered staying home, but then decided it would be better for Brent to see her surrounded by admiring men, as she surely would be at the Bodelon dinner. She chose a dress of palest taffeta, the color of celery, because it was a warm evening and the color was cool; she slipped into dark-green velvet slippers and tied back her hair with green velvet ribbons.

Susanna was in a light-hearted and excited mood, and the effect was devastating on all of the gentlemen present. Everyone was talking about the hunt and ball to be held at Bartlett Hall, the country estate of Sir Edmund Bartlett in Surrey, during the following weekend. The Bartlett brothers, Malcome and David, both of whom had shyly proposed to her, were attentively at Susanna's side.

When Susanna told them she would be busy for the weekend and could not attend the festivities, Alicia Bodelon, exquisite in floating black chiffon, had narrowed her violet eyes and asked if Susanna was going to be out of the city. As she made a noncommital answer, Susanna was thinking that Lady Bodelon continued to wear black only because it suited her and set her apart from the other women. Alicia's black evening frocks were of rustling taffeta, delicate lace or filmy chiffon and cut low to show milky-white shoulders.

"You look lovely tonight, Miss Marshall," Malcome Bartlett was saying. "How can we bear not to see you all weekend? You haven't told us why, either."

"Father will be disappointed," David put in. "He likes to have the prettiest women at his hunt ball. He thinks it is the event of the year."

"Whatever you have planned for the weekend," a clipped voice said from just behind her, "it must be extremely important to you." Nicholas Kirby's presence cast a momentary pall on Susanna's happy mood.

"Yes, it is," she said.

"A secret, I take it?"

Susanna merely smiled.

"Involving your Uncle Rowan?" Kirby persisted.

"I say, sir," Malcome Bartlett protested, "it's hardly done to interrogate a lady."

"The lady in question is in London under the auspices

of Lord Bodelon's estate and is under my protection. I have the right and indeed the duty to make myself fully aware of her comings and goings. Actually, I am merely surprised that Miss Marshall chooses to insult your father by refusing his invitation."

Alicia joined the group with a rustle of black taffeta petticoats and added, "I'm afraid our young American friend has much to learn and does not realize how much she embarrasses us at times."

Susanna glanced from one to the other and resisted the strong temptation to tell them she expected to spend the weekend in the arms of her lover, but the thought brought a mischievous glint to her eyes and she dimpled as she said to the Bartletts, "Being new here, I foolishly made other plans before I knew of your father's hunt ball. Do forgive me."

Nicholas Kirby's blinking eyes went from her face to her body, and he shrugged and moved away.

Alicia looked at Susanna for a long moment and then said coolly, "You must enjoy English hospitality while you can, my dear, and not turn down too many invitations. After all, one does not always know when one's fortunes—or popularity—might suddenly wane, does one?"

There was a sudden flutter among the women present, and Susanna heard one of them murmur, "Who is that divine man with Emma?"

Looking across the room, Susanna saw a tall, black-haired man, tanned to swarthiness, eyes that glowed with excitement and zest for living, muscled shoulders and broad chest tapering to lean hips and long, strong legs. Brent was dressed in evening clothes, as finely tailored and well fitted as any present, and he followed Emma across the room with his rolling sailor's stride, eyes taking in everyone and everything.

They stayed at the party until the first departures made it correct for them to leave. After their first greeting, they had spent little time together. Susanna remained surrounded by the young Englishmen, while Brent was quickly engulfed in admiring women. That

Lady Bodelon would flutter violet eyes at him Susanna expected, but she was amused and a little saddened to see plain little Emma fix adoring eyes on the darkly handsome American.

In the carriage en route to Essex Square, Brent had taken Susanna's hand in his and they had sat in silence, watching each other, unaware of anything but their physical closeness.

I love him so, Susanna thought, I've longed for him so, I don't care about anything else . . . it doesn't matter that he doesn't love me enough to marry me. All the guile and coquetry she had practiced, all her newfound sophistication were forgotten as every inch of her body responded to his nearness.

She dined with the English aristocrats as though she were one of them, to the manner born, Brent was thinking. There wasn't another woman in the room as exciting or beautiful. She was like a flamingo in a flock of sparrows. Every man back there wanted her, and tonight they'll imagine she is the woman lying with them, but she is mine.

All the months of absence and longing had honed their desire to a fine edge of need that was savagely sweet. In her room they went dumbly into each other's arms. They made love the first time still partially dressed, then Susanna removed the rest of his clothes and kissed his lips, his ears, his throat and chest; took the sponge from the hip bath and sponged him all over, slowly, methodically, caressingly. He watched as she removed her stockings and sponged her own body, standing naked in the lamplight. The dark eyes ran slowly over her full breasts with nipples of palest pink, tiny waist, hips that were narrower than was fashionable, legs that were longer and slimmer than those of other women he had known.

At first their conversation had been whispered words of passion and joy at being together again, neither of them mentioning their parting at Nassau. Now Brent extended his arms and she went into them, thrilling to the embrace of hard muscles and the coarse black hair on his chest that rubbed excitingly against her breasts.

"Ah, Susanna, my sweet girl," he said softly, "I want you so. God, how I missed you . . . seeing you sail away from me at Nassau. Let me hold you for a moment longer, and then you must take me to see our son."

Susanna sat up abruptly, pushing her long hair from her eyes. "He isn't here, Brent. The Army frightened Mizjane . . . she didn't know what they wanted with her. They are in North Carolina. It's a long story, but Rowan promised me—"

"Rowan? Is Marshall still with you?" There was an edge to his voice. "You didn't marry him, did you? I noticed they addressed you as Miss Marshall tonight. But since there was no sign of him . . ."

"Do you mean you wouldn't care if I had married him?" Susanna said, shivering suddenly although the room was warm.

He smiled and pulled her down so that she was lying on top of him and his organ was stirring again against her legs. "Of course I would care. I want you all to myself. I was just teasing. When I docked in Liverpool I went directly to Mr. Bulloch to get my orders, and who should I run into but your old traveling companion, Marshall. Needless to say, I immediately inquired as to your whereabouts . . . and when Marshall was a little reticent about giving me your address, I simply went to a colonel on Bulloch's staff and got it from him. Actually, I was just going to ask the colonel to get it from Marshall for me. I was surprised to find that our people know all about you, however."

He did not add that he had been told they were all well aware of Susanna's whereabouts, that she was already notorious not only for her possible value to the Confederate network of agents in England, but also because it was a huge joke the way the English aristocracy was blithely accepting a little whore from some Virginia bordello into their exclusive ranks.

Susanna felt a stab of hurt and said, "You mean . . . if you hadn't met Rowan accidentally, you wouldn't have come to see me?"

His dark eyes flickered. "Of course I would, but I would have had to search London for you after I got here. I saved valuable time in being able to come directly to you. I also found out you were using the name Marshall. I was just teasing you about marrying him . . . so let's not talk about him any more. Unless you have some confession to make? You haven't been letting him make love to you, have you?"

Susanna buried her face in his chest and moved her legs so that the hot swelling of him slipped into her, and Brent's eyes closed as she raised her body over him, moving in slow circles, gripping him with her thighs, encircling him with a silken vise that held, then released, slipped away and returned until he was gasping and forgetful of everything but the wonder of her and the delight she gave him. He did not mention Rowan again that night except to tell her, just before dawn, that if the Army could not bring their son to her then he, Brent, would do so. Indeed, not only would he bring his son, he would lay the moon and stars at her feet.

They made love, drinking deeply of sensual pleasures that blotted out all other feelings save those of fulfillment of the demands of their bodies. In the mad rapture of it all, Susanna gave no thought to the consequences of their being discovered, or the wisdom of giving herself so completely to Brent. She cried aloud in ecstasy as the moving hardness within her penetrated to the innermost core of her being and exploded into a torrent of joy that swept through her total being. A faraway voice was speaking softly: "We belong together for always, always . . ."

"Brent, Brent—I love you so desperately . . ." The words seemed to come from some deep well inside her.

Before Brent's arrival in London he and Rowan had surveyed each other across the age-darkened oak table in the public bar at the Pig and Whistle. The air about them had crackled with their resentment and enmity.

"I understand, Major, that you have instructions for me regarding the *Agrippina*. I'll have ale, barman," Brent said.

"Keep your voice down, and don't mention the name of the tender again," Rowan said after the barman had moved away. The glint of steel flashed from his gray eyes.

"A thousand pardons." Brent's voice was mocking. "I forget the surreptitious nature of your business, Major. I'm not versed in sneaking around behind people's backs to get what I want."

"Oh?" Rowan raised an eyebrow. "I take it you are not referring to your personal life when you make a statement like that?"

Brent smiled slowly. "There is no need for any further discussion of that particular subject, Major. I have already obtained Susanna's address. I also learned a little about you, sir, and your background. Taking your disadvantages into account, not least of which being your lack of breeding, I shall overlook your churlish innuendoes rather than soundly thrashing you as I would were you a gentleman."

Rowan's hands were gripping the underside of the table, but he smiled also, his eyes burning with white flame. "Well, now, Lieutenant Chaloner, I wouldn't want to deprive you of the pleasure of calling me out, just because I'm not a gentleman."

Brent's shoulders moved slightly and his hand flexed around the tankard of ale as his eyes flickered over Rowan. Although they were the same height, Brent's powerful shoulders and chest, his arms and hands, were those of a man who had fought wind and tide and more than once an errant yardarm. He looked disdainfully down Rowan's lean frame.

"Don't tempt me again, Major. You threw a lucky punch that night in Nassau, and your military friends quickly broke up our scuffle before I could teach you a proper lesson. I was Navy boxing champion for four consecutive years, and I wouldn't prove anything to myself by fighting you. You see, my friend, I was always told to ignore the bleating of my inferiors rather than soil my hands on them. But more than that, I don't want to get in trouble with the Army and spoil my chances for assignment to . . . you know what. Besides, I doubt Susanna finds you interesting. You aren't man enough for a girl like her."

"You say 'a girl like her.' What sort of girl is that, Chaloner? Is she one of your inferiors too? What plans do you have for her?" There was a rapier edge to Rowan's voice.

"Well, well," Brent grinned, amused. "I do believe the poor swine is smitten with her."

"You haven't answered my question."

"And you haven't given me my orders about the tender in London. I came here to get those orders, not to discuss some—"

'Yes?" Rowan's voice was deadly quiet.

Brent laughed and drained his glass. "Very well, Major. I'll answer your question. Now what is it exactly you want to know about Susanna and me? Surely you must already know she bore my son? That she was my woman? What is your question, Major?"

"Are you going to marry her?" Because if you hurt her again, you won't live to sail on the *Agrippina*, he thought to himself.

Brent threw back his head and laughed harder, and as Rowan began to rise, white with anger, he said quickly, "Sit down, Major, and tell me how we are going to get our supplies on board the tender. And in return I'll explain the difference between my class and yours. You see, gentlemen don't take whores to be their wives."

Outside the open window the stars were spinning dizzily into a pink void and a nightingale sang its achingly beautiful song. Brent lay still now, breathing deeply. Content, Susanna lay beside him listening to the sound of his breath and the song of the bird outside. But another sound was intruding into her consciousness.

A timid knock on her bedroom door, and then a louder knock which continued for several seconds. Susanna slipped on her dressing gown and went to the door to find Morgan, her maid, standing in the hall.

"Please miss, excuse me, miss. 'e said it was a matter of life and death, miss, or else I wouldn't of disturbed you."

"Who said this?" Susanna asked impatiently.

"Your uncle, miss. Mr. Rowan. 'e's downstairs in the

parlor and says 'e must see you right away, it's a matter of life and—"

"Yes, yes. I shall be down in a moment." Susanna closed the door and looked across the room to Brent, lying on the bed, his arm extended about the warm hollow where she had lain beside him. He had been asleep but now was stirring, running one hand through tousled black hair, searching for her with the other hand.

She went to his side and bent to drop a kiss on his cheek. "I shall be back in a moment, my darling. Go back to sleep," she whispered.

Down in the parlor Rowan was standing at the window watching a silver dawn burst through the trees in the square. There was a tired droop to his shoulders, and when he turned as she entered the room, his voice was hoarse and he spoke rapidly.

"We need your help, Susanna. There is something we have to know, and I believe you can find out for us."

"No. I can't help you now. Brent is here."

"You must. It's his neck too if we fail."

"What do you mean?"

"Sit down. We must talk. I had your maid bring us some coffee . . . over there on the sideboard. Pour some, will you?"

This was not the easygoing, bantering Rowan she had known. This was a stranger full of authority and urgency. Susanna sat down and began to pour the coffee.

"Susanna, last November Yankee marines boarded a British ship—the *Trent*—and seized two Confederate commissioners, James Mason and John Slidell, who were en route to England and France. The British were furious, of course, and it looked for a time as though England might go to war with the Union because of the incident."

Susanna listened silently. With the dropping of Rowan's mask of nonchalance, there was something very commanding about his manner.

"Then Prince Albert died of typhoid. His death seemed to calm tempers, and the Yankee State Department was able to resolve the whole mess by releasing our commissioners and apologizing to England. There was then a tremendous feeling of relief in England that war had been averted, and with relief came anger that we, the South, had brought about the situation in the first place."

Susanna rubbed her eyes sleepily and sipped the coffee. "What has this to do with us? I thought we were here to get ships built."

"We did build a cruiser, Susanna. She sailed in March, and we had the devil's own time getting her to sea. Her name is *Florida*. And that brings me to the point. We have a second cruiser ready—she's lying in the Mersey right now. She's the reason I need your help and, incidentally, the reason your planter-sailor friend is here."

"Brent?" Susanna's interest was captured.

"What I am trying to tell you is that because England came so close to war, there is a great deal of sentiment in this country against violating the Queen's Neutrality Act. Mr. Dudley—he's the American Consul in Liverpool—has been suspicious about our ship in the Laird shipyards . . . remember, I pointed out Birkenhead to you when we docked at Liverpool? It's just across the river, and our ship is an imposing structure, even to a landlubber like me. Number 290 is the most graceful, fastest ship we'll have, and she'll give the Yankee shipping hell if we can get her to sea."

"Is Brent going to sail on her?" Susanna asked, a note of fear creeping into her voice at the thought of losing him again so soon.

"Not exactly," Rowan answered.

"What does that mean?"

"Susanna, the less you know, the better. Right now our main concern is getting the ship out into the open sea before the British government realizes she was built to be a Confederate cruiser and seizes her. We have an English captain who will take her out, minus any warlike trappings, and he is the soul of discretion. But we're caught in a net of Northern agents, and they're rapidly gathering information about the ship. The Yankees even hired an English barrister to present the case for detaining the ship. In fact, the chief law officer of the Crown, Sir John Harding, had detention papers on his desk when he died suddenly, which gave us a few more days' grace."

"Died? Did we kill him?" Susanna cried.

"He had a stroke," Rowan answered tersely. "Susanna, the people you've been meeting at Alicia's parties, the Bodelons' friends, you know that many of them are connected with the Foreign Office?"

"No, I didn't. I knew the Bodelons were in shipping, that's all."

Rowan picked up her hand and held it, despite her efforts to withdraw from him. "We have to know how much time we have to get Number 290 out to sea. There's a big soirée being held down at the Bartletts' estate this weekend. Susanna, you have to go down there and find out what's happening about our ship. Sir Edmund Bartlett is with the Foreign Office. Perhaps you can learn something from those two sons of his who have been mooning over you."

"But why can't you find out?"

"Because I have to return to Merseyside immediately and try to keep things under control there." And because these are my orders, like them or not, he wanted to say, but added instead, "I have to keep any eye on Consul Dudley and the customs people and . . . anyway, you'll find out from the sleeping prince upstairs that he won't be able to grace your bed for the weekend. He has work to do also."

Susanna jerked her hand away from him, looking away. "How did you know he was in my bed?" she asked in a very small voice.

"You told me he was here as soon as you came downstairs, and that dewy-eyed look you have didn't come from sleeping all night." No other man ever put those stars in your eyes, Rowan thought miserably, least of all myself. All I was ever able to do was act like a surrogate for your blasted sailor . . . I should have had more pride. I have to treat you like the Confederate agent you're supposed to be, or I'll go out of my mind. . . .

Susanna did not meet his gaze. "I don't know *how* I am to find out what you want to know."

"I shall leave that to your ingenuity. Do whatever you have to do." Rowan was angry, at himself and at her.

"By the way, it's Sir Edmund's birthday celebration. We have to know when the Foreign Office is going to act —hours of warning could be the crucial factor in our plan. I shall be at the Pig and Whistle on Water Street; I have a room there. As soon as you know something, get on a train and come to me. We can't risk the telegraph wires."

"This is Friday. Must I leave today?"

"Look," Rowan said impatiently. "Chaloner will make his excuses and leave, probably within the hour. What the hell kind of man is he, anyway, to let you come from his bed to see me alone?" Rowan gripped the table top, fighting the savage urge to race upstairs and pound Brent Chaloner to a pulp. It was only the limpid, adoring look in Susanna's eyes that kept him from doing so. If Chaloner could make her look like that, then for her sake, Rowan would control himself. Perhaps Chaloner had merely been baiting him in Liverpool and had proposed marriage after all. There was no doubt what Susanna's answer would be, if he did. Rowan cursed himself inwardly for being a fool ever to have hoped otherwise.

Susanna felt the color begin to stain her cheeks. "I believe you only told me Brent was involved in this to make me go to the Bartletts'."

"Number 290 has to sail without guns, ammunition, anything that would give away the fact that she is a warship," Rowan said. "A second ship will carry all of these supplies and rendezvous with her at an island off the Azores. Your Brent Chaloner will be on that second ship, the tender."

"When will he sail?"

"We're working on the final details of a plan now, but the more time we have the better, and safer, for all concerned. That's why we have to know if the Foreign Office is planning to seize the cruiser and when."

"Very well. I'll send a note to the Bartletts right away that I shall be able to go to their ball. By the way, are you going to call your precious ship by a number all her life? Or do you have a name for her?"

"She'll be called the *Alabama*," Rowan answered.

It was much later that Susanna remembered she had not told him of Jacob Drost's visit.

9

A light rain had fallen during the night and the sun
came up on Saturday, July 26, to find glistening teardrops
on the roses that climbed about the latticed windows of
Susanna's bedroom in the east wing of Bartlett Hall. She
pushed aside the bedcurtains with their metallic spangles
and stepped onto a Savonnerie carpet that had been
made for Louis XIV.

Bartlett Hall had been built in the seventeenth century by a spirited and original baronet who had wanted
a home more than a fortress, and he had filled the
Jacobean mansion with the works of many artisans.
Susanna stood for a moment at her window, looking
down on velvet lawns and arbors disappearing into the
woods, beyond which spirals of smoke rose from the
chimneys of the tenant farms. The serenity of the setting
and the grandeur of the furnishings, no less than the
vast H-shaped hall itself, made Susanna wonder why
the Bartletts bothered with political activities which took
them away from their magnificent home.

Two hundred miles to the north in a public house
near the Liverpool docks, Rowan paced his room cursing
himself for not defying orders and telling Susanna of
the dispatch received from North Carolina two days
earlier. There was no doubt whom Susanna would blame
for the tragedy. Yet Rowan was under military orders,
and every move he made, every word he uttered, had
consequences for all of the Confederate agents in England.
He had been ordered to withhold the information from
Susanna until after her visit to Bartlett Hall and the other
plans that were being made for her.

Breathing the fragrant morning air of the rainwashed

countryside, Susanna thought about Brent and was happy. She had traveled down to Surrey on the train the night before, only slightly concerned that Malcome Bartlett had misunderstood her message and believed she might have had a change of heart about marrying him. The brothers met her at the station, a pair of shy country boys, despite their having recently come down from Cambridge. Malcome was twenty-three and David a year younger. They looked like eager young colts, Susanna thought, in their riding boots and tweeds.

The guests gathering at Bartlett Hall seemed legion. Alicia Bodelon and Emma, Tom Douglas and his family, Nicholas Kirby with a woman half his age, whose presence did not keep Kirby's eyes from straying repeatedly in Susanna's direction, and Jacob Drost, alone and sinister. Other guests continued to arrive far into the night.

Emma attached herself to Susanna's side at breakfast, confessing that she disliked hunting and would not be riding to the hounds. Her mother had insisted she come, she said, as they stood at the sideboard, serving themselves from the chafing dishes.

"She keeps hoping I'll meet some eligible young man and he will propose to me," she whispered, blushing.

"Do you like any of the young men?" Susanna asked, although in her mind she was trying to formulate a plan to get the information Rowan needed.

Emma looked with some distaste at a platter of grilled kidneys surrounded by red circles of fried tomato, then she went to the next dish and lifted what appeared to be a flat brown fish to her breakfast plate. "The Bartletts aren't too bad. Quite intelligent, really," she answered in an offhand manner, then added, her eyes lighting up, "But how dull they all seem compared to your friend Lieutenant Chaloner."

"Emma, what *is* that?"

"What? Oh—this is a kipper. Smoked herring. Have you never seen one before? Try one, these look good."

"No, thanks. I'll have some ham, I think. Is either David or Malcome in the Foreign Office, like their father? I suppose they told me, but I've forgotten."

They took their plates out onto a sunny terrace where small tables had been arranged under umbrellas for the overflow of guests. Freshly cut daffodils nodded from silver vases upon snowy tablecloths.

"Sir Edmund wanted one of them at least to go into the diplomatic corps, but they both would really rather be country squires. Sir Edmund always relied on tenant farmers to cultivate his land, but his sons seem to love the country more than the city, and they have both studied the new methods of agriculture. They probably feel two members of their family in the Foreign Office are enough. Their uncle—Lady Bartlett's brother—is also in the Foreign Office, you know."

"Mmm, I see," Susanna murmured, deciding it would be a waste of time to play up to Malcome and David. She would have to get the information directly from their father. She had met Lady Bartlett's brother briefly— a rather deaf old gentleman who attended social gatherings reluctantly. She smiled as Lady Bartlett, a small, nearsighted woman who peered anxiously at the world without her lorgnette, passed their table.

"Is Lieutenant Chaloner . . . do you . . . is he one of your suitors?" Emma asked, a pink flush showing beneath her sallow skin.

"No. Just an old friend from Virginia," Susanna answered. The plain little Emma's face lit up when she spoke of Brent, and, pondering upon this briefly, Susanna decided he probably had the same effect on all women and Emma was just more transparent than most.

After breakfast Susanna went up to her room to dress for the hunt, paused at the mirror to admire her new forest-green riding habit with the striking plumed hat to match, then went down to the courtyard, where the guests thronged among grooms and horses. She asked Malcome to choose a mount for her, then disappeared back into the house, leaving him to search fruitlessly for her. Her host, she knew, was not riding with his guests because of an attack of lumbago.

Inquiring of the butler, Susanna was told that Sir Edmund was in the wine cellar selecting wines for dinner. Unlike his sons, Sir Edmund was obviously a man who took life's pleasures where he found them. His aristocratic handsomeness was still evident, despite advancing middle age and some carelessness about his appearance. The graying hair and sidewhiskers suggested a dignity belied by merry eyes that were full of the devil. He reminded Susanna of the gentleman callers who had visited her aunt's house on Blossom Street.

Looking up from the dusty wine racks, Sir Edmund was surprised to see the pretty American girl coming down the cellar steps toward him. He knew both of his sons were smitten by the girl and felt interest stabbing at his own groin as he looked at her tiny waist and softly rounded breasts. There was a faint perfume to her hair as she came closer, smiling at him bewitchingly and showing dimpled cheeks, but it was the look in her eyes that made him straighten up slowly as his heart began to hammer.

"Do forgive me for creeping up on you like this," Susanna said, "but I'm hiding from everyone because I really don't like to hunt."

He started to say something he hoped would be comforting, but it came out as incoherent stammering.

"Besides," Susanna was adding sweetly, "I wanted to wish you happy birthday and give you my gift in private."

"Oh, ah, my dear . . ." he mumbled, feeling like a fool at the weakness that had come over him, which had nothing to do with his lumbago.

"You see, I didn't know it was your birthday until I arrived," Susanna lied. "And I didn't have time to get you a real present, so I wanted to give you this."

She looked down shyly, then, without warning, suddenly pressed herself very close to him and kissed him on the mouth. At the taste of her lips he was galvanized into action and, before he realized what was happening, had slipped his arms around her waist and was kissing her in no fatherly way. Why, the little minx actually had her tongue between his lips and . . . good gracious, how did it happen that all of a sudden the buttons on her riding habit were undone and her blouse open, and his hand was closing over a firm young breast, the nipple of which was hard as the diamonds that bobbed so beckoningly on shell-pink ears.

Panting, wild with excitement, Sir Edmund staggered as though drunk, the cool darkness of the cellar closing around him.

The next moment she had pushed him away and was sobbing into her hands.

The awful realization of what he had done swept over Sir Edmund like a gust of icy wind. He leaned back against the wine rack, sending a bottle crashing to the stone floor, while Susanna cried harder and tried to cover herself up, tugging ineffectively at her blouse.

Sir Edmund brushed his hand across his brow in dumb horror, then began to pat her gently on the wrist to try to calm her.

"There, there, my dear. Oh, please forgive me, I don't know what came over me," he was saying in a strangled voice. "You're just so beautiful, so . . . oh, please don't cry."

Clumsily he helped her with the stubborn buttons, the soft flesh tantalizingly near to his shaking fingers, then fumbled in his own pocket for a handkerchief to dry her tears. Susanna allowed herself to be taken into his arms, laying a tearstained cheek on his shoulder, as he apologized over and over again.

At last she looked up shyly and said, between sobs, "Sir Edmund, we were just swept away for a moment, that's all. You are forgiven, for how could you know what a silly, helpless thing I am? And you are so important . . . with the Foreign Office and everything and this huge house . . . I just didn't think anyone as important as you would even notice a girl like me. . . ."

"Oh, my dear," Sir Edmund said, breathing a sigh of relief, "believe me, there isn't a man here who hasn't noticed your beauty. I've envied my sons on many occasions when they've danced with you and squired you about town."

Susanna's eyelashes fluttered slightly and she drew a deep breath, causing her soft breasts to press against his shirt. "You see, Sir Edmund, I really came to you because I'm so afraid . . . oh, I did want to wish you happy birthday . . . but I'm so afraid . . ."

"Now my dear little girl, what can you possibly be afraid of? Tell me and I'll have the young scoundrel horsewhipped, whoever he is. . . . Oh, surely it isn't Malcome or David?"

"Oh no, nothing like that. It's my Uncle Rowan," Susanna said quickly. "He's going to be in great trouble and I shall have to leave England if he goes . . . and I did so want to be able to get to know you better, Sir Edmund. . . . I had not been unaware of you also. . . . Your sons are charming, of course, but alas, I seem to be the kind of girl who is drawn to more mature men . . ."

Susanna smiled against his shoulder as she felt his chest puff up. She had often wondered how Pansy and the other girls on Blossom Street had endured making love with the older gentlemen callers, and all at once it seemed it really would not be too bad after all. There was a kind of gentle dignity about an older man, and, what was even more surprising, Susanna was experiencing a twinge of desire herself, which she put down to being plucked so unceremoniously from Brent's embrace the previous day.

"But why would you have to leave? Tell me, my dear, what kind of trouble is he in?"

"There is a ship," Susanna said softly, with a glance toward the closed cellar door, "being built in Laird's shipyard in Birkenhead. My uncle wants to buy it for some American friends, but the British government may seize it."

Sir Edmund stiffened, his expression changing as he held her away from him and looked searchingly into her face.

"I want to stay here so much," Susanna said before he could speak, "I would do anything . . . anything at all . . . just to find out if that ship is going to be detained. Just a day or two of notice . . . I wouldn't want to get anyone into any trouble, but if the ship were going to be seized anyway, at least my uncle would have a little time to extricate himself from the agreement. Oh dear, I wish I had a protector. Someone strong like yourself, to lean on . . . then I would not be so dependent upon my uncle."

She swayed toward him again and her arms went up around his neck. Sir Edmund battled with his conscience while his lips were pressed to that fragrant chestnut hair. The die had been cast over that damn ship in the Mersey anyway. It would take three days to clear all the necessary documents, but it was certain the Crown would seize the ship next Tuesday.

Sir Edmund wavered, feeling like a man swimming against a strong tide, but his honor managed to prevail.

"My dear . . . I'm sorry, I would do anything in the world for you . . . but I cannot divulge state secrets."

Susanna went back upstairs, leaving an apologetic and highly aroused Sir Edmund in the cellar. Except for a pair of scullery maids in conference with Lady Bartlett glimpsed through the half-open door of the kitchen, everyone appeared to be outside. Susanna paused. An appeal to another woman? The plan was only half-formed as she pushed open the kitchen door.

Lady Bartlett looked up, squinted at her guest and said, "Are you lost, my dear? You will miss the hunt."

"May I have a word with you?" Susanna said hesitantly. The clatter of hooves reached them through the open window and Susanna worried that Malcome would come looking for her.

"It's the hunt, Lady Bartlett," Susanna whispered as the two maids went back to their chores. "I'm simply terrified of horses and I wanted to hide all by myself for a while . . . and there's a letter I must write. I didn't want to go to my room, as my friends would find me there. I wondered if there is a study I could use?" Don't say too much, she was thinking.

Lady Bartlett's lorgnette slipped from her nose, a gesture conveying exasperation. She herself would dearly have loved to be riding out instead of planning meals.

"My husband prefers that the guests do not use his study, or indeed any of the rooms in the west wing, but I'll clear off my desk for you if you wish. I have one in the sewing room."

The sewing room was adjacent to the kitchen, and

Susanna waited nervously as Lady Bartlett moved her household ledgers. When at last the door closed behind her, Susanna listened for a moment to the retreating footsteps, then went out into the empty hall and darted past the kitchen. Knowing her bedroom was in the east wing, she had little trouble finding the west wing. But which room was Sir Edmund's study? She went along the ground-floor hallway, trying doors and peering into rooms. Nothing that looked like a study. Upstairs was an elegant upper landing with linenfold panels and all the doors were unlocked but one, she learned as she twisted the doorknob. That had to be the study. Her heart thudding, she went into the adjacent room and over to the window. There was no balcony. She was in a bedroom, a rather plainly furnished one compared to her own. Then she noticed the inner door connecting the room to its neighbor.

Holding her breath, she slowly pushed open the door, revealing a room crowded with books and dominated by a massive, cluttered desk. It seemed to take an agonizingly long time to scan all of the papers. Nothing made any sense to her, worded as it was in the jargon of officialdom. Sir Edmund was evidently a somewhat untidy person; he had left documents and letters scattered all over the surface of the desk, and some were piled on the leather chair and in heaps on the floor.

Susanna was about to turn away in defeat when she caught sight of one piece of paper, neatly folded and carefully placed beneath a heavy glass paperweight. In all of the disorder, that one sheet of paper was important enough to warrant special care. She unfolded it with trembling fingers and the words leaped out at her:

. . . believed to be destined for the Confederate States of America . . . that said vessel is in actual fact a warship . . . detention will take place forthwith . . . when all necessary protocol observed we anticipate this will be Tuesday, July 29th . . .

She had just replaced the letter when she heard the sound in the adjoining bedroom, a slight clearing of the throat. Sir Edmund! She would have to bluff her way out somehow. Then her eyes went to the door leading to the landing and she saw the key on the inside of the lock. Swiftly she crossed the room and slipped through the door just as she heard Lady Bartlett's voice call out, "Edmund . . . is that you?"

She was on a train for Liverpool that afternoon. There was no time to announce her hurried departure to anyone but Emma, who had promised to make her excuses. Watching the English countryside go by the window of the Liverpool express, Susanna's thoughts were not on the importance of the information she had obtained, but on the uneasy feeling she had had since leaving Bartlett Hall that she was being followed. It had begun as she slipped out of her room and started down the deserted hallway, her bag clutched in her hand. A door closing quietly behind her, then the creak on the stair, but, turning, she had seen no one.

The first-class section of the train was almost empty, but several times she had thought there was someone in the aisle outside her compartment. Once she had gone to the door and looked out in time to see the door of the next compartment closing.

As they traveled north she could see storm clouds gathering on the horizon to the west, and by the time they arrived in Crewe station, large raindrops were splattering against the windows. Susanna had been alone in the compartment for over four hours and was glad when two men boarded the train at Crewe and asked if they might be permitted to share her compartment.

The men were neither young nor old, and Susanna noticed little about them except that they spoke in accents she recognized as those of Lancashire and their clothing looked like that of seamen. Both men wore beards, which also seemed to proclaim them to be sailors. No doubt en route to a ship in the Mersey.

Looking at the heavy rain, Susanna wished someone was meeting her in Liverpool. The train stood an interminably long time in Crewe station and she fidgeted anxiously, wanting to be with Rowan and have the message delivered.

When at last the train steamed into Lime Street station, rain was falling in torrents and lightning whipped the leaden skies in the wake of great rolls of thunder.

Clutching her cloak close to her body, Susanna extended her hand to be helped down by a porter.

"Someone meeting you, miss?" he inquired. "Or would you like me to get you a cab?"

She looked up and down the long platform at the people waiting, half hoping to see Rowan's rangy figure sauntering toward her, but of course he had no idea when or if she would be arriving in Liverpool.

"Yes, please, would you hail a cab for me?"

Following the porter as he carried her single bag, Susanna again felt a prickling sensation at the nape of her neck. She wanted to turn and see if someone was following her, but forced herself to keep her eyes on the porter's retreating back.

At the entrance to the station the porter waved down a hansom cab and helped Susanna into it. She told the driver to take her to the Pig and Whistle on Water Street, then settled back to pull the damp hood from her hair.

The next moment two men were in the cab with her, crushing her in the narrow space, a hand clamped over her mouth, and the cab lurched off over rain-soaked streets as she struggled to free herself from the suffocating hand.

"You promise not to scream?" a rough, Lancashire-accented voice hissed in her ear. She nodded, her heart pounding against her ribs, and her breath wheezing in her throat. The hand was lowered from her face and she looked into the bearded faces of the men who had boarded her train at Crewe.

The driver of the cab huddled deep in his Garrick, and the rumbling thunder would probably muffle her screams, she decided at once. Taking a deep breath, she said in as calm a voice as she could, "And what may I do for you gentlemen?"

The man next to her snorted. "You're a cool baggage, ain't yer? Aye, lass, there is sommat as you can do for us. You can tell us what that uncle of yours and 'is friends are going to do about the ship in Laird's yard."

"What ship?" Susanna asked innocently.

For answer the man reached over and jerked her cloak aside, his fingers tearing at her bodice.

Susanna stifled a scream as she felt his nails against her bare flesh, then his hand closed viciously around her breast and began to tighten until she bit her lips in pain.

"All right—wait . . . please," she gasped.

"That's better, lass." the man said, and although he relaxed his grip, he continued to fondle her breast while the other man leaned forward to get a better view.

She fought to clear her senses, to think, what to tell them . . . how to escape.

"They are planning to try to make a run for it," she said, "but not until next weekend." Surely, she thought, they will be gone by then—the letter said the ship was to be seized in three days' time.

"Then why did you make such an 'asty departure from his lordship's place?" the other man asked.

So, she had been followed all the way from Bartlett Hall. Jacob Drost, it had to be he . . . and these men were in his employ. But who had seen her leave besides Emma?

"I wanted to be with my uncle," Susanna said, feeling the loathsome hand begin to tighten again, "because one of the gentlemen there made . . . improper advances . . ."

The two men sniggered at this, and the first one nudged his companion. "Can't say as I blame 'im, can you?"

"Come on, let's be off before the cabbie out there wonders what we're up to," his companion said.

As the cab slowed for the next corner, the horses' hooves sliding over the cobbled street, the two men jumped to the pavement and were lost in rain and darkness.

It was midnight. Susanna, wrapped in a warm blanket, was sipping hot milk laced with brandy. She had locked the door after Rowan left to deliver her message to Mr. Bulloch.

Rowan had listened, white-lipped, as she told him of the two men, and had smashed his fist in impotent fury when she was finished. After he calmed down, he told her there was more danger lurking on the streets of Liverpool and they were far from getting the *Alabama* out to sea. The Yankee Consul, Dudley, was in a frenzy of activity and knew, for sure, that they were planning to slip the cruiser out somehow. Dudley was burning the wires to London and the Foreign Office to try to get the detention order put into effect. Now they knew exactly when this would be, there was one man who might be able to help them simply by disappearing for a day or two while they completed their plans.

"You've been through a lot today," Rowan had said, "but I'm afraid I don't know any other agent who can keep that man from doing his duty for the Crown by detaining our ship."

"What man? Who are you talking about?" Susanna had asked sleepily.

"The collector of customs, Susanna. He is the one who will be given the order to seize our ship. We shall have to keep him out of the way for a day or so. . . . But sleep now. I've got to get your message to Bulloch."

The rain had slowed to a misty drizzle as Rowan walked down the floating gangway to the Birkenhead ferry. The ferries crossed the river infrequently during the hours of darkness, and it was going to be a long, damp wait. Someday, he was reflecting, some enterprising engineer is going to bridge this river here, or put a tunnel under it. So many things in the world needed attention, and wars and politics kept men from more useful endeavors.

The Confederacy's Chief of Overseas Purchasing, James Bulloch, had taken a room in Birkenhead while presiding over the matter of the *Alabama*, and Rowan cursed the delay in crossing the river to take Susanna's message to his chief. Susanna . . . he still had to tell her of the dispatch from North Carolina. After all she had gone through today, to have to reward her so . . .

In his absorption with his thoughts of Susanna, Rowan was careless and did not see the two figures detach themselves from the shadows as he left the Pig and

of the river. Rowan released the man, wiping the blood on his jacket.

"Listen to me. You spread the word. I'll kill any man who goes near the girl again. Understand?"

He reached inside his coat for a handkerchief to wrap around his bleeding hands, and when the ferry touched the dock he swung himself over the rail and jumped before the gangway was lowered.

Number 290 was an impressive sight. Her timbers were of the finest English oak, every plank hand-picked. Two hundred and twenty feet long, barkentine-rigged, with extra-tall masts and an engine that would drive her almost fifteen knots when she used both steam and sail.

On the night of July 28, the 290 was anchored at the public landing stage in Liverpool. Mr. Bulloch had been informed by a "private but most reliable source" that he had three days before the Foreign Office's detention order would be carried out. Upon receipt of that message, he decided that the 290 must leave England within forty-eight hours.

On the night he received the warning, Bulloch wrote letters of instruction. To the captain of the tender *Agrippina*, in London, he sent orders to sail for the Azores and prepare for a meeting with the cruiser. To his special assistant aboard the *Agrippina*, he reiterated his orders to recruit as many of her crew as possible for Southern service.

To the English Captain Butcher, who would be taking the 290 out of the Mersey, he sent Rowan with the highly confidential information about the ship's route and rendezvous, including directions for transferring command to Captain Raphael Semmes, formerly of the *Sumter*.

Another of Bulloch's agents was charged with securing a tug to accompany the 290 down the Mersey, and on Monday night, July 28, 1862, all was in readiness.

Aboard the *Agrippina* was the equipment that would turn Number 290 into the deadliest cruiser ever to sail the seas: coal, cannon, including a 100-pound Blakely rifle, ammunition, uniforms. Next morning Number 290 would leave Liverpool, ostensibly on a trial run, loaded with local dignitaries, flags flying. There was no need for customs clearance; she would return with the tide.

All along the Mersey, sailors aboard the other ships sighed in envy at the sheer beauty of her as she glided by. Down on the sands of the small holiday resort at the mouth of the river a handful of bathers looked up idly as the ship went by. They could hear the laughter, the sound of popping corks and the clinking of wine glasses.

Late in the afternoon of the 29th, the guests on board the 290 were told that it would be necessary for the ship's trials to continue into the night and, since the food and wine were depleted, they would be sent ashore in the tug so thoughtfully provided.

In London, orders to seize Number 290 were being shuffled between the Foreign Office and the Treasury and then to customs officials.

In Liverpool, Consul Dudley was frantically trying to find the local collector of customs and get him to hold the ship until its status could be clarified, but that official was mysteriously absent from his post.

He was, in fact, lying naked upon a sheepskin rug in a private home in the outskirts of Birkenhead in a particularly lovely section of the Wirral peninsula. Oddly enough, although he felt that lethargic satiety that comes after an excellent romp with an experienced wench, the details of what had actually happened seemed to elude him.

The girl was sitting in the window seat, admiring the view. The sun gilded her chestnut hair with bronze highlights and dappled her creamy shoulders with entrancing patterns. She was wearing an evening dress . . . odd, he was sure she had undressed with him.

He remembered dining with her the previous evening. . . . there had been others present then . . . the champagne . . . so much champagne. He had stumbled out of bed this morning and managed to get as far as the rug before collapsing again. This morning she had hinted at some of the pleasures they had shared the previous night. Yes, it had been a good romp, he was sure. It was a pity he could not remember anything that had happened. He had had far too much to drink and his head hurt. Well, no matter, she wanted to detain him, keep him from going to his duties, he was sure of that. She had been a little coy this morning and insisted he take her riding along the river. Perhaps he would be able to persuade her to return here later . . . ?

Not that he needed any inducement to be absent from his office at this time. He had walked warily for days, fearful of being placed in a position of being forced to stop Number 290 from leaving the Mersey. The collector of customs was, in fact, a heavy speculator in cotton.

Fortunately, Susanna did not know her presence was unnecessary. I am not really being unfaithful to Brent, she was telling herself. All I actually did was flirt a little and talk a great deal. And he is certainly in no condition to do anything this morning. I may have been compromised for my country, but I haven't been seduced. My country, she thought wonderingly. Mine and Rowan's and Brent's and our son's. Perhaps now the *Alabama* has escaped they will let us go home again.

And Brent, sailing for the Azores on the *Agrippina*, watched the coast of England recede into the mist and thought fleetingly of Susanna. He would return to her . . . and think of her in those heady moments of danger and pleasure that were inseparable and which he craved even more than Susanna's warm embrace.

In the open sea, the 290 was safely steaming toward their rendezvous and would soon be renamed *Alabama*, while in a grimy Liverpool public house, Rowan fell into an exhausted sleep, one handkerchief-wrapped hand slowly dripping blood onto the floor.

10

No, Susanna said in a stricken voice. "No, no, no!" she screamed, beating her fists against Rowan's chest, oblivious to his swollen and bruised face and mangled hands. When he did not flinch under her blows she turned from him and sank to the floor, burying her face in her hands.

"Susanna, oh, God, if I could have prevented it . . . " Rowan said brokenly. "I didn't know . . . "

She looked up at him, her face contorted with anguish. "If you hadn't made me come to England without her she'd be alive. I'll never forgive you . . . I'll never work for the Confederacy again. The Yankees are right, you don't believe black people are human . . . you don't think it matters what happens to them. Oh, Mizjane, Mizjane, you were my mother, you were more to me than a flesh-and-blood mother. . . ." Susanna stopped speaking, her eyes widening with a new fear. "Little Brent! My baby . . . what about my baby?" she screamed louder.

"He's safe. Susanna, please—he's safe. Mizjane took him to your Aunt Rhea. That's how she was caught."

"Caught!" Susanna echoed. "Why was she running?"

"It was all a misunderstanding."

"Misunderstanding! She's dead!" Susanna stared at him for a moment and then her shoulders began to shake. Rowan let out his breath with relief until he realized she was convulsed not with tears but with wild uncontrollable laughter. She rolled on the dusty carpet, shrieking hysterically, until he pulled her to her feet.

"Susanna! Stop it! In the name of God, stop!"

"Oh, no, it's all too priceless . . . too useless . . ."

Rowan pulled her roughly to him and held her close despite her struggles until her laughter became dry sobs.

"How did it happen?" she asked at last.

"Come and sit down and drink this brandy and I'll tell you all I know."

Susanna gulped the fiery liquid. *Dead. Mizjane is dead. I'll never see her again.* The words pounded in her head.

"You know she had been evading us. Our people were watching your aunt and caught a boy taking a message to her from Mizjane. They followed him back to the house where she and the baby were hiding. They searched the place but they managed to elude the searchers. I'm afraid one of the troopers became impatient and made some threats against the people who lived there for harboring a mammy who had kidnapped a white baby."

"Mammy! Kidnapped . . ." Susanna repeated in horror.

"Susanna, I don't know all the details," Rowan went on, the pain in her eyes tearing every nerve in his body to shreds. "It seems that night Mizjane managed to get to your Aunt Rhea's house. The troopers went in after her and she was seen running from the back door, carrying a bundle they thought was the baby. Things get confused in the report here . . . but she reached the docks, or a bridge, I'm not sure, and dropped the bundle down into the water. Her closest pursuer thought she was throwing the baby to his death and he opened fire. It was only after she was hit that they discovered it was only a log of wood wrapped in a blanket. Mizjane had wanted to lead them away from the baby. She had left him in your Aunt's house with Emerald."

"Where was Aunt Rhea?"

"She wasn't home. It seems only Emerald was there, and she was hysterical with all the shouting and confusion. After the men realized Mizjane hadn't thrown the baby from the bridge, they went back to your Aunt Rhea's house and saw your son. I give you my word he's alive and well. Since there was no one to bring him to England, they left him in your aunt's care. I have her address. I thought perhaps it better if he stayed with her until our work is done—it shouldn't be too much longer."

"You say a trooper killed her?"

"I'm not exactly sure it was a trooper." Rowan looked away, his eyes bleak. Silently he wished he could cut out his own heart to undo what had been done.

"It was a patroller, wasn't it?" Susanna demanded. "You let a patroller shoot her down in cold blood. Why didn't you send the bloodhounds after her too? She was a free woman . . . she gave her life for my child and she died like a runaway slave."

Susanna refused to travel with Rowan to London. She refused to speak to him the next day when he told her he had some news she might be interested in hearing. It was only when she arrived back in Essex Square that she opened her reticule and found the note, clumsily printed by Rowan's injured hand.

Susanna:
There are no words to tell you how desolate I am. I have been ordered back to Virginia. Our friends would like you to remain in London until I return for you.
My heart aches for your loss.
As ever, Rowan

He would have sailed from Liverpool, she supposed, and would now be on the high seas.

The first day back in London she was besieged by visitors, most of whom were concerned about her sudden disappearance from Bartlett Hall. Emma had apparently told everyone she had been called away on a personal matter.

Susanna announced that there had been a death in her family and that since she was in mourning, she would not be receiving visitors for a time.

As the days slipped by, Susanna spent more and more time in her room. She seemed to be constantly tired, and put this down to grief over Mizjane's death. She ordered several black gowns and began to wear them, which discouraged visitors after their initial sympathy call, except for Lady Bodelon, who called to inquire if perhaps Susanna was considering returning to Virginia and to hint strongly it would be advantageous to do so.

She longed for her baby and was sorry she had not insisted she be sent home to him, especially since she could have sailed with Rowan. There had been no word from Brent, but he was at sea. He had promised to bring her son to her, but Brent's promises were will-o'-the-wisps at best. As her listlessness became more pronounced with each passing day, she spent her waking hours reliving the hours she had spent with Brent before he sailed on the *Agrippina* for his rendezvous with the *Alabama.*

He had awakened in her bed, stretching luxuriously, and, as Rowan had predicted, Brent had told her that he must leave immediately to board a ship that was preparing to sail at a moment's notice.

"But we haven't talked about anything," Susanna had protested.

The dark eyes turned opaque. "I promised I would go and see our son, bring him to you if I can. But I'm a sailor, Susanna, I spend long periods at sea. I cannot tell you when I will see him . . . or when I will see you again if you insist on staying here in England. I did offer to make a home for you in Nassau."

"I have to stay here, for a while longer," Susanna said, wanting to tell him about her bargain for her aunt's freedom, yet not wanting him to know what Rhea had done to necessitate this.

"So be it. You have a fine house and you are far away from the fighting. I am sure I will be able to get to England from time to time. If you need money . . . clothes . . . ?"

"No. I don't need any of those things."

"Then what? I've told you I love you. I meant it."

"We've had one night together and now you are leaving."

"We have a war to win. In the Navy, particularly, every man counts. It's difficult to recruit sailors, Susanna. Even the Northerners with their endless supply of immigrants can't fill all their ships."

"You will go to see our son as soon as you get back to North Carolina? And see if Aunt Rhea is all right?"

"Yes, I promise." He caught her to him again. "Susanna, wait for me. Be true to me. Don't let anyone else love you."

She did not dare mention marriage again. What purpose would it have served? Bitterly she thought of the lonely nights and suppressed desire she would have to endure. So be it—she would not couple with another man.

Now in the sultry late-summer days in Essex Square she slowly began to realize what ailed her. She was again with child. Brent's child.

The immediate problem that presented itself was what to do to conceal her pregnancy from the London crowd. Already the two maids in the house were eyeing her with a knowing look. She dared not consult a doctor, although she could not remember feeling so tired and ill while she carried little Brent. For once she wished briefly that Rowan were there to tell her what to do. He had always managed to cheer her up when she was downhearted, or at least make her so indignant that she forgot what had been making her blue.

Soon it became necessary to raise her top hoop and wear a shawl when her maid brought her food tray. Susanna worried that Lady Bodelon, or worse still, Nicholas Kirby, would discover her condition. She wondered lethargically how she would find her way back to America without Rowan if she was turned out of the house on Essex Square for scandalous behavior.

Emma called regularly, trying to divert Susanna's attention from her grief by bringing news of their friends and also what was happening in America. As the summer faded into autumn, all the news was good.

The South was clearly winning the war. General Lee had split his army and invaded Pennsylvania. They were fighting in Yankee territory and winning great victories. And a Rebel raider named *Alabama* was wreaking havoc with Yankee shipping.

All of Emma's efforts to kindle a spark of response in her friend were to no avail. Susanna had no interest in the war that had killed her beloved Mizjane, taken everyone she loved away from her and thrust her into this foreign country. The stirrings of patriotism and her elation at helping the *Alabama* escape faded before the realization that for all her grand illusions, Brent still considered her a woman of easy virtue to be used and as quickly forgotten. She cursed herself for a fool and wished passionately she were back in Blossom Street so she could go to the old woman who killed unborn babies.

She must go home—she could not face the London set. She had to be far away in her shame, away from the stares and whispers and heaven only knew what other humiliations. She would get through this somehow, and never, ever again would Susanna Brigid O'Rourke live for any man.

Susanna was no longer the vivacious girl whom Emma had grown to love. This Susanna was shockingly pale and spent her days lying limply on a chaise longue. Emma tried to understand Susanna's grief, but it was difficult. The woman who had died had only been a kind of nanny. But then, Her Majesty was still lost in her grief for her dead Prince Albert. Emma supposed that it took some people longer to recover from the loss of a dear one. Emma herself still missed her father, but in some strange way, Susanna seemed to have taken his place.

In spite of her weakness and lack of interest in news from home, Susanna's interest was aroused when in October 1862, the English Chancellor of the Exchequer, William Gladstone, made a speech that electrified the world.

"Jefferson Davis and other leaders of the South have made an army, they are making, it appears, a navy; and they have made what is more than either—they have made a nation."

The effect of these words on both North and South was devastating. Clearly it was only a matter of time before England recognized the Confederacy. Had Queen Victoria's government decided to intervene in American affairs?

Now that the South appeared to be marching toward victory, the strong pro-South sentiments in Parliament surfaced. Everyone was sure the North's military disasters and Lee's march into Maryland heralded the end of hostilities.

While Lord Palmiston, Gladstone and diplomats from

England, France and Russia met to propose and argue over mediations to bring about an armistice, an end to the blockade and formation of two separate countries, Emma finally realized how desperately ill Susanna was.

"You must allow me to bring a doctor, dear," she said firmly, looking down at the dark circles under Susanna's eyes and her sunken cheeks.

"No. Emma, please, no." Susanna clutched weakly at her hand and Emma was horrified to feel how fiercely the fever burned in the limp fingers. "I must go home. I can't stay here. It will be all right for me to go now; the war is almost over. . . . You see, I had made a bargain I had to keep . . . but it won't matter now we've won the war. . . . I must go to North Carolina to my aunt. . . . Please, Emma, dear sister . . ."

She's delirious, Emma thought in dismay. "Susanna dear, you can't leave us. I don't think you are strong enough to travel. You must let me bring a doctor to you."

"Emma, listen to me. I have to trust you, I have to tell you . . ." Susanna's voice was so low that Emma had to bend over her to hear.

Hesitantly, slowly, Susanna told Emma the whole story, including the fact that she was carrying a child and had a second child by the same man, who was not her husband. The only thing she did not reveal was the identity of the man.

When she finished, Emma's eyes were shining with sympathy and love. She bent to gather Susanna's wasted body into her arms.

"You are my sister . . . oh, Susanna, I am so happy you are my sister," she said, tears slipping down her cheeks to rest on Susanna's burning brow. "I had been so drawn to you from the first moment we met, and now I know it was because you reminded me so much of Father. . . ."

Susanna was too weak to protest this infamy. "Will you help me . . . to get to my aunt and my little boy? I want to have this baby in my own country," she whispered. "If you could get me on one of your ships going to Bermuda or Nassau . . ."

"But my dear, you're so ill. Couldn't you have the

baby here and then go? I shall take care of you."

"It would cause a scandal, Emma. I would have to move from this house and lose my bequest. I have no money of my own to support myself."

"I will support you," Emma said firmly. "You would move into our house."

"No, no . . . please, Emma." Susanna had a chilling vision of living under the same roof with and at the mercy of Alicia Bodelon. "It isn't just that . . . it's my little boy. I miss him so desperately . . . and sometimes I am so homesick. . . . I know I would get well again if I could just go home."

"Very well, my dear little sister. But you must promise to come back as soon as you are well. I should never be able to rest, thinking of you in the middle of a dreadful war. Now you must rest, I will take care of everything."

Susanna nodded weakly and lay back on her pillow. It would be all right now, she thought. She would return to Aunt Rhea in Wilmington . . . the war was almost won. They would make a home for themselves and the two babies, and she would raise her sons to be honorable toward women.

Within three days Emma brought word that a passage had been secretly arranged on one of the Bodelon ships. Emma had told no one who the passenger would be, and when embarkation time came Susanna would be quietly slipped aboard and everyone would be told she had returned to her own country for a visit. Emma also brought a bitter-tasting concoction she had secured from a pharmacist friend which he said was a tonic specifically for Susanna's condition. It made her feel a little better, but she slept a great deal of the time and even when awake the world did not seem real to her.

It had been some weeks since anyone except Emma had called out of respect for her period of mourning, but flowers and messages arrived almost daily from the Bartlett brothers, Tom Douglas and several other young men. Quite soon after her return from Liverpool, Susanna had also received a small velvet case containing a pair of emerald earbobs. The accompanying card read simply:

"To match the fire in your eyes—E. B." Edmund Bartlett. . . . Had Susanna felt stronger she would have
returned the gift, but the stones glinted wickedly at her
and, mesmerized, she slipped the gold wires through her
pierced ears and her spirits were momentarily lifted.
Emeralds did bring out the green of her eyes.

Nicholas Kirby was away on a business trip, and Dobbs
had requested some time to go and visit an aging relative, since there was little to do in the house while
Susanna was not receiving visitors. Susanna had agreed
to this gladly, and when she knew her passage had been
arranged, she sent the other servants to seek other
employment, telling them she would be closing the house.
Meantime one maid could come in on a part-time basis.

The outside world had begun to fade from her thoughts.
She was conscious only of the terrible lethargy that had
her in its grip. A week before she was to sail for Bermuda she was rudely awakened from an afternoon nap.
The sound that had disturbed her seemed to be coming
from the room above. A scraping, then a muffled thud.
Silence for a moment, then the same sounds, but from a
different direction. Susanna struggled to clear her head
and come fully awake. Again a board creaked over her
head. She reached for the bell cord to summon a servant,
then remembered she was alone in the house.

The rooms above her were used by Nicholas Kirby,
but he had been gone for several weeks. There was a
creaking on the stairs coming down to her floor and
then a footfall on the landing. Now the intruder was
in the room next to her. A door or drawer slammed
shut . . . footsteps as someone walked by the door.

Susanna sat up, blinking as the room swam slowly
around her. She tried to remember what day it was.
Was it morning or afternoon? When did the maid come
in? But no maid ever banged doors and moved about
so noisily.

"Who is it? Who is there?" she called out.

There was no response.

Trying to think back to before she had fallen asleep,
she vaguely remembered that the maid had already been
there. She had left a tray of food before departing.

Yes . . . there it was, the silver covers still on the dishes, the tray on her bedside table.

"Emma?" she called. "Is that you, Emma?"

The footsteps were in the hall again, heavy footsteps. A man's footsteps.

"Who is it? "Who is there?" she called again.

A door closed across the landing, but there was still no response to her question. Someone was slowly and methodically searching the house . . . and he did not care to be quiet about it.

Susanna struggled to her feet, the room swimming before her eyes as she did so. She had been too weak to dress for several days, so pulled on a robe over her nightgown.

Dragging herself to the door, she was sure she would faint at any moment. There was a painful stabbing sensation in her side and the baby in her womb felt heavy as lead. As she reached her bedroom door there was another thud and then a muttered curse.

Swaying unsteadily on her feet, she reached the door and threw it open. All the other doors on the landing were open, and a small table had been knocked over outside her door. Gripping the wall for support, she edged toward the sitting room across the landing, where the sounds were coming from. Passing the spare bedroom, she saw that the wardrobe doors hung open and all the drawers in the chest had been pulled out. Clothing and books were scattered about the floor.

The floor seemed to be slanting unevenly as she reached the open doorway and saw that someone was ransacking the room—a tall thin figure who spun around and fixed watery eyes on her.

Jacob Drost dropped the writing case he was holding and moved toward her, kicking aside an overturned chair as he did so. Susanna clung to the doorjamb for support, her mouth dry. Drost reached her side and his bony fingers went around her arm. She struggled, her nails raking his cheek, fists flailing at that hateful face. She twisted away from him and tried to run, but he caught her and pulled her back. Now she kicked at him and swung her elbow into his stomach with her last ounce of strength.

"You little . . . " she heard him mutter as he struck her, and for a second everything disappeared into blackness and she almost fell, but he was dragging her back to her room and the pain in her side brought her back to consciousness.

"All right," Drost said, flinging her on the bed. "Where is he and where are the warrants?" He began to pull the clothes from her wardrobe and throw them to the floor.

"Who?" Susanna tried to speak clamly. She could feel perspiration dripping from her head as she inched across the bed to the bell pull. Oh, please, she thought, let the maid have returned.

Drost looked at her just as her hand closed over the pull. "Nobody home but you. But thanks for the idea, you wildcat."

He seemed to have receded a great distance from her and his voice came from far away . . . but he was not far away, because he had torn down the bell pull and was tying it about her wrists. The room went dark as she felt his hands tear at her robe and nightgown, then he was fastening the cord to her ankles. Great tearing pains were coursing through her body and she closed her eyes and lay there, hearing the sound of her nightgown being torn, wanting to retch but too weak to do anything but pray for deliverance from this nightmare.

Suddenly he slapped her across the cheek. "Open your eyes, you bitch. I mean to know where Marshall is and if he's spent those warrants yet. You'll get no mercy from me, lady. I hate your kind worse than any other scum I know. You'd sell your body and your soul and your country, wouldn't you, no-good bitch . . . "

Susanna lay still, wishing she could die. Just before he hit her again she looked into his eyes and saw an overwhelming hatred reflected there. Some demon other than war possessed Jacob Drost. Then his fist smashed into her face.

Merciful darkness closed in and she gratefully slipped away. Down, down a long tunnel and out into the open sea. Misty sea, gray waves bore her away toward the rising storm. There was a sudden agonizing pain and then she was in a void.

"Mr. Bulloch is dining with friends and can't see you now," the aide said to Rowan. "What are you doing back in Liverpool without being ordered to return anyway?"

"Because the Scottish sea monster isn't for sale at any price," Rowan said, "and because I got word from a contact here that another of our agents may be in danger." He kept his voice low, looking around the hotel restaurant but not finding what he sought.

"They are in a private banquet room," the aide said. "Which agent? We'll warn him."

"Look, I'm not going to waste time here. My informant tells me every Union agent in the British Isles has been searching for me and that another known Confederate agent in London also dropped out of sight lately. Then Jake Drost suddenly gave up chasing me all over Scotland. He hasn't turned up in Liverpool, so I can only assume he now knows where Susanna . . . the other agent is hiding. I have to find her first—or him—and stop him."

"I'm sure your little friend from the bordello can take care of herself," the aide said smoothly, "and Mr. Bulloch will want a full report on your failure to acquire the Scottish ram."

"Keep your voice down, damn you. You can report my failure to Bulloch and tell him if any harm comes to that girl I expect to be in a murderous mood when next I see him. I'm leaving for London."

The aide watched as Rowan walked to the hotel lobby, then shrugged and returned to his dinner, unaware that Rowan was creating a disturbance at the desk and drawing considerable attention to himself. Normally soft-spoken, he was bellowing at the clerk that James Dunwody Bulloch had refused to see him and that was all the thanks he got for all of the trouble he had gone to. He lingered in the lobby while the clerk hovered nervously and then Rowan shouted that he was going back to his lodgings and to hell with J.D. Bulloch.

A similar scene took place a short time later at the Pig and Whistle public house, but now it appeared that Rowan was suddenly and severely under the influence of drink. He staggered about the public bar informing everyone present that yessir, one Rebel could lick a dozen Yankees . . . maybe even a hundred . . .

When he was satisfied he had called enough attention to himself, he slipped outside to a starry night and a blow on the head from behind.

They dragged him into the rear of the deserted fish market and three of them held him down while a fourth poured a bucket of foul-smelling water over his face, leaving him gasping for breath and covered in fish scales.

"All right, Reb," the wielder of the bucket said, "you've led us a merry chase. Now you're going to tell us what Bulloch wants you to buy with the warrants . . . and where it is." And the empty bucket came clanging down into his face.

"Drost . . . " Rowan formed the word through the swelling of his lips. "Jake Drost . . . I want to talk to him . . ."

"Drost ain't here. You'll talk to us." A foot came down on his stomach, winding him.

"Drost . . . " he gasped out again.

"Where is Jake?" a voice said somewhere over Rowan's head.

"He got word from his friends in London that the girl is still in her house . . . never left, it seems. She'd sent her servants away and was holed up there all alone. Jake is leaving on the midnight train to find out what she knows."

"What about the warrants, Reb?" Where've you been and what have you been up to lately?" the voice close to Rowan's face said.

Blood was trickling from the corner of his mouth. He spat and said, "Can you get to the station . . . stop Drost from going to London? I'll talk to him . . . tell him everything. The girl doesn't know, I swear on my mother's grave. Keep him away from her . . . I'll tell him . . . "

"You'll tell us, Reb. It's too late to beat that train out of the station."

Rowan tried to roll away from the flailing boots, tried to protect his face from the fists, but there were too many of them.

They left him battered and bleeding in a litter-filled gutter, whispering her name to the stars that blinked over soot-blackened chimneys. They knew no more than before, and he was alive because a prowling cat had jumped onto an off-balance fish box and sent it crashing to the ground. Fearing the arrival of the peelers, they had vanished into the night.

The Northern press had dubbed her "the phantom cruiser." She would appear suddenly in the South Atlantic, or off the South African coast, or in the China Sea. No ship was safe from the swift marauder, no one could predict where she would strike next.

On this particularly searing afternoon, the *Alabama* was at anchor in an African bay, beautiful as a swan against an azure sky and mirrored sea.

On her decks some of the seamen looked longingly toward the white beach and wished they had been chosen to go ashore in the longboat for supplies. Even a few hours with the solid earth under their toes . . . and the slavers had not touched this stretch of coast; the natives in their canoes and the women on the beach smiled and looked toward their ship without fear.

Brent, in charge of purchasing fresh food, had finished this task, set the men to loading the boat, and wandered down to a rocky cove. Their time ashore was brief, only what was necessary to take on supplies. Brent looked toward his ship lying safely beyond the teeth of coral in the shallow waters lapping into the bay and he felt a surge of pride. Surely no more graceful lady ever sailed the seas. Proud, defiant, an aristocrat of her kind.

Two dusky-skinned girls were dragging a net containing several large crabs up the beach. The girls wore only brightly colored skirts, pulled between their legs and tucked in at the waist, no doubt as a convenience while struggling in the water with the nets. Their supple young bodies glistened in the sunlight and they laughed and chattered to each other as they came toward him.

My ship and my woman, Brent was thinking. They both have the bearing and grace of ladies that conceal their deadly purpose. Ah, Susanna, he thought, my destiny is not to spend my days pining for a woman whose morals are those of a man.

The girls on the beach could have made a detour and gone the other way, but, still giggling, they continued toward him. Brent leaned against the wind-bent palm, its stem rough with old leafbases, and waited. They smiled at him as they came closer, showing white teeth and little pink tongues. He smiled back and his hand snaked out and ripped away the skirt of the nearest girl. Dropping the crabs, they ran, giggling and stumbling on the rocks. Brent followed the naked girl as she ran along the palm-fringed beach to where sand dunes rose above the sluggish waters.

He caught her by the legs and they rolled down into a sunny hollow, birds shrieking overhead, stubby grasses jabbing sharply through his shirt as he landed on his back, the girl on top of him.

The hair between her legs was crisply curled and wiry to the touch as he ran his hand over it. The brown breast was elongated, but firm, and he pulled it down to his mouth. She laughed again and wriggled and his fingers had parted the curly hair and found moistness.

She sat up and watched with great interest as he removed his clothes and kneeled above her, pointing to his erect organ. Misunderstanding, she came up on her knees and tried to pull him into her.

"No. Not there . . . here," he said, and touched her lips.

She smiled and lay down on the sand, enjoying the game but not understanding it. Brent sighed, then rolled her over and entered her from the rear. He did not want to look into the soft brown eyes. After a moment the thought occurred to him that women who did not speak his language could not make demands on him and it was better that way. There were too many women in the world to be true to just one, no matter how fascinating.

Susanna's first sensation was the shivering of her aching body and the restraints upon her hands and feet. Jacob Drost was sitting in a chair beside the bed, going through a dispatch case that belonged to Rowan. The room seemed to have taken on an oppressiveness. Blurred objects took on sinister forms. The draperies had been closed, shutting out most of the light, and the single lamp beside the bed cast a ghostly glow on the gaunt features of her tormentor.

"So. You're awake. You ready to talk to me now? Tell me what you know about the ram. The warrants ain't here. Did he buy it yet?"

"I don't know . . . what ram is. . . . Please, some water . . ."

"Look, Marshall was in Liverpool with enough cotton warrants to buy a whole navy. We know Bulloch is up to something, but whatever he wants to buy is not being built in the Mersey. Then Marshall drops out of sight. Into thin air. You'd better tell me where he is or you're going to be sorrier than you are now."

"*Alabama* . . . that was what we were . . . "

Drost's face was close to hers; she could smell his fetid breath and felt waves of nausea rising again.

"She sailed months ago. Your Rowan Marshall went back to Virginia and returned with warrants worth a fortune."

"Don't know what warrants . . . are . . . "

"Cotton futures. Just like money. What does he want to buy?"

His hand closed around her throat and she gasped as she tried to suck air into her starving lungs.

"It's for the ram, ain't it? The Scottish ram. That's where your friend is. Come on, damn you, tell me where he is. I've got to stop him before he buys that ram. We don't want . . . "

Susanna was slipping away into unconsciousness again. For a moment it seemed that Mizjane was hovering over the bed, looking down at her, arms outstretched. Then

there was a great pounding in her ears, louder, louder.
No, it was not in her ears. Someone was pounding on
the door below, running up the stairs, bursting into the
room. Drost released his hold on her throat and long,
tortured breaths escaped from her as she tried to open
her mouth to scream.

Dimly she heard a familiar voice, and then a crash
and a hail of curses and grunts. Drost was thrown back
violently against the bed, twisted himself to his feet and
then crashed again into some unseen body. Susanna
heard the slap of knuckles on flesh and bone and someone
fell heavily to the floor.

Raising herself up on one elbow, she could see two
figures now. They rolled on the floor, then one was
free and smashing his fist into the other. Susanna closed
her eyes and lay down again. She knew she should escape
now, but her legs refused to move. The two figures
crashed about the room for what seemed an age and
then at last were still.

He'll come and kill me now, she thought with terror.
He'll kill me because I don't know where Rowan is,
or what a cotton warrant is, or what a ram is . . .

Gentle hands were lifting her, comforting arms encircling her. "It's all right now, Susanna my darling. I'm
here, my brave little girl."

Susanna let go of her senses. She floated away again
on a clear blue sea, and everything would have been
perfect but for the pains that came each time a wave
broke on the shore.

11

SHE had been floating for a long time. The slow swaying motion was soothing to her pain-wracked body. During the dream faces came and went. Hands touched her. After a time the pain subsided except for the burning needles when she tried to move her legs. She tried to speak to the blurred faces in her dream, but only one word ever managed to make itself heard through parched lips. A name she called over and over again.

When the red haze at last lifted from her eyes she looked up at a lamp, swinging slowly back and forth from the ceiling . . . and a round window on the wall . . . beyond which was a pewter mass that swelled and churned restlessly. She was in the cabin of a ship, lying in a bunk. She tried to raise her arms to pull herself upright, but found she was bound loosely at the wrists. She screamed then, for she knew Jacob Drost was coming back to kill her.

"Susanna, no, don't . . . it's all right, it's me. We just tied you so you wouldn't fall out of the bunk when we roll." Rowan's voice, Rowan's hands, gentle yet strong, sending reassuring messages through her numb body by the touch of his fingertips.

Dear God, thank you, she thought.

She looked up at Rowan and saw joy mingled with relief in his eyes. "Thank God," he breathed. "You know me now, Susanna? You know where you are? You're on a ship, going home to your baby and your aunt."

"Jacob Drost?" Susanna questioned, horrified at the painful croaking that was her voice.

Rowan had freed her wrists and was massaging them

171

gently. "I should have killed him," he said savagely, "but I didn't." He brought a cup of cool liquid to her lips and Susanna sipped it gratefully.

"I thought you had gone back to Virginia. . . . Where did you come from?"

"I wanted to keep you out of it. After those two brutes got hold of you in Liverpool I vowed you would have no part in any more of our work. I wasn't very successful, was I?" he asked bitterly. "You see, I did make a fast trip home. I didn't get a chance to get to Wilmington to see your aunt—I'm sorry, Susanna, but I had to turn around and come right back. I spent a short time in Liverpool and then had to go to Scotland." There was a long scar down one side of his face.

"Scotland? But why didn't you let me know?"

"I thought I was protecting you. Did Drost say anything about the Scottish sea monster to you?"

"No. He talked about cotton, I think. Warrants, or something like that."

"It's a kind of certificate guaranteeing that cotton will be delivered at a fixed price. It's the most valuable currency we have."

"What did you say about a sea monster? And how did you know Jacob Drost . . . " Susanna found it difficult to formulate her thoughts. There was something missing; she was not sure what it was. As though part of her had been left behind somewhere.

"It's a special kind of ship, Susanna. A ship that will win the war for us. If we can build a fleet of rams we shall win. It's the most deadly weapon ever devised."

"You are building them in Scotland?"

"The first one, yes. Number 61."

"You and your numbers . . . " Susanna said wearily, feeling the need to sleep creep over her again.

"I got word from one of our people in Liverpool that Drost had lost my trail and was believed headed back to London. I knew he was going to try to find out from you where I was, so I caught the next train south. Thank God I was only hours behind him, but Susanna, honey . . . I wish I could have got to you first." Looking into Susanna's haunted eyes, Rowan reflected bitterly that the more he tried to protect her, the worse she seemed to fare, and he wondered if he would have the strength to take her home, go away and forget her.

"If I had been stronger . . . " Susanna said sleepily. "I hadn't been well. . . . " She moved her hands, resting them on the hollow of her stomach . . . and then knew what it was that was missing.

"My baby! Rowan . . . "

"I'm sorry, Susanna. Your baby was dead. The doctor had to take it from you. We thought you were going to die too." Rowan's compassion and pain was plainly written in his clear gray eyes, in the gesture of his hand pushing back his lion's mane of hair from his brow.

Oddly, Susanna felt only relief at his announcement.

The weather was good for the time of year, and as the ship sailed into sunny southern waters Susanna spent more time on deck, rapidly recovering her strength. There was a doctor aboard the ship, and he kept close watch on her.

When she was almost fully well again he sent his nurse from the cabin and said to Susanna, "Now look here, Mrs. Marshall, I have a few blunt words of advice for you, and I don't want any blushing or tears. You are not to have any more babies for several years, do you understand? At least three or four years. Now I am going to tell you how to avoid having them."

Susanna listened intently, and when he had finished she said, "Yes, doctor, I understand. Now can you tell me how to gain a little weight? I'm far too thin."

Her eyes went to the porthole, to the pencil line of green on the horizon. They would be in Bermuda within hours. Her spirits lifted. Home . . . and her baby . . . Aunt Rhea . . . and Brent.

Late in 1862 rumors were already rife in the Confederate Navy about the Scottish sea monster being built in Glasgow, forerunner of a fleet of terrible, piercing rams. Brent Chaloner was among the first of Captain Semmes' officers to inquire about volunteering for service aboard an ironclad ram.

"Is it true the ram has five inches of armor sheathing

and a displacement of over three thousand tons?" he asked his captain. "I hear the first is two hundred and seventy feet long on the drawing board."

Captain Semmes smiled. Some of the rumors about the rams were wildly exaggerated, but this young officer's information was close to the facts. "Number 61 not only has the armor, but it's backed by two nine-inch layers of teak, one horizontal and one vertical. And it has a fifty-foot beam," Semmes replied.

"Guns?" Brent asked, his dark eyes gleaming.

"Ten on each side. . . . She's sharply pointed bow and stern and the bowsprit is hinged to be lifted during ramming. But for the moment, Lieutenant Chaloner, you're more valuable to the Navy where you are."

"If we get a fleet of rams, sir, we'll be able to sweep the blockaders from every Southern harbor. And smash the Northern ports until they beg for mercy."

"I'll make a note of your request for service aboard a ram," Captain Semmes said reluctantly. Lieutenant Chaloner was a brave and daring officer and would be difficult to replace. Still, he was right that the rams would take the war to the Northern coastal cities and the Confederate ports would immediately be opened for commerce. The secret weapon of the war between the states could win the war for the South.

Brent had transferred to the *Alabama* at the time of the rendezvous with the *Agrippina*, knowing full well that the *Alabama* was designed to stay at sea for long periods, having the capability of carrying extra supplies and ammunition and also having condensers for saltwater conversion. She was the finest, fastest raider the South had, and therefore Brent was compelled to serve aboard her—even though it meant he could not keep his promise either to see his son or to return to Susanna.

Yes, the *Alabama* was the scourge of the seas, and Brent was proud of her. But his blood churned with excitement when descriptions of the rams reached him. Nothing like a war to move old institutions forward. A new navy with fighting ships such as the world had never seen were emerging from this conflict.

As it happened, however, Brent was to leave the

Alabama sooner than he expected, and not to take command of a ram.

The morning had dawned hot and calm. It seemed the ship was floating on air instead of water, so calm was the sea. No breeze stirred the rigging, and the sky was an oppressive white ringed with gray on the distant horizon. Brent was off duty, and as his quarters were stifling, he made his way topside.

They had taken a ship the day before, and there were women among the prisoners, including a fresh-faced miss with blazing green eyes who had reminded him, disturbingly, of Susanna.

Captain Semmes' orders were uncompromisingly rigid in regard to female prisoners. They were to be left strictly alone. However, the ship was at sea for long periods of time, and their time in port too brief to allow shore leaves for all. The men were restless, and there had been mutinous mutterings among some of them. Except for the officers, who were all Southerners, the crew was made up of a motley array of seamen from the waterfronts of Liverpool and other foreign ports.

As sailors, it offended them to burn the ships they captured, but there was no choice, for there was no port to which they could take prizes. More and more they felt like the pirates the Northern press claimed they were. Officers, including Brent, were regarded with hostility and suspicion. There had been several incidents that made both captain and officers jumpy, and some had taken to wearing sidearms at all times.

Nerves were strained to breaking point, and the presence of women prisoners aboard did not help. As Brent came topside one of the sailors swabbing the deck kicked over his pail, sending a stream of filthy water in Brent's path. He stopped, his glance sweeping from the sailor to his two companions, who paused, mops held more in the manner of clubs than cleaning tools. Like lightning, Brent reached for the first sailor's mop, grabbed it and swung it in an arc, catching all three off guard.

"Out of my way and watch what you're doing with that blasted water. You want someone to break his neck?" He smiled, but it was a smile that froze the blood of all three, and they moved aside to let him pass.

Sweat was beading on his forehead, not from the encounter but from the sultriness of the day. They were headed into a storm, a big one, and everyone knew it. He felt the need to find a quiet place to himself. A difficult task on board a cruiser jammed with crew and prisoners, to say nothing of the booty they had taken. Making his way aft, with no particular destination in mind, he suddenly found his way blocked by several men.

He could have turned back without losing face, but there was something in the expression of the man nearest him that made Brent hesitate. Then he heard a slight sound, a whimper like an animal in pain . . . cut off abruptly.

Brent's fist went into the belly of the nearest man and his knee into the groin of the second, and they fell back, cursing, revealing the two men who were dragging the girl toward the forecastle. Frightened green eyes beseeched above the hand clamped over her mouth; her blouse was already rent from collar to waist. She had undoubtedly felt the heat belowdecks and come up for air, stumbling unknowingly into this group.

"Let her go," Brent ordered.

"Come on, sir," one of the men holding her said ingratiatingly, "we ain't gonna hurt her. Just a bit of fun . . . she'll enjoy it as much as us. She ain't a lady anyway, she's an actress . . . been on stage in Paris, and you know them Frogs." He snickered, and the man nursing his belly let go to give Brent a nudge in the ribs.

"Take your hands off her or you'll spend the rest of your life in the brig," Brent snapped, mentally assessing his chances against the four of them if they chose to disobey, and it was certain they would.

He sprang first at the men holding the girl, surprising them into releasing her. He had sent one sprawling on the deck and was closing with the other when the first shrieking gust of wind hit the ship.

The tempest was upon them in an instant. With the wind came racing black clouds. They could see giant raindrops striking the surface of the sea several yards from the ship while the sun still shone on the deck where they stood. Suddenly white foam appeared atop the waves, a huge swell caught them, and the deck lurched beneath them as they staggered to regain balance.

"To your stations, you bilge rats," Brent yelled, and as the full fury of the hurricane lashed the ship, the four men obeyed.

Rolling before the mountainous seas, her decks awash with salt water and torrential rain, the ship groaned as the wind screamed through the rigging. Stumbling across the sloping deck, Brent reached the girl and held her as a huge wave broke over them.

Gasping, his hair plastered over his face, feet slipping from deck to bulkhead as he tried to keep his balance, he dragged her to the nearest refuge, a starboard gun turret. A tarpaulin had been lashed over the turret in anticipation of the hurricane, and they crawled under it as the ship went down into an endless trough.

Inside the turret, the rolling of the ship sent them crashing back and forth against metal and each other. In the semidarkness their eyes met and held as though they were the last two people on earth.

The ship had turned into the storm now, and instead of rolling she pitched forward, riding up the waves and sliding down the other side, vibrating as though she would split her hull. Brent put out his hands to hold the girl and touched bare, wet breasts. She came into his arms instantly, her mouth on his, and he was tearing at her soaking skirts while she clung, sobbing, about his neck.

They went up into the pinnacle of another wave and the ship hesitated at the pinnacle, caught in space before sliding forward. In that split second the girl wrapped her legs about his body and he thrust his bursting organ into her. The next moment his ejaculation sent a shudder through his body and all was suddenly still.

"What happened?" the girl whispered in the eerie silence.

"We are in the eye of the hurricane," Brent said. "It isn't over, but we should get you back to your cabin while we can and I should be at my station."

"You were too quick for me," she replied. "Come to my cabin with me."

"After the storm is over, I'll come to you then," Brent promised.

But when the storm was over she had changed her mind and tearfully reported that she had been brutalized and raped by one of the officers.

Captain Semmes had no wish to punish one of his best officers, and besides, it was only the girl's word against Chaloner's. How the devil he had managed to have intercourse with her in the midst of the worst hurricane of the year was a mystery anyway. Brent was quietly put ashore at their next port of call for reassignment to another ship, with the promise that he would return to serve on the *Alabama* when they were sure the girl would not press the incident further.

Brent was sent back to blockade running until the matter was forgotten.

"I never asked how it was you are traveling with me," Susanna asked as they sat on the verandah of the Bermuda hotel watching a crimson sun slip into the sea. "I see you are wearing uniform again. I'd forgotten how handsome you look in gray and gold. Matches your hair and eyes."

"Why, Susanna, you must be mellowing a little toward me. I swear I've never had a compliment I value more," Rowan answered, grinning. "And as to my returning with you, I requested it. Mr. Bulloch agreed it was the least I could do since you had served your country well in helping get the *Alabama* under way and had suffered at the hands of a Yankee agent. But tell me more about how handsome I am." The old devil-may-care gleam was back in his eyes.

Susanna smiled. "I never thanked you for saving me from him."

"But you lost your baby. I was truly sorry about that."

"No. There was something wrong before then. I was ill the whole time. I should have seen a doctor. I never asked if it was a boy or girl. It doesn't matter now, I suppose."

"A boy, I believe. Emma would know. She told me how desperate you were to get to Wilmington and about how she had a passage arranged. The doctor said you weren't going to recover, and it was she who insisted I carry you on board the ship and take you home. She was convinced you would recover at sea. She said her father had an affinity with the sea and always went on long voyages when he was troubled or ill. I agreed with her, but for another reason. You love a sailor, not the sea. A sailor whose name you called over and over in your delirium."

Susanna looked at him sharply, but he was expressionless. "She knew that she and I shared the same father. I told her when I became so ill."

"I gathered that. I got the impression she would do almost anything for you. She asked me to beg you to return to England with your son."

"I shall never go back. I would always see Jacob Drost bending over me. Perhaps she will visit us when the war is over."

"Yes, perhaps." Rowan was silent. The Southern victories they had thrilled to before leaving England had been won at terrible cost, and he did not know if the South had the men and materiel to pay so dear a price again, but there was no need to mention this to Susanna.

"I suppose you will stay with your aunt in Wilmington?"

"If she has room for us." Susanna had been expending all of her energy on the task of recovering physically and had not worried about the future beyond regaining her strength for each coming day. It crossed her mind now that she was totally without means. Aunt Rhea had supported her until she went to England, when her expenses were met by her father's bequest. Since Aunt Rhea had fled from her business and was living with Henri Duvalle, Susanna was not sure what her status with them would be.

Rowan was regarding her gravely. "I might be able

to talk the Army into giving you some sort of payment for your services," he said.

"How do you always know what I am thinking?" Susanna was not angry. "Let's wait and see if I need it first."

"Have you heard from Chaloner?" Rowan asked suddenly.

"Please, don't let's argue. I probably won't see you when we get home."

"I was merely asking a question, not arguing."

"No. I haven't heard from him."

"I suppose you still believe you are in love with him? You haven't learned yet that undying love exists only in literature, and that what you felt was only infatuation and that longing in the loins that can sometimes bind two totally unsuited people together."

"I thought we weren't going to argue."

"You said that, not I. If I thought I could convince you of your folly in waiting forever for that sea rover of yours, I'd argue all night."

"Then I'd better bid you good night and retire. I expect we shall make another fast run into port under cover of darkness?"

"Susanna, wait a minute. When we do sail, I want you to dress as lightly as possible. No hoops or heavy skirts, and wear your lightest slippers all the time we are at sea."

"Why, for goodness' sake? So you can come to my cabin and take advantage of me?" Susanna asked laughingly.

"Yes, something like that." But Rowan did not laugh with her. Lines of concern etched his normally bantering expression.

Two days later, many hours before their ship was ready to put to sea, Rowan went onboard, still uneasy, and talked at length with pilot, skipper and chief engineer. The flues and fireboxes were clean, the boilers would be at peak efficiency, and a good supply of smokeless coal was on board, he was assured. Still, Rowan could not dispel the warning of disaster he felt in his bones.

Just before they reached the coast, on the last night out, a swirling, all-enveloping fog shrouded the ship as she edged inshore in an effort to avoid the Yankee patrol boats. The engines were silent. Those on board awaited daybreak, nerves taut, afraid to speak to one another for fear of being heard across the dank water.

Unknown to Susanna, who sat in her cabin wondering why Rowan paced the cold deck, a thousand Enfield rifles were stowed in the hold of their ship.

By dawn they were poised for the dash into harbor. But mists obscured the channel markers and the pilot protested that even his skill could not get them through. The rifles had to be delivered, the skipper insisted, they would have to take a chance. Better to go aground than to let the precious cargo fall into the hands of the Federals.

Susanna had just decided to dress in warmer clothing against the damp chill of the mist when Rowan knocked urgently on her cabin door.

"Take off your shoes and everything else except your pantalettes," he ordered.

"Don't be ridiculous, Rowan, we can't make love now."

"Do as I say, Susanna, please. I've got a strange premonition that we're going to be in for a swim, and I don't want you pulled down by heavy clothing."

She could see from his face he was in deadly earnest. She had stripped to pantalettes and chemise when there was a grating crash and they were flung to the deck.

"We're aground. Come on, it's not far to shore," Rowan shouted, and, taking her hand, he pulled her from the cabin.

The ship was listing heavily to starboard so that the water seemed only inches away. Slipping, sliding, they made their way to the rail, and Susanna could see the gray sweep of the beach through the mist and, just below the ocean surface, the jagged rocks that had torn the hull. The ship shuddered convulsively, throwing several men into the water. Others were frantically bringing items up from below, which they no doubt hoped to salvage.

"She's taking on water fast, Susanna. We have to

jump and swim for it," Rowan said. "Come on, I'll hold your hand and we'll go over the side."

Susanna gasped at the shock of the cold water and in her surprise swallowed hard instead of holding her breath. She came up coughing, with Rowan treading water at her side.

"I forgot to ask, did they teach you to swim at the Academy?" He was grinning in his usual unconcerned way.

A brief picture floated across Susanna's mind. Of Mizjane taking her down to the deserted beach as a small child, wading out with her, showing her how to float, to swim, as Mizjane had swum in the warm Caribbean in her own childhood.

Teeth chattering, hands turning blue, Susanna struck out for the shore. Turning, she saw Rowan coming after her with an easy crawl.

"I see you are taking me home the same way I left," she called over the bobbing waves to him. "Without any clothes."

Paddling up beside her, he blew water at her. "It was time for you to stop wearing those dreary mourning dresses anyway."

At last they were riding the breakers toward shore and then the sand was beneath their feet. They lay at the water's edge, breathing heavily. No other survivors had yet reached that part of the beach.

"Are we in Yankee territory?" Susanna asked, shivering. "Will they rape me if they find me without clothes like this?"

"I doubt it. You look all blue and covered in goose-bumps. Very unappetizing." It was, he thought, a better answer than telling her she would be raped or hurt over his dead body.

"Oh, you!"

"Well, we'll know in a minute. Here comes someone."

Two men were running toward them, one white and one black. Rowan moved in front of Susanna, shielding her with his body.

Helping them to their feet, the white man spoke in a soft Carolina drawl. "Been watching you since dawn, figured you might run aground. You're the third ship to come too close to shore here." He was wrapping a blanket about Susanna while his servant did the same thing for Rowan.

"It's essential that I be on my way to Virginia as soon as I can find some clothes . . . and the lady has to go to Wilmington. Can you help us?" Rowan asked.

"My man here will be happy to take the lady in to Wilmington, and we can find some dry clothes for both of you back at the house, although the selection won't be great, I'm afraid."

Susanna gave a last look at the ship, rolling on her side in the dissipating mist, and thought of Brent, somewhere out there in the same ocean.

12

SUSANNA was dismayed when the carriage came to a stop on a mean-looking street lined with shabby houses. "Are you sure this is the right address?" she asked the driver.

"Yes'm, ah's sure. If you' pardon me, ah's best be gwine back now."

Susanna did not blame him for wishing to depart—the neighborhood was unsavory to say the least. She had gone first to the address Rowan had given her for Aunt Rhea. There the maid told her it had been some time since Captain Duvalle and his friends had rented the house. Rhea O'Rourke had, however, come back later to leave a forwarding address.

Surely, Susanna thought as she approached the battered front door, the maid has given me the wrong address. A feeling of dread swam coldly through her veins.

A slatternly black girl responded to the knock on the door, and it took Susanna a moment to recognize Emerald. She was dressed in a dingy calico dress that did not appear to have been washed for weeks. Her feet were bare and her sullen features pinched with hunger.

"It's me—Miss Susanna. Don't you recognize me, Emerald?"

"Ah knows who yo' is," Emerald said, holding the door wider for Susanna to enter.

If I weren't so tired, I'd teach her some manners, Susanna thought as she stepped into a tiny hall. The house was even more dilapidated inside than out. Peeling wallpaper revealed cracked plaster, and it appeared the inner doors had all been torn from their hinges. Susanna could see a boarded-up window in the room directly ahead, which appeared to serve as a bedroom for several people, as there were three straw mattresses on the floor.

"Dear God!" Susanna said quietly. "Where is my aunt and where is my son?"

Emerald shuffled her feet uneasily in the dust that coated the floor, not raising her eyes to meet Susanna's appalled stare. Panic gripped Susanna. She seized the girl by the shoulders and shook her. "Where are they?" Her voice rose to a scream.

"Yo' baby he's next do'," Emma cried, her eyes rolling in terror. "Ah doan' know where Miz Rhea am. Ah ain' seen Miz Rhea all day. Ah done left de baby with de neighbor woman."

Susanna drew a deep breath. She was shaking so badly she feared she might faint.

"Emerald, take me next door to my baby. What about Captain Duvalle? Where is he? No . . . tell me on the way."

"We ain' seed him. Ah doan' 'member when. Ah specks ah cain' 'member much when ah is hungry all de time."

Emerald pushed open the door of the house next door, and Susanna's nostrils were immediately assailed with the stench of stale bodies, vermin and urine.

Half a dozen small children, all black, played on the floor while a grossly fat Negro woman and a wizened white man copulated on an ancient bed in the corner of the single room.

Emerald looked away and Susanna swayed unsteadily on her feet as the scene etched itself into her memory in all its nightmare detail. Pulling himself upright by the sagging springs of the bed was an almost naked white baby. His ribs stood out above his distended belly and his spindly legs wavered precariously, but sheer determination to stand on his feet was written in every straining ten-month-old muscle of his little body.

Susanna swept her son into her arms, her tears of anguish falling on him as she held him close.

The woman on the bed looked at her and grinned an unconcerned greeting while raising her immense hips to meet the furious onslaught of the old man, whose breath rasped in his lungs with every labored thrust.

Susanna started toward the door through which Emerald had already departed, then stopped in her tracks as she realized what the children were playing with. Several fat cockroaches scurried toward her, to the accompaniment of yells of encouragement and the placing of imaginary bets.

Smothering a scream, Susanna detoured around the racers and plunged through the door and into the street.

Back in her aunt's house, a tight-lipped Susanna surveyed Emerald. "Get me a bowl and some warm water," she commanded.

"Ain' no water—" Emerald began.

"Get it, or I'll beat your hide, damn you." Susanna tried to keep her voice calm so as not to frighten little Brent, but he was regarding her with quizzical black eyes and playing with a strand of her hair.

Emerald disappeared again into the street and was gone for so long Susanna was afraid she had run away, but at length the girl returned with a small bowl and a kettle of water.

Susanna tore off her borrowed petticoat and bathed her surprised baby while Emerald watched.

"When was he last fed?"

"A doan' know."

"What is there to eat in the house?"

"Corn pone, ah guess."

"No milk?"

"Milk?" Emerald's voice was so incredulous Susanna might have been asking for the moon.

Little Brent was tenderly wrapped in the other half of Susanna's petticoat, and, suddenly content, he fell asleep in spite of his empty belly. Susanna looked with distaste at the mattresses on the floor, but placed the baby down on one and went to see what was in the kitchen.

Emerald followed her and watched impassively as she looked through the empty cupboards. There was a partly eaten corn pone and half a bottle of whiskey.

"All right, Emerald," Susanna said, turning to the girl.

"First tell me how you dared to take my son into that house with that awful woman next door when he was left in your charge."

"She ain' no awful woman. She's jes' doin' what we all do to keep from starvin'," Emerald responded with some spirit. "An' ah were'n sposed be lookin' after yo' baby. Miz Rhea done tole me to walk downtown, but ah ain' gwine. Ah is unwell."

Susanna clutched the rickety kitchen table for support. "Aunt Rhea sent you to walk the streets! Oh, I can't believe this. . . . What has happened? Where is she?"

"Ah specks she'll be back terreckly . . . if'n she cain' pick up some sailor."

"Aunt Rhea . . . is out picking up sailors? Dear God, what has happened?" Susanna realized that she had not eaten since leaving the ship. She sat down on the single kitchen chair.

Slowly, she got the story out of Emerald. When Rhea had first come to Wilmington she and Henri had shared a fine old gabled house with Henri's first mate and his woman. In addition to Emerald, there had been two other servants. When the Confederate troops came around and started asking questions about a black woman bringing a white baby to them, their neighbors had grown suspicious of the group—Henri with his foreign accent was undoubtedly a speculator and who knew what else. Their house was probably full of hoarded supplies while decent folk went without the necessities. And the story of the black woman running off with a white baby . . . everyone knew there was a danger of a slave uprising.

Wilmington was now the main port of access for the blockade runners, since Charleston was sealed off tight by Yankee gunboats. Connected to Richmond by rail, Wilmington was the center of a national scandal that precious food rotted in wayside stations while the Army to the north went hungry. Trains went through carrying wine and other luxuries that sold for higher profits. Moreover, warehouses throughout Wilmington bulged with blockade-run cargoes being held by speculators while prices rose almost hourly.

One night Henri Duvalle and his first mate were set

upon by an angry mob as they came from their ship. The two Frenchmen had departed the next morning and not returned since.

Rhea had squandered most of her own money furnishing the house, and without income she quickly fell behind in the rent. They were evicted and their furniture confiscated. Rhea and Emerald had brought the baby to live with the black family who had sheltered Mizjane, but all of their menfolk had been enlisted in the Army and sent north to dig breastworks for the troops. Left behind, the women were soon starving and eventually drifted off in search of their men.

Even those who had jobs were in scarcely better circumstances. The tightening blockade and rampant inflation, plus the inadequate manufacturing and transportation facilities, meant hardships to every Southerner. In Wilmington the expensive hotels and restaurants swarmed with wealthy blockade runners and speculators, and their free spending brought even greater inflation and shortages to the poorer classes.

When Rhea, in desperation, had brought home some sailors and suggested Emerald entertain them, Emerald had cried and pleaded she didn't want to be a bad woman, apparently forgetting she had originally applied for that very same work back on Blossom Street. Rhea had entertained the sailors herself, but there were too many good-looking young women for the sailors to choose from, and Rhea's lonely night walks became less and less fruitful. Out of hunger, Emerald had at last complied, but apparently did all she could to avoid the chore.

Susanna looked around the dismal house with its pitiful broken sticks of furniture and straw mattresses and had a quick vision of the elegantly furnished house on Blossom Street.

"But why didn't she just go back to Blossom Street?" she asked Emerald. Surely entertaining Yankees could be no worse than this. There was a tin box on the kitchen table, and Susanna was studying the brownish contents curiously.

"De house done burn down. De Confedruts done set fire to de shipyards and some of de sparks blowed over and burn down de house. Miss Pansy she came by and done told us."

"What is this stuff in the box?" Susanna asked.

"Coffee," Emerald answered. Actually it was a mixture of parched rye and sweet potatoes which was boiled to produce a poor substitute for coffee.

"You'd better make me some," Susanna said, "and then I am going to clean up this mess while you go and sell my earbobs."

She slipped Sir Edmund's emeralds from her pierced ears, thinking regretfully of her luggage aboard the ship, of the comfortable if somewhat gloomy house on Essex Square . . . all of which seemed as far away as her carefree childhood. If only she knew how to get in touch with Rowan . . . but he would be well on his way to Virginia by now. He would have the address of the gabled house they had first called at that day looking for Aunt Rhea, and probably the sympathetic black maid who directed them here would do the same for Rowan, or any messenger he would send. But how to survive in the meantime? Three women and a baby to be fed.

"Get as much as you can for the earbobs. Be sure to tell them they are real emeralds," she instructed, "and then go and buy food. Be sure to bring some milk for the baby. And save some of the money, I need a new dress."

Emerald's eyes rolled at this last statement. There were no new dresses being made or worn by anyone she knew.

The dress Susanna had borrowed had belonged to a farm wife several sizes larger than Susanna, and the faded calico had seen better days.

Susanna set about sweeping the floor with a depleted broom she found that had been propping a board over a broken window. She tiptoed around the sleeping baby, giving him a fond glance. For all his thinness, he was beautiful. Put a little meat on his bones and he would be fine. She looked at the other two mattresses on the floor. If they were used for the purpose she supposed . . . well, there would be no more of that.

She was about to start scraping the grease from an iron skillet when her Aunt Rhea returned with an elderly gentleman who was wearing militia uniform. If he was an example of the men defending the town, Susanna thought, it must mean that their victories in the North had taken all the young men from the home front. But it was at her aunt that Susanna looked in horror, scarcely recognizing this scrawny, sunken-cheeked woman with frizzed red hair as the beautifully gowned, jewel-bedecked Rhea O'Rourke of the sporting house on Blossom Street. Rhea was as shabbily dressed as Emerald, and there was a distinct tidemark around her wrinkled neck.

The old gentleman on her arm was staggering and laughing in a high-pitched way that plainly said he was very drunk. Probably too drunk to really see Rhea or her surroundings, Susanna decided. Rhea's eyes widened as she saw Susanna, then tears started to slip down her rouged cheeks and they were in each other's arms.

The baby awoke and began to cry and the old gentleman blinked in all the confusion until Susanna told him to go next door and he would find what he was seeking there. As his drunken giggling faded away, she thought of the huge Negro woman on the bed and smiled to herself.

"Welcome home," she muttered over Rhea's shoulder to the reflection in a cracked looking glass nailed to the wall.

"Haven't you any money at all?" Susanna asked Rhea. Susanna had slept fitfully beside her baby, whose hunger had been temporarily appeased with warm water sweetened with a little molasses. The bitter-tasting coffee was serving as breakfast for the two women.

"Oh, Susanna, I've been so foolish." Rhea dabbed her eyes with a filthy lace handkerchief. "I brought a trunk of my things here—and some jewelry. The Negro family Mizjane had been living with were here then. But one morning I woke up and found they—and the trunk— were gone. I guess they went north to find their menfolk."

"We'll think of something, don't fret. But I don't want you walking the streets any more." Susanna surveyed the empty room. "Where is Emerald?"

"Expect she went next door to see if Jassie has any thing to eat."

"Jassie?"

"Jasmine . . . that very fat Negro woman. She's been very good to us, helped us out so many times."

"Why haven't you sent Emerald out to find work? Surely there must be a house in town that can use her? You taught her how to dress hair and take care of clothes."

"Oh, honey, the town is full of Negro girls coming in from the country. Probably escaped slaves. Anyway, they can't get positions unless they have a recommendation from someone."

"Then she will have a recommendation. She will be one less mouth to feed. Do you have any writing paper?"

"Writing paper! Why, Susanna, honey, I don't have any toilet paper. . . . Oh, I'm sorry dear . . . I didn't mean to be vulgar . . . I tried, really I did . . . to make a home for your baby. I bring home gentlemen callers but they all want to . . . do strange things with me . . . not like the gentlemen callers on Blossom Street. These aren't gentlemen at all, really . . . coarse sailors and peculiar old men who are making money from the blockade but can't make love unless we go through all sorts of strange rituals. And, well, some of the younger ones want to put it . . . oh, I can't say . . . and I don't think that is right . . . to say nothing of . . ."

"Yes, yes. You won't have to do it any more, Aunt Rhea, I promise," Susanna said quickly, not anxious to hear any further details of the depravities to which her aunt had been subjected. "When Emerald comes back I want you to tell her to get some water and bathe herself and wash her dress. I am going out to get some writing paper for a letter of recommendation for her and for me. From now on you will stay home and take care of the baby. I don't want him to go next door to Jassie . . . kind-hearted soul though she may be. Do you understand?"

Rhea nodded, only too happy to have someone tell her what to do. "Oh, honey, I forgot to tell you. Emerald brought back your earbobs last night. She was afraid to tell you, but she can't sell them, they would think she had stolen them. Here they are. You try to sell them, won't you?"

Susanna's borrowed slippers had been made for dancing in some far-off forgotten world and had never been intended for the long walk downtown. Limping, her feet hurting, she stopped at the first street in the commercial part of town. The first building on the corner was a bank. The Merchants' and Seamen's Bank, the gold letters proclaimed across the front window. A bank would have paper, at least.

An elderly teller, looking at her disdainfully, showed her into the manager's office after she insisted, noisily.

"Good morning, ma'am. I am Benjamin Kresser. What can I do for you?" He, too, was old. Pink-faced and bewhiskered and with a paunch his frock coat did not conceal. He was quite tall, Susanna noticed as he stood up to greet her.

"I would like to sell my earbobs," she began, her eyes taking in several sheets of notepaper lying on his desk.

"Might I suggest a pawnshop?" he said curtly. "Banks do not buy jewelry."

Susanna fluttered her eyelashes upward and swayed slightly. "I'm sorry . . . but I really came to see if you have any work. I was very good at arithmetic whilst studying at the Misses Elmrods' Academy for Young Ladies. . . . Perhaps helping with your accounts in some way?"

He put his hand under her elbow to steady her, his eyes going over her as he helped her to a chair. Her clothing was shabby and she was a little pale, but she did not have that hungry alley-cat look that many poorer women were acquiring, nor the anemic vaporings of women who, while not starving, were unable to cope with the shortage of food. Moreover, she was clean and her hair looked freshly washed.

"Come, my dear, ladies are not employed by banks," he said in a less gruff tone.

"But I know I could do the work . . . at the Academy

I used to astonish my teachers with how fast I could add up and subtract, really. It's just a matter of seeing the figures in groups, rather than individually. . . . "

"I might know of someone who could give you work of a more suitable nature. . . . I suppose you have a husband away fighting somewhere?"

"No, sir, I am alone in the world," Susanna said sadly.

He smiled slyly and leaned forward. "Perhaps we can even find someone to buy your earbobs." He placed a hand on her knee. There were no hoops beneath her skirt, and her petticoat was serving as swaddling for her baby. She felt the heat and sweat of his plump fingers through the calico.

"Would you like to work for your breakfast?"

"If you mean will I climb into bed with you for the price of a meal, the answer is no," Susanna said, rising to her feet and tilting her chin scornfully.

"Now, now, miss, don't put on haughty airs with me. If you were really a lady you would be blushing and stammering instead of flashing your eyes at me," Kresser said. "And I do know where you can find work. I'll even give you a note of introduction. You do sew, don't you?"

"Yes, I suppose I do. What do I have to do for the note? I've already told you—"

"I promise I won't lay a hand on you," Kresser said.

"Nor anything else?"

"My word on it. I'll buy you a meal first and write the letter for you, then afterward you are free to go."

Susanna thought of little Brent, sucking furiously at the molasses-flavored water, stopping occasionally to give a short cry of disappointment. You'll have milk tonight, my darling, she thought grimly.

Benjamin Kresser pulled the shades down on the carriage windows. They drove in stony silence to the outskirts of the town and then past an old farmhouse to a group of buildings set apart. Smokehouse, barn, shed. Susanna did not look around. Her breakfast lay heavy in her stomach and she did not want to think about what she was going to do. Kresser produced a key to the barn and they went inside.

Susanna saw the swing first. It was suspended from the roof by swaying ropes, moving slightly in a draft over the hay-strewn floor. She caught her breath, thinking instantly of her swing in the garden at Blossom Street. Shivering, she looked around. The swing, a couch, nothing else.

"Come now, it isn't that cold in here," Kresser said, fastening a heavy padlock on the inside of the door.

"Now you understand exactly what you are to do and say?" Kresser asked. "Word for word, in the exact order I told you? Or shall we go over it again?"

"No. I know what you want me to say and do," Susanna said, unfastening her dress with icy fingers.

Kresser went to the couch and lay down, covering himself with a blanket, while Susanna stripped and climbed onto the swing.

"Very well. Begin now."

She glided forward on the swing, slowly, then backward. "Benjy!" she called out, something cringing inside her. "Benjy, you mustn't watch that dreadful woman." She swung higher. "I'm going to tan your hide. . . . " She hesitated, forgetting what came next, her eyes going around the walls, looking everywhere except into those terrible watching eyes.

She let the swing come to a stop, climbed down and went slowly to where the riding crop hung on the wall. Her lips were blue with cold and her throat dry as she raised the crop and brought it down with all her might on the heaving blanket.

13

THAT Christmas was a time of celebration in the hearts, if not on the plates, of every Southerner. The Yankees were being soundly licked and one or two more victories would see the end of the war. No matter that everything was scarce and newspapers were filled with the scandals of food speculation and shortages of medicine with which to treat the increasing numbers of wounded and sick filling Southern hospitals. The blockade runners were kings of Wilmington, despite the knowledge that too frequently the bounty they brought in was more than a little frivolous.

All over the South, factories of every size and capability had sprung up overnight like toadstools in a damp field, working day and night to turn out the materials needed for the army. In what had formerly been a private home, looms and spinning wheels retrieved from the attic were humming under the hands of women, many of whom had never before worked outside their own homes. Now, with menfolks gone, or dead, they were only too glad to strain their eyes far into the night weaving material for uniforms. Among the women was Susanna. Without Benjamin Kresser's note to the owner, Susanna would not have the job, for there were more penniless women than there were spinning wheels.

After a few days of backbreaking toil, she used her precious lunch period to approach the Army for help. The uninterested lieutenant told her he knew nothing about any Confederate intelligence service and if she did not know the name of Rowan Marshall's battalion or regiment, or where he was stationed, there was no way for her to send him a wire. Too late, Susanna regretted not listening more carefully when Rowan had told her what his plans were.

Her needs were too immediate to press the matter further. She quickly returned to the looms. At least it provided food for all of them, especially the baby, and an end to her aunt's sordid endeavors. She sent Emerald to call upon the houses in better neighborhoods to see if anyone wanted a ladies' maid, bearing a letter written on purloined notepaper purportedly from a fine old Norfolk family who had reluctantly let Emerald go when they evacuated the town. Emerald had not yet secured a position, despite her impressive letter of recommendation, and Susanna's salary barely fed the three women, since Susanna insisted the baby's needs be taken care of first. Little Brent was walking now, his gibberish becoming words, and he was a constant source of joy to Susanna, although she worried that he was not being fed properly.

The hard work and poor food, coming so soon after her illness, were taking their toll with Susanna. She was painfully thin and her eyes were large as a cat's in her shrunken face. Christmas brought only a brief respite from work and worry. She listened dispiritedly as her fellow workers rejoiced over the victory at Fredericksburg and Burnside's humiliation and with only slightly less enthusiasm sang carols celebrating the birth of the Prince of Peace.

Susanna's every waking moment was filled with one thought, one purpose in life. Somehow, she must raise enough money to take little Brent, Aunt Rhea and Emerald back to England, away from the gnawing hunger, the pinched faces and the eternal talk of war and bloodshed. So tired was she that she no longer thought of Brent or the possibility of finding his family in Georgia.

The months between Christmas and the spring of 1863 saw a lull in the South's offensive and a time of unremitting toil for Susanna. Had she owned any suitable clothes, she would have considered finding a rich food speculator to entertain, but her rags, the calluses on her hands and her thinness, she knew, were hardly what rich speculators were looking for in the way of entertainment.

Besides, she told herself, she despised all men. Brent, who had used and deserted her; Rowan, who had done the same, although not in quite the same way; Henri Duvalle, who had left her aunt destitute; and the men in Washington and Richmond who made this war that took food out of the mouth of her child.

Then one day in early spring, a long-delayed letter arrived from England. It had been sent in care of her Aunt Rhea to her first address in Wilmington and had waited there until the maid could be persuaded to take it to "that trashy neighborhood."

Opening the letter, Susanna realized that in her hunger-induced stupor, she had completely overlooked the obvious solution to her problem.

My dearest sister,

Why have you not written? Or answered my letters? I obtained your aunt's address from Mr. Marshall when you were leaving on the ship. I do hope I have the right street and number. I cannot tell you how dull my life or how lonely London is since you left.

Her Majesty is still in deepest mourning and there is no life at court at all. I believe Nicholas Kirby may ask me to marry him. I don't want to, yet sometimes my loneliness is unbearable.

Mother is in the south of France on holiday. She is quite well but, like the Queen, refuses to stop wearing black. How I wish you were here so I could ask your advice about Nicholas. He interferes more in the Bodelon Line's business than I care for and spends too much time in the offices in the company of our clerks.

We are glad to read of your victories against the North. The political drawings you used to hate so much in *Punch* seem to be changing very subtly to indicate that we may soon formally recognize the Confederacy.

Please write and tell me what you are doing and all about your life. The secrets you confided in me will be safe and I promise to burn your letter, if necessary, so it does not fall into the wrong hands.

Susanna turned the letter over and wrote on the back of the parchment pages. She told Emma that she wanted to return to England with her aunt and baby. Emerald would have to be left behind, Susanna decided, since there was no way to explain to Emma the responsibility she felt toward the girl. Besides, Emerald surely could have found some kind of position by now had she really been trying. Susanna did not go into detail about her circumstances, but merely said her situation was somewhat distressed and asked if Emma could arrange passages to England.

While Susanna waited impatiently to hear from her half-sister, a second letter arrived, postmarked from a hospital in Richmond. It was from Rowan, and it too was brought by the maid from Rhea's former address.

My dear Susanna,

Are you enjoying life in the perfumed confines of your aunt's home? No doubt with every young buck for miles calling to take you buggy riding? If so, spare your old friend a kind thought—and if possible a brief letter to cheer his boredom.

As you know, I had every intention of avoiding the mud, the hardtack, and anything even remotely resembling battle. But alas, the best-laid plans of mice and men went awry, and I found myself in a place called Marye's Heights with a lot of gentlemen in blue suits wanting to play king of the hill with me.

Fortunately, my good looks are intact, as are all necessary portions of my anatomy. So fear not on that score. Still, a small problem with my leg and foot will keep me from coming to see you for a time.

I beg of you, do not do anything hasty while I am not there to watch over you. Especially in regard to the black-hearted pirate we know so well. Now, now, don't get your Irish up . . . try to envision how pathetic I look, all wrapped in bloodstained bandages and boredom, and be a good girl and write me a nice letter telling me how much you miss me and yearn for my embrace. I trust your son and aunt are well.

Respectfully yours . . .

Susanna smiled, in spite of herself. Rowan could not even take being wounded seriously. She supposed he did at least have a reason for not coming to see her. She read the letter again, sitting on the broken kitchen chair, and then looked at the straw mattresses on the floor and began to laugh. Perfumed confines, indeed! Oh, that was too priceless. Through the windows overlooking the street she could see Negroes and poor whites dressed in identical rags shuffling about aimlessly. Young bucks taking her buggy-riding! She laughed so hard that little Brent came to her knee and looked up at her hopefully.

"Mama find sumfing to eat?"

Susanna's laughter died abruptly and she pulled her son close in a fierce hug.

She wrote to Rowan, all around the edges of his letter, telling him that she was returning to England as soon as Emma Bodelon could arrange it. She did not go into details of her life at present. If he wanted to see her as the belle she had been in England, so be it. She wished him a speedy recovery, mailed the letter and put him out of her mind.

On April 1, a week before the first fleet of Federal ironclads sailed into Charleston Harbor and Wilmington became the last port of access for the blockade runners, Susanna received word from England that their passages were booked on a Bodelon ship leaving Bermuda. At first elated, Susanna then realized with dismay that she would have to find a way to get the three of them to Bermuda. She wished she had been more honest with Emma and told her how desperate their financial straits really were. Emma had probably not given a thought to the problem of the distance from the Carolina coast to Bermuda.

Susanna made an announcement that night to Rhea and Emerald over a dinner of cornbread and a few black-eyed peas.

"Half rations for the three of us. And Emerald, either you find some paying work tomorrow, or out you go."

Emerald rolled her eyes and began, "Ah cain' gits no work, ah done tried an' tried . . ."

"If Jassie can get work, so can you," Susanna said pointedly. "And Aunt Rhea, I am going to try to find some material for a new dress."

"A new dress! Oh, how lovely, honey. I'm so tired of wearing this old rag—"

"Not for you," Susanna said brutally, "for me. Someone has to go and find a sympathetic blockade runner who will take us to Bermuda, and I don't suppose either of you want the task? Emerald, you go out and spread the word on the street that we will pay handsomely for a length of dress material. I managed to sell my earbobs today."

She shuddered, recalling her visit to Benjamin Kresser to ask for the name of the person he said would buy her earbobs. He coyly suggested another trip to the barn and Susanna had told him he would either tell her where she could sell the earbobs or she would stand in front of his bank and tell everyone who came near he had made improper suggestions to a poor seamstress. Kresser had looked into her cold green eyes and given her the name of a madame of his acquaintance who was always looking for gewgaws for her girls. When Susanna had pressed her advantage and asked him to give her the name of a blockade runner who might take her to Bermuda, Kresser had snorted derisively. "For that kind of information we go to the barn," he said.

The three women, aided by the plump Jassie, sat up all night sewing the poor-quality muslin into a dress. The skirt was skimpy and the bodice cut so low it exposed most of Susanna's breasts, but it was a pretty pale green and with a touch of Rhea's rouge on her cheeks and lips, Susanna was transformed, if not into a lady, at least into a lady of the evening.

Aching with fatigue, as the dawn broke Susanna left them to put the final stitches into the hem while she prepared to go to work. She fed the baby and put him down to play while she drank the bitter liquid they called coffee. Her tired eyes slowly became aware that something was wrong as she watched her son playing on the floor.

"How long has he been crawling like that?" she asked sharply. "He was walking so well. Why is he crawling all the time again?"

When she first arrived in Wilmington, the first thing she had seen was little Brent trying to stand up. He had been an early and determined walker. Now he pulled himself listlessly with one arm and, after little progress, quickly gave up trying to move at all.

Susanna gathered him up into her arms, feeling the

thin little body curve into her. His legs were dreadfully
spindly and his little hands touched her without energy,
but his black eyes glowed brightly.

"He gwine into de rickets if'n you' not careful,"
Jassie said.

"Rickets!" Susanna exclaimed in horror. She spent all
of her small salary on food, but every week the prices
went up and it bought less. The blockade runners brought
in more taffeta and coffee and wine these days than
food. There were speculators who met the ships, bought
their cargoes and stowed them away in warehouses.
Sometimes a cargo would change hands many times
before it eventually found its way to market.

Little Brent needed good food and a doctor. They
had to be on that ship to England.

"Emerald, you mind what I said. You've got to find
work for yourself. Here, give my breakfast to the baby,
I'm not hungry. I shall be going out tonight right after I
get home from work, so have that dress ready and ironed.
And Aunt Rhea, I shall need your slippers—they aren't
as worn as mine."

The women at the looms were given a short break at
noon, and as soon as they were dismissed, Susanna walked
to the Merchants' and Seamen's Bank. Benjamin Kresser
avoided her eyes when she entered the front door, but
followed her into his small private office.

"What do you want this time?" he asked, darting a
furtive glance over his shoulder at his teller.

"Passage for myself, another woman and a baby on
a ship to Bermuda. I shall have to leave within the week."

"That," Kresser said, laughing, "is going to cost you
more money than you'll make in a year, including the
price you got for your emeralds."

"I want you to introduce me to the captain of a blockade runner. I'll do the rest."

He looked at her shrewdly. "You aren't worth it any
more, my dear. You're too thin and tired-looking. There
are plenty of plump young things in the bordellos."

"Let me worry about that. Will you introduce me
to someone who can help me get to Bermuda?"

"For the usual price," he said, looking away from her.

"After I meet him. I must meet him tonight. After the arrangements are made . . . I'll go with you to the barn then."

"I'll send my carriage for you this evening."

She looked down quickly before he saw the gleam of satisfaction in her eyes. She had no intention of keeping her word about the barn once she knew the identity of a blockade runner. She thought of little Brent, dragging himself limply across the floor. Yes, my darling, she thought grimly, I'll lie for you and cheat and kill for for you.

Kresser's carriage caused some interest among the Negroes on the street when it arrived to pick her up that evening, and they offered vulgar comments when she came out of the house.

Since Lincoln's Emancipation Proclamation a new type of black had emerged in the South, swaggering, insolent and looking for retribution to descend on the heads of their tormentors in the form of the blue tide from the North they knew would surely come soon.

Fortunately for Susanna, Jassie came bursting out of her front door armed with a broom and quickly cleared a path through to the carriage.

Dressed in her new gown, wearing Rhea's slippers and with the last of Rhea's cologne in her hair, she rode in Kresser's carriage to a brightly lit café, where the banker huddled in a corner awaiting her.

In the artificial light and with Rhea's rouge on her cheeks, some of her old beauty was visible. Only her eyes were different. Several of the men lounging about the bar sat up to take notice as she entered.

"Well . . . that dress is an improvement," Kresser said grudgingly.

"Where is he? You said he would be here."

"All in good time. I promised to feed you also, so sit down."

Susanna's anger returned when the food was served. Oysters and fat shrimp, dripping butter. Fresh bread and wine. She thought of the cornbread her baby would have for his dinner.

"You realize he will want to be paid in advance?" Kresser said.

Susanna swallowed some wine and felt it burn its way to her empty stomach. She tried a mouthful of shrimp but was afraid she would gag and so washed it down hurriedly with more wine, leaving the rest of her food untouched. She felt reckless, light-headed, and able to kill, if necessary, to gain her ends.

She gasped when a powerfully built black man, wearing sailor's clothes, entered the café and approached their table. It was unthinkable for a Negro to enter a white café, but this man looked about him boldly and obviously feared no consequences.

"He is Jamaican," Kresser whispered, "and owns his own boat."

The man towered over their table, his face breaking into a wide smile.

"Miss O'Rourke, may I present Captain Soloman."

White teeth flashed again and an enormous hand closed over Susanna's shaking fingers.

"Come, we will talk," the Jamaican said.

"Go with him," Kresser instructed. "I don't want you discussing anything in my presence."

Soloman led the way to a room at the rear of the café, through beaded hangings. He waved his hand indicating the room, furnished with a table, chairs and several couches. "I eat in here. You want more food?"

"No—thank you, I had dinner."

Soloman rang the bell and a waiter appeared almost instantly with a tray of bread and fruit. A second waiter came hard on the heels of the first with two bottles of wine.

Susanna sat down nervously, wishing her dress were not cut so low. Like most Southern women, even those of her Aunt Rhea's profession, the fear of physical contact with a black man was inbred in her.

"Benjy tells me you want for sail to Bermuda," Soloman said, his voice deeply resonant and reminding Susanna of a contracted form of the British accent. "You got plenty of money and plenty nerve?" He deposited nearly a whole banana into his mouth and swallowed, then downed half a bottle of wine almost in a single gulp.

"How much money?" Susanna asked, her voice wavering from fright. "There are three of us . . . and a Negro girl . . . one is a very small baby, wouldn't take much space on a ship . . ." She was thinking feverishly that Emerald might be the answer, that perhaps he would accept favors from Emerald. She did not know her fear and consternation were written plainly all over her face.

"You 'fraid of Cap'n Solly, girl?" The white teeth flashed again.

Susanna squared her shoulders. "No. I'm not afraid of anything. I just asked how much money you want to take us through the blockade to Bermuda. I'm anxious to get there as soon as possible. You will be sailing this week?"

"Oh, aye, that I will." He laughed, a great booming laugh that made Susanna draw back in her chair.

"That Benjy Kresser . . . he's a funny fella," Soloman said, wiping his eyes. "He think all black fella want is to have white woman. He tell me little white miss ain't got no money to pay her way. Solly just humor him, see, tell him I go to meet little white miss. And Benjy Kresser, he say . . . you make arrangements with the girl, can I watch?" Soloman's laugh rang out again and Susanna felt the blood drain from her face.

"Captain Soloman, I couldn't . . . I wouldn't . . . consider . . . " she began.

"In actual fac' old Solly is just a gambler." He slapped the table at the hugeness of the joke on Kresser. "Old Solly make a heap of gold running the blockade and lose it all first time he see a poker game! Best damn blockade runner you ever see, 'cause old Solly need the money to pay gambling debts."

"How much money would you want to take us?" Susanna asked.

"Ship a cargo or a body . . . take anything for money."

"How much?" Susanna asked again.

"Five hundred—in gold. No Confederate paper." His voice was suddenly brisk. "You got that much?"

"I'll get it. When do we sail?"

"Bring the money to the dock—my ship is called

Celestine—two nights from now. What's your name, miss."

"Susanna O'Rourke."

"I like you, Susanna O'Rourke. Maybe you come with money, maybe not. But you ever get your hands on a cargo, you let me know—I take it through for you. These fellas here in town, all try to cheat Cap'n Solly . . . think he stupid, see . . . old Solly ever stop gambling he's going to buy the whole town!" He drank the rest of his wine and laughed again, slapping his huge thigh and laughing until the tears ran down his shiny cheeks.

Susanna stood up and pushed aside the beads, hurrying out into the night air, away from the sight of Benjamin Kresser, who still huddled at his table, mouth open, eyes fixed on her as she stumbled to the door.

Outside she almost collided with a bearded sailor, who put out his hands to support her. "There now, girlie, what's your hurry? Will you take a drink with a lonely sailor?"

"No," Susanna began, then looked up at the man and saw he was fairly young and was wearing a Navy officer's uniform.

Seeing her hesitate, the man said, "I was going to a party and my lady friend changed her mind. Want to come?"

Susanna forced her lips into a smile. "I do seem to have lost my escort," she said, "and have no other plans for the evening." Five hundred dollars in gold, she was thinking—there wasn't that much money in the entire town. She did not look closely at the building to which she was taken. It was not as brightly lit as the café they had just left, but there was a uniformed doorman who admitted them after a whispered word with her escort. They had walked the few blocks, the man slipping his arm about her waist in a familiar manner.

They went through a circular hall to an inner door, also protected by a doorman.

"Lonnie Burke and friend," he told the man, who promptly admitted them. "What's your name, honey?"

"Brigid," Susanna answered.

"Thought you were Irish . . . those eyes and that hair. You're not a professional, are you?"

"No. I work in a factory, weaving cloth for uniforms. I need money desperately—" She broke off; she should not have said that. Desperation was not something men found attractive in women. That much she had learned from Brent.

"Oh, and what do you need money for?" They were in an opulently furnished room filled with sailors and girls. Lonnie called out greetings as he pushed his way through the crowd to a table.

"What is this place?" Susanna whispered.

"Just a club—a private club for seamen. What did you say you needed the money for?"

"To get to Bermuda."

Lonnie sat down and studied her. "I didn't have in mind paying quite so much for the pleasure of your company," he said. "Unless you're not planning to sail for a year or two." He laughed loudly. "Why do you want to go there anyway? Stay here—at least whatever you do you'll do it with your own people." He leaned forward and looked at her more closely. "You'd be a pretty little thing if you weren't so thin. Want to be my girl?"

"I have to get to Bermuda. I'll do anything . . . " It was hopeless, she knew. Five hundred dollars in gold . . .

Lonnie motioned for a waiter to bring drinks, then said, "Well, if you want money that badly . . . the biggest money to be made is in the back room with the groups."

"Groups? Of what?"

He grinned. "Girls. They entertain in groups. Put on a show up on the stage . . . and then the audience bids for them. The only thing is, everything they do with anyone from the audience is done right there on stage too. They're always looking for new faces. . . . We could go and watch for a while if you like, then you could decide."

Susanna swallowed hard. "Yes, yes . . . let's go."

She drank the whiskey he passed to her, and his face promptly went out of focus as she drained the glass.

The room was dancing dizzily in front of her eyes, music and laughter running together in a sound that droned in her ears. Lonnie leaned forward and pulled one of her breasts from the bodice of her dress and he was talking, laughing, and she was there and yet not there. Through hazy eyes she could see his dark hand on her breast, through fogged senses feel him pinching her nipple to make it stand upright, and somewhere in the endless droning sound in her ears his voice was telling her something . . . what . . . ?

She was on her feet and he was leading her through the crowd of chattering, shrieking women, many of them with clothes as much in disarray as Susanna's bodice.

They were in a different room now; the lights were much dimmer and there were four girls on a small stage in the middle of the room. Shadowy figures sprawled about on the floor in a semicircle about the stage. Susanna's eyes peered through the darkness but saw only vague shapes. The whiskey had joined the wine in her empty stomach and her mind had left her body. It was as though she were floating somewhere above it all.

Her escort was pulling her down among pillows piled on the floor, dragging her skirt up as he did so. Susanna looked toward the stage at the four girls who were performing there . . . blinking her eyes, not wanting to see what she was seeing . . . feeling the groping hands beneath her skirt. Then she was on her feet again, naked, swaying dizzily, and someone was pushing her toward the stage, telling her to climb up and show them what she could do, and the other girls stopped to look at the scrawny newcomer.

The whiskey and wine were demons battling in her stomach and her head was filled with exploding lights. The lights faded as the noise ebbed away from her and she felt her legs give way and would have fallen had not someone caught her in his arms.

She was dreaming, of course. It couldn't be Brent who carried her away. Away from that evil throng . . . up the stairs to a private room. Flinging her on the bed and then, cursing her, thrusting his organ into her dry and protesting flesh with no preparation and no tenderness, taking her roughly, hurting her . . . until she could feel no more pain, just numbness and then nothing.

14

SHE awoke to find herself in a strange bed, a weight upon her feet. Her head ached and nausea made her clutch her bare stomach. The weight on her feet was Brent, sitting watching her, smoking a long cigar.

"Would you put that out . . . please? I feel ill," she said through cracked lips.

He went on smoking, eyes black as coal. "So you came to this? And all the while I was wondering how to get back to you in England."

"Came to what? Brent, I was never in this place before last night, you must believe me." She put up her hand to her burning head, trying to think clearly.

"It doesn't matter. It's your life."

"No . . . Brent, listen to me. I was desperate. Our son is ill and I have to get back to England. I needed money. . . ." She was going to make it sound worse, she realized dully, but went on, "I had to get to Bermuda. A man said he would introduce me to the captain of a ship . . . only he was a black man . . . Brent, please excuse me . . ."

She plunged out of bed, leaping toward the bowl that stood on the washstand, and clung to the cold marble as she lost the meager contents of her stomach. Brent made no move to come to her, but stubbed out the cigar.

"Why did you leave England? No one knew what you were there. I could have come to you without embarrassment."

"Damn you! Damn all of you," Susanna said, fighting not to burst into tears of shame and humiliation. She staggered toward the bed. "Where is my dress?"

"You had no dress when I found you," he said curtly.

She had sold her earbobs for that dress, they had sat up all night sewing it. Vaguely she thought of the food she could have bought.

"I shall need something to wear so I can leave here," she said, pulling a sheet around her.

"Are you telling the truth about wanting to go back to England?"

"We have passage on a Bodelon ship. Brent, I came home to get our son. I didn't know Aunt Rhea was destitute . . . and I'd been ill, I didn't plan things very well . . . I've been working in a factory."

His expression did not change. "Very well. I'll take you to Bermuda. I have time for a run before I rejoin my ship."

"Your ship? You never wrote to me, Brent, never told me where you were or what you were doing. I would have asked for help if I'd known where you were."

"There is no way to send a letter from the high seas, Susanna. I was on the *Alabama*. I shall be rejoining her shortly, but keep your mouth closed about it. Seems like it was providence that delayed me here, to make one last run through the blockade with you. I shall take you and your son through and give you what money you need to keep you out of places like this."

"Brent . . . please don't look at me like that. I can't stand the look in your eyes, it's tearing out my heart. I'm not a prostitute."

"I'm sorry, I can't help the look in my eyes. And I haven't called you a prostitute."

"No," Susanna said, looking away, "you didn't have to."

They went through the blockading squadron silently, in total darkness. Rhea and Susanna huddled in the tiny cabin, keeping the baby quiet. No sound, they were warned, until they were through the circle of Yankee ships.

At the last minute Emerald had refused to go with them, fearing running the blockade more than the hardships in Wilmington. Susanna managed to persuade her employer to let Emerald take her job at the spinning wheel.

Brent had provided clothes for the three of them. He had looked at his son with eyes that showed no feeling and had been coldly polite to Susanna and Rhea, no more. He never asked to speak to Susanna alone, never spoke to little Brent. On the rare occasions when Susanna was able to read any emotion in his face when he looked at her, that emotion was a combination of disgust and disappointment. She had tried to explain, to tell him all that had led up to that horrible night, but he would avert his eyes, and at last she gave up trying because her pride would not let her grovel.

Then one day, they were on the Bodelon ship, eating good food, and everything that had happened since she and Rowan had swum for the Carolina shore began to recede in her mind. The only visible sign of the hardship and deprivation she had left behind on that distant shore was a certain calculating brittleness she had acquired. The dull ache she felt when she thought of Brent lessened as she began to lavish upon her son all the love his father had spurned.

Emma was waiting for them in Southampton and hugged Susanna joyfully, trying not to show how shocked she was at the other girl's thinness and pallor, despite the long ocean voyage. Emma was horrified too at the strange new look in Susanna's eyes. Little Brent was back on his feet and getting stronger each day, while Rhea was every inch the dowager aunt in the clothes Brent had provided.

"Oh, I'm so glad you're home, Susanna," Emma exclaimed. "You must never leave again. Everything is ready for you on Essex Square. . . . I was so sorry you lost your baby. You were so ill when I last saw you, but I'd hoped during all these months . . . "

"I'm all right." Susanna's lips smiled, but her eyes did not. An unpleasant memory was stirring. "Does Jacob Drost still come around to see your mother and Nicholas Kirby?"

Emma shuddered. "No. We haven't seen him."

"I don't remember much about what happened that day," Susanna said as they moved through customs and Rhea began to charm the inspector who was checking their meager baggage.

"It's better you don't, dear. But I must tell you that if I had not arrived shortly after Rowan . . . well, I tremble to think what would have happened to Jacob Drost. Oh, Susanna, Rowan was like a wild man. Even when I brought the doctor and he had taken care of you, Rowan still refused treatment, although his poor face was unrecognizable and the doctor said two ribs were cracked. It took all of our efforts to calm him. But he wouldn't let us send for the authorities to deal with Jacob Drost. He said he would deal with him later." Emma paused for a moment, and when Susanna made no comment she added, "I told everyone—including Mother—that you were going to bring Rowan's child back to England, and when you didn't return I said that you were having a holiday."

Susanna laughed mirthlessly. It had been quite a holiday. Her child addressed her as "Mama" and she did not intend to have him call her "Aunt" for the benefit of London society, but she did not say this to Emma.

Emma was laughing delightedly at little Brent's antics, and as he looked up slyly at his newfound friend, Susanna's heart fluttered. She saw Brent's dark-eyed glance on their child's face. Brent . . . who could fix those black eyes on her and every nerve in her body would respond. No! she told herself. Don't think about him. Think about the new, independent Susanna, free of him.

Susanna arrived back in London just as a curious conflict was coming to a head.

This was the affair of the cruiser *Alexandra*, a name Susanna found on everyone's lips and filling the newspapers.

Following the escape of the *Florida* and *Alabama*, British government officials, prodded by Consul Dudley in Liverpool and Secretary Seward in the United States, had seized a small steamer at Liverpool.

On the day the order was issued to seize the *Alexandra*, the collector of customs asked whether the ship, "if registered and duly cleared, is detainable, having as yet committed no offense against any law." The half-century-old statute which set out rules for Britain's neutrality contained ambiguous phrases that were proving totally inadequate to deal with the case of the Confederate cruisers.

Consul Dudley had been gathering evidence against the ship and had proof, he believed, that it was designed for the same nefarious purposes as the *Florida* and *Alabama*. Anglo-American relations, shaky since the Confederate commissioners were seized aboard the *Trent*, were again strained.

Officials suspected that the *Alexandra* had been built by pro-Confederate Englishmen as a gift for Jefferson Davis, although technically the British firm retained title to the ship and they had no proof of Confederate connection.

The time had come for a test case. The British Court of the Exchequer, sitting in Westminster before the Lord Chief Baron and a special jury, opened the trial of the *Alexandra*, charging its owners and agents with violation of section seven of the Foreign Enlistment Act: "that the defendants did equip, furnish and fit out . . . and knowingly assist and be concerned in the equipping, furnishing and fitting of said vessel with intent to employ her in the service of foreign states with intent to cruise against the Republic of the United States . . ."

And Susanna barely had time to unpack before Rowan Marshall appeared at her door.

Like herself, he was thinner, and he walked with a cane, but his gray eyes were as reckless, his grin as infectious, and his manner dashing as ever. He was handsomely attired in a fine broadcloth jacket with velvet lapels and so impressed Morgan, the maid, that she took his hat and promptly collided with the hall stand as she stared at their good-looking visitor.

Susanna hugged him happily, brushing aside a guilty tear as he limped into the drawing room. He had written to her several times in Wilmington, but she had always

been too tired to reply after the first note she had sent
to the hospital to tell him she planned to return to
England. Now she saw he had obviously been wounded
more severely in the leg than he admitted, and she felt
sorry she had not answered his letters.

"Why are you back here?" she asked, after sending
Morgan to bring wine and cake.

"To see you, of course, and to meet your son at long
last." Rowan smiled. His eyes devoured her hungrily.

"I mean really, why are you really here?"

"That is why I am really here, but as to why the
Army let me come, I volunteered to come to London
to keep a finger on the British pulse, as it were, in regard
to the *Alexandra* trial. Since I'm not much use at marching through the mud any more, they were glad to be
rid of me."

Little Brent came rushing in on the heels of Dobbs
and for a while chattered excitedly to the tall, golden-
haired man who spoke in a familiar accent and bounced
the child on his remaining good leg.

"Brent, darling, run away and play now," Susanna
said at length, "and you may take a slice of seed cake
with you." Her face glowed as she watched him run away.
She knew now that with proper nourishment those little
legs would grow more sturdy each day.

"A fine boy, Susanna—you must be proud of him,"
Rowan said. "You're lovelier than ever, by the way.
Although I do detect something missing. . . . Have you
finally quelled the torch you were carrying for the in-
trepid blockade runner and sailor *extraordinaire?* You
seem to have lost that limpid, adoring look that always
lingered in your eyes."

I lost that when I nearly starved to death in Wilmington," Susanna said shortly, and found herself telling
Rowan all that had happened, although omitting the
night she had met Captain Soloman and Lonnie Burke,
and not mentioning that it had been Brent who brought
them out of Wilmington. When she had finished, Rowan's
hand closed over hers.

"I'm sorry, Susanna. That wasn't as I imagined you
were living. But for God's sake, why didn't you write

and tell me? I would have come hopping to you on one leg."

"At first I didn't know where you were . . . I don't know . . . then you were in the hospital. Rowan, when one goes hungry day after day, something happens. Everything becomes an effort . . . just to breathe takes all one's strength. It's impossible to think rationally. Besides, why should you care what happens to me?"

"Why indeed," Rowan said in an odd voice. Then, leaning forward, he took both of her hands in his. "The last few months have changed both of us, Susanna. I suppose you know that some of our leaders believe the war is lost?"

She looked at him, startled. "But all the victories . . . we are winning . . . why, there was another Southern victory at Chancellorsville . . ."

"Susanna, no. Listen. That isn't where we are losing. We are losing at sea. This trial of the *Alexandra*, no matter which way it goes, we're sunk. The South's last hope is the rams . . . remember the Scottish sea monster? Our hopes were pinned on a fleet of rams like her . . . already being built. But we'll never get them. Susanna, I fought at Fredericksburg. I saw men without shoes, doubled up with dysentery, and Yankees coming up the hill in wave after wave. Oh, sure, we held them off, we licked them. But when we lose one of our boys, there's no replacing him. For every Yankee lost they have a dozen more. Right now they're recruiting over in Ireland . . . which makes this *Alexandra* trial even more of a farce."

There was such intensity in his grey eyes that Susanna squirmed uncomfortably. He had always taken such a light tone about everything, including the war, that she was unprepared for words that she knew were coming from deep in his heart.

"I used to joke about it, Susanna, but I was as patriotic as the next Southerner. No one wanted us to win more than I. It wasn't that I believed slavery was right, but we'd have freed the slaves ourselves without Yankee interference. How many of our boys who are fighting and dying ever owned slaves? Many of them never even saw a slave. I believed in a shining new country, Susanna, starting out without the mistakes the first country made . . . building a new nation. Before we seceded the states were too spread out . . . the country too huge to be efficient. Split into two nations, allied and friendly, we could have built the dream for everyone. What did we in the South have in common with an Irish immigrant in New York, or a wheat farmer in Iowa? No more than an English miner or millworker has in common with the man working in the French vineyards—who are geographically closer together than we are. I believed all this, I truly did, God help me."

"But I don't understand," Susanna said. "Feeling like that—"

"I don't feel like that now, Susanna. That dream is dead. We have to build a new dream."

Susanna withdrew her hands uneasily. "Rowan, I remember you always said we were only licked when we believed ourselves to be licked. I wish you wouldn't talk like this. You sound like a traitor."

Rowan laughed, a short hard laugh. "Unlike the fearless Captain Chaloner, I suppose. By the way, he is only a captain on his blockade runner. In the Navy he is a lieutenant. Not that I wish to belittle him in any way."

"I don't want to quarrel with you, Rowan. And if you really want to know, I don't care much one way or the other about the war. I just don't want little Brent to overhear you talking about defeat. I've already decided what my dream is, you see. I'm going to be very, very rich."

"And do you have any plan in mind to achieve this end?" Rowan asked gravely. He had spent a month's pay on his broadcloth jacket in an effort to distract her attention from his shattered leg.

"Oh, let's not be serious any more today. Let's go riding down the Row—oh, I'm sorry, I forgot about your leg. We'll take the carriage and go for a turn around the park. I'll get little Brent."

It seemed as though the interlude in Wilmington had been only a bad dream. Susanna was swallowed up in the social life of London, although Alicia Bodelon gave her a cool reception and Nicholas Kirby watched her more closely than ever. Susanna had the feeling she was tolerated in their set only so that they might keep closer watch on her. She was sharper-tongued than before and quick to take offense, so that both Alicia and Kirby became more guarded around her, but when she wanted to be, she was the old Susanna around the young men who came calling and who found her as fascinating as ever.

Dobbs and her maid, Morgan, had returned to Essex Square before her return from America, and Susanna hired a new cook and kitchen maid. The staff were a little surprised at the new interest Susanna showed in the household provisions; she seemed to need to reassure herself constantly that there was enough food on hand.

Rowan again made trips to Liverpool, but they were less frequent than during their first sojourn in England and Susanna saw him constantly. Little Brent soon became a fervent admirer of Rowan, as he was the first adult male the child had known intimately. Rowan had infinite patience with children, tempered with the right degree of firmness, and little Brent told Susanna one day, in solemn amazement, "Uncle Rowan thinks I'm a real person!"

Emma confided that Nicholas Kirby had proposed and her mother was pressing her to accept so they would have a man to head the Bodelon shipping line. Susanna privately thought that if she were given the opportunity Emma had—that of running the shipping line herself—she would have jumped at the chance. She said, surprised, "Are you going to marry him?" Emma might be plain, but Nicholas Kirby was more than old enough to be her father.

Emma looked away and her sallow skin turned crimson. "I'm in love with someone else," she said, and the tone of her voice precluded further questioning. Susanna knew only too well the pain of loving someone. Secret, and probably unrequited, love must be even worse.

If she had had time, she would have wondered who the recipient of Emma's devotion was, but life was too full of interesting and exciting things to do. There was lost time to be made up, time to laugh and dance and eat to her heart's content, but always, at the back of her mind, were her desire to be self-supporting and the plans she was forming toward this end.

These plans became more necessary when Nicholas Kirby visited her one day and put his cards, very bluntly, on the table.

"Your father made this bequest because he wanted you and me to share this house on a permanent basis," he said to her utter astonishment. "I promised him I would marry you and take care of you, to ease his conscience and pay a debt I owed him. I gave him my word I would marry you if you came to England. However, since he is no longer with us, I do not feel bound by this promise. Besides, he did not know that you were desirable enough to choose your own husband. He thought of you only as a bastard without family or dowry, probably looking somewhat like his plain Emma."

"Why are you telling me this now?" Susanna asked.

"Because I want you out of this house. I intend to marry little Emma and through her gain control of the Bodelon ships. Houses in this part of London are hard to come by. But more than that, my future mother-in-law, the fair Alicia, does not want you to remain in London. And I need Alicia's help to get Emma to marry me. Believe me, my dear, if I did not need the Bodelon wealth, the prospect of marriage to you would be far more exciting to me. Yes indeed, far more." His eyes darted over her body, which was slowly losing the angular contours and regaining its former curves.

"I don't suppose you are going to tell me what debt you owed my father that prompted him to extract such a promise from you?" It was certainly no surprise that Lady Bodelon disliked her so.

"No. I wouldn't care to be vulnerable a second time. In any event, your father's bequest stipulates that you are not to besmirch his name in any manner, and I happen to know you have, shall we say, besmirched it, on at least two occasions, in this very house. Of course, I know that young Marshall is not really your uncle, but everyone is whispering about a possibly incestuous relationship with him. It would not be difficult for me to get the solicitors to set aside the bequest. I am giving you the opportunity to bow out of the picture gracefully for the sake of my bride-to-be's feelings toward you. I shall expect you to be out of the house by autumn."

"One thing puzzles me," Susanna said. "Why do you want Emma? If you want the Bodelon Line, why not Lady Bodelon herself? She's nearer your age, to say nothing of being far more attractive."

Kirby gave a grotesque smile and paused for a moment before replying, his thoughts on Alicia Bodelon. "Because, my dear, Lord Bodelon left everything to his daughter, Emma, except for our mutual bequest. His widow was cut out of his will entirely. She lives solely on her daughter's charity. Someday you will have to read your father's diaries, if Alicia hasn't destroyed them. I discovered them hidden in this house after your father died, and I gave them to Emma. You may find several entries of personal interest. Now, I'm not a vindictive man . . . I shall be happy to assist you in any way I can. My advice to you would be to marry one of the Bartlett brothers and bury yourself in the country . . . although I don't know how you will explain the child."

"I take it you know little Brent is my son?"

"I do now," Kirby replied. "I think you were foolish to name him after his father and then try to pass him off as your nephew, but rest assured, your secret is safe with me, although I would advise you to keep the boy out of Alicia's way. Fortunately, with your American habit of addressing the child by various forms of endearment rather than his given name, it may be that people have forgotten the name of your good-looking sailor friend." He paused, stroking his upper lip with one finger thoughtfully. "You know, my pretty little miss, if you would like to bestow some of your favors in my direction I could make life much easier for you. I've always been attracted by you—"

"I find you disgusting," she said loudly, but she was glad that Dobbs and the maids were just down the hall and moving about audibly.

That evening Susanna told Rowan of Nicholas Kirby's visit, although omitting most of the details of their conversation.

"So he suggested you marry one of the Bartletts," Rowan said. "Would you consider marrying anyone?" The old watchful look was back in his eyes, but Susanna did not notice.

"Don't be silly!" she retorted. "I shall never marry anyone. I could become Sir Edmund"s mistress—I'm sure he would set me up in a house somewhere and be more than generous. I've been receiving flowers and notes from him ever since I returned to London." And, giggling, she told Rowan of the day she had tried to extract the information from Sir Edmund about the proposed seizure of the *Alabama*.

Rowan stared at her for a long time. "Susanna . . . sweet little Susanna," he said slowly, "what did we do to you?" But Susanna knew he was teasing, because he smiled an odd sort of smile when he said it and added, "But don't set up house with that old fool. Wait, we'll think of something."

"Rowan, you are becoming my old friend and confidant, did you know that?" Susanna said lightly. "But I haven't asked what you have been doing. How are things in Liverpool?"

"Bulloch is becoming more of an Englishman than the English," Rowan said, easing his injured leg into a more comfortable position. "I have a feeling that whatever the outcome of the war, J. D. Bulloch is going to remain right where he is. I came back to London because of the trial, by the way . . . the Crown versus the cruiser."

"Does your leg hurt much?" Susanna asked.

"No, I hurt too much somewhere else to notice the leg."

"Where's that?"

A fleetingly serious expression gave way to a grin as Rowan glanced downward. "In that portion of my anatomy that becomes very active whenever I am in your presence."

Susanna smiled back, her eyes lighting up mischievously. "And is it active now, this very minute?"

"Oh yes, very active."

"Then let us do something about it. Aunt Rhea has taken little Brent to a circus, his very first. We are alone . . . and if Nicholas comes back, what more can he do?"

And so they lay on the rug in front of the fire and made love, leisurely at first, but with rising passion. Susanna ran her hand sympathetically over the ugly scars that covered his leg from battered knee to misshapen foot and then, teasingly, laughingly, told him to lie still and she would do all the work. Rowan made a great pretense of lying immobile on his back, hands under his head, eyes half-closed, while she lay on top of him, her weight lightly on her knees, but after a while his arms came around her hungrily and, lifting her hips to the pillow he pulled from the couch, he entered her with a swiftly drawn breath of pleasure and need, supporting himself awkwardly on one knee.

Susanna looked up at him tenderly. "I've needed this, Rowan," she said softly.

For a second his eyes clouded and he said, "Not *this* don't say *this* . . . say, I've needed *you*, Rowan. My God, Susanna, how are we ever going to make a courtesan out of you if you keep using the wrong words?" But his voice was joking, in spite of the look in his eyes, so Susanna laughed happily with him and moved her hips faster as he penetrated deeper and she came fully alive again for the first time in months.

Afterward, when she lay contentedly in his arms, he stroked her hair and daydreamed that he had met her long ago, before Brent Chaloner had come along, and that he and not Chaloner occupied that special place in her mind and thoughts. But would it really have made any difference, he thought, when she saw him as an "old friend and confidant"? Except, of course, when they made love . . . and then she closed her eyes and imagined she was lying in Brent Chaloner's arms and Rowan would tell himself that it would be the last time . . . he would go away and never see her again.

Would he, he wondered sadly, even be missed if he were to go away forever?

In the confrontation between the Crown and the cruiser, the inexperienced Solicitor General, Roundell Palmer, was no match for Sir Hugh Cairns, a gifted barrister, and England's best trial lawyer, George Mellish, who put on a flamboyant courtroom show that sparkled with sheer wit. They demolished key witnesses for the prosecution and appealed to their countrymen's sense of justice and, not least, their economic self-interest.

They stressed that the Foreign Enlistment Act was not meant to prohibit all commercial dealings in ships of war with belligerent countries. Cairns pointed out to the jury, "You have the power to paralyze the commerce and industry of our ports." He then hinted darkly that shipbuilding would be driven to a neighboring country—knowing Englishmen were not about to relinquish anything to France—and ended with a plea for a verdict against the Crown and for the defendants.

Without hesitating for more than a minute, the jury did indeed return a verdict against the Crown in favor of the defendants. And the day after the verdict was returned, Susanna had a visit from an old adversary.

Dobbs came into the solarium where she was arranging a vase of flowers and announced that there was a gentleman to see her and that he had already taken the liberty of fetching Mr. Rowan down from his room to be present during the visit.

"Oh, and why did you do that, Dobbs? Is the gentleman here to see Mr. Rowan or to see me?"

"It's Mr. Jacob Drost, mum," Dobbs said. "I thought perhaps he should see both of you."

15

SUSANNA entered the room with angry words on her lips, though Rowan raised his hand to silence her. Jacob Drost was sitting in a leather armchair, his face set in an expression more of resignation than of belligerence. "What is that man doing in my house? Why haven't you thrown him out?" Susanna demanded, ignoring Rowan's upraised hand and the fact that with his cane taking most of the weight of his right leg, Rowan was incapable of throwing anything.

"Will you please sit down for a moment and listen to me, Susanna?" Rowan said.

"Better do as he says," Jacob Drost offered laconically.

"If you will tell me why you are receiving this man in my house," Susanna said angrily, "after what he did to me—"

"Susanna, I half killed him for what he did to you. What I didn't know—what we both apparently were wrong about—was his motives for what he did."

"I don't understand." Susanna looked with loathing on Drost's sunken features and felt a cemetery chill.

"Susanna, he's a Confederate agent."

Susanna's mouth dropped open. "You're joking. He can't be. Why, he tried to get information out of me, he . . . he . . . " She tried to remember what he had wanted from her, but the details were blurred.

"Nevertheless, he is one of our own agents. I have been informed of this by Mr. Bulloch himself. Here is the letter, and I know J. D. Bulloch's handwriting as well as my own. It seems Mr. Drost here was employed by one of our Senators to keep an eye on my friend, Mr. Bulloch, and on how the Navy and Army were handling matters in England. The senator—whom neither Mr. Bulloch nor Mr. Drost will identify—was concerned about our relations with Great Britain. Mr. Drost was under orders to report everything we did back to Richmond. Mainly, he was to keep Mr. Bulloch from purchasing the Scottish ram."

"But he's a Northerner," Susanna said in disbelief.

"There's more than a few Northerners on the side of the South," Drost offered, his voice bleak as ever. "And as for manhandling you, miss . . . well, I thought you were involved in something nasty."

"What?" Susanna asked.

"Nicholas Kirby was running Bodelon ships into New York, picking up guns and ammunition and selling them to the South, with payoffs to the right officials in New York and a guarantee of their ships getting through the blockade. I thought you were involved . . . being friendly with the Bodelons."

"You see, Susanna," Rowan put in, "it didn't matter where our supplies were coming from, but I happen to know that some of the goods Kirby was bringing in were bad . . . guns that backfired and shells that wouldn't explode. It was something we had been investigating to try to find the shipper. I guess it was because of this that J. D. Bulloch finally learned about you, Drost?"

Drost's pale eyes were expressionless. "Bulloch found out because the Senator was ready for him to find out."

Rowan looked at the man for a long moment. "I had planned to kill you," he said finally. "It's going to be difficult to work with you. I'd prefer not to. And I do intend to wire Liverpool for confirmation that this letter is indeed from Mr. Bulloch."

"Ain't come to work with you," Drost said to Rowan. "It's the girl we need."

Susanna shivered. She would never be able to accept this gauntly ugly man as a fellow Confederate. "The last time I was asked for my help, I ended up getting roughly handled in a carriage in Liverpool. Were those thugs your men?"

Rowan leaned forward. "That's a fair question. And

to it I'd like to ask about a certain group of Americans who beat me one night and called me "Reb" and knew all about you. Strange behavior for fellow agents, wouldn't you say?"

The pale eyes blinked once. "You know well enough this country is full of men working both sides of the fence. I paid Englishmen and Americans to work for me, and if they had the right information, it didn't matter to me where they came from. Senator didn't want Bulloch buying the Scottish ram."

"And what does the Senator want now?" Rowan asked.

"Same thing we all want. A fleet of rams. Now the Crown has lost the *Alexandra* case and England may be on the point of recognizing us as a nation. Now is the time to get them."

"But you just said you had orders to stop Rowan from getting the Scottish ram," Susanna said.

"We didn't want that ram, at that time. Now Laird's yard is building two rams in Birkenhead, and we want those and more like 'em."

"And where do I enter into your plans?"

"Your friend from the Foreign Office . . . Sir Edmund Bartlett. We want you to compromise him. He has to be blackmailed. Understand it's something you're good at."

Rowan had risen, unsteadily, to his feet, his face white with rage. "By God, Drost, I don't care if you are on our side. I'm going to kill you—"

"Rowan." Susanna laid her hand on his arm, "It's all right. Let's hear him out. I want to know what it is exactly that he has in mind."

"Your friend Sir Edmund," Drost said, "is powerful not only in the Foreign Office, but in other government circles. Seizure or release of the rams is in his hands. We want to be sure he makes the right decision. We know it was through him you got the information about the detention order for the *Alabama*. He has to be thoroughly enmeshed this time. A scandal to ruin his career and family . . . unless he does right by the rams."

A chill went slowly up Susanna's spine as she thought of Sir Edmund, with his merry eyes and gentle courtesy, but the shell that encased her heart prevented the feeling from penetrating very deeply. Momentary misgivings were replaced by something else as she said, "And now, Mr. Drost, let me tell you what I want."

Rowan gave her a quick look of amazement, but she ignored him and went on, "My services for the Confederacy are no longer free. I want a sum of money placed in a bank in Bermuda at my disposal and a letter of credit in my hands before I do anything with Sir Edmund."

"How much?" Drost asked, without blinking. "We'll ship it in gold to a shipping agent of your choice. There ain't no banks in Bermuda."

"I don't suppose you'd marry me?" Rowan asked later that evening. He held his breath waiting for her reply, but kept his voice light.

"Don't be silly." Susanna chuckled. "I will go to bed with you . . . after I've tucked the baby in."

"I was thinking of saving you from a fate worse than death and all that," Rowan drawled, his eyes watching her intently.

"Sir Edmund? Oh, he isn't that terrible," Susanna said casually. Rowan, she was thinking, is the only man I know who jokes about marriage.

"Susanna . . . if you're doing this out of some misguided sense of patriotism . . . "

"No," Susanna said quickly.

"You wouldn't do it for the money, I know that. Susanna, the rams will prolong the war . . . "

"Please, Rowan." Susanna's eyes were cold. "I do not want to discuss it now."

"All right, let's not discuss the war. Let's talk about you . . . and Sir Edmund."

"What I do is not your affair," Susanna snapped. "Now what is it you wish to know about Sir Edmund?"

Rowan looked at her, a puzzled expression on his face, as though she were suddenly a stranger to him.

"Nothing," he said at last. "I'm afraid of what you'll say. But tell me, why did you ask for your ill-gotten gains to be shipped to Bermuda?"

"Because there is a large and terrifying black man who has a ship called the *Celestine*—his name is Captain

Soloman—and he is going to buy cotton for me and run it into Bermuda. Then it is coming here on Bodelon ships. And my original stake from the Confederacy will really turn into ill-gotten gains after I store my cotton in Liverpool for a while. The collector of customs up there is also a friend of mine, if you remember, and I'm sure he will assist me with arrangements at this end."

"You never cease to amaze me, my Susanna," Rowan said, shaking his head. A cold knot of despair constricted his throat. This new money-hungry Susanna was further from his reach than the sweet and vulnerable child who loved another man. Rowan spent all of his army pay on necessities . . . not the least expensive of which being the information he was forced to buy from time to time.

"You don't know the half of it," Susanna said. "I decided after working in that miserable factory in Wilmington and . . . all the other things that happened to me there . . . that I would never be poor again, and I won't. Not only am I going to take money from the Confederacy, but I'm also going to accept gifts from Sir Edmund and convert them to cash, and that money is going into cotton too . . . and maybe I'll buy guns and run them the other way. The only people who were eating well in Wilmington were the speculators . . . and that's what I'm going to be, a speculator."

"And a very ruthless one too, I'm sure. I'm not sure I would have told you my feelings about the South losing the war had I known you were going to ravage the carcass. No matter what I personally feel about the outcome of this conflict, I am going to do my duty by my country until the last minute. There's got to be an honorable solution somewhere." He gave her a rueful grin, and added, "Well, I must be on my way. I'm sorry I can't take you up on your kind offer to share your bed, but I have to go to Liverpool." He got up slowly, still looking at her worriedly. "Susanna . . . despite Bulloch's vouching for Drost, I don't trust him. I wish you'd reconsider working for him."

I've already spent the money he's going to pay me, in my own mind anyway, Susanna thought. Aloud, she said, "I rather like Sir Edmund, actually. He treats me as though I were a lady. I shall only associate with men who do treat me like a lady from now on . . . except for you, of course." The last was added mischievously but did not bring the expected grin from Rowan.

"Please beware of Drost."

"Rowan . . . wait a minute. The two rams . . . if they get away, will they put English captains on them as they did with the *Alabama*?"

"No, in view of how smug everyone feels about the outcome of the *Alexandra* trial they'll probably brazenly send one of our Navy officers to each. Why?"

"Because I've just thought of another condition I am going to impose on my old friend Mr. Jacob Drost," Susanna said, her eyes flashing ominously. "He is going to request that a certain lieutenant be relieved from duty on the *Alabama* to come here and sail one of the rams out of the Mersey."

Rowan did not speak, but looked at her for a long time, his face ashen and his fists clenched in a gesture of mute despair. She did not notice, however, as she lay on the floor with her son, helping him stack the large wooden blocks one on top of another.

Alicia Bodelon watched Susanna over the lace edge of her fluttering black fan. The girl was surrounded by all the most eligible young men in London, as usual, each of them vying for her attention and hanging onto her every word. Alicia was not listening to what Nicholas Kirby was telling her, she was straining to hear what Susanna was saying to her circle of admirers that caused them to laugh so heartily and press even closer to the young American girl.

"You aren't listening to me, Alicia," Nicholas said. "And we must decide quickly whether we should take what profits we can and extricate ourselves from the venture. Ever since the object of your present jealousy returned to London she has done nothing that the Union representatives would be interested in . . . and Marshall has been too wily for us. Since we have nothing to sell them, the Northerners are not so willing to let us sail into

New York without inspecting our cargoes quite thoroughly when we leave."

"Why don't we just make up some story about what she is doing and sell it to those men in Liverpool?" Alicia said from behind her fan.

"You really do hate her, don't you?"

"Those men you sent after her should have spoiled her looks. That would have taught her a lesson."

"Be patient, my sweet. We are watching her every move, and we know she must have a reason for playing up to Sir Edmund Bartlett. As soon as we find out what it is . . . but we mustn't overplay our hand. I've hounded her about moving out of Essex Square. Perhaps that will precipitate something with old Bartlett." Nicholas glanced around the room and his gaze rested briefly on Emma, who sat contentedly on the sidelines watching Susanna hold court, love and pride written plainly on her sallow features.

"You know, Alicia," Nicholas continued, "if I'm not able to convince your timid little daughter to marry me soon, we are both going to be in a lot of trouble when our debtors refuse to be placated. I had hoped for at least one more shipment from the North to the South, but without the cooperation of our friends in New York . . . and we can't bribe them, we don't have the means. No, we need information to sell in Liverpool."

"I've talked with Emma. She will be eighteen soon, and then there will be nothing either of us can do. She is so like her father, so unwavering when they set a path for themselves . . . I look at her and wonder what part I ever played in her creation. Now please excuse me, Nicholas. If you won't do anything about . . . that woman . . . then there are some things I can do."

Her smile was brittle as she went past Susanna to where the butler stood in the hall, directing the footmen with their trays.

"While I think of it," she whispered to the impassive butler, "I want you to take a note with you the next time you go to the wine merchant, the grocer, the greengrocer, fishmonger . . . "

It was several days before an embarrassed Dobbs came

to see Susanna to tell her that their credit had been cut off with all of the local merchants and that they would soon be without provisions. Susanna listened with astonishment, then sent Dobbs out again with cash to buy what they needed. He returned, red-faced, to tell her that he had been informed that their business was no longer desired.

"This is ridiculous. We must have food," Susanna said, and her old fear of her baby going hungry whipped icily through her mind. "I shall go and see them myself."

In the grocers' and greengrocers' shops, the shop assistants told her they had been ordered not to supply her household and did not know why. Those were the owners' orders, and they had the right to refuse service to anyone they chose. When she questioned them further, they did not meet her eye and quickly escaped to serve other customers.

Susanna stood outside the shop for a moment, fighting a rising sense of panic. Across the street a sign swung above a diamond-paned shop window proclaiming, "Wines and Spirits." The wine merchant was standing outside berating a dustman whose horse was slowly chewing up the foliage in the windowbox. Crossing the street, she caught up with the wine merchant as he was about to disappear into the gloom of his establishment.

"Wait . . . I am Miss Marshall," she said breathlessly.

The man frowned and stepped aside to bypass her. "Your business is not wanted here, ma'am. Good day to you."

Susanna slipped quickly between the merchant and the door of his shop. "I believe I am entitled to know why, sir."

"As I understand it," he said pompously, "you will shortly be deported back to where you came from . . . because of the unnatural acts you have committed."

Susanna gasped. "What are you talking about?"

"We have laws in this country, miss, and you can be had up for certain things."

"Had up? What do you mean?"

"Put in jail, miss. Newgate," he said with relish.

"Jail . . . surely you are joking. On what charge, and who is bringing charges against me?"

"A gentleman does not speak of such things, ma'am."

"A gentleman be damned," Susanna said. "Either you tell me exactly what it is you are talking about or I shall stand here until you do." She had not realized it, but she was brandishing her parasol threateningly and several passersby were turning to watch.

The merchant looked into the green daggers of her eyes and backed off in alarm. "Incest . . . they say you have committed incest."

Susanna walked slowly back to Essex Square. Alicia or Nicholas Kirby had to be behind this. Of course, even if she were charged with the crime it would come out in court that Rowan was not really her uncle. All they could be charged with was fornication. She wasn't sure, but she believed that to be against the law also. Queen Victoria's moral standards were high. Rowan would know. But Rowan was up north and Susanna's needs were immediate. Supplies for her household. There was nothing else for it—she would have to go to someone powerful for help. If she had wavered about Sir Edmund before, she was now committed to a course of action. She stopped at the corner of the street and hailed a hansom to take her to Sir Edmund's office, not pausing to think it would have been wiser to wait for an opportunity to meet him in less conspicuous surroundings.

July came and warm dust settled on the city. The street vendors pushed their carts laden with overripe fruit and wilting vegetables, while news filtered across the Atlantic of severe reverses for the Confederacy.

There had been a battle at a place called Gettysburg, and after a long siege, Vicksburg had fallen, giving the Union troops control of the Mississippi River. The Confederacy had been sliced in two. Some Englishmen were breathing sighs of relief that Britain had not made a commitment to the South during the Confederate Army's victorious march into Northern territory the previous year.

Rowan had received confirmation from James Bulloch that Jacob Drost was indeed working for a Confederate

Senator, and Sir Edmund Bartlett was quietly negotiating the purchase of a small mews house, through his private solicitor, for a Mrs. Wilford . . . a name chosen by Susanna without explanation. She had not moved in yet, but continued to live in seclusion in Essex Square, visited only by Emma Bodelon, and they had used the mews house only for assignations.

Although Sir Edmund had been able to quell the rumors flying about London and persuade the authorities they were merely the result of a jealous woman's tongue, he had not been able to dissipate society's suspicion that where there was smoke there was fire or to prevent Susanna's subsequent ostracism, and she was no longer invited to any social activity. For Susanna's part, she was too busy with other matters to worry about the lack of parties and was not surprised to find the world of commerce was much more interesting than the gay social whirl. No wonder men had kept this fact to themselves for so long.

She met Sir Edmund in out-of-the-way tea shops, or rode with him in a closed carriage whenever he was able to slip away from his office. He walked with a jaunty air and was wearing new clothes, and his eyes fairly danced with merriment.

He would hold her hand, kiss her as wonderingly as a schoolboy and tell her how beautiful she was. At first Susanna had been prepared to be revolted by the caress of an older lover, and she had steeled herself to endure but feel nothing. After all, what more could happen to her? The diamond-hard façade she had acquired in Wilmington was her defense against any encroachment on either her feelings or her conscience. But Sir Edmund was so pathetically eager to please her, so humbly grateful and affectionate, that she was touched in spite of herself. The first time he took her to the mews house and made love to her, she closed her eyes and pretended he was Brent, but she soon began to feel genuine affection for Sir Edmund himself. He was fun to be with and surprisingly proficient in his lovemaking, having replaced the impetuous youthful urge with a mature, savoring approach that was at times serious and at times hilarious.

"Ah, sweet little girl, my old John Thomas is in seventh heaven since you came into his life," he murmured one lazy afternoon.

"Don't call him old," Susanna remonstrated, and her hand darted out playfully.

"But he never stood up for himself like this for years before you came along. . . . Oh, Susanna, yes, do that again, please!"

Susanna laughed. "You are so easily pleased, Edmund. What games would you like to play today? But wait, did you bring me a present?"

"You are like a child waiting for Father Christmas when it comes to presents, aren't you, my pet? I suspect you had a deprived childhood. Yes, of course, I brought you a present . . . although why do I never see you wearing any of the presents I bring you?"

"Because, sir, you insist I remain naked whenever we are alone together."

"That is all too true, I am a decadent old man. I brought you another emerald. . . . It fascinates me the way emeralds make your eyes glow with green fire . . . how they set off your hair. See, I will place this emerald . . . "

Susanna rolled on her back, laughing and pretending to push him away. It was all part of the game. Later the emerald would be slipped into her reticule.

Much of their time together was spent in pleasant conversation or that silent companionship that requires no words. With Sir Edmund, Susanna felt a security she had not known since Mizjane was snatched from her life.

Rhea O'Rourke stuffed herself daintily with pasties, steak and kidney pies and cream buns and grew plumper day by day. Her good looks had returned, and at Susanna's insistence she chose a wardrobe less flamboyant than she had worn in her Blossom Street days.

It was clear Rhea need only remain a "widow" until she chose one of the gentlemen who found her accent and the way she had of making a man feel like a king irresistible and begged her to marry him. Rhea had no difficulty finding admirers from the vast middle classes of England who knew little and cared less about the machinations of high society. Upon Susanna's advice, she took none of her beaux to her bed, but did allow a little friendly fondling of her person in dark carriages and moon-drenched gardens.

A nanny had been employed to care for little Brent, who grew stronger, and more like his father, every day. He would strut and swagger and was the terror of the other infant boys who played with him in the park. He was eighteen months old. Emma Bodelon worshipped him and confided to Susanna that she longed for a child of her own. It was clear that Her Majesty was never going to recover from her grief over the loss of her beloved consort, and there was no future in court for Emma. Nicholas Kirby was pressing her to marry him.

"He wants to marry you to gain control of the Bodelon ships, Emma," Susanna told her bluntly. "And you don't love him, you told me you were in love with someone else."

"I know why Nicholas wants to marry me, but at least he could give me children. My someone else will never marry me—it is a hopeless love."

"But why?"

"Because he loves someone else."

Looking into the tortured eyes, Susanna had a sudden flash of understanding. Emma had never told her who that someone else was, because that someone else was close to her, to Susanna.

"Emma, it isn't Rowan, is it? Because if you think he loves me, you're completely wrong. There is only a . . . camaraderie . . . between us of shared times and experiences."

Emma turned her plain little face away. "No, it isn't Rowan. Perhaps I will marry Nicholas."

"Suit yourself. I think the importance of marriage is vastly overrated anyway, out of all proportion to its value to women. Look at me—I have a son and all the benefits of marriage, with none of the problems and heartaches."

Emma tried not to blush at Susanna's frankness, studying her pale hands folded on her lap with great care. "You don't . . . you didn't love little Brent's father? You don't love him now?"

The green eyes that regarded her glittered oddly, like a cat's. "Oh, yes, I did once. Not now. Now I love my son, fiercely. And you and Aunt Rhea . . . not quite so fiercely, I'm afraid. It's strange, but once I believe I loved my country too. That love I seem to have replaced with the love for money. I shall probably go to hell when I die for all this. Oh, Emma, men complicate things so, you can't let yourself love them, or you'll just be hurt."

When Emma left, Susanna sat down at her desk and wrote another long letter of instruction to Captain Soloman of the *Celestine* and a second letter to her shipping agent in Bermuda. She was too busy with matters of business, with consular invoices and bills of lading, to be concerned with the fact that she was now totally shunned by London society.

The following day Emma returned, carrying a leather-bound notebook. "Susanna, after we talked yesterday . . . I . . . something frightened me . . . some awful change that has come over you, a brittleness, a hardness that wasn't there before. You are my darling sister, and while you don't love me fiercely, as you say, I'm afraid I do love you fiercely. Nicholas found father's diaries in the townhouse after he died. There were several which would be of no interest to you. But this particular one I've brought . . . well, it didn't make much sense to me until you came to London and told me who you were. Now I think you should read it."

And so Susanna sat down to read the words her father, Edward Bodelon, had written all those years before. The early pages were written in a boyish scrawl and showed evidence of both age and damage, probably by water or some other liquid; certain letters and words had been obliterated. The journal appeared to have been begun on the long sea voyage from England to the Indies, young Edward's first sea voyage.

Becalmed, we float endlessly on a hot yellow sea and I dream of a soft mist dancing on green English meadows and the dear friend of my childhood telling me of the distant islands.

I shall hate Father *forever* [underlined with vehemence] for sending her ,away. His new wife, he said, would not tolerate her presence. She would offend my new mother. A pox on my new mother, I say.

Several pages following this entry were blank and several more had been ruined by fading and water damage. Then Susanna was able to read:

How long ago I wrote those words, made that first long voyage to Spanish Town—the white sands of Montego Bay. I had thought with manhood would come a lessening of the pain I felt at losing Jane, but each time I return to these islands I think of her and wonder what became of her. There is a man in Port Royal who may be able to help me. He was with Father on that last voyage, when he took Jane from England and never brought her back—but instead presented me with my pale English stepmother.

I closed my ears and my heart to Father's explanations—did I not know that he had loved Jane? Had I not burst upon them in their chambers and found them locked in a lovers' embrace? Could she not speak with scholars, move with grace among her fellow beings, and teach a boy to swim, to watch a bird, to read beyond written words, to laugh, to be honorable? Had she not been educated as well as the pale Englishwoman? Did she not feel more than the . . .

Susanna pored over the words, a buzzing in her ears as realization came, straining her eyes to decipher the faded words. There was nothing legible for several more pages, then:

Triumph! I have found her—and by what a series of coincidences and mishaps! She is with a family in Virginia. She is older, she no longer has the tinkle of laughter in her voice, and her eyes are terrible to see, yet she tells me she is happy. How can she be happy? She is a slave! She, whose ancestors fled to the hills from the Spaniards—descendant of proud maroons— she was bought at the block. . . . Father in heaven . . .

The family who have her have two daughters. The younger one is very pretty. Jane tells me the younger one is her favorite. The girl has astonishing green eyes with little golden lamps glowing in them. Her name is Susanna. . . .

Susanna's heart was beating in slow, distinct thuds. Jane . . . her Mizjane . . . had brought Edward Bodelon and her mother together; that was how they had met. That was the secret Mizjane had kept from her all those years, the reason she had never spoken of Edward Bodelon.

Reading on, it was quickly evident that Edward was falling in love with the first Susanna. He could not wait to get back to Virginia and cursed the time he had, of necessity, to spend in England. His father had died and he had inherited both the title and the fleet of ships, and his stepmother was urging him to marry, to produce an heir.

I asked her today if I may speak to her parents and ask for her hand in marriage. I could not believe it when she said I could not. Have I been so blind? I was so sure she returned my feeling for her that I did not question for a moment that she loved me. She does not love me, however. She knows what my father did to her Miss Jane and she says she cannot forgive or forget. She has begged her parents to free Jane at once, and for this at least, I am glad, for I believe her parents will comply, they are so obviously adoring of their younger daughter.

Susanna looked up from the journal, bewildered. Her mother had refused to marry Edward Bodelon! She moved rapidly through the following pages to find an answer to what had happened . . . how she, Susanna, had come into being. There were pages of details of Edward's travels and other friends and acquaintances and the mention of several other women, and then one poignant passage:

It is no use. Every time I look upon another woman I see her, in my waking and in my sleeping. . . . I think I shall go mad if I cannot possess her. . . .

There were no more legible entries after this, and Susanna was about to close the book when she noticed that the lining of the back of the leather cover was curling slightly. Slowly, with infinite care, she peeled back the page that had been fastened down, tucked into the leather cover and carefully hidden under a blank liner; the page that neither Alicia nor Emma, nor anyone else since Edward had written it, had seen.

May God have mercy on my soul for what I did. I write these words so that I may remember for the rest of my life my crime, my shame.

I went back to Virginia to tell Susanna I must marry— to beg her again to be my wife. I was resigned, I believed, to the fact that if she refused I would come home to England and marry Alicia.

Susanna was scornful, she said she was glad I loved her and could not have her, she said it made up for what my father had done to her dear Miss Jane, that the sins of the fathers were being visited upon the sons. She taunted me, flaunted her beauty, laughed at me when I begged for mercy.

We had walked along the beach while her coachman waited. All at once I could stand her laughter no longer. I seized her and dragged her back into the cove, out of sight—and I took her, there on the sand, by force.

I had not meant to write of this—my shame is too great. I am married to Alicia. We married as soon as I returned to England, and Alicia was already with child when I received the massage from Virginia that Susanna had borne my child. I made haste to return immediately to find her, but upon my arrival learned that her parents had died of yellow fever and the two girls and Jane, and my baby, were gone. I could find no trace of them. Illness forced me to give up the search and return to England.

I meant to go back, but always something prevented me—perhaps knowing I would have to look into those eyes again and feeling I would not be able to bear what I would see there . . .

Susanna closed the diary. She was glad it had been her mother who had refused to marry her father and not the other way around. She did not want to think of the circumstances of her conception. If she had not been born out of love, she had received love a thousand-fold from Mizjane . . . Mizjane, killed by the war. Damn their war, it was not going to touch Susanna or her son again.

She sat for a long time holding her father's journal as though the worn leather could somehow transmit to her what kind of a man he had been. Emma had loved him so . . . and from his own words he had sounded sensitive. Yet he had raped her mother. And what of that first Susanna? Had she really hated him so much . . . enough to lead him on and then make a mockery of his love for her? At last Susanna rose and went into the solarium where Rhea was indulging her favorite occupation, that of consuming a large box of bonbons while glancing at the more lurid of the weekly news sheets.

"Aunt Rhea," Susanna said, pulling a chair closer to her aunt's chaise longue, "I want to know all about my mother and Lord Bodelon. Everything."

Rhea's hand leaped to the lacy jabot at her throat. "Oh, Susanna, honey . . . "

"I have read my father's diary. I know that it was my mother who refused to marry him. Not the other way around. Now I want to know everything. I'm no longer the little girl you kept hidden from the world, Aunt Rhea . . . the sordid facts of life are well known to me."

Rhea sighed and did not speak for a long moment, trying to find a reason not to, but when Susanna's green stare did not waver, Rhea said, "Very well, dear. But I do declare it might be better for you to let it all rest. You see, my dear little sister was madly in love with another beau. She had loved him since . . . oh, I don't know when. But he was the town ne'er-do-well, a gambler, a drunkard, not received anywhere. He'd been called out by every father and brother in town for compromising their daughters and sisters. His name was

Drew Mackay and he was a good-looking rascal . . . bold, black eyes and a black mane of hair . . . reminded me a little of . . . well, no mind. I used to pretend to Mama that Susanna was in my room with me and we were gossiping or doing our embroidery . . . and she used to climb out of the window and go and meet Drew. Oh, she loved him so."

"Did she . . . did they . . . ?" Susanna had a sudden wild notion. What if she were not Edward's child after all, but Drew Mackay's?

"Oh no!" Rhea exclaimed. "I know for a fact that no matter what everyone said about him, he was a perfect gentleman with your mother. He wanted to marry her. And honey, if you could have known your mother . . . she was, well . . . I don't know how to explain to you what happened."

"Aunt Rhea, she's long dead, and it can't hurt her now. You and I are women of the world, as much as we like to pretend otherwise. Tell me, I must know."

"Well, she was a very strong-willed girl, much more so than me. She always said she would die rather than go to her marriage bed not a virgin.

"Well, that young Englishman kept coming around and our parents were really impressed with him and wanted her to marry him, but she was planning to elope with Drew just as soon as he could get enough money. Being a gambler, he was always without funds, it seemed. And when Susanna told me they were the same Bodelons who had owned Mizjane and sold her off after so many years she said she was going to use that as a reason for not accepting Edward. She just couldn't tell anyone about Drew . . . Father would have killed him, I believe. And then, that dreadful day . . . Edward took Susanna down to the beach. She was out of her head with pain and shame when the coachman brought her home . . . blood all over her. No, honey, there's no doubt who your father was. Anyway, our parents weren't home and Mizjane and I took care of her. Then later when Papa found out she was . . . *enceinte* . . . we moved away to avoid the scandal. Susanna never told Drew we were going . . . she sent him a note that she had changed her mind about marrying him. She told me she couldn't—she loved Drew too much. She couldn't face him in her shame, carrying another man's child. And then the poor little thing died giving birth to you . . . and our parents dead of the yellow fever so soon afterward . . . "

Susanna stood up slowly. "Thank you, Aunt Rhea." Her mother had loved desperately and uselessly too, to say nothing of her father. In a moment of black despair, Susanna wondered if it had always been her destiny to do the same.

16

Rumors were rampant. The South expected seizure of the rams at any moment, while the North expected escape. In England, no one could find out for sure who owned the ships in Laird's yard.

A telegraphed reply to the question came from Lord Cowley, British Ambassador in Paris: "Ironclad vessels are not for the French government." From Brussels it was reported that "the King of Belgium has written to the Queen of England urging detention."

And in mid-August, treasury agents of the Crown in Liverpool noted the arrival of a Confederate Navy officer and assumed he had come to take the rams out of Britain.

Susanna would later assume that Brent had come because she had requested Jacob Drost to send for him. In actual fact, Brent had long ago volunteered for the mission. He did not know when he arrived in Liverpool that his superiors had already canceled his assignment. He was told to leave Liverpool, to go anywhere for a few days until new orders arrived for him. Brent took the train to London.

Getting out of the cab in Essex Square, he wondered briefly if Susanna would see him. He had not been exactly gallant on that last dash to Bermuda. Upon his return to Wilmington, he had learned from Lonnie Burke that Susanna had told the truth about their encounter, and moreover Lonnie had seen her running from a meeting with Captain Soloman, the black blockade runner. With time in port and out of curiosity and no less a sense of rage that a woman he cared about had sold herself, Brent had then gone to see Soloman and finally Benjamin Kresser. From the latter he learned that Susanna had indeed been working in a factory to support herself and family.

Still, the circumstantial evidence had been overwhelming, even Susanna would admit that. How did Brent know, even now, what had taken place before he had entered the club to see the naked Susanna about to ascend the stage? Brent clutched a small velvet case in his hand containing a silver-filigree brooch, a peace offering.

Dobbs came to the door. "I'm sorry, sir, milady isn't at home. No, sir, I do not know where she is or when she will return. . . . The child, sir? Yes, he and his nanny are in the park. Possibly by the lake—the lad has a sailing boat he's very fond of, sir."

Disappointed, Brent found his way to the park and strolled around the lake, examining each small boy with a starched nanny at his side.

Brent recognized his son at once. Black hair and eyes, small feet planted firmly astride, arms belligerently akimbo as he argued with his nanny, who was trying to stop him from plunging into the cold water to salvage his sinking ship. As Brent watched, the boy turned and floundered into the water in the wake of the sailing boat, while his nanny screamed. In three strides Brent was beside her and splashing into the water after the boy, who too late found the lake deeper than he expected. Back on the bank, Brent wrapped his jacket about the boy.

"You don't remember me, do you?" he asked his son, waving aside the fluttering nanny, who was trying to thank him.

"No." The boy searched his memory for a moment and then added, "You talk like Uncle Rowan."

Brent gave a rueful smile. "Actually no, I don't . . . my accent is from Georgia and much more refined than your . . . Uncle Rowan's. Come on, nurse, we'd better get the boy home for a change of clothes."

"You know Uncle Rowan?" the boy asked.

"And your mother . . . very well." Brent turned to the nurse and asked where Susanna was.

"At the Bodelons' I expect," she replied.

"My boat!" little Brent shouted with alarm.

"I have it here under my arm. You like boats, do you?"

"Yes. I'm a sailor."

Brent looked down at the boy in his arms, wet black hair plastered about an earnest little face. My son, he thought wonderingly. Mine and Susanna's.

He turned to the nanny, hurrying along at his side. "It's no farther to the Bodelon house than to Essex Square, just the opposite direction, if my memory serves me correctly. Let's take him there. I'm anxious to see his mother . . . and the Bodelons, of course."

Emma Bodelon avoided his eye when she said she did not know where Susanna was. However, she went on quickly, there was going to be an engagement party at Bartlett Hall down in Surrey the following day. David Bartlett was going to marry a local girl, and everyone would be there. Brent could travel down with her and Lady Bodelon, if he wished, as Susanna was going to be there.

Brent smiled down at her. "Yes, thank you. I'd like to do that."

Sir Edmund Bartlett felt he had a lot in common with the young calf that was cooking on the spit in preparation for the feasting. Susanna had insisted on being invited to David's engagement party, and Sir Edmund hadn't the heart to refuse. The poor girl had not had any invitations since Alicia Bodelon had started those vicious rumors. Susanna had suddenly wanted to dress up and dance and be surrounded by people, and it seemed a small request. But Sir Edmund knew from past experience that his wife's nearsighted peering was actually a defense against intrusion by the outside world; she felt in pretending not to see others, they would not see her. His wife liked to be left alone, with her horses and her flowers. His wife, did, however, see all too clearly what was going on around her when she chose to do so. Sir Edmund feared that if he looked at Susanna in his wife's presence, she, and everyone else, would know that he was bedding the girl on a very regular basis. Then too, he did not want to spoil David's engagement party by having a scene with the other guests protesting Susanna's reappearance in their midst.

Fortunately, Susanna's uncle was going to bring her to the party, and Sir Edmund expected that Rowan Marshall would monopolize a great deal of Susanna's time, since he had been away for some time and only recently returned to London. Nevertheless, Sir Edmund had not been able to resist buying an exquisite emerald brooch for Susanna, a green heart set in a cluster of diamonds. And he knew that if the opportunity arose and he could slip off for a few minutes from his guests . . .

Alicia Bodelon had come down with her daughter. Emma seemed more vital today, possibly because she was gazing, enraptured, upon a dark-haired young man who accompanied them and who reminded Sir Edmund, disturbingly, of someone he knew but could not bring to mind.

Sir Edmund took another gulp from his brandy glass before going to mingle with his guests. Susanna had not come downstairs yet; he must compose himself before he saw her. Gad, he felt like a boy every time she came near him.

Lady Alicia was bringing her dark-haired young man to meet him. Alicia certainly could find an unending supply of nice-looking young chaps . . . it was well known that Alicia took only young men to her bed, and he supposed that since she was attractive enough to get them, one should not feel resentful about this.

Through the brandy haze, Sir Edmund's glance fell on Alicia's companion, and he began to choke as he inhaled his drink into his lungs. Someone was thumping him on the back and, purple-faced, he nodded dumbly that yes, he was all right, as Alicia introduced him to Mr. Brenton Chaloner. Susanna had even given the child his name. . . .

Susanna came down the stairs with Rowan at her side and her Aunt Rhea a few steps behind her. They were talking softly and laughing together in a very intimate manner, and both Sir Edmund and Brent watched their descent with some dismay. Susanna was wearing a white satin dress, its skirt caught up in festoons to reveal a deep-green velvet underskirt. The tiny bodice ended in a mass of green and white tulle petals which spilled over to her arms in puff sleeves that left her shoulders bare. She wore a single square-cut emerald on a fine silver chain about her throat, and emerald earbobs danced as she moved, swaying first toward dimpled cheeks and then back toward the deep waves of chestnut hair. Behind her, Rhea O'Rourke was every inch the dowager duchess, in pale lilac with demure pearls at her throat and a feathered fan in beringed fingers.

Brent moved through the crowd and stood at the bottom of the great curved staircase as they came down, but Susanna did not look at him—she was deep in conversation with Rowan, who held her elbow with one hand and supported a stiff leg with a cane in the other hand.

Confidently, a smile hovering about his mouth, Brent waited for her to see him, to break free of Rowan's hand and come running to fling herself in his arms. Slowly the green eyes met his.

She did not run. She nodded coolly, then turned back to Rowan and continued speaking, casting a glance over her shoulder at her aunt, who smiled and said something in return.

"How nice to see you again, Brent," Susanna said, her voice impersonal, as they reached the foot of the stairs. "I hope you are well?"

"Very well, thank you. You look magnificent, Susanna," Brent said, in some awe.

"Thank you." Susanna did not stop.

Brent nodded respectfully toward Rhea, ignored Rowan and said, "Susanna . . . may I . . . "

"Perhaps later, Brent. I shall have to check my dance card to see if I have any dances to spare. You will have to excuse me now—I haven't seen Rowan for some time and we have much to talk about."

Brent stood aside as the orchestra struck up a waltz. He watched as they went to the chairs encircling the ballroom and sat down, still deep in conversation. Almost immediately, a red-haired young man went over to them, spoke to Rowan and then whirled Susanna out onto the floor. A moment later someone claimed Rhea. A group of young men were soon hovering nearby waiting to dance with Susanna, all of them oblivious to the thinly veiled hostility on the faces of the other women, who made it clear they resented her presence.

There had been an awkward moment when Susanna first arrived, but Rowan was at her side and none of the ladies had ever been able to resist his charms. The fact that he had been wounded and came limping in on a cane drew attention away from Susanna, and in the outpouring of sympathy everyone seemed to overlook the fact that if Susanna was guilty of the crime society was whispering about, then so too was Rowan. As soon as the ladies began to flutter about the wounded warrior, the young men lost no time in surrounding Susanna. None of them believed the rumors anyway, as it had always been obvious to them that Rowan Marshall had a habit of speaking bluntly to Susanna, as one would to a close relative.

Brent stood alone, watching Susanna dance, until there was a gentle tug on his sleeve and he looked down to see Emma Bodelon at his side. "Lieutenant Chaloner . . . I don't think she was expecting you," she said, blushing. "I know you don't know anyone here . . . perhaps you would like to sit with Mother and me?"

"Thank you," Brent said shortly. He was angry, but other than the furrow that had appeared between his eyes and a slight tightening of the mouth, no emotion showed as he followed Emma.

For most of the evening he watched Susanna dance with every young man present, and several times with their host, Sir Edmund. Rowan, his leg stiffly out in front of him, watched indulgently, his eyes, like Brent's, following Susanna everywhere.

At last Brent could control his anger no longer, and he abruptly strode into the middle of the floor and tapped Susanna's partner on the shoulder, took Susanna into his arms and left the bewildered young man standing amid the dancing couples.

"That is not an English custom, Brent," Susanna chided,

her eyes narrow. "You could have come and asked Rowan if you might dance with me, like a gentleman."

"I'll not ask Rowan for something that is mine," Brent snapped, his hand tightening on hers.

"Yours?" Susanna raised an eyebrow, breathing steadily in spite of the fast waltz turns he led her into.

"Susanna, look, I'm sorry about our last meeting. Let's get away from here so we can talk."

"Talk, Brent? When did we ever talk? Oh, you talked and I listened, many times. What you really mean is, let's get out of here and find a bed somewhere."

"Susanna, no . . . please. I don't feel like that. Seeing you here, like this . . . you could pass for a lady anywhere, I know that . . . I want to treat you like a lady."

"And propose marriage?" Susanna's voice was so soft he almost missed the words.

For an instant the picture of his son, lying in his arms, came back to him. He hesitated, but the pause was long enough. Susanna twisted out of his grasp and sped quickly from the floor, to be swallowed up in the crowd that surged about the orchestra dais as Sir Edmund rose to make the engagement announcement.

Immediately afterward, the refreshments were served and both Sir Edmund and Susanna disappeared. Brent went up the stairs, to search the floor below, but they were gone. Many of the guests were taking advantage of the interval between dances to stroll the lush grounds of Bartlett Hall. The August evening was warm and the girls went without wraps, moving through the flower gardens and shrubberies like so many bright moths clustered about the lanterns that had been strung from the trees. Something nagged at Brent's thoughts as he searched, something in the way Sir Edmund had held Susanna when he danced with her, something about the way he looked at her. Brent turned and went back to the house, stopping one of the footmen who hurried by with trays of champagne glasses.

"Does Sir Edmund have a private suite of rooms—a study, perhaps?" he asked.

"I believe so, sir. I'm only here for the evening, I'm

not on the staff. But I did take a glass of brandy up to a room on the second floor of the west wing before the guests arrived."

Brent went quickly through the house and up the stairs, noting that both Rowan and Sir Edmund's wife were clearly visible in the ballroom below. He met Sir Edmund and Susanna coming along the upper hallway toward the stairs. They walked side by side, holding hands like children and whispering conspiratorially.

"Susanna, I must talk to you alone."

"Brent! What are you doing up here?"

"Young man," Sir Edmund said quietly, "it would be quite improper for the young lady to see you alone. You may say anything you wish to her . . . in my presence."

For a second Brent wanted to smash the old fool in the face, but he restrained himself in view of Susanna's amused stare. He found himself saying, foolishly, "It's just that I had a present I wanted to give you, Susanna." He fumbled in his pocket and produced the filigree brooch.

"How nice, thank you," Susanna said. "Here, you can pin it to my dress next to the one Sir Edmund just gave me."

Brent looked down at the emerald heart, nestling among its diamonds, in the green and white petals of Susanna's dress. He put the simple filigree broch back into his pocket. "I'll call on you at Essex Square tomorrow afternoon, Susanna. Good night. And good night to you, sir."

Long after the other guests had retired to their rooms for the night, Brent paced up and down the deserted terrace. If there had been a train back to London, he would have taken it, but as it was he would have to wait until morning. There was a grandeur and spaciousness to Bartlett Hall that reminded him of his own home in Georgia, despite differences of architecture and the patina of age here that his own home had not yet acquired. He was filled with rage at the certain knowledge that Susanna's favors were no longer his alone . . . worse than that, he was cast aside tonight for an old man with a paunch and an inane expression on his face.

"Lieutenant Chaloner . . . " a voice said softly. Emma stood behind him, her eyes wide with concern. "I saw you down here . . . and wondered . . . are your accommodations all right?" Her voice was a flutter of butterfly wings, and the plain little face was contorted with an agony of shyness.

"Oh, yes. They're fine. It's such a beautiful night it seemed a pity to waste it sleeping," Brent answered and stopped to lean against the flower-topped stone wall that encircled the terrace. Emma hesitated, unsure whether to go or stay, and in the first light of dawn Brent saw that the middle button of her basque was not fastened. She must have seen him from her bedroom window and dressed hastily to come down to him.

Casually he reached out and pulled the button into the buttonhole. "How kind of you to be concerned about me," he said, feeling her jump at his touch. Her scrawny breast heaved as she drew in her breath sharply, and there was dismay and unutterable joy mingling plainly on her face.

She may not be pretty, but she is a woman, he thought as he slipped his other arm around her waist and drew her to him, bending her backward and seeking her mouth with his. She trembled in his arms, her breath caught in her throat, as she was crushed in that hard embrace. Hesitantly she raised her thin arms about his back, brushing him as lightly as bird's wings, then his tongue was parting her lips and he could taste her tears spilling down her cheeks.

When his hand slipped inside her chemise and found the small breast, she stiffened and, sobbing, pulled away from him.

"Oh . . . please . . . Lieutenant Chaloner," she gasped. "It's wrong to . . . oh, dear . . . it's not that I . . . "

She did not run away, but stood looking at him like some dumb animal he had whipped, pleading with her eyes for forgiveness.

He looked at her for a long moment, without compassion. Colorless, shapeless little creature. The memory of Susanna's voluptuous curves, the fire in her eyes and in her caress, the bewitching spell she could cast on a man, came to his mind through a haze of anger and disappointment.

"Go back to bed, Miss," he said at last to Emma. "You're not ready for a man yet, and what I need tonight is a woman."

Blinded by her tears, Emma stumbled silently away.

It was a different Susanna who greeted Brent the following afternoon in Essex Square. She drew him into the house, closed the door and whispered that everyone was out and they were completely alone.

Several wine decanters and glasses were set out in the drawing room, and because it was a warm afternoon and a fire was unnecessary, the empty grate had been filled with masses of fresh flowers. Susanna had replaced the heavy draperies at the windows with an open-weave material that let in filtered sunlight and air, and when Susanna turned and smiled at him in that setting, the effect was curiously more erotic than in a moonlit bedroom.

He felt his blood churn as she moved close to him, her dimples dancing wickedly as she said softly, "Brenton Wilford Chalenor, you handsome devil, you. You are going to spoil all the ladies in London with your good looks. How will they be able to compare all the other mortal men to you? They will hate their husbands and beaux." She was looking at him in a way that made him catch his breath.

Then she put her arms about his neck and pulled him down to kiss her, her hands sliding down his back, lifting his jacket and pulling up his shirt to glide over bare flesh.

He drew away, gasping for breath. "Susanna . . . what is all this about? The cold shoulder last night, and now today . . . "

She dropped her hands and went to the sofa, sitting down and pulling her feet up under her in a very unladylike way. She was wearing a light housedress of some filmy material with, it appeared, very little under it. She smiled. "But I thought this was what you wanted, Brent. I've been learning a lot about the games men like to play. I thought yours was the game of blowing hot and then cold. First you want me, then you loathe me. First you want to make love to me, then you want to leave me. Don't I have the rules right? Cold last night and now warm today . . . very warm, Brent."

She slid one leg out of the housedress and extended it on the sofa, reaching up to unpin her hair at the same time.

"Susanna, I met our son . . . talked with him. You're doing a fine job of raising him. . . . "

"You met him before, remember? On the ship to Bermuda. We had to sit in the cabin and keep our hands over his mouth to stop him from crying out and giving us away to the Yankees. He was very frightened . . . and he cried a lot in those days. You see, he was always hungry."

"Susanna . . . don't . . . " Brent said miserably.

"Oh, you wanted to talk about something else? Let's see if I can guess what." Susanna knitted her brows together and propped her head with one hand in a pose of great concentration, then slowly started to untie the ribbons that held the front of her dress together.

Brent went to the sofa, sat down beside her and said, "I'd like to say I'm sorry."

Susanna turned her fiery green stare on him. "Sorry for what? That your son went hungry?"

"That—and everything else that happened to you. What are you to that old man—Bartlett?"

"His mistress. But don't worry, he won't be needing me this afternoon. Do you have any other questions?"

Brent drew back slightly. "I see." He was silent, staring moodily in front of him.

"I'm doing it for the glorious Cause, you see," Susanna said. "Any day now poor Sir Edmund will be confronted with the evidence of his indiscretion by a gentleman named Jacob Drost—the deed to the house Sir Edmund bought for Mrs. Wilford. How do you like that pseudonym? And in return for our silence, Sir Edmund will allow the rams to leave the Mersey. I take it you will be on one of the rams?"

"Susanna . . . oh God, whose idea was this?"

"Drost's, of course—whose did you suppose? I'm certainly not clever enough to think of it all by myself. I'm only a body, you see, not a mind—a body to be used by whichever man needs a body at the moment. And by the way, the body isn't too much the worse for wear, as you can see."

She tore away the last fastening ribbon, ripping the material in her haste and anger, and then she stood up and kicked off her dress to stand naked in front of him.

"We can start again, Susanna . . . " Brent stood up and took her into his arms. "It doesn't have to be like this. You must come back with me."

"Back? Where? To Georgia . . . or to Wilmington? To starve to death among the cockroaches?" she flared back.

"Susanna, Susanna." He buried his face in her hair. "I love you . . . forgive me . . . please, Susanna."

The scent of her hair was in his nostrils, her bare flesh warm under his hands. He lifted her into his arms, laying her down gently on the sofa, kissing her mouth, her eyes, her hair, the soft hollow between her breasts; then she was kissing him back, eagerly, passionately.

He was poised before that moment of eternal wonder, ready, about to enter her, when suddenly she wriggled free, and, losing his balance, he rolled to the floor as she leaped to her feet. She snatched up her torn dress and looked down at him triumphantly.

"No, my dear Brent. Not this time. Not this time, my sweet." And she was running from the room, slamming the door.

He needed salve for his wounded pride, and he needed a woman to finish what Susanna had started. It mattered little which woman. At Susanna's door he was confronted by the arrival of an ornate carriage.

"G-g-good afternoon, Lieutenant Chaloner," a softly sweet voice said. Emma's plain features were tinged with pink, her eyes downcast, and he could see a pulse beat in her throat. There was no hint of remonstration for his churlish behavior earlier.

"She isn't home. No one is. Will you drive me somewhere?" Brent said, smiling at her.

"Oh, yes . . . just tell the coachman." Emma's face lit up and her heart was a beacon in her eyes as he climbed in beside her.

"Is your mother home?" he asked.

"No . . . " Always a little tongue-tied in the presence of men, Emma was struck dumb by the memory of the stolen kiss at Bartlett Hall. In all of her sheltered existence, she had never been confronted with the sheer masculine power Brent exuded, and she was both terrified and excited.

"Then let's go to your house," he said with a sidelong glance.

Emma kept her eyes fixed on her pale hands, which were twisting her gloves into knots. "We could have tea . . . " she whispered.

Brent smiled again, his teeth white against his tanned skin, but there was no matching warmth in his eyes. His senses were still filled with Susanna, the scent of her in his nostrils, the taste of her on his lips, the pain in his loins that was more anger than need.

Emma did not ask the maid who brought the tea tray to remain with them, despite the impropriety of entertaining a man alone in the drawing room. Emma picked up the silver teapot and spilled tea on the cucumber sandwiches as she poured, and the teacup rattled against the saucer when she handed it to him.

Brent took it from her and placed it on the table beside him. He was well aware of her innocence and awakening feelings for him. For a moment he thought of his mother and sisters . . . ladies like Emma. She would suffer his lovemaking in pain and embarrassment merely to please him. Damn it, that was how it should be; a woman was not supposed to enjoy it, it was a man's pleasure. Damn Susanna. Damn all women, good and bad.

He took the teapot from her shaking hands and returned it to the tray, then pushed her down against the dusty velvet of the sofa and crushed her with his weight as he sought her lips. For a second he hesitated, looking into the staring eyes that were already filling with tears. She was plain to the point of ugliness, but she was ready to face dishonor for him, and to a woman like Emma, dishonor was worse than death itself. Still he felt no pity, merely revulsion that she was not beautiful.

"Brent . . . " the words were torn from her throat, "I . . . love . . . you . . . "

"Good. I don't make love to women who don't love me," he said and kissed her roughly, his hands tearing at her dress.

"Please . . . Brent, dearest . . . don't take me here . . . like this," she pleaded.

A quick vision of his mother and sisters flashed unbidden into his mind again, and he sat up. Nice women did not do this and were not forced to do it. Of course, one could always give them a false sense of security by becoming engaged to them . . . but it wasn't really worth the trouble. The streets of London were crawling with women.

"Forgive me, my dear Emma. I was quite carried away by your charms," he said sarcastically. "My impetuousness will surely spoil my chances of finding favor in your eyes."

Emma wept for happiness, oblivious to the mockery and contempt written on the darkly handsome features.

Informed sources believed the government was about to confiscate the rams. The *Florida* was cruising off the coast of the British Isles and, some said, was waiting to accompany her more formidable sister ships out of the Mersey. But then everything came to a standstill, the summer doldrums were upon England, it was August, and the population, including those in government, went on holiday.

Rowan came to see Susanna, bringing a small bunch of violets from a street seller. "I think Drost is ready to pounce on Sir Edmund," he said. "The first ram is ready to sail. So everything is coming to an end. Once the rams are under way, I shall no longer be needed in England.

Nicholas Kirby is telling everyone he is going to marry Emma and move into Essex Square. What will you do?" He did not dare mention Brent Chaloner, who was in the forefront of his mind.

"Oh, no, Rowan, I don't want you to leave England," Susanna said, pulling out a chair for him. "Thank you for the violets. Why do you have to go back? Surely you can't fight with your bad leg?"

"Ah, Susanna, you always know how to bolster my pride!" Rowan said. "There must be something I can do back in Virginia. Perhaps my law training . . . which, incidentally, will be useful when the Yankees put us on trial at the end of the war. We haven't enough food to feed our own Army, let alone Yankee prisoners, and after they're through punishing us for that, they'll move in and take whatever is left. The only way we can fight them then will be within the framework of the Constitution."

"Is it coming to an end? I'd hoped to run some more cargoes through."

"Have you no decency, Susanna? I never thought you'd be among the jackals."

"You said yourself we're going to lose. If we're going to lose anyway, I for one don't intend to be left at the mercy of the Yankees. When one is rich, one is safe from all enemies."

"You do plan to go home then? I feared you'd decided to remain in London permanently." A small hope was born again.

"Oh no. I shall go back home when the war is over. As for now, I shall set up my own establishment when and if Nicholas marries Emma. A couple more of Captain Soloman's famous runs through the blockade and I shall have enough money."

"And Sir Edmund? Are you going to throw him to the wolves?"

"Do you care?"

"Yes. I care that you have turned into a ruthless, selfish little—"

"Rowan!" Susanna was genuinely hurt. "You've never spoken to me like that before . . . you always accepted everything I did and laughed about it, or at least you didn't call me names. You don't have any right to sit in judgment about me and Sir Edmund. You did send me to him in the first place, you know . . . to say nothing of the customs man in Liverpool when you wanted to get the *Alabama* out."

The look in Rowan's eyes was that of a man who has looked into the depths of hell, but he said with a thin veneer of his old jocularity, "I guess a little sexual fun never hurt anybody, not them and not you. That isn't what I mean. I mean, how can you let Drost blackmail Sir Edmund into letting the rams out—"

"I have no intention of doing so," Susanna said. "But I was going to keep quiet about it. I was afraid you would want me to go through with the odious plan. I thought you were as anxious as Drost to get the rams out."

"No. I believe it will be a grave mistake if the Crown lets the Confederacy have them. They can only prolong the war now, without changing the result."

Susanna was feeling an inexplicable wave of relief to have regained lost favor in Rowan's eyes, and she said quickly, "I never actually moved into the mews house, or even signed the deed, you know. We were just renting it until the papers were signed. I won't move in. I'm going to tell Sir Edmund everything tonight, and take my chances he will understand. I hate to hurt him, he's been so kind . . . and I'm going to return the money Drost gave me. I can now, because between the jewels I sold and all the profits I made, I can easily afford to give it back."

"I don't know if that will be enough to satisfy our friend Drost. You'd better let me handle him."

"No, Rowan. I want to have the satisfaction of flinging it at him. You can be present, but let me get the money first. And then when everything is taken care of and I'm in my own house, I swear I am going to be sweet and kind again and not the heartless creature you think I am." She dimpled suddenly and impulsively leaned forward to kiss his cheek.

"I don't suppose you'd consider marrying a stiff-legged

lawyer with no future? I mean, if you don't have anything better planned?" His clear gray eyes were wide with hope that was lost on Susanna.

She smiled. "Now, Rowan, why spoil a beautiful friendship? You and I are the only man and woman in the world who can be completely honest with each other. No secrets, no pretense. Would you like to make love? I haven't made love with you since I've been seeing Sir Edmund. I'm really quite fond of him, but he doesn't set my blood on fire as . . . " She broke off, suddenly shy.

Rowan misunderstood her hesitancy. "No thanks, Susanna, I have to leave. But Chaloner is still in town, I believe, so you can have the real thing if you've a mind. I'm tired of being his proxy." He turned his head so she would not see his misery, afraid the pounding of his heart must be as audible to her as it was to him. Unconsciously he drew himself to his full height, erect with military bearing despite his wounded leg. A shaft of sunlight caught him in the face as he turned, gilding blond hair and mustache and lighting the gray eyes that were filled with a doomed recklessness that would have startled Susanna had she seen it.

"Rowan . . . no . . . " Susanna began, for she had not been thinking of Brent, but of Rowan's exciting and tender lovemaking.

At that moment little Brent came bounding into the room, followed by Rhea.

"Susanna, honey, I have some bad news, I'm afraid," Rhea said.

Susanna went white and clutched the table for support. "Brent?" she asked in a faint whisper.

"No. It's Sir Edmund Bartlett. Heart failure . . . honey, I'm afraid he's dead."

17

THE day after the funeral Susanna had a visitor. Lady Alicia Bodelon paced up and down in front of the drawing-room fireplace, flitting across the room like an angry black cat. She turned as Susanna came into the room, violet eyes coldly appraising the black dress Susanna wore.

"So, you are in mourning, my dear. How quaint . . . mourning your lost benefactor."

The polite smile of greeting faded from Susanna's face. "Lady Bodelon—" she began.

"We shall forget all the little niceties. You will pack your things and be out of this house today."

"I had planned to leave. There is no need for this," Susanna said quietly.

"There is every need. How do you think I've felt, seeing you here in this house? Receiving you in my house? Watching you ingratiate yourself with my daughter? You . . . you . . . Oh yes, I know your mother was my late husband's whore. How dared he flaunt you like this? How dared he suggest Nicholas marry you? I knew from the start, of course, but that stupid will . . . that stubborn Mr. Tweedye. There was nothing I could do until you showed your true colors. We could prove nothing about the child you passed off as your nephew. But we found out about you and Sir Edmund, we have proof now, and Tweedye will have to set aside the will. And you . . . you will be deported from the country."

"I'm sorry I've caused you so much distress," Susanna said. "But you speak unjustly of my mother. She was not your husband's whore. He raped her. The proof is in

259

his own words, in the diary Emma has. The last page was sealed, I did not tell her."

Alicia's lips were white. "How dare you make such accusations against my dead husband, you . . . "

"Lady Bodelon, I do not intend to hear any more of this. I shall pack and leave. I had intended to anyway as soon as the funeral was over." Susanna turned to leave the room but Alicia caught her by the arm.

"Don't ever come back, do you hear?"

Susanna pulled her arm away and ran from the room.

Events had crowded one upon the other so rapidly that Susanna had not had time to wonder why Jacob Drost had not returned to demand repayment of the money he had given her to compromise Sir Edmund. She was overwhelmed with guilt and grief in equal portions. She and Sir Edmund had sinned, and he was dead and she must surely be punished too. The mortal fear of hell and damnation drove all other thoughts from her mind.

Rowan had begged her to return to Virginia with him, but he was sailing on the morning of Sir Edmund's funeral and she would not hear of it, telling Rowan that she would never return to war and misery and she never wanted to see him, or any other American, again as long as she lived. She had sinned for her country, and now she must pay for it by living in exile, alone and unloved.

When Rowan tried to tell her her reaction was normal, it would pass, that she was not a sinner, she turned on him in rage and told him it was all his fault. She hated him, she had always hated him.

Rowan stood quietly for a moment, the color drained from his face and his eyes clouded, then he said quietly, "All right Susanna, I guess I can understand that. Still, if you are going to stay here, there is something I want you to have."

He pressed something small and sinister into her hand.

"It's a derringer, Susanna. I'm going to show you how to use it. I want you to promise me you'll keep it with you at all times. I don't trust Jake Drost . . . and I never want you to be at any man's mercy again."

"I should use it on you," Susanna stormed at him.

"Everything that has happened to me is your fault." She continued to berate him as he patiently explained how to use the tiny gun.

Tight-lipped, he bade her goodbye. She watched him go and then flung herself on the bed and cried until there were no more tears.

After her interview with Alicia Bodelon, Susanna went to her room to pack while Rhea kept little Brent occupied and away from his sad-eyed mother.

The curtains had been drawn to proclaim the house in mourning, and the room was dark and oppressive. Vaguely she was aware of the chime of the doorbell below, but paid no heed until her bedroom door was suddenly and violently kicked open. Jacob Drost and Nicholas Kirby stood on the threshold, and there was no doubt from their manner that she was in deadly peril.

"You ain't going anywhere," Drost said slowly, "until after you've been to Bartlett's widow to tell her if the Laird rams aren't seized by the Crown, the fact of his affair with you will be spread all over London."

"Seized . . . " Susanna repeated, bewilderment momentarily overcoming her fear.

There was a smirk about Nicholas Kirby's lips and the hot look of lust in his darting eyes as they went over her half-dressed body.

"Seized," Drost said again.

"You tricked us," Susanna said faintly. "You are a Yankee spy . . .you are not one of our agents."

"Oh, don't feel too badly, old girl," Kirby put in. "Our resourceful friend here managed to trick Mr. James Bulloch and all of his staff, including your Rowan Marshall. You see, while Mr. Drost does indeed work for a Southern Senator, they are both Northern sympathizers."

"Shut up, Kirby," Drost growled. "Now, miss, we are going to visit a grieving widow."

Susanna was thinking rapidly that Rowan could not save her this time, he was already at sea, and downstairs was her son and Aunt Rhea. They must not be placed in jeopardy. Aunt Rhea had no doubt sent the two men upstairs believing they had business to discuss with Susanna. Rhea never interfered with Susanna's business dealings. Susanna felt sick. She could not bring shame and dishonor to the Bartlett family, no matter what happened to her personally.

"Wait a minute, Jake old fellow, what's the hurry," Kirby said. "You do owe me something, after all. If I hadn't sent you the telegraph you wouldn't have known your chicken had died before you could get him plucked."

"You'll get your payment. Now let's go."

"I've always fancied the girl, you know," Kirby said, moving into the center of the room as Susanna backed away from them. "We can spare a little time, surely?"

"You'll not take her in my presence," Drost said. "Women disgust me."

"Wait . . . " Susanna cried. "It will be your word against mine, about Sir Edmund and me. You have no proof . . . " She must play for time, time to think. Her skin crawled with revulsion as she looked across the room at Kirby with his slack mouth and hideous little eyes. "What good will it do to go to Lady Bartlett? How can she bring about seizure of the rams?" Behind her back Susanna's hands slid along the dressing table, frantically seeking something with which to protect herself. Talcum powder, a lamb's-wool powder puff and her cologne bottle . . . Lying on the bed and out of her reach was her reticule, and inside it the tiny derringer Rowan had given her. But it contained a single bullet . . . there were two of them. Besides, would she really be able to use it?

"You are forgetting," Kirby said, "that Lady Bartlett's brother is also a member of the Foreign Office. And we do have proof, my dear. The estate agent for the mews house will be able to identify you as the mysterious Mrs. Wilford for whom Sir Edmund was buying the house and with whom he had several tête-à-têtes . . . you underestimate the strict moral code our dear Queen Victoria has imposed upon all of us. The Bartletts will move heaven and earth to see that a scandal does not erupt involving their family name. Lady Bartlett and her brother have powerful friends who will do as they ask without needing a reason. . . . But enough, our friend Mr. Drost grows impatient."

"No!" Susanna shouted recklessly. "I won't do it. I won't be a part of it. And I'll find a way to fight you . . . stop you, somehow. I'll tell them you paid me—I don't care about myself, it doesn't matter any more. I'll tell everyone you paid me to make a scandal but Sir Edmund would have no part of it."

Jacob Drost stood in the center of the room, staring at her malevolently, his face a mask of hate and cold fury.

Kirby coughed nervously. "It would be better if we could have her cooperation, old boy. Keep it quieter and neater, so to speak."

"She'll cooperate," Drost said slowly. "She'll do exactly as she's told. Now I'm going downstairs to fetch her child up here . . . and I believe she'll soon be begging us to let her go to the Bartletts."

The room rushed away from her for a second and a white light exploded inside her head. Her thumb went under the glass stopper of her cologne bottle and she flung bottle and stinging contents into Drost's eyes as she sprang at him, screaming at the top of her lungs for Rhea to take the child and run.

Cursing, he wiped his eyes with one hand as his other hand balled into a fist and smashed into the side of her head, sending her sprawling backward on the bed. Kirby stood frozen, watching, his mouth agape.

Susanna felt the breath leave her body, faintness begin to overcome her. Drost had turned his back and was walking toward the bedroom door . . . to go and bring little Brent . . . Frantically she hung onto consciousness, her fingers fumbling with the reticule that lay beside her.

The derringer was in her hand and she had squeezed the trigger. Through the mists swimming before her eyes, she saw Drost crumple to the floor and Kirby drop down onto his knees to turn that gaunt body over and search for life. Kirby stood up slowly.

Susanna raised the tiny gun again and pointed it at him. "Don't come near me . . . there's another bullet for you," she screamed. She could hear Aunt Rhea at the foot of the stairs, shrieking her name, and she called back, "Stay down there, I'm all right. Stay with the baby."

"Don't—shoot," Kirby said, running his tongue over his lower lip. "Please. He's dead. I don't care about your affair with Bartlett . . . there's nothing I want from his family . . . Drost was the only one who had anything to offer me, and he's dead. Please . . . "

Susanna's breast was rising and falling rapidly, and her eyes were wild as she again pointed the gun at him.

"Wait—I'll get rid of the body for you," Kirby shouted.

Susanna lowered the derringer. "All right . . . but keep your distance. Now I'm going downstairs to Aunt Rhea, and after you hear us leave, you may do whatever is necessary."

She stood up, stepped over Drost's body and reached for her cloak. She was curiously detached and calm. There isn't anything else that can happen to me, she thought, I've committed the ultimate sin. Murder. And now I must surely face damnation.

Susanna took little Brent and Rhea to the mountains of Wales. Morgan, her maid, had told her of the peace and isolation of her village there, and Susanna rented a cottage and left her mail uncollected at the post office in the town with the unpronounceable name.

She spent quiet days and sleepless nights when she cringed in horror at the specter of the murdered Drost, afraid to sleep for fear of his haunting her nightmares. And she had killed Sir Edmund too, she was sure. She was filled with remorse and utter desolation. Only her son, with his needs and his love, pulled her back from the pit of despair.

Meanwhile, the cumbersome machinery of government moved slowly during September and nothing was resolved about the rams. Tired of waiting for orders that never came, angry that no one would tell him where Susanna was, Brent Chaloner requested permission to return to the *Alabama* as soon as she put into port . . . any port, he would go to her.

The days grew shorter and the leaves turned. Susanna

was unaware that in October the Crown took full posses-
sion of the rams, moored them in the Mersey under
British naval guns with armed guards aboard. The death
knell of the Confederacy had been tolled as surely in
Birkenhead as in Vicksburg.

Rhea suffered her niece's silent torment and gloom
until just before Christmas and then begged to be allowed
to return to all of the friends she had made in London.
Reluctantly, Susanna decided to go into town and collect
their mail.

She was in one of those periods of life when everything
slows to a snail's pace and the mind and body seem to
turn inward. There was a garden around the cottage,
where hollyhocks and lupins and rambling roses had
flourished all summer, and she spent her days tidying up
the remains, rebuilding the low stone wall that kept her
garden from spilling over into the narrow lane leading
to the village. Susanna and her son explored the countryside in long leisurely walks. But none of this eased the
constant loneliness she felt. She had been fond of Sir
Edmund, but not to the point of need, and she could
not define the emptiness that now enveloped her.

Little Brent had playmates in the village, bright-eyed
little Celts with their strange guttural language that was
nevertheless melodic and pleasant to the ears. The Welsh
congregation in the little chapel sang like a heavenly
choir, and Susanna and little Brent attended services
regularly, although they could not understand a word
either sung or spoken. The Welsh hymns were stirring
songs of their bygone warrior days and reminded Susanna
somehow of the struggle going on in her own country.
Vaguely she wondered if she were homesick. Had she
somehow acquired that desperate love of country that
surpasses all other loves and loyalties? That same love
that had driven Brent and Rowan, and perhaps even
Drost too. Perhaps if she were also an ardent fighter
for her country she would be able to think of Drost as
an enemy . . . that she had killed a Yankee . . . and
his ghost would not stare at her as she lay awake at night.

Now the wind that came down the mountains was
cold with the chill of winter, and frost gilded the window

panes in the morning. At Rhea's urging, she went to town to see if there were any invitations to London at the post office.

There were several letters. Letters from Bermuda, letters from Liverpool . . . one from the Merchants' and Seamen's Bank in Wilmington, who handled her merchandise there. There was also a letter for Rhea, and two others, which Susanna held in her hand, unopened, all the way home. She opened Brent's letter first.

My dear Susanna,

I tried to see you so many times. Your neighbors told me you had moved away, which was confirmed by the Bodelons. I have asked Emma to mail this to you.

Susanna, what can I say to make you believe I do truly love you and your son, very much? I have tried to forget you, but I cannot. We are at sea for long periods of time—I told you that. It isn't that I don't think of you. I promise to write the first time we are in a civilized port.

I did not get a chance to tell you that I had been home to see my family, just before we met in Wilmington. I could not believe the changes, how desperate the situation is on the home front. My younger brother is fighting in Virginia, and both of my sisters are planning to marry boys I remember as being children, who are now in the Army. But everything will be restored to normal as soon as we win the war, of that I'm convinced.

We never know where we will be when we see land, but if there is some way I can get to London, I will try again to see you. Please, Susanna, I want to talk, really talk to you about your future. There is no point in your writing me, I don't know where I shall be—we are the "phantom" raider, almost literally. Wait for me.

Brent

Curiously unmoved, Susanna dropped the letter to her lap on top of the business letters and the ones from Emma begging her to return to London. Nicholas Kirby had left the country, Emma wrote, and Jacob Drost had disappeared too . . . she hoped they had both gone for good. She missed Susanna desperately.

Susanna saved Rowan's letter for last, looking at the

tattered envelope for a long time before opening it, seeing Rowan's gray eyes smiling at her, the lock of hair forever falling over his forehead, his rueful grin. She settled down in front of her coal fire, a crisp apple from the tree that nudged the kitchen window in her hand, and slowly, with eager anticipation, opened the letter. She had missed Rowan's wry comments, his teasing, the comfort of having him near.

I am commissary officer, so feel quite close to you, since we are in the same line of business—in a way. Alas, my training for this was sadly neglected and I despair of ever acquiring your taste for commerce.

You must bear with me if I sound morose, but I have decided to write what I was never able to tell you in person, for I have a strange premonition I may never see you again.

You see, my Susanna, I have loved you to distraction from the moment I first saw you, sitting on the swing behind your aunt's bordello on Blossom Street. You were wearing a white dress trimmed in pink, and I thought you were the most exquisite, most desirable creature I had ever laid eyes on.

Susanna glanced away from the sheet of paper held in her trembling hand, her heart beginning to beat in almost audible cadence against her ribs. It was as though Rowan were in the room with her, speaking the words, so strong was the feeling sweeping through her.

I must confess next that it was I who maneuvered you into going to England. Forgive me, but at the time I was prepared to do almost anything in order to see you again, to be near you.

When I enlisted, I requested placement in a position where my legal training might be useful (not being a fighter, as you know!) and was eventually asked if I would be prepared to serve as an agent overseas. Someone with a knowledge of law—and, of course, our law is based upon British common law—and who could interpret maritime and other laws was needed in England, where we hoped to build a navy.

England! As soon as it was suggested, I thought of

you and your bequest. I also thought of you being safely away from the fighting and—even more important—your aunt's bordello. Not that I have anything against the latter. It's just that you were born to love, and paid whores lose that capacity after a time. I knew you would not go to England unless I presented a very valid reason —and, of course, that reason was your aunt. Please believe me, I did not accuse her unjustly—but when she was arrested it did seem that providence had presented me with the opportunity I needed. I quickly suggested that a female agent with connections in high places in England would be extremely useful. And so I told my superiors about you, Susanna, and since they intended to release your aunt after a stern warning about keeping her mouth closed about our ships' movements and a couple of days detention . . . the rest you know.

How could I have known what a tangled web all parties would weave in England? Agents working against each other and nobody knowing for sure what the ultimate goals were, Englishmen for us and others against us— and this before we even began to deal with the Yankees. Old Jake Drost is a case in point—and here I must add that there are rumors that one of our Senators is a Union sympathizer (I felt a definite chill when I heard that, in case it is the Senator that Drost is working for). Please, please beware of him, Susanna.

But I digress. I was in England with you, nothing else mattered. Had I known you would be in danger, I would have faced a firing squad before taking you there. But alas, we cannot always see into the future.

And so I waited, waited like a fool, for you to forget your black-eyed pirate. Don't you see, Susanna, he belongs to an age that has already passed him by? He isn't one of us. He should have lived a century ago, not now. His family exploits black slaves and he exploits women—seeing both blacks and women as subhuman, yet demanding from them loyalty and chastity above and beyond his own, and all the while he speaks of his breeding and his honor. But enough.

You are intelligent, Susanna, if a trifle young and not yet versed in the ways of the world. I was sure sooner or later you would see him for what he really is.

But you didn't, you haven't—and now it is too late and I realize my love for you is as hopeless as yours is for him.

Why do I tell you all this now, when it is too late to change the inevitable end? Perhaps some part of me wants to feel that you will think of me when I'm gone, and know that I loved you.

You see, I told my commanding officer today that I can no longer fulfill my duties to the commissary—to preside over putrid food that will be fed to men already half-dead from dysentery. I told him my leg is now completely healed and it is time I fight for my country with a gun in my hand. Perhaps you will be proud of me, maybe I will distinguish myself on the field of battle, in spite of myself. I hope I die well, Susanna. I want you to be proud you knew me, for I fear I won't see you again. But I will love you through all eternity.

Susanna sat for a long time staring into the fire, the uneaten apple still in her hand. Tears misted over her eyes and a terrible pain formed somewhere in her heart. The clock on the mantlepiece chimed suddenly, filling the room with the soft melody of Westminster bells, and she started, looking around as though seeing her surroundings for the first time.

What am I doing here? she thought in alarm. My country is in its death throes, and the man I love is going to his death and I sit here in an alien land and feel nothing. . . .

Rowan! His eyes of steel and that tawny mane of hair that was forever hanging over that dear brow. He had been there whenever she really needed him . . . no matter what he said about planning it all. When her aunt was arrested . . . during the storm at sea . . . when Jacob Drost attacked her . . . when their ship went aground . . . he had been with her in moments of fear and danger and triumph, and never, ever, had he condemned her, judged her, or looked down on her until the moment he thought she might blackmail Sir Edmund, and then he had spoken only to prevent that from happening. He had joked and made light of problems, had read her mind, suffered her insults and rages, and had been a father to little Brent, the son of a man he despised. Dear Rowan, who hid his infinite patience and love under a cloak of jest and pretended exasperation and whose comradeship she had taken so blithely for granted. It had always been the two of them against the world.

She looked down at the letters lying on the hearth rug. Brent's and Rowan's had fallen from her grasp and lay side by side. Rowan was right—she had never loved Brent. Brent was the first man she had ever known and she had endowed him with all the mystical attributes of a missing father, a storybook hero, and a fantasy lover. Had she been born in another place, another time, Brent would have been her schoolgirl crush . . . and in later years she would have remembered him fondly, but without regret.

She thought of all the shared moments with Rowan that had slowly brought love. Rowan, who knew all there was to know about her and loved her anyway . . . Rowan, whose first concern, even in their love-making, had always been for her and not for himself. How could she have been so blind?

Voices reached her—Aunt Rhea and little Brent in the kitchen, calling to her. Rhea came in, holding the child's hand. She was pink from the cold air.

"Did you go to the post office, dear?"

"Yes. There's a letter for you."

Susanna handed it to her and gathered Brent into her arms, where he wriggled and said, "Bwent a big boy bach."

Startled, Susanna looked down at her son. "What did you say? What was that word you used?"

"Bach. It's a Welsh word, dear," Rhea said. "He knows several."

"Aunt Rhea," Susanna said, "I'm going home. If you want to go back to London, I believe I can set you up in a modest way until you decide which of your gentlemen you want to marry."

"Home!" Rhea exclaimed, her hand to her throat. "But you can't . . . oh, honey, have you forgotten what it was like . . . moldy cornbread and worms in the peas . . . and no dresses and all those awful old men . . . oh, honey, no, I can't allow it," and she began to cry, crumpling her letter in her hands. "And what about little Brent? You can't take him back to all that misery."

"It's his country too, Aunt Rhea. We shall have to face whatever comes. Anyway, I have money now, and you know as well as I do that money can buy anything, even in the middle of a war. I have cotton sitting in a warehouse in Liverpool and the price is going up every day, and I have goods in Bermuda and Wilmington. My friend Captain Soloman thinks it is great sport to have a woman buying cargoes for him to run through the blockade . . . especially since I give him a share of the profits instead of a flat fee such as he gets from other shippers."

"Honey, I don't know where you learned all these things," Rhea began fretfully, and Susanna tried to hide her resigned smile. It was typical of Rhea to feel a woman was sullied by entering the man's world of commerce, while rationalizing the selling of women's bodies.

"In any event, as soon as I can sell the cotton in Liverpool I am going to sail to Bermuda. Have you decided what you are going to do?"

Rhea blushed becomingly. "Well, I am rather fond of that nice Mr. Cholmondeley, the publican."

"I will go back to London with you. I want to say goodbye to Emma before I leave . . . but I must go home as soon as popssible." She felt another stab of pain as she looked down at Rowan's letter. He was quite certain he was going to be killed . . . and Rowan's premonitions had an uncanny way of coming true.

"No!" she said, not realizing she was speaking aloud. "He can't be killed, not now that I know I love him."

"Susanna, dear . . . you mean Brent? Have you heard from Brent?"

Susanna looked at her. "Not Brent. Rowan. It's Rowan I love, Rowan I'm going home to. I'm going to marry him. He asked me, you know . . . twice. Only I never gave him the right answer."

There was so much to do. Susanna impatiently tried to work around the clock to get everything done, but still the days slipped away from her. The cottage had to be closed, their belongings packed . . . then she decided she had better go to Liverpool to handle the sale of her cotton in person, rather than trust some middleman. She sent Rhea and little Brent to London with reservations at a hotel and went north herself.

She was astounded at the price her cotton brought and the ease with which she was able to handle the brokers and buyers. When I return home, she thought, I shall go into the import and export business, just like Nicholas Kirby. Rowan can practice law and perhaps run for some public office, in order to be sure the old wrongs are gone forever, and I shall build a business. We will fare very well in putting the country back in order, for we will be needed. She thought, fleetingly, of Brent and his place in the new order of things . . . and wondered if there would be a place for someone experienced in slaveowning and plundering on the high seas. It did not seem likely.

Then she was on a train to London, and Rhea met her at the station accompanied by a white-whiskered, ruddy-cheeked gentleman with a slight stammer and a great deal of love shining in his eyes for the elegant Southern lady he was to marry. She can forget her past here, Susanna thought, Aunt Rhea can be a lady here. It seemed odd that this was so, but Rhea spoke in the softly charming accent of Virginians, and that, while wearing the right clothes, was all that it would take in England.

They were married in a simple civil ceremony, and after they were dispatched to Southend on a honeymoon, Susanna and Emma went back to Susanna's hotel room to talk.

"Does your mother know you came to Aunt Rhea's wedding?" Susanna asked.

"I didn't mention it. She knows you are here, of course."

"I take it you know of my last encounter with your mother?"

It was obvious that Emma did not. "Susanna, whatever she said to you, I am truly sorry about it. I really am. I cannot excuse her, even if she is my mother. Indeed, I have issued an ultimatum to her in regard

to her treatment of you, and I promise you things will
be different. I wish you would find it in your heart to
forgive her and remain in London."

"I'm sorry, Emma. I'll miss you, but I have to go
home. I have to go to the man I love. He needs me."

"Rowan?"

Susanna looked at her in surprise. "How did you know
it was Rowan when I didn't know myself until very
recently?"

"It was very obvious, dear . . . and I knew how
much he loved you. He told me, when you lost your baby
and were so ill just before you went home. He said if
you died he didn't want to live either. There was always
something right about the two of you together. That was
why I—"

"But Brent . . . " Susanna began and stopped as Emma
looked away, but not quickly enough. Susanna saw the
naked truth the downcast eyes tried to hide.

"Emma," Susanna said, the light slowly dawning, "when
you told me you could not marry Nicholas because you
loved someone else . . . it was Brent, wasn't it? Oh,
my God, no. . . . "

"Susanna, please. It's all right. I knew he was in love
with you. How can I compare with someone as beautiful
as you? Every man you meet must love you. I knew
Brent had eyes for no one else. And, of course, when I
met your son . . . I knew Brent was his father. I was
surprised, because I was so sure that you and Rowan . . ."

"Emma, Brent is . . . " Susanna fumbled for words.
She wanted to spare her sister the pain of loving Brent,
but how could she, who had been his willing slave herself
for so long?

"You and Rowan will be very happy together, Susanna," Emma said before Susanna could think of anything to say. "Now I want to tell you something that
concerns only us two."

Susanna had not been prepared for what Emma told
her next. Her father's will, leaving almost everything to
Emma, had specified that when she became eighteen
she would have full control of her resources. Emma was
going to be eighteen shortly, and had already seen her

solicitors and Mr. Tweedye and made arrangements for ownership of several Bodelon ships to be transferred to Susanna, who was, of course, a Bodelon also, by birth if not by name. Emma had decided she could not bear to be parted from her half-sister, and this way they would have a link across the ocean that separated them.

After her protests and surprise subsided, Susanna thought wryly that good fortune seemed to come in greater abundance when one did not really need it. Still, she would be independently wealthy from now on, and that was what she had once wanted more than anything else in the world. Now all she wanted was for Rowan to be alive to know she had at last come to her senses, about many things.

Before Emma left her that evening, Susanna also learned why their father had cut Alicia out of his will so completely. As a small child, Emma told Susanna, she had learned to cover her ears to blot out the sound of her parents' quarrels, the vicious words flung in anger behind the closed bedroom door. She grew up knowing that when her father went away on his long sea voyages, his house and his bed were occupied by young men. Many young men, always different young men. Boyish young men who whistled and patted the shy little girl on the head as they raced up the stairs to Alicia's room. Lord Bodelon had, of course, eventually returned home and caught his wife in bed with one of the young men. He had told her then that she could remain in his house but that she would get nothing when he died.

At last Emma stopped talking, and Susanna, her eyes heavy, suggested they retire as she had so much to do the following day.

They had to wait until after Christmas for passage to Bermuda. Fewer ships sailed the Atlantic now because of the danger of being caught in a confrontation between Federals and Confederates, including, of course, the deadly raider *Alabama*.

Susanna had written to Rowan, pouring out her heart and love, but there had been no reply and she became more apprehensive as each day passed, wishing she could be on her way to him. Home and Rowan, it was all she could think about. What if he did not receive her letter in time. . . .

She began to see him everywhere, his clear gray eyes laughing at her, his devil-may-care grin. How recklessly gallant he looked in his uniform . . . surely no man had ever looked more handsome than Rowan with his golden hair and gray eyes matching the colors of his uniform. The cleft in his chin . . . the wayward lock of hair falling determinedly over his brow . . . the lean, rangy body . . . the way he touched her, gently, wonderingly. He haunted her waking and her sleeping, and her body and soul yearned for him until she could not bear it.

They had Christmas dinner with Rhea and her beaming husband. A fat goose stuffed with chestnuts and sage-sprinkled bread, rich plum puddings ablaze with blue fire, mince pies by the dozen. Little Brent, surrounded by gifts and love, plaintively asking *when* he would see Uncle Rowan. Susanna dared not think of Rowan now. If I don't think it . . . it won't have happened . . . he will be alive. I must never think he is dead . . . we're only licked when we want to be licked . . . but why hasn't he written?

18

SHE had been the scourge of Yankee shipping for almost two years when, in June 1864, she sailed into Cherbourg Harbor to refuel and rid herself of barnacle encrustations.

Brent Chaloner was on the *Alabama's* deck, wishing it were England, instead of France, that beckoned across the misty water. Susanna and his son were in England and only twenty-odd miles away, though it might as well have been the far side of the earth.

Brent had thought a great deal about Susanna since their last meeting. When the war was won, perhaps then he could present them to his family in Georgia as a *fait accompli*. Perhaps marriage would be the only way he could ever really be sure of Susanna. All his instincts rebelled against the idea of marriage to a woman of her morals, yet he could not put her out of his mind.

Less than a week after the *Alabama* arrived in Cherbourg, the U.S.S. *Kearsarge* sailed down the Dutch coast and anchored off the mouth of Cherbourg Harbor, ready for combat. Captain Seemes immediately issued the challenge—he would be out to fight in two days.

Fifteen thousand Frenchmen lined the bluffs that sunny Sunday morning as they sailed out into the English channel to meet the Union ship. The *Alabama* was by far the more graceful, but its beauty was lost on Brent. He was aware only of the savage pounding of his heart as they closed with the *Kearsarge*.

They opened fire with a full broadside from their starboard guns, the shots shaking the rigging of the Union ship. The second broadside did more damage, but the

Kearsarge continued to steam closer, her guns silent. The *Alabama* was built for speed and flight, and Captain Semmes had hoped to keep the enemy ship, a true man-o-war, at a greater distance. Closer . . . now they were less than a thousand yards apart.

Commanding the starboard guns, Brent ordered the third round to be fired, and the Union ship opened fire simultaneously. The two vessels circled one another, guns flashing fire, but there was a sinister difference in the effect. The Southern ammunition had been supplied by blockade runners from Latin America and was of inferior quality. The *Alabama's* crew cursed with frustration as their shells failed to explode time and time again. Meanwhile, the eleven-inch Dahlgren guns of the *Kearsarge* lobbed shells into their ship with deadly accuracy.

To Brent it seem that the *Alabama's* impending defeat foreshadowed the demise of the Confederacy. The way of life he had fought for was coming to an end. Yet some stubborn streak in the core of his being could not acknowledge defeat.

The sound of tearing timbers, the crash of falling rigging and the anguished moans of the wounded echoed in his head as he shouted orders until there was no one left at the guns to obey them. At last, through the smoke, he saw the enemy ship moving in for the kill.

Wiping the sweat from his eyes, he staggered about the battered remains of the once graceful and proud *Alabama*, now listing heavily. Great holes torn in her hull, her rigging all but gone, the engines and boilers blasted apart, she was no longer responding to the wheel. He stumbled over lifeless bodies, slipped on the blood that ran like a tide over the decks, ignored the feebly clutching hands and whispered pleas for water.

He caught one sailor about to clamber over the rail and viciously dragged him back to the sloping deck. "God damn you, we're not finished yet—back to your station," he shouted, seeing what the sailor had seen— a sleek British yacht watching the contest from a safe distance.

"Aye, sir," the sailor answered, ashamed, and turned

from the rail, blood oozing from his shoulder as he moved.

The next moment Brent stared in disbelief as the sailor's body was blown apart, and then Brent was thrown headlong to the deck, tasting his own blood, feeling the crushing blow as a great rushing noise assaulted his ears and an inky fog closed his eyes.

She had gone to Richmond and searched for Rowan. There was nothing left of the regiment for which he had been commissary officer and to which she had sent her letter. After the regiment had been decimated by fearful casualties, the remaining officers and men had been reassigned, sometimes several times. She went to every army post, asked everyone who would listen to help her find him, begged for information. Everyone was too busy, too weary to care. She was one of thousands of women who did not know what had happened to their men. Fearfully she had searched for Rowan's name on casualty lists.

Troops had been moved by rail from Richmond in the longest and most spectacular movement of men in war in history; maybe he was one of those men? There had been bloody battles, staggering casualties.

She found the offices of Davies, Hamilton and Son, Attorneys at Law. They would surely know which regiment Rowan had been transferred to, where he was. But their offices were boarded up, and the proprietor of the business next door told her Mr. Davies and Mr. Hamilton had joined the militia after young Mr. Hamilton had been killed at Gettysburg. Silly old fools, with their rheumatics . . . neither of them had lasted the winter. No, he didn't know Mr. Rowan, he had taken over the business next door after they left. And he limped away to attend to a client, his wooden stump clumping across the floor.

Susanna worked in the hospital. It passed the time and made her feel useful. When she saw golden hair beneath bloodstained bandages she would hurry to see if it was Rowan. He isn't dead, he can't be dead. If

I keep him alive in my heart, if I keep searching for him, he will be alive.

Then, at last, a faint hope. They were exchanging prisoners. Only the severely wounded and ill at first. She waited and worried. Searched their faces. Oh, it wasn't fair. Why couldn't she have known it was Rowan she loved when he was only an arm's reach away from her?

Slowly, inexorably, the blue tide was sweeping down from the North, and as the Confederacy began to writhe in its final agony, Susanna forgot her vow to be rich, to be a great lady. She turned over her hard-won blockade goods to the Army, hoping perhaps some of the food would find its way to Rowan. She toiled in the hospital until she collapsed from fatigue, and when her son was afraid because of the gaunt and grim-faced adults who surrounded him, Susanna told him stories of their gallant victories, of the brave men of the South . . . men like his Uncle Rowan, who were fighting and dying . . . and achingly, humbly, Susanna O'Rourke acknowledged in her own heart the pride and love for her people and the land in which she had been born. Above all, she had learned compassion amid the awful suffering and gallantry of her fellow Southerners. But Rowan, oh, Rowan, why couldn't you be here to see me as I really wanted to be all along . . . not as I tried to be to accommodate others, or because of dreadful circumstance?

And, at last, she found his name on an old casualty list, from months before: Marshall, Rowan Charles, missing in action.

From far away, he heard Captain Semmes' voice. "We are sinking. We'll try to make shore." Dejection and defeat in that voice. Surely that was not the same man who had boldly challenged the *Kearsarge*? But the pain was too great, and Brent drifted off again on a darkly heaving sea.

He could hear the Confederate shore batteries. They would make it to the bar, he knew that. Be bold, slip right through the blockading gunboats and to hell with them . . . more dangerous by far were the shoals . . . mustn't run her aground . . . was that the sound of surf breaking on a beach? Sharply pointed coral reefs were tearing at his vitals, he could see the dagger-sharp points just below the surface of the channel. Nassau . . . was he sailing into Nassau? Susanna had been there, so long ago. He should have married her then, made the child legitimate.

"The British yacht," a voice was saying, "if she'll take us aboard we'll be in neutral hands."

"Sir, the *Kearsarge* has lowered boats to pick up survivors," another voice said.

"Damn it, I'm not going to be picked up by the bastards."

"Ahoy, *Deerhound*!"

Deerhound . . . he had seen that name somewhere . . . yes, on the side of a British yacht . . . this was not Nassau, nor Cape Fear . . . he was in the English channel on the *Alabama*, and she was sinking.

"Take me with you." He tried to say the words, but no sound came from his bleeding lips and his limbs refused to move, no matter how he strained. It was as though all his bones had been crushed to powder.

Movement nearby—a foot brushed by his face and the jarring pain gave him the strength to wrench his hand free and grasp the man's ankle.

"Take me with you . . . want to fight again . . . don't want to be prisoner . . . " Was he saying the words aloud, or was it all in his head? He could feel himself slipping into oblivion again.

"This officer is alive, sir," a voice said over his head, and the next moment someone was pulling the great weight from his body and he realized he was not paralyzed, but held fast by wreckage. Strong hands pulled him to his feet and the black fog lightened to a red mist filled with blurred images.

"Come on, sir, the English boat is standing by. You'll be having tea and crumpets before you know it."

News of the sinking of the *Alabama* came as another

shattering blow to the Confederacy, although every Southerner was relieved when they heard Captain Semmes and forty-one of his men had been picked up by the British yacht *Deerhound*. Safe in England, the men were now being fêted as heroes.

Susanna saw Brent's name on the list of the men who had escaped and thought of him briefly. Perhaps he would go to see Emma in London. Perhaps he would decide that the legitimate daughter of a British nobleman was a fitting bride to take back to his plantation. Someday she would meet Brent again and tell him she wished him well, but that was all.

She went repeatedly to Army headquarters, trying to learn if Rowan were a prisoner, if someone could tell her what "missing in action" really meant. A sympathetic officer promised he would let her know at the hospital if there was any word. But so much time had gone by . . . surely if Rowan were alive there would have been word of him?

Late one afternoon the Army surgeon told her there was an officer waiting to see her outside, and her heart leapt. Rowan! It had to be. Her feet flew. Outside, he was outside waiting for her! Her heart sang.

The officer was an older man, deeply etched lines in his face, his eyes dulled from the sight of too much carnage to be aware of the dead and wounded being unloaded at the hospital doors. His uniform was slightly better than the tatters Susanna was accustomed to seeing and his shoes almost intact. Respectfully he bowed to her and introduced himself. Susanna did not hear his name. A great avalanche of pain was sweeping her away as he drew a letter from his pocket. It was her letter to Rowan.

"No . . . " she whispered. "No . . . it can't be."

"And when I got back one of the officers told me I'd find you at the hospital," he was saying.

She stood perfectly still, frozen in the sunlight, her eyes fixed on the letter in his hand. She could not speak.

" . . . a gallant officer and gentleman, ma'am. Told me to come and find you if I made it back, just in case. He wanted you to know he'd got your letter. Strange it was, ma'am, he fought so recklessly and never got a scratch. The day your letter came, he told me he was going to be damn careful not to get killed or taken prisoner, and damn it—oh, pardon me, ma'am—but that very night the two of us blundered into a Yankee encampment when we were out foraging and we were taken prisoner.

"And one day the Yankees said if the Reb officers would go west and fight Indians for them, they'd be exchanged after a time . . . and hell—oh, beg your pardon again, ma'am—we figured it was better than rotting in a prison camp. 'sides, we didn't figure breaking our word to damn Yankees counted for anything anyhow. Determined to get back to you he was, ma'am. Carried your letter on him . . . see, this is just the envelope I have, with your name on it so's I wouldn't forget. He told me you said you'd let the Army know your Richmond address in case you hadn't heard from him before you left England. Told me first chance he got he was going to hightail it back to you and to hell with any promises made to damn Yankees. But, well, when it came down to it . . .

"We were just a small scouting party see, ma'am. Six of us. The Yankee officer sent us back to warn the fort and said he'd hold 'em off as long as he could. That's when Major Marshall slipped me the envelope and gave me the wink that it was my chance to make a break. Then the major says he's going to stay with the Yankee officer, to give us more time to get back to the fort. Well, two of us made it out of the canyon . . . me and a Yankee corporal. He went to the fort and I just kept coming on home to fight in the real war. I don't know what happened to the major and the Yankee officer."

Susanna swayed against the wall of the hospital, her mouth dry, trying to thank the man for coming to see her. Rowan had stayed with a hated Yankee! She could not believe it.

But he survived, he must have survived, somehow.

The wounded came in carts layered one on top of

another, a filthy mass of suffering that moaned feebly
and bled freely but never complained. With women who
had never before seen a naked male, Susanna washed
powder-blackened bodies, bandaged, swabbed, mopped
feverish brows, picked off lice, swatted flies and wept
when boys too young to shave died in her arms. She
looked upon a lost generation of manhood, flower of a
doomed nation, and her soul bled for them. Surely there
had never been men more gallant, more brave.

She was bending to hear the whispered words of a boy
from Tennessee who had lost his right arm and leg,
writing a letter to his mother for him, when a voice
spoke from behind her.

"Susanna . . . they said I'd find you here and I didn't
believe them."

She spun around. He was not lying on a bloodstained
litter, he was on his feet, smiling, his arms outstretched.
She ran into that embrace and time stood still for a
long blissful moment. He kissed her slowly, wonderingly, and she was laughing and crying at the same time
and it was the first time in her life she had ever cried
for happiness. She pushed him away and looked at him.
He wore a nondescript butternut-color uniform instead
of the handsome gray and gold, and his toes showed
through his shoes, but he was in one piece. She ran her
hands gratefully down his arms, glad there were two, and
looked down at his legs. The hospital was full of limbless
men.

"I'm all right. My leg is still a little stiff." He smiled
at her, clear gray eyes reflecting her own joy and his heart
thumping happily in cadence with her own.

"God, you look wonderful . . . like a dream come true,"
he whispered.

"Oh, Rowan, you frightened me so! A man came and
told me you had stayed with a Yankee officer. Something
about Indians attacking a fort. I knew he must be
mistaken . . . but he knew about my letter to you—had
the envelope. Oh, Rowan, I was so afraid for you."

Rowan kissed her eyes and her nose and her lips. He
had carried the wounded Yankee officer back to the

gates of the fort, alerted the sentry and then disappeared back into the desert. But Susanna did not need to be told this, not yet.

"Where is the boy? Where's Will?" Rowan asked.

"Will?" Susanna said, puzzled.

"You said you'd named him Brenton Wilford. I'm going to call him Will, because by coincidence my grandfather's name was William. You don't mind? I'm not quite noble enough to be able to call my son Brent . . . without the name sticking in my throat."

"No," Susanna said, "he's young enough to get used to a new name. And I like Will, it has a good sound. And while he's learning a new name we can teach him to call you something other than "Uncle Rowan," since you are going to . . . since you and I . . . "

Someone was whispering her name and she turned to look down into the smiling eyes of the boy from Tennessee. "Ma'am . . . you can write my letter some other time," he said. "Now you all go on home with your husband, hear?"

Susanna smiled happily and slipped her arm through Rowan's. "Come on, husband, let's go and make it legal before you go rushing off to war again."

"Susanna, there is one thing I have to explain about our forthcoming honeymoon," Rowan said, as they picked their way carefully through the litters of wounded men.

"Where shall we go, how much time do you have?" Susanna asked, a dreamy look in her eyes.

"Would England be all right? They've asked if I could go back and get just one more cruiser out—"

"Rowan! Oh, no . . . you wouldn't!" Susanna didn't know whether to scream or hit him in rage.

"Honey, the war is far from over . . . but I guess it's only fair to tell you that one more cruiser probably won't make much difference."

"We're only licked when we think we're licked," she chided. "I suppose you have another mysterious number for this ship?" She sighed, but she knew this time she would gladly work for the Cause, lost though it may be.

Rowan grinned. "We're going to name her *Shenandoah*."

Epilogue

LONG after the war ended, the C.S.S. *Shenandoah* would roam the North Atlantic and Arctic oceans destroying Union shipping. She would not surrender until seven months after Appomattox, the last cruiser to lower the Confederate flag.

And when at last she was chased halfway around the world and forced into the Mersey, Brent Chaloner would watch bitterly as his ship was boarded by British officials at Liverpool and the colors were finally lowered.

JANETTE SEYMOUR

PURITY'S PASSION

She was Purity, a maddeningly beautiful woman who wanted to save herself for the one man she had always loved – the man who rescued her from the horror of the French Revolution, who found her a place in England's aristocracy and who refused, because of a painful secret in his past, to open his heart to her longings.

And she was Passion, a woman who drove men wild with desire, who submitted to cruel tormentors, a blackmailer's demands, a hypnotist's powers and an innocent young man about to die. But she, while giving her body, steadfastly refused to give her heart.

CORONET BOOKS

ALSO AVAILABLE FROM CORONET BOOKS

All these books are available at your local bookshop or newsagent, or can be ordered direct from the publisher. Just tick the titles you want and fill in the form below.

Prices and availability subject to change without notice.
